"If you get any more dragons, remember, Turquine's the name. Fast, efficient service, no supernatural monster too large or too small. Cheerio for now."

Turquine vaulted onto his horse, which sagged slightly; then he trotted away, making a sound like a panel-beating contest. When he was out of sight, Florizel slowly turned round and looked at the dragon.

For obvious reasons, it didn't look back at him. Its eyes were open, and there was dust on its eyeballs; its yard-long jaws were slightly open, and Florizel could see teeth as long and yellow as bananas, and a cushion-sized segment of pink tongue. In spite of its size it looked very, very real, and as sad as road kill. No, he thought, I'm definitely not having fun. In fact, why don't I just go back where I came from and get a real life?

This is real, said a little voice in his head. *And it's not right.*

The Outsorcerer's Apprentice

Tom Holt

www.orbitbooks.net

Orbit
Hachette Book Group
237 Park Avenue, New York, NY 10017
HachetteBookGroup.com

First U.S. Edition: July 2014

Orbit is an imprint of Hachette Book Group, Inc. The Orbit name and logo are trademarks of Little, Brown Book Group Limited.

The Hachette Speakers Bureau provides a wide range of authors for speaking events. To find out more, go to www.hachettespeakersbureau.com or call (866) 376-6591.

The publisher is not responsible for websites (or their content) that are not owned by the publisher.

The characters and events in this book are fictitious. Any similarity to real persons, living or dead, is coincidental and not intended by the author.

Library of Congress Control Number: 2014935545
ISBN: 978-0-316-36879-7

10 9 8 7 6 5 4 3 2 1

RRD-C

Printed in the United States of America

Once upon a time there was a story. It was about magic and the magical land, and the right here and the very much now. It was about wizards and dragons, profit and loss ratios, doughnuts, manpower coefficients, crystal portals, a handsome prince, a poor but feisty peasant girl, Vivaldi, a unicorn, a LoganBerry XPXX3000, coffee stirrers, goblins and high-speed broadband. It starts off "once upon a time". It goes like this—

The long shadows of a summer evening were falling across the meadows as Buttercup walked from the village to the big woods. In the basket over her arm she carried her father's supper: bread and cheese, an apple and half a jar of pickled walnuts. As she approached the eaves of the wood, a rabbit poked its head out of its burrow and looked at her.

"Hello, Buttercup," it said.

She looked at it. "Get lost," she replied.

The rabbit twitched its whiskers. "It's a lovely evening," it said.

"It's always a lovely evening," Buttercup replied. "Go nibble something."

"You seem upset," the rabbit said. One of its ears was drooping adorably across its face. "Is something the matter?"

Buttercup reached into the basket, found the apple, took a quick but sure aim and threw. She hit the rabbit just above the eye, and it vanished back down its hole. Buttercup retrieved the apple, wiped the smear of rabbit blood off it with her sleeve and put it back in the basket. She felt a little better, but not much. A song thrush perched in the low branches of a sycamore tree opened its beak, thought better of it, and flew away in a flurry of wings.

Twenty yards or so inside the wood, Buttercup met an old woman sitting on the trunk of a fallen tree. She was wearing a big shawl, with a hood that covered her face. "Hello, little girl," she said, in a dry, crackly voice. "And where might you be going on such a fine evening?"

Buttercup stopped, sighed and put down her basket. "You're new here, right?"

"I come from a village twelve miles away, across the Blue Hills," the old woman replied. "I've come to visit my son. He's a woodcutter."

Buttercup slowly shook her head. "I don't think so," she replied. "Look, we both know the score, right? Now, since you're not from round here, I'm going to give you a break. I'll count to five, and if you just get the hell away from me and don't bother me again, we'll pretend none of this ever happened. If not," she added, "well."

The old woman laughed shrilly. "What a funny girl you are," she said. "Why don't you—?"

"One."

The old woman hesitated for a moment. "Why don't you come with me to my cosy little house, and I'll make you a nice cup of—"

"Two."

"Tea," the old woman said, but there was a faint feather of doubt in her voice. "And biscuits. And gingerbread. You like gingerbread."

"Three," Buttercup said. "And gingerbread sucks."

"All nice little girls like gingerbread," the old woman said. "Everybody knows that."

"Four."

"Did I mention that I'm actually your long-lost aunt from over Green Meadows way?" the old woman said, edging a little closer. "I haven't seen you since you were—"

Buttercup breathed a long, sad sigh. "Five," she said, and

put her hand inside the basket, which also contained, as well as the bread, cheese, apple and pickled walnuts, the small but quite sharp hatchet her mother used for splitting kindling for the fire. "Sorry," she said as she swung the hatchet; and the wolf wriggled frantically to free itself from the old woman's clothes, but it wasn't quite fast enough. The hatchet caught it right between the eyes, and that was that.

Buttercup stooped to wipe the hatchet blade on the moss growing on the side of the fallen tree. She looked at the wolf. It was lying on its side, its eyes wide open and empty, its tongue poking out between its jaws. She felt sorry for it, in a way, but what can you do?

Five minutes or so later, she found the wolf's little house. Sure enough, there was a round table covered with a chintz cloth, a rocking chair and a small upholstered stool. On the table she found a teapot, two cups, a plate of scones, ham and watercress sandwiches, jam, clotted cream and the inevitable gingerbread; also butter knives, forks, spoons (electroplate rather than actual silver, but still worth something) and, on the wall, a cuckoo clock. She emptied the teapot, the butter dish and the cream pot, then scooped everything into her basket (apart from the gingerbread, which she chucked out for the birds) then closed the door behind her and walked away, doing sums in her head. Sixpence for the tea set, maybe a shilling for the cutlery; no idea what the clock was worth, but—

"Buttercup?" She looked up and saw a tall, fair-haired young man standing in the path looking at her. He had a big axe over his shoulder. He'd been running. "Are you all right?"

She shrugged. "Hi, John," she said. "Why wouldn't I be?"

John was peering at her, as though something wasn't quite right but he couldn't quite figure out what it might be. "Oh,

I don't know," he said. "Though they're saying there's been wolves seen in these parts, so I thought—"

"John, there's always wolves in these parts," she said wearily. "Also bears, trolls, lions and at least six gryphons. Which is odd," she added, frowning. "Makes you wonder what they live on."

A shadow fell across John's face. "Children, mostly," he said. "Which is why—"

"Yes, but they don't," Buttercup pointed out. "Think about it. When was the last time a child got eaten this side of the Blue Hills?"

John gave her a bewildered look. "Why, only last week, little Millie from the mill was nearly gobbled up by a troll at Cow Bridge. If my uncle Jim hadn't come along with his axe at just the right—"

"Exactly," Buttercup said. "Sure, there's ever such a lot of close shaves, but somehow there's always a woodcutter passing by at exactly the right moment, so no harm done. Doesn't that strike you as a bit—?"

"Lucky." John nodded. "Just as well. I've killed seventeen wolves, two trolls and a wicked witch already this week, and it's only Tuesday. Really, it's not safe for a nice girl like you alone in these woods."

"John, it's perfectly safe, that's the *point*." She sighed. "Don't worry about it," she added, as John's puzzled frown threatened to crush his face into a ball. "And thanks for being concerned about me, but I'm fine, really."

John slumped a little, then shrugged. "OK, then," he said. "I guess I'll go and chop some wood. But if you do happen to run into anything nasty, you just holler and I'll be—"

"Yes, John. Oh, one other thing," she added, as he turned to go.

"Yes?"

"Want to buy a clock?"

A little later, lighter by one clock and richer by ten shiny new pennies, Buttercup arrived at the shed in the woods, where her father and three uncles were busy at their trade. She opened the door and walked in. "Hi, Dad."

"Hi, poppet." Her father looked up from the forty-foot plank he was planing. "Is that supper?"

"Yup."

"Just put it down on the bench," her father said. "We'll get to it as soon as we've finished these boards." He crouched down, squinted along the plank, marked a rough spot and stood up again. "Guess what," he said, "we had a visitor today."

Buttercup was unpacking the basket. "Don't tell me," she said. "The wizard, right?"

"Sure. How did you guess?"

"It's always the wizard, Dad."

With just the right degree of pressure, her father eased a wisp of wood off the plank and brushed it away with his hand. "And he had someone with him. A man."

"Yes, Dad. Hey, I got you something nice for your supper tonight. There's scones, ham and watercress sandwiches, jam—"

"Sounds great. No gingerbread?"

"Sorry, Dad."

"Never mind," her father said indulgently. "Put the kettle on and make us all a nice cup of tea."

Obediently she knelt to light the stove, which had gone out. "I met John the woodcutter's son on the way over," she said.

"He's a good boy, that John," her father said, pausing to put an edge on the blade of his plane. "You could do worse."

She knew better than to tell him what she thought about that. "Dad," she said, "I was wondering."

"Yes, poppet?"

"What do John and his dad do with all the wood they cut? Only they're always out there working, when they're not killing wolves and all, so they must cut a whole lot of wood."

"Very hard-working family," her father said with approval. "Not short of a bob, either. I heard they got a clock."

"Two now," Buttercup replied absently. "So, they cut all this wood, and then they sell it," she said. "In the market?"

"Well, yes."

She nodded. "Dad," she said, "who buys it?"

He looked at her, as if she'd started talking in a language he couldn't understand. "Well, people. You know. People who need wood."

"But everybody's got plenty of wood, Dad. I mean, there's John and his dad and all his family, and there's you and Uncle Joe and Uncle Bob and Uncle George, and you've got all the offcuts you could possibly use, and there's old Bessie in the cottage down the lane, and every time you see her she's out gathering sticks in the forest, and that's *it*. So, who buys all the wood?"

Her father's face froze; she could see him thinking. It was like watching a small man dragging a big log uphill. "Folks from the town, I guess. They'll buy anything, townies."

"I see," she said. "They come all the way from the town, through Silverleaf Forest and Big Oak Forest, fifteen miles on potholed roads, just to buy wood. And then they cart it all the way home again. Dad, what's wrong with this picture?"

"What picture, poppet?"

She sighed. "Forget it, Dad. Your tea's ready."

She poured tea into four tin mugs, and started dividing up the wolf-spoils between four tin plates. It'll be different, she thought, once I've saved up enough money to get the hell out of here. And, at the rate she was going, that wouldn't be too long now. Every wolf-in-granny's-clothing she ran into netted her at least a shilling – three, if they had gold earrings – and, at an average of two a week, the old sock under her mattress was starting to get encouragingly heavy. There was, of course, the small matter of who bought the stuff, but she preferred not to think about that.

"Seriously, though," her father was saying, "it's about time you were thinking about getting wed, settling down. You'll be nineteen in October."

"Sure," she replied, looking away. "And then who'll bring you your supper?"

"Well, you will, obviously. But—"

"I have no intention," she said firmly, "of getting married. Not to anybody, and especially not to any of the boys round here."

Her uncles were grinning. "Is that right," her father said.

"Yes. For a start, there's only three of them. And they're all woodcutters."

"What's wrong with that?"

"Are you serious? You know what happens to woodcutters' families while the men are out all day."

Her father shrugged. "Well, there's wolves and witches and trolls and goblins and stuff, but it's all right. The woodcutter always comes home in the nick of time and – well, it's all right. I mean, when was the last time anybody actually got eaten this side of the Blue Hills?"

She felt like she was chasing her own tail. "That's not the point," she said. "Think about it, will you? Being married to a woodcutter, I mean. Quite apart from the danger from *wildlife*, you've got an entire community whose livelihood depends on selling firewood to people who travel twenty miles over bad roads to buy something they could get just as cheap, or cheaper, a couple of hundred yards from their own front door. I mean, what sort of economic model is that?"

She stopped. Her father and uncles were staring at her, and she couldn't blame them. She had no idea what she'd just said. It was as though the words had floated into her head through her ears and drifted down into her mouth without touching her brain. Except that she knew – dimly – what they meant. "Ecowhatty what?" her father asked.

A sudden flash of inspiration. "Sorry, Dad," she said. "I was talking to the wizard earlier. That's a wizard word."

Her father scowled at her. "I told you," he said, "you're not to go talking to the wizard. Didn't I tell you?"

"I'm sorry," she said quickly.

"Things happen," her father said gravely, "to young girls who talk to wizards."

"What things?"

Her father looked blank. "I don't know, do I? *Things*. You're not supposed to do it. All right?"

She nodded meekly. "Yes, Dad," she said. "It won't happen again, promise. Only," she added (and if there was a hint of cunning in her voice, she masked it well), "what's wrong with talking to wizards, Dad? You do it. All the time."

"Yes, but—"

"And the wizard comes in here all the time, most days, in fact, and nothing bad ever happens. Well, does it?"

"No," her father admitted. "But that's because *I* talk to him. It's different."

"Sure it is, Dad." She paused, choosing the moment. "Dad."

"Yes, poppet?"

"Why does the wizard come round here all the time?"

Her father relaxed a little. "To see how we're getting on with his job, of course."

"The planks."

"That's right."

"Remind me," she said. "What exactly does the wizard want all these planks for?"

Her father smiled. "He's building a house. You know that."

She nodded. "That's right, so he is." Another pause. "How long've you and Uncle Joe and Uncle Bob and Uncle George been making planks for him?"

Her father frowned. "You know, that's a good question. George? How long's it been?"

Uncle George counted under his breath. "I reckon it's been upwards of forty-seven years now, Bill."

"Forty-seven years," Buttercup repeated. "The wizard's been waiting to build his house for forty-seven years. Don't you think—?"

"What?"

"Well, isn't that a bit odd? I mean all that time. And there's other carpenters. Don't you wonder why he hasn't gone and got some of the planks he needs from somebody else?"

"Ah," Uncle Joe broke in. "That's because we make the best planks this side of the Blue Hills. And wizards want only the best. Isn't that right, boys?"

A chorus of agreement, against which she knew she'd make no headway; so she nodded, and said, "Right, I understand now. You can see why I was puzzled."

"Course you were, poppet. You're a girl. Girls don't understand about business."

No, she thought, but I know what an economic model is. *How* do I know that? "Dad," she said.

Her father sighed. "Yes, poppet?"

"Just one more thing, Dad."

"Well, sweetheart? What's on your mind besides your hair?"

There would never be a better time to ask. That didn't necessarily mean that this was a good time; just not as bad as all the others. "That pair of shoes Cousin Cindy sent me," she said. "For my birthday."

Her father smiled. "The red ones."

"That's right."

"They're good shoes," he said. "Really well made and stylish. And plenty of wear left in them."

"Yes, Dad."

"Hardly worn at all, in fact." Her father grinned indulgently. "Of course, now she's married to that prince, she can have all the shoes she wants. Must be great to be rich, hey, poppet?"

"Yes, Dad."

Her father sighed wistfully. "Still, it was good of her to think of you. And they fit all right, don't they?"

"Yes, Dad. They fit really well."

"Well." He shrugged. "That's all right, then. Everybody's happy."

"Yes, Dad. See you back at the house."

She walked home slowly, deep in thought. She was so preoccupied that she didn't seem to notice the bird with the gold ring in its mouth, or the old woman gathering sticks who, if she'd stopped and offered to help her with her heavy load, would undoubtedly have granted her three wishes, at least one of which would've been worth having. Dad had been right, she decided, about two things, but not the third. The shoes from Cousin Cindy did fit, really well. And everybody was happy. But it wasn't all right. Far from it.

At the last moment, the dragon miscalculated. As the knight crouched before it, frantically scrabbling for his fallen sword, it couldn't resist the temptation to rear up and spout a flowery jet of kingfisher-blue fire through its craggy nostrils. A little voice in its head said, *No, you really don't want to do that,* but it paid no attention. It had won, and it loved to show off.

Which is why, at the very last moment, the knight managed to get one finger round the pommel of his sword, hook it towards him, catch it with his other hand and hold it out quite still as the dragon lurched down on him for the kill. The sword's point went into the dragon's armpit with the minimum of fuss, like a needle into cloth.

The knight let go of the sword and staggered back. The dragon looked slowly down and saw the hilt, which was all that remained visible. "Oh," it said.

The knight had regained his balance and was walking backwards. He stopped after nine paces. Dragonfire, as they both knew, has an effective range of eight yards.

"Sorry," the knight said. "Nothing personal."

For the first time in its thousand years of existence, the dragon knew what it was like to feel weak. Suddenly, all that strength, which it had taken for granted for so very long, wasn't there any more. It took all its reserves of courage and determination to lift its head a little. Then it fell over. The ground jarred its head as it landed, making it wince.

After a little while, it heard the knight say, "Excuse me, are you still alive?"

"Mphm."

"Fine," the knight said pleasantly. "No hurry. You just take your time."

He wanted his sword back. Well, of course he did. The dragon tried to draw in a deep breath, for a final foe-incinerating blaze of glory; but it was hard, so very hard, and deep inside it could feel the embers of its internal furnace starting to go cold. Oh well, the dragon thought; it's been a good life, plenty of flying around and crunchy people and expensive armour glowing cherry-red. No hard feelings. Then it remembered there was something it was supposed to do at this point; and, being a conscientious creature, it resolved to make the effort. It opened its cavernous mouth – painful and difficult, like flexing a knee after you've been sitting in one position for too long – and said, "Listen to me."

"Sure," the knight said amiably. "Fire away."

"Learn your destiny," the dragon said. It had no idea where the words came from; they were urgently inside it somewhere, like a large egg in a small chicken, and they needed to come out before – well, the end; because otherwise it wouldn't be right, somehow. Dragons have a strong sense of right and wrong, which is why they always wipe their feet after bursting into a crowded mead-hall. "You must ride to the forest of Evinardar, beneath the White Mountains of Glathinroth, where you will find—" The dragon hesitated. "Excuse me. Are you listening?"

The knight looked up from the book he was reading. "Sorry?"

"I said, are you listening to me? This is your destiny."

The knight marked his place with a dandelion and closed the book. "Sorry, yes, that's fine. Go to the forest of Evinardar, beneath the White Mountains of Gladinroth—"

"Gla*thin*roth."

"Whatever," the knight said. "And there I shall find a crystal cave where awaits a twelve-fingered giant; if I overcome him, I get to claim the golden chalice of Northestroon, and so on and so forth. Sorry," he added with a slight smile, "heard it all before, actually. And to be honest, I can't say I'm all that bothered. All a bit too New-Agey for me, I'm afraid."

It occurred to the dragon that maybe it wasn't the first of its kind this knight had killed. It felt a faint pang of irritation, but no matter. "I forgive you," it sighed. "Go in peace."

"Jolly good," the knight said absently. "How are you feeling?"

"I go to join my ancestors in the heart of the Great Fire," the dragon said. "Soon I shall be at one with the elemental force from which we all derive our being, and from whence—"

"Splendid," the knight said, munching an apple. "Don't let me keep you."

"But you must know—" the dragon started to say; and then it stopped, because it didn't feel at all well. And then it died.

The knight saw the light in the great creature's eyes go out. He finished his apple and stood up, wincing as his horribly abused muscles made a formal complaint to his brain, then went over to the corpse and pulled out his sword, which he wiped carefully on the grass before sheathing it, because swords cost money. As he turned and walked away, he was doing mental arithmetic under his breath.

They were all waiting for him at the bottom of the hill. He

paused to flick out an apple pip that had got lodged between his teeth, then strolled down to join them.

"Sir Turquine," the king said, in a strained voice. "Have you—?"

The knight nodded. "All done," he said. "Now, I'll be needing a large cart—"

His words were drowned by an eruption of wild cheers from the soldiers and courtiers, while the king closed his eyes in silent thanksgiving. The knight waited politely until they'd quietened down a bit and he could make himself heard. "A large cart," he repeated, "and if you could spare a dozen men for the afternoon, I'd be ever so—"

A choir of local children broke out into a hymn of thanksgiving, while a large, plain girl tried to hang a garland of flowers round his neck. He fended the flowers off as tactfully as he could, and cleared his throat loudly. The king raised his hand and the children fell silent, though their mouths continued to open and close for some time. "Sir Turquine," the king said. "We are forever in your debt. Thanks to you, the long night of horror and fear—"

"Yes," the knight said. "So, as I was saying, if you just let me have a large, stout cart and ten men—"

The king looked at him as though he'd suddenly turned green. "Nothing," he said, in a slightly snarky voice, "will ever be able to express our true gratitude. However, half the kingdom and my daughter's hand in marriage is, I believe, the traditional reward."

The knight's lips were tightly pursed. "Terribly sweet of you," he said. "But, thanks but no thanks. Really."

"Sir Turquine?"

The knight sighed. "No offence," he said, glancing briefly upwards as though gauging the time of day by the position of the sun, "but honestly, I'd rather not."

The king frowned. "Perhaps I haven't made myself clear,"

he said. "As a reward for your heroism, I would like you to rule half my kingdom and marry my only daughter, the heir to the throne. To bestow any lesser reward would—"

"Yes, got that, thank you," the knight said, in a very clear voice; so clear, in fact, that the children all took a step back, and the chancellor ducked smartly behind the archbishop. "Like I said, desperately generous of you, but I'm not what you'd call the ruling type. Also, if memory serves, your northern provinces are in open revolt, your economy's just gone into triple-dip recession and the dragon burned down all the frog-apple trees, whose fruit is your country's only export and source of hard currency. It's terribly feeble of me, I know, but I prefer my rewards just a bit less challenging."

"My daughter—" said the king.

"Don't let's go there," the knight said. "No, honestly, it's been a real treat for me, and a privilege to have been of service, but what I'd really like is a nice strong six-wheeler hay cart and the loan of half a dozen strong men for a couple of hours, and then we can call it quits. Agreed?"

It occurred to the king that taking offence with the man who'd just killed the invincible dragon might not be the wisest thing he'd ever done. "Agreed," he said. "One cart, six men. If that's what you really—"

"Yes. Thank you."

A soft red sunset had begun to fill the sky when the knight, seated on the crossbench of a heavily loaded cart, rolled up the long, narrow road that led through the high pass in the Blue Mountains and down into Sair Carathorn, the Wizard's Vale. Pulling gently on the reins, he paused for a moment to gaze out over the harsh, wind-scorched fells towards the obscure horizon, beyond which lay the Seven Kingdoms and, further still, his half-forgotten home in Westeresse. One day, he thought; one day, perhaps, but not yet. Not, in fact, for as long as humanly possible, unless they'd eventually got around to doing something about the drains, and his people had finally lost their ancestral passion for double-fermented pickled cabbage. With a soft word of command he urged the horses on, and began the long descent into Sair Carathorn.

When he reached the gate in the stockade, the gatekeeper grunted reluctantly and let him pass, although technically it was already past curfew. He drove across the empty square, jumped down and tied the reins to the hitching-post in front of the great bronze doors of Enith Carathruin, the Abode of the Wizard. The night shift could take it from there, he decided. What he wanted most of all was a drink.

The taproom of the Blue Boar was almost deserted, but for a solitary figure sitting beside the fire, his hood drawn down to obscure his face. Nevertheless, the knight took his pint of ale and sat down beside him.

"Bedevere," said the knight.

"Hello, Turkey." Sir Bedevere yawned, and put his mug down on the floor. The innkeeper's whippet got up from under his chair, sniffed the mug and walked slowly away. "Any luck?"

Sir Turquine shrugged. "One," he said. "Bit on the small side, but what the hell. You?"

"Three," Bedevere replied. "Mind, you should've seen the one that got away."

Turquine suppressed a frown. "Three," he said. "Not bad."

"Small ones," Sir Bedevere said. "I'll be lucky if I get nine shillings for the lot. Still," he added, "nine bob's nine bob."

"Quite," Turquine said. "Where did you—?"

Sir Bedevere made a slightly vague gesture with his left hand. "Some place out east I'd never even heard of. Remarkable, isn't it, how many of these little tinpot kingdoms there are in these parts."

Turquine nodded thoughtfully. It was, in fact, a subject to which he'd given a certain amount of bemused thought over the past few years. Practically every valley south of the Mouthwash was a tiny independent entity, with its own king, royal court and interchangeable simpering princesses; and, it went without saying, its own dragon. Not that he was complaining, needless to say. Even so; how had it come about that way, he couldn't help wondering. How did they all survive? What did the people of these miniature principalities all do for a living? It couldn't be trade, because they were all dirt-poor. Not agriculture, because most of the land was barren scrub, and the few acres that weren't tended to be infested with a ridiculously large population of dragons. Still, he told himself, there was bound to be a perfectly simple explanation, which everyone else knew except him, and he didn't want to make himself look stupid by asking. Besides, the more dragons the better, as far as he was concerned.

Even so—

"I had a narrow escape with one of them," Bedevere was saying.

"Oh yes?"

Bedevere nodded emphatically. "Buggers ambushed me," he said, "on the way back from the lair. Flowers, bridesmaids, brass band, little kids throwing rose petals, bishop in a red dressing-gown, the full nine yards. I had to pretend I was already married before they let me go. And even then they gave me a bloody funny look. I think they'd probably been checking up beforehand." He sighed. "That's not right, if you ask me. Leaves a nasty sort of taste in your mouth, that sort of thing."

"You've got to be so careful," the knight agreed.

"Too right. You know, sometimes, for two pins I'd pack the whole thing in. Still," he added thoughtfully, "nine shillings, in these hard times."

The knight sipped his beer, shuddered, and put the mug down on the floor. "What I want to know is—" He stopped, having realised what he'd just started to say. But there was no going back. "What I want to know is, where do all these dragons come from?"

Bedevere looked at him. "You what?"

"All these dragons." The knight couldn't remember when he'd felt so foolish. Still. "Think about it. How many have you had this month? Nine? Ten?"

It was one of those things you simply didn't ask. "Actually, twenty-six. Not, if you don't mind my saying so, that it's any of your—"

"Sorry," the knight said quickly (and he was thinking; twenty-*six*? At, say, three shillings a head? My *God*.) "You've got to admit, though, that's a lot of dragons."

Bedevere shrugged. "Loads more where they came from."

"Exactly," the knight said, "that's my point. That's a hell of a lot of dragons."

Bedevere sighed. "You're not going to turn out to be one of those wretched tree-hugger types, are you? Because dragons are pests, they burn crops and eat sheep. They kill people, for crying out loud. If it wasn't for us—"

"Of course," the knight said quickly, "I wasn't suggesting otherwise. I just can't help thinking—"

"I can." Bedevere stood up abruptly. "Good lord, is that the time? Think I'll turn in. Nice bumping into you and all that. Cheerio."

After he'd gone, the knight sat alone for a long time, thinking; twenty-*six*. That's three pounds nine shillings. That's—

He stood up, yawned and stretched. His earlier exertions, together with a long ride on an unsprung cart, were beginning to set hard, rather like slow-drying plaster. I'm getting too old for this, he thought. He was twenty-two.

By the time he reached the wizard's house, the night shift

had finished skinning and quartering the dragon; they'd hung the quarters on a great steel frame on little wheels, and the bronze doors were open so they could take it inside. Through the open doors Turquine caught a glimpse of a vast, high-ceilinged chamber, brilliantly lit, its walls and floor white as snow. It was filled with row upon row upon row of skinned dragon quarters on steel frames, hundreds, thousands, of them. A bitter chill from inside wafted over him, and he shivered. The night-shift foreman was marking one of the quarters with a stencil. He turned to Sir Turquine, and grinned.

"You all right, mate?" he said.

Turquine nodded. "That's a lot of —"

"Yeah, well." The foreman shrugged. "You go on down the office, they'll give you a blue form and a receipt. All right?"

"Thanks," Turquine said. He was peering over the foreman's shoulder. Right at the back of the great white chamber, set into the furthest wall, he could see – what? A gateway? A portal? It was round, maybe fifty feet in diameter, surrounded with a sort of golden-brown frame that glistened and sparkled in the pure-white glare, as though studded with thousands of diamonds, though the hole in the middle was as black as soot. The men working inside had loaded a dozen racks of dragon quarters on to a crane, which swung across into the black hole in the centre of the portal; a moment later, the crane swung back again, empty.

The foreman was looking at him. "All right?" he repeated.

"What? Sorry." Turquine got the feeling he wasn't entirely welcome. "I was just—"

"Go down the office," the foreman said firmly, "they'll give you your blue form and your receipt, and then you can get paid. All right?"

"Yes, right." For some reason, the look on the foreman's

face made Turquine nervous, in a way dragons never did. Not live ones, anyway. "Thank you."

"'S all right," the foreman said, still looking straight at him. "Mind how you go."

He went to the office, where a very old man in a brown coat and a curious flat-topped cap gave him his blue form and his receipt, smiled and put up the "Position Closed" sign before he could say anything. He looked round, but the only other living creature in the office was a very tall, thin young man, leaning against the wall, eating a sausage. He didn't look as though he was in any position to answer difficult questions, though he nodded politely as Turquine walked past him into the cold night air.

The drill was, you took the blue form and the receipt to the other office, right round the other side of the building, where you got your money; but the other office closed at dusk and didn't open until three hours after daybreak. Turquine glanced down at the blue form, and was pleasantly surprised; 907 lbs @ 15d./cwt = 6s. 2d. Six shillings and twopence. A warm smile spread over Turquine's face, like spilled oil on water. Six bob. Hey.

He went back to the inn and asked for a beer. "The good stuff," he specified.

The innkeeper looked at him. "You sure?"

Turquine nodded. "I can afford it."

The good stuff was still pretty bad, but it was unimaginably better than the other stuff. Turquine sat by the fire, nursing his beer, staring into the flames. He was trying to remember what it had been like, before the wizard came. He found it remarkably difficult. How old would he have been? Hard to say. Nine, twelve, something like that; he was pretty sure he'd been in the dragon-slaying business for four years, and he'd won his spurs when he was eighteen. Of course, those four years had felt like for ever.

Yes, but it was so much better now, wasn't it? He unfolded the blue form and looked at it, just to make sure the numbers were still there. Six shillings and twopence. The family estate, to which his father and now his brother had devoted their lives, brought in a gross income of one pound two shillings and fourpence (in a good year, when the harvest didn't fail and the chickens didn't get fowl pest), and that put their family in the top third of the nobility; new shoes once a year, fresh cabbage leaves for the outhouse and half a bottle of malmsey wine at Candlemas. Before the wizard came, any transaction involving six shillings and twopence was big news, the sort of thing they'd be talking about in the inn and the smithy from lambing through to blackberry-time. Now, though; now, a no-account younger son like Bedevere (a nice enough chap in his way, but scarcely the sharpest bodkin in the quiver) could earn himself three pounds nine shillings in a single month, and for doing what? Pest control. Forty-one pounds a year for being basically a glorified rat-catcher.

And what was good for the younger sons of the nobility, of course, was good for the kingdom; all that extra money in circulation, leading inevitably to prosperity for all. True, there wasn't much sign of it to the casual observer. The villages were still poverty-stricken, mostly because of the depredations of the dragons, but no more so than before; about the same, in fact. Turquine thought about that. If the wizard hadn't come along when he did, they'd presumably still have had the plague of dragons (where *did* they come from? Good question), but without the vital cash boost to the economy that the wizard provided. Without the wizard, in fact, they'd be in all sorts of trouble, though of course it was no use trying to tell that to the average peasant-in-the-stocks. That was the trouble with ordinary folk. They simply couldn't get their heads around the complexities of economics.

He lapped the last half-inch of his beer round the bottom of his mug, watching the white specks of dead yeast scurrying in the eddies like carp in a pond. Two things, a wise old man had told him once, that you don't ask about: what the meat is in a shop-bought meat and turnip pie, and where anything worth having comes from. Wisdom indeed. True, the same old man had then sold him a cow that died three days later, but there you go. Life is really just a river; it moves on, and all sorts of stuff ends up in it.

Next day, he went to the desk in the other office and got his six shiny silver coins and his two rather world-weary coppers. He put the coppers in his pocket, then trotted along to the shimmering white marble building that housed the Consolidated Wizards Bank. Reckless courage, the willingness to risk everything on a desperate million-to-one chance, is the hallmark of the hero, except where money is concerned. But what could possibly be safer than a bank?

"Three pounds," the girl behind the counter told him, "nine shillings and fourpence."

Sir Turquine scowled. "That's not right."

The girl checked her ledger. "Sorry," she said. "Three pounds, nine shillings and fourpence *halfpenny*."

Knights are trained from boyhood to treat all damosels with chivalrous respect; even so, Sir Turquine couldn't help making a growling noise in the bottom of his throat, like an angry dog. "That's more like it," he said. "Thank you so much."

"Have a nice day."

The next time, she didn't hesitate. The moment she saw the little stooping figure tottering up the path in front of her, she reached into the basket, grabbed the hammer she'd borrowed from her father's workbench and swung hard. There was a chunky noise and a shrill yelp, and she stepped back to give the wolf room to fall.

"Right," she said, pulling off the dented straw bonnet to reveal two pointed grey ears. "I want a word with you."

The wolf looked at her with pale yellow eyes. "Oh," it said. "It's you."

Buttercup frowned. "You know me?"

"Heard of you," the wolf replied. "Oh yes. Where I come from, we know all about *you*."

"Really?"

"The Angel of Death, that's what you're known as."

Buttercup couldn't help feeling mildly smug. "Is that right."

"Yes."

"Fine. So why'd you keep coming? You know it'll all end in tears."

The wolf shrugged. "We're wolves," it said simply.

Buttercup grabbed the nearest ear and twisted it hard.

"That's not good enough," she said. "I mean, it doesn't make *sense.*"

The wolf looked at her. "Sense?"

"That's right," she said eagerly. "Come on, think about it, for crying out loud. You're wolves, right? Presumably you live in some sort of pack, up in the Blue Hills."

The wolf's other ear was flat to the side of its head. "I'm not telling you where," it said firmly.

"I don't want to know," Buttercup said. "Really."

"Yeah, right."

"Really. I mean," she went on, "what actual threat do you pose to us? None whatsoever. Because it's always the wolf that gets killed, never the cute little girl. Look, how many raids do you do every week? Two? Three?"

"Not telling."

"At least two, often three. And what happens? The wolf dies. You always lose."

"I know what you're doing," the wolf said. "This is advanced interrogation techniques, right? First you destroy my self-esteem and sense of individuality, then you force me to tell you where the pack hides out, so your woodcutter pals can come and slaughter us. Well, you're wasting your breath. I won't talk. I *won't talk.* Got that?"

"You are talking," Buttercup pointed out. "In fact, shut up a minute and let me finish. Two raids a week, let's say, fifty-two weeks a year, that's a hundred and four dead wolves, out of a pack of what, two hundred and fifty? No, I'm not asking you," she added quickly, as the wolf started shaking its head frantically, "I'm just trying to make the point. In evolutionary terms, what you're doing is genetic suicide."

The wolf's eyes were perfectly round, and Buttercup had never seen such terror. Compared with it, the fear of death was mild apprehension. "Evo-what?"

Buttercup shivered slightly. The words, the long words

she'd never heard before but which she understood implicitly, were coming more and more frequently, and she wasn't sure she liked it. "It doesn't make *sense*," she translated. "If you carry on like this, you'll all be dead. Extinct. No more wolves. So—" She took a deep breath. "Why do you do it? Why?"

The wolf looked confused as well as terrified. "We're wolves. We need to eat."

"Then why the hell don't you eat sheep? The hills are covered with them."

The wolf hesitated. "I don't know," it said. "I guess we've never— I don't know."

"And anyway," Buttercup ploughed on, "you *don't* eat little girls. You try to, but you *always fail*. How come you haven't all starved to death long since?"

The wolf's eyes were a mirror of spiritual agony. "I'm not answering any more questions," it said.

"Come on," Buttercup said, "this is for your benefit as much as mine. Why don't you starve?"

The wolf's eyes turned glassy. "Wolf," it said, "beta male. Serial number zero zero zero six three seven."

"Answer me," Buttercup yelled, shaking the wolf by the throat. "Answer me and I'll let you go, all right?"

She'd done it this time. "You'll what?"

"Let you go."

"*You can't do that.*" The wolf was shocked, as though Buttercup had suggested something unspeakably obscene. "Don't you understand? We're the bad guys."

"No you're not," Buttercup said. "That's the point."

"Of course we're the bad guys." The wolf was trembling uncontrollably. "We're wicked predators who sneak down from our lair and gobble up innocent—"

"No you *don't*," Buttercup howled in his face. "You come down here, over a hundred a year, and we *slaughter* you.

You're a goddamn *endangered species* because of us, you're *victims*. Don't you see that, you stupid bloody poodle?"

The wolf composed itself, acquiring a strange, sad dignity as it looked past Buttercup at the relentlessly blue sky overhead. "Wolf," it said. "Beta male. Serial number zero zero—"

"You're an ecological disaster waiting to happen," Buttercup screamed, then broke off. The wolf was dead. She let go; but she knew from the lack of cramp in her fingers that she hadn't strangled it, you have to squeeze really hard, and your hands are stiff for days afterwards. It had just died.

"That's *silly*," she howled at the sky, but no reply came.

She knelt down and pulled its shawl respectfully over its face. A wolf, the ancestral enemy, as stupid as a brick, but within its own frame of reference it had died with honour. (And another thing; what happened to all the dead wolves, anyway? Nobody ever buried them, so the woods should be littered with shawl-shrouded bones. But the next day they were always gone, without fail.) Looking down into its empty eyes, she felt a pang of guilt. But it wasn't me, she reminded herself, I didn't kill it, it just died.

Animals don't just die.

She picked up her basket and went on her way through the dappled gallery of the woods, stopping from time to time to watch a scampering squirrel or a gently grazing deer. Animals don't just die. I didn't kill it. Therefore—

Therefore, somebody else killed it.

Don't be so silly, she told herself, carefully stepping over a big red toadstool with cute white spots. No arrow wound, no wound of any sort. Poison? A remote possibility, but she didn't think so. Nobody would dream of putting down poison, for fear of harming the squirrels, badgers, hedgehogs, pixies, gnomes. And anyway, why would anybody want to kill— Why would anybody apart from the woodcutters and herself want to kill a notoriously harmless wolf? Unless—

I won't talk, it had said, inaccurately. Now she thought about it, the wolf had been far more afraid of interrogation than mere death. Leaving aside the impossible problem of how you kill a wolf without leaving a mark or even being there, suppose the wolf had been killed to prevent it from betraying some secret. Was that possible? She thought about it. It struck her as pretty far-fetched, but she could just about imagine circumstances in which somebody might just do such a thing.

Advanced interrogation techniques. Were they, she asked herself, words that had suddenly appeared in the wolf's head, completely unfamiliar but perfectly understood, because it had needed to know their meaning? Maybe, maybe not; but someone or something had trained that wolf how to resist aggressive questioning – not very well, admittedly, but presumably the concepts involved had been as unfamiliar to the wolf as economic models and evolutionary dead ends had been to her, just a short while ago. In which case, it hadn't done too badly.

She frowned. If someone was doing this, he, she or it wasn't very nice. Suddenly she grinned. Not being very nice was a bad career move in these parts. Sooner or later, they always got what was coming to them. So, maybe there was a woodcutter's axe with his-her-its name on it somewhere. And why the hell not.

A round, pink face appeared above a bush beside the track; it was wearing a green cap with a red feather, and a mildly bewildered expression. She sighed. "Hi, Tom," she said.

Tom the woodcutter was even taller, broader and fairer-haired than John the woodcutter, though there wasn't all that much between them in the gormlessness stakes. Both of them, in fact, were bottomless pits into which gorm vanished without trace. "Hello, Buttercup," Tom said, and stepped out from behind the bush. He had his axe on his shoulder. The edge, she couldn't help noticing, had recently been honed to razor-sharpness.

"Fancy meeting you here," she said.

"What? Oh, I was just—" He stopped, and his eyebrows met. It was like watching a fight between two crazed hedges. "You all right?"

"Why shouldn't I be?"

"Um. Well, they do say there's wolves been seen in these parts lately."

She nodded her head at the sad bundle on the ground. "Who told you?" she said.

"What?"

"About the wolf. Who told you it'd be right here, precisely now?"

"Nobody told me, I just—"

"Just what?"

"Thought there might be, well, you know, someone in trouble."

"You heard the screams and came running."

"What screams?"

"Quite." He looked like he wanted to make a run for it, but she fixed him with a stare, folded her arms and waited. "Well?"

"Well what?"

"Why did you think there'd be someone here needing saving from a wolf?"

"I don't know, do I? I just thought—"

"You're lying." As soon as she said it, she wondered why. It was such a bizarre thing to accuse anybody of, let alone Tom the woodcutter. "Someone told you. Who was it? Was it the wizard?"

"What? No, of course not."

There are some people whose lies are a lot more reliable

than most people's statements of truth. Whenever Tom told a lie, his ears went red, his nose twitched, his eyes blinked rapidly and he started to sweat. There aren't many things in this life you can absolutely depend on, but Tom's lies were rock-solid.

"It *was* the wizard. Wasn't it?"

"No. Yes. Well, sort of. Not really." He backed away and bumped gently into a tree, which swayed visibly. "I – I don't know. Honest."

"Tom." She gave him three seconds of the stare, then switched to sweet and winsome. "It's all right," she said, smiling as pleasantly as she knew how, "you can tell me."

He shook his head. "No, I can't."

Try something else. "You can tell me," she said reasonably, "or I can hit you with this hammer."

"Buttercup?"

All right, then, not that. "Sorry, Tom, just kidding." She sighed. This was getting tedious. "Look," she said, trying not to plead. "*Why* can't you tell me?"

"Because I don't know." She looked at him, and he was genuinely miserable. "It's just that sometimes—"

"Yes?"

"When I'm in the forest, cutting wood," Tom went on, looking away, "it's like I hear this voice in my head saying, Go to such and such a place, and when I go there, usually there's this little girl just about to be gobbled up by a big bad wolf or a wicked witch or a troll or something. So then I smack the wolf with my axe, and—"

"This voice," she interrupted. "It's the wizard, right?"

"Sometimes I think it might be," Tom said uncertainly. "Except, I've never actually heard the wizard say anything, so how would I know?"

Suddenly she felt very tired. "Fine," she said. "Well, thanks anyhow. You've been a great help."

"No I haven't. The wolf was already dead when I got here."

"Yes," she told him. "That's what was so helpful."

She watched him to see if that might possibly sink in, but it didn't; she could almost watch it bounce off and dissipate in the empty air. "Well," she said, "don't let me keep you."

He nodded, half turned, stopped and blushed like a sunset. "Buttercup."

"What?"

"Um. Would you like to go to the Spring Dance with me?"

"No. Goodbye."

He drooped, then shouldered his axe and shambled off into the trees. She couldn't help feeling just a little bit sorry for him, but not enough. He's another victim, just like me, she thought. The difference is, he doesn't know it. That's quite a difference.

She became aware of the pressure of the basket handle on her arm. Her father and uncles would be expecting their dinner. She looked round briefly, but she couldn't see the wolf's cosy little hut; the hell with it, they'd have to make do without their ham and cucumber sandwiches for once. (Query: where do wolves get ham and cucumber sandwiches from? And how does a wolf, a quadruped lacking an opposable thumb, dress itself up in a shawl, bonnet and button-up boots? And why, come to that, did her father and uncles insist on having their workshop in the heart of a dark, wolf-infested forest when there was a perfectly good barn out the back of the house which nobody ever used for anything?)

I have to get away from here, she thought. I need to get right away – five miles, even ten, assuming the world was that big; the other side of the Blue Hills, at any rate. Things would have to be different on the other side of the Blue Hills; no wolves, no woodcutters, and maybe just possibly, things would make *sense*. She cast her mind back, trying to retrieve any information she'd gathered over the years about the big wide world. Well, to start with, there was the town. Lots of people lived there; they bought loads of wood, so at the very least it'd be warm there, and practically everything came from there, all the clothes people wore and the tools they used, so she wouldn't need to take anything with her, except money, and she'd got quite a bit of that stored in the sock under her mattress. And maybe, just maybe, there were other towns even further away, beyond other hills—

One day, perhaps. Right now, she had to take the food basket to the workshop, and then it'd be time to go home and boil the copper for washing the clothes, and then there were floors to sweep and the carrot bed to weed, and all the other things that needed to be done, and there wasn't anybody else to do them. She wasn't absolutely sure that that made sense either.

She walked round a bend in the road, then stopped dead. Standing in the middle of the path, holding the bridle of a milk-white horse, was a young man with long golden hair. He was dressed in green velvet, with a red cloak and shiny black boots, and there was a sword hanging from his belt. It wasn't exactly clear what he was doing. He had a little rectangular black and silver box nestled in the palm of his hand, and he was prodding at it with his thumb and frowning. She'd never seen him before, needless to say, but there was absolutely no doubt in her mind about his identity.

One day, they kept telling her, your prince will come. Well, he just had.

In the vast, echoing space of the Halls of Udrear, half a mile underground and lit by the wild flickerings of a thousand pine-resin torches, two mighty armies confronted each other in dead silence. On one side, the grim dwarf-host of Drain son of Dror son of Druin stood motionless in serried, geometrically perfect ranks and files; on the other, the goblin horde of King Mordak seethed like a cesspool in an earthquake. The thick, damp, smoky air felt heavy with the miasma of five hundred years of war, a physical presence that lay like a crushing weight on the shoulders and neck of every warrior present. For a long time they stood, their eyes full of the enemy. Then Mordak took a step forward – one step, but everyone present would have sworn the earth shook. Opposite him, Drain clenched his empty hands until his knuckles showed white, and advanced precisely one step to meet him.

Iron-clad toe to iron-clad toe; they were so close that the tip of the dwarf's beard was almost touching the goblin's sixth chin. Their eyes met; the hatred, the disgust and the hope—

"Well?" Drain said.

Mordak's deep voice seemed to rumble up out of the mine shafts under their feet. "It's time."

"Bags I go first."

Mordak drew in breath for a great shout of refusal; but all he did was nod his enormous head. "Fine," he said. "You can go first."

Drain hesitated. In his mind's eye he could see ninety-seven generations of his ancestors, looking down at him from the gates of Nargoprong, waiting for him to screw up. The entire future of dwarfkind rested on the choice he was about to make. And if he should fail— He steeled his heart, lifted his head and in a loud, clear voice said, "I spy with my little eye something beginning with F."

Mordak blinked. "Eff?"

"You heard me."

Mordak breathed out slowly through the three slits just above his upper jaw that served him as nostrils. Eff, he thought, for crying out loud. "Fire."

"No."

Eff. Apart from fire, what was there in the Great Hall that began with F? Soldiers, lots of soldiers, in armour, holding weapons. And that was about it. He racked his brains for abstruse military terminology. "Phalanx?"

"Phalanx," Drain said smugly, "begins with a P."

Mordak's eyes widened; two of them, anyway. "Does it?"

"Yes. Look it up."

Which left just one more guess; and if he guessed wrong, the five hundred year war would be over and he'd have lost. By the terms of the armistice (which he'd proposed, argued passionately for in the teeth, the yellow, split-ended teeth, of furious opposition from every single goblin clan chieftain under the Mountain) the dwarves would then be entitled to vacant possession of the entire network of mines, from Drubin's Gate to the Nazerbul. It didn't bear thinking about.

Eff, for pity's sake. By the rules of the contest, thrashed out over the course of two years by five hundred negotiators from each side, he wasn't allowed to look round, to see what Drain could see. He had to rely on his memory and, Thun preserve us, his imagination.

Flames? Fighters? Wasn't there some sort of rare, obsolete throwing-axe whose name began with F? No, howled a little voice inside him, it's nothing like that, it can't be. Remember, Drain's a dwarf. Dwarves are *devious*.

The dwarf-lord cleared his throat. Time was passing. If Mordak didn't answer in five seconds, he'd lose by default.

All right, Mordak thought desperately. The rules say it's got to be something he can see from where he's standing; but he knows he daren't lose, so it can't be anything I might possibly guess. What, within the parameters of the rules and, as a dwarf would define it, the truth, would he know I'd never ever say?

Suddenly he relaxed, and knew that he'd won. Put like that, there could only be one answer.

Mordak smiled, revealing all his teeth. "Friend," he said.

Drain went white as a sheet. "Sorry. Didn't quite catch—"

"Friend," Mordak repeated, loud and grimly clear. "That's the answer, isn't it?"

"Um," said Drain. "Best of three?"

"Friend," Mordak boomed, and his voice ricocheted off the vaulted roof like catapult shot. "Well?"

Twenty thousand dwarves and twenty thousand goblins held their breath. Then Drain mumbled something to his shoes. It sounded like *ymblmbl*. "Say again?"

"Yes."

It was one of those trigger moments; when the destiny of the Three Races hung on a tiny detent, like the slim steel spur lodged in the nut of a spanned crossbow that keeps the string from slamming forward and launching the arrow. It would only take the smallest pressure to release it; some fool drawing a sword or nocking an arrow on a bowstring, or dropping a clattering spear on the granite floor. The last time two armies of this size had been this close to each other under the Mountain, the battle had lasted three days and there had been just one survivor, and they'd had to hire in outside contractors to clear away the dead.

"Just to clarify," Mordak said. "That means I've won."

The dwarf didn't speak. Mordak hadn't expected him to. As soon as Drain admitted defeat, the dwarves would come out swinging; a fraction of a second later, the goblins would retaliate in kind, and forty thousand sentient beings would set about the congenial task of turning every living thing in the Great Chamber into pastrami. It was probably just as well, Mordak told himself, that I've prepared for this moment.

"Tell you what," Mordak said, "let's call it quits."

The dwarf's head snapped up. "You what?"

"Let's do a deal," Mordak said, and his voice seemed like it was coming from a long way away and belonged to someone else. "Your lot can have all the mine workings south of this room, and we'll have everything to the north. Well?"

Imagine how you would feel if forty thousand and one people were staring at you, convinced you'd gone off your head. But at least they weren't shooting. "Just like that?"

"Yup."

"We'd have all the mines *south* of this room, and you'd have all the mines *north*—?"

Mordak nodded. "That's the general idea. So?"

Drain lowered his voice to a harsh whisper. "But you won."

Mordak nodded. "So I did," he hissed back. "And in two minutes, unless we can pull this off, these idiots are going to start slaughtering each other. Not to mention," he added with feeling, "us. But if we do this deal, they'll all be so bewildered and confused they won't know what to do, which means you and I can slip away quietly, and maybe just possibly we'll both still be alive this time tomorrow."

"But—"

The dwarf had spoken automatically, because anything a goblin says to a dwarf has to be contradicted immediately. "Hang on," Drain said. "That's not such a dumb idea."

"Thank you so much."

"But—"

The inner conflict raging inside the dwarf's small, round head was fascinating to watch; like a fight to the death between three goldfish. "But that'd mean *peace*."

"Good heavens, so it would. There's a thing. Still—"

"No," Drain whispered nervously, "no way. They'll tear me limb from limb."

"Not," Mordak hissed, "necessarily. Just stop and think, will you? What does peace actually *mean*?"

Behind him, Mordak could hear twenty thousand goblins starting to mutter. "I don't know, do I?" Drain said helplessly. "There's never been—"

"Peace," Mordak said, quickly and urgently, "means no more fighting. Also, it means an end to the ruinous expense of training, equipping and supplying two ridiculously large armies, which is bleeding both of us white. It means an opportunity to stand down the armed forces, fire the existing generals and get new ones who aren't actively plotting against us, recruit and train up a decent professional standing army to replace the useless, sloppy, bolshie bunch of draftees we're both lumbered with, and take a bit of time and a bit of care to get ready for the *next* war—"

"Ah!"

"—At the end of which, our combined forces will have wiped the Elves off the face of the Earth. *That's* what peace means. Well?"

"*Ah.*"

Mordak allowed himself a brief, happy grin. "Thought you'd get the hang of it," he said, "a bright fella like you."

He'd won. He knew it. Goblins and dwarves hated each other; of course they did. But *everybody* hated the Elves; and why not? Bunch of stuck-up, supercilious, patronising, bleeding-heart-liberal-intellectual tree-huggers, it made his blood boil just thinking about them. If peace was what it took to nail every last Elf to a tree by the tips of its pointy ears, it was a small enough price to pay. And Drain might be thick as three lead bricks, but he had to see that, too. Didn't he?

"Done," Drain said. "You got yourself a deal."

"Thanks," Mordak said. "Friend," he added. That got him an extra special dwarven nasty look, but he felt he deserved a little self-indulgence.

He let Drain do the speech; and, to be fair, the little chap did it pretty well. He talked about new beginnings and a bright new dawn for their children and their children's children, about understanding and reconciliation and kicking twelve kinds of shit out of the Elves; and by the time he'd finished forty thousand battle-hardened warriors were standing around with stunned expressions on their faces, and five centuries of war were suddenly over, just like that—

I did that, Mordak thought. And then he thought; *why* did I do that?

Well, he told himself afterwards, as he sipped a well-earned margarita from the jewel-encrusted skull of his predecessor (the gemstones picked out the words WORLD'S BEST BOSS; goblin craftsmanship at its finest), obviously I did it so that we can go after those bastard Elves and sort them out once and for all. And then he played a little game; substitute dwarves for Elves and Elves for dwarves, and see what difference it makes.

None whatsoever.

Yes, but— He frowned. Fine. First we deal with the Elves. Then we can break the alliance and sort out the dwarves, after they've done most of the hard work annihilating the pointy-ears. Put like that, it made perfect sense. One thing at a time, and only an idiot fights a war on two fronts. Yes. Of course.

And was that the real reason? No. Thought not.

What's got into me? He scowled at his drink and put it down. While we're on the subject of things that only fools do, how about lying to yourself? Other people, fine, no problem; yourself, no. The *real* reason—

Was that the war was *stupid*. The war meant that 75 per cent of the goblin workforce was fighting the war, costing him money, when they could be working down the mines, earning him money; sure, the war was about who controlled the mines, but so long as it lasted, ownership was irrelevant, because practically nobody was working down there. Also, a hell of a lot of goblins were getting killed, and maybe that wasn't such a good—

He cringed. He was starting to sound like an Elf. No, worse than that (because Elves had no problem with wars so long as they weren't actually doing the fighting). He was starting to sound like a *human*.

Yuck.

After we've done the Elves and the dwarves, he promised himself, the humans are definitely going to be next. Absolutely. No question.

His predecessor was grinning at him. As well he might; Ugrok had been a good, traditional, uncontroversial Goblin King, loved and respected by his surviving subjects. A robust approach to diplomacy and a fine head for military strategy (and here it was, empty; Mordak reached for the bottle and poured himself a large brandy) He'd never have made peace with the dwarves, just because some wizard—

No, we won't go there. Mordak sighed. Too much think-ing made him dizzy, and right now the room was slowly churning round and round. Keep it simple, he told himself, keep it real, keep it *goblin*. The only reason I just ended the war was so I can start it again. Put like that—

Put like that, it was silly; also, it wasn't true. But not to worry. A goblin needs truth, the old saying went, like an Elf needs intestines. With a conscious effort, he turned his atten-tion to more important things; like, for example, how to screw the dwarves to the floor over this new treaty without actually breaking it. That was more like it. North and south of the Halls of Udrear; he was quite proud of that one, given that the richest veins of The Stuff lay directly underneath the Halls, and therefore weren't covered by the terms of the agreement. Of course, Drain was too stupid to realise that. Or was he?

Slowly and carefully, Mordak devised a plan of campaign. It was, he told himself with pride, typically goblin; cunning, vicious and morally bankrupt. Much more like it. His self-esteem restored, he drained his brandy, waddled into the kitchen, dumped his empty mug in the headwasher and strolled out through the Royal Mews to take the evening air.

Which was particularly fine tonight. Mordak's sensitive nose easily discerned the various trace elements – sulphur, magnesium, a dozen different isotopes of silicon; in spite of everything, he'd managed to keep Shaft Nine in full produc-tion 24/7, and by the smell of it they were bringing the day shift's production to the surface right now. He wandered across to the pit head to see for himself, and was rewarded with a view of sixteen large wooden trolleys, drawn by captive dwarves, laden with rough-hewn blocks of glowing yellow rock.

Ah, the glory of it. *Mithuriel*, the Elves called it; *blastein*, in Dwarvish; to the goblins, it was simply The Stuff – a hard grey rock that, under certain circumstances, shone with a pure yellow light. Kings and archpriests slaughtered each other for a peanut-sized chip of it to place on their crowns. Dragons sat on it, trolls ate it (but there you go), Elves wrote scratchy sounding violin sonatas to celebrate its ethereal beauty; and the wizard *bought* it, top dollar, cash on the nail and keep it coming. Forty-five gobbos a ton. You could buy a lot of war with that sort of money.

He watched them load the raw blocks into the derrick, then strain against the bars of the capstan that turned the winch that swung the crane up and into the soot-black hole in the middle of the huge diamond-encrusted golden-brown circular Portal set into the back wall of the cavern. A moment later, the crane basket came back empty, and that was it. For some reason, Mordak found it vaguely unsatisfactory, as though there should be rather more to it than that. Like, what did the wizard actually do with a hundred and seventy tons of The Stuff; where did it go to, and what exactly lay on the other side of the black hole, beyond which no goblin had ever ventured? Not venturing, however, was an express term of the contract, on pain of forfeiture of a nine-figure sum. So; no venturing, or else.

There were theories, of course. Professor Magluk of the Goblin Institute of Alchemy had postulated that the black hole led to a transdimensional interface, in effect a sort of hiatus hernia in the gullet of space/time, and that there must be some unique property in The Stuff that allowed it to pass through the interface without being subject to quantum disruption, in accordance with Ngyuk's Third Law, or otherwise the wizard would end up with a teaspoonful of irradiated grey ash for his money, which was improbable— On the other hand, Academician Snatbog of the Goblin Association for the Advancement of Science had recently made a very good case for arguing that the black hole was in fact the imaging chamber of a functional teleportation device, presumably powered by an artificially created quantum singularity, with the power to transmute matter into energy and, by folding the fabric of the continuum back onto itself into a sort of Mobius paper chain, transport inanimate objects across the boundaries of alternate universes (in accordance with multiverse theory) to a preordained location. They were both good theories, and Mordak would have liked to have seen them taken further. Unfortunately, being goblins, Magluk and Snatbog had sought to resolve their differences by means of a duel to the death, in the course of which both of them had perished, so the question was, for the time being, unresolved.

She looked at him. He looked at her. The horse shuffled a bit and ate a nettle.

She'd heard the two words all her life; *handsome prince*. They went together so closely it was hard to think of them being used separately. *Ugly prince* or *handsome woodcutter* simply wouldn't mean anything. And, at some point in her early childhood, a vague mental image had coalesced in the back of her mind; a tall, blond, curly-haired young man with a small nose, big ears, a white horse and a perpetual cheesy grin. The truth was, she'd never really *liked* handsome princes in stories. They were too easy, too convenient. The girl, stupid or spineless, gets herself locked up in a tower, put to sleep for a hundred years, poisoned with a magic apple; but not to worry, because some day, just in the nick of time, her prince will come and he'll take care of everything; all she has to do is look fragile and decorative. To a girl who'd spent her eighth birthday prising the gold fillings out of the upper jaw of the dead witch she'd just brained with the kitchen hatchet, the picture didn't seem right. Besides, she didn't like curly hair on men, and horses made her sneeze.

"Gesundheit," he said.

But this prince was different. He was – well, let's not use

the H word, not when there's terms such as cute, gorgeous, well fit and so forth, which haven't been devalued by a lifetime of negative connotations. True, he was tall, and his fair hair was a bit curly, and his horse was indisputably white. Other than that, he was nothing like the soppy halfwits of her imagination.

"Excuse me," he said (and his voice was soft and surprisingly deep; the handsome princes in her head all squeaked like hamsters) "I'm not from around here. Would this be the Forest?"

On either side of the track, the trees crowded round, their spindly heads swaying in the gentle breeze.

"Yes," she said.

"Ah, fine, that's all right." He was scowling at the box in his hand, as if it had done something wrong. "Can't seem to get a signal, for some reason. Are you local?"

"What?"

"Do you live round here?"

Dammit, she was going to blush. She tried to fight it, but it was no use. "Yes," she said.

"Splendid, maybe you can help me. My name's—" Was it her imagination, or did he glance down at the back of his hand, "Florizel, and I'm the new prince. What I mean is, my father's just become king, so I'm sort of going around the place, checking stuff out, just a sort of preliminary fact-finding initiative, kind of thing. You know."

Odd. Handsome princes wandered around the place all the time, but they were hunting or hawking or exercising their horses, they didn't find facts. She'd always assumed they had people for that. "Oh," she said.

"That's right," said Prince Florizel. "And sounding out local people in, you know, local communities. Seeing what their concerns are, what they want from their public services, all that. Schools, infrastructure, integrated transport networks."

He was trying to stuff the little grey box into his tunic, but there wasn't a pocket where he was trying to put it. "Anything you'd like to, you know, put on the agenda?"

"Excuse me?"

"Is there anything you feel the government ought to be doing that it isn't?"

Government. Now there was a word. She'd never heard it, but she knew what it meant. So, apparently, did he. But that was all wrong, she thought. We don't have government, we have kings and handsome princes and pretty, airheaded princesses with wicked stepmothers. And as for *infrastructure—*

"Actually," she said, "there is one thing."

"Yes?"

"Wolves," she replied. "Do you think you could do something about the wolves?"

Prince Florizel looked distinctly apprehensive. "There's wolves in these parts?"

"Oh yes." She nodded vigorously. "Loads of them."

"Ah." He frowned. "But, you know, there's a lot of nonsense talked about wolves. The truth is, they're quite shy animals really. Very intelligent, highly developed social structure, and they hardly ever attack humans."

She looked at him. "Oh yes they do," she said. "Well," she added, "they try."

"Do they?" He looked worried.

"All the time, they're a real nuisance. I've had to kill six this week already."

"My God. Well," the prince said quickly, "I can see we'll have to do something about that."

"Oh, they don't *hurt* anybody," she said. "But if they keep coming down here and getting killed, pretty soon there won't be any left, and that probably wouldn't be a good thing. Would it?"

"Ah," he said. "In that case, maybe a carefully orchestrated relocation programme, naturally taking care not to upset the ecological balance in the local habitat." He reached towards the pocket that wasn't there, realised the grey box was still in his hand and prodded it several times with his fingertip. "Well, I've definitely made a note of that," he said. "We'll get on it right away. My father the king, I mean."

"That'd be . . ." Highly unlikely? A miracle? "Very nice," she heard herself say. "Really kind of you, and your father. What was his name again?"

This time she watched, and he definitely read the name off the back of his hand. "Hildebrand," he said. "The First. We're a new dynasty."

"Oh. What happened to the old one?"

"They retired. Abdicated. " Prince Florizel was picking at his cuff. "Gone far, far away. So we're in charge now, Dad and me. Anyway," he went on briskly, "wolves, yes, got that. Anything else?"

She hesitated. It was something that had always bothered her, but a little voice in her head was telling her that when you meet your handsome prince, socio-political issues shouldn't be foremost in your mind. But what the hell. "Actually," she said, "there's one thing I'd really like to ask, if it's all right. About kings and stuff."

"Fire away."

"Where?"

"Please ask your question."

"Oh, right." She took a moment to order her thoughts, because the question – well, it was kind of slippery. It had taken her a very long time to formulate it, mostly because the same little internal voice that was currently urging her to lead the conversation round to an entirely different topic had always told her not to be so silly, every time she'd tried to figure it out for herself. Now, with Florizel only a few inches

away from her, it was as if a battle was going on inside her
between the question and the voice. But she knew, she suddenly realised, which side she wanted to win. She took a
deep breath. "It's like this," she said.

"Yes?"

"Well." She looked straight at him. "You know when
there's a giant, and it goes round burning down villages and
destroying crops and all that stuff, and nobody can defeat it,
so the king sends out heralds to say that any hero who kills
the giant will get his daughter's hand in marriage and half the
kingdom." She paused. Florizel was frowning slightly. "With
me so far?"

"What? Oh, yes, definitely."

"And then the hero comes along and he kills the giant
and he gets the princess and half the kingdom, right?"

"Yes. Yes, I suppose so." Florizel gave her a big smile. She
couldn't help feeling it was intended as a distraction. "But of
course giant attacks are very rare. There is no cause for
alarm."

"Rare-ish," she said. "Six in the last hundred and fifty
years."

"Is that right? Well, fairly rare, then. Not something you
really need to be concerned about."

"Which means," she ground on, "that in the course of the
last century and a half, the size of this kingdom has halved *six
times*."

"Um."

"All right," she continued. "Let's say for the sake of argument that the kingdom started off with an area of three
million hectares, which is probably the bare minimum
required to sustainably support, say, five major cities, given a
basically agrarian society. You'll agree, I'm sure, that any
geopolitical entity with less than five major urban centres
would properly be classified as a duchy or principality rather

than a country, according to accepted international diplomatic protocols."

"I guess."

"Well then, subdivide three million by fifty per cent six times, and you're left with a surface area of 46,875 hectares, which is clearly insufficient to sustain one city of, say, twenty thousand inhabitants, not to mention the cost of a royal court, centralised administration and bureaucracy and a standing army. Then, when you factor in the knock-on effect of economic disruption caused by a series of unanticipated partitions, not to mention loss of confidence in the currency and the concomitant pressure on sovereign debt—" She stopped and breathed out slowly. "It doesn't make sense," she said. "Does it?"

There was a long, awkward silence. "You thought of that all by yourself?" Florizel asked.

"Yes."

"Dear God." He blinked twice, then broadened the smile until she could almost hear the tendons in his face creaking. "You're a pretty smart girl, you know that?"

"Yes. But how does it *work*?"

The smile was still there, but now she reckoned she could see things moving behind it. "How come," he asked her, "you know about hectares?"

"I—" She narrowed her eyes. "Come to that," she said, "how come *you* know about hectares?"

"Look." The smile had gone now. "It's perfectly simple. For a start, it's a big kingdom. Very, very big. Also, you'll probably find that on at least one occasion, the king didn't have a son, so when he died his son-in-law the giant-killer inherited his throne, so the kingdom was put back together again. Or maybe he inherited a chunk of another kingdom, as the result of a carefully planned dynastic marriage. Or something like that. The point is, it *does* work and it *does* make sense, and the only reason you can't see it is because you're a girl from a stupid little village and you don't know about important stuff like politics. All right?"

She thought about that for a moment. Then she stamped on his toe. "I see," she said. "Thank you so much for explaining it to me."

He'd closed his eyes. Now he shifted his weight slowly from one foot to the other and hopped towards the horse, which was eating bracken. "My pleasure," he said. "Any time."

"You won't forget about the wolves, now will you?"

"I'll try very hard not to."

"You shouldn't let your horse eat that stuff. It makes them sick."

"Does it? Ah well." With visible effort, he put his stamped-on foot in the stirrup and hoisted himself into the saddle. "Well, I'd just like to say what a pleasure it's been meeting you."

"Likewise."

"I'd like to say that, but I can't, because it isn't true."

"Always tell the truth," she told him. "It's what princes do."

"You don't say. Well, goodbye for now."

"Bye."

He nudged the horse with his heels and rode away, wincing slightly as he rose to the trot. *I just assaulted a member of the royal family*, she told herself, as he ducked under a low branch just in time, then got hit in the face by a broad spread of chestnut leaves. *That's — not right.* But it had felt right at the time. Oh yes.

Geopolitical entities, she thought, as she walked slowly down the path. Hectares. Sovereign debt. The words had bubbled up in her mind like silt from the bed of a stream, as soon as she'd thought of the idea that needed them to be expressed with. Had they been there all along, she wondered?

She couldn't have made them up, because *he'd* understood them. And his explanation; well, it was so full of holes you could strain soup through it, but it was— She frowned. It had sounded like it came from the same place her own thoughts came from, wherever the hell that was. So—

There was a dear old lady hobbling up the path towards her, her face buried in a shawl. Oh damn, she thought, not *now*.

—So maybe he did, too. Now there was an interesting idea, and one that didn't need long, difficult words. She lifted her head, settled the basket comfortably in the crook of her arm and quickened her step. As soon as the dear old lady came within hailing distance, she gave her a terrifying scowl and yelled "GO AWAY!" at the top of her voice. The dear old lady froze, looked at her, wriggled out of the shawl with a splendidly fluent movement and dashed off into the trees, its tail between its legs.

"That's better," she said, to no one in particular. "Thank you."

She walked on a few steps, then stopped dead, turned round and ran back. She found the place where she'd stood talking to Prince Florizel – the horse had thoughtfully left a brown pyramidal marker for ease of identification – and dropped to her hands and knees, scrabbling in the leaf mould until she found what she was looking for.

When she'd trodden on Florizel's foot, he'd dropped his small grey box. She'd seen it fall, out of the corner of her eye, but at the time she'd had other things on her mind. She picked it up and looked at it. She'd never seen anything like it before. It was a little bit like a small roof tile, except that it had a piece of glass set into it; decoration of some kind, she guessed, like the numbers and letters laid out in neat rows underneath. She turned it over in her hand, but the back was quite plain.

Why would a grown man carry around a roof tile with him? And when she'd told him about the wolves, he'd prodded at some of the decorative letters, almost as if he was making notes (but there was no ink, no goose quill, and she couldn't see anything written anywhere). She frowned. Neat rows of letters; all the letters in the alphabet were there, and never the same one twice. It reminded her of the slate her mother had made for her when she was learning how to read: but Florizel was a grown-up and had seemed reasonably intelligent, even if he was obnoxious, so presumably he already knew how to read. There were other symbols as well as letters and numbers, but she had no idea what they were supposed to be.

She stared at the box for a while, then shrugged. If he valued it, sooner or later he'd be back to look for it. Probably as well to keep it safe till he returned. If it was just left lying there in the road, it might get ruined by the dew or run over by a cart. And if he didn't come back for it, then maybe someone would give her sixpence for it in the market. Hard to see what anybody would want with such a thing, but, then, people bought all sorts of junk. She put it in her basket and covered it up with a bit of cloth.

Once upon a time there was a young farm boy who lived with his grandmother in a small cottage on the edge of the big forest. Though they were good and honest they were very poor, so once a week the boy took a basket full of jars of his grandmother's home-made nettle jam to sell in the market. But for some inexplicable reason not many people ever wanted to buy the home-made nettle jam, and so as often as not the boy brought most of it back again, and they had to eat it themselves, which made them very sad. And so they got poorer and poorer and thinner and thinner, and eventually there came a day when nobody bought any nettle jam, and the boy was left to make his way home, wondering what on earth his grandmother was going to say when he showed up with a full basket.

He was so busy thinking about this that he almost didn't notice the old man sitting on a tree stump beside the road. He was tall and thin with a long grey beard and a long walking stick and a pointed hat like an upturned ice-cream cone. The hat alone should have been enough to tell the boy that the old man was really a wizard; but he was so preoccupied with the thought of the unsold jam and what his grandmother would have to say about it that he only realised what the old man truly was when he noticed that he wasn't sitting on the tree stump but was in fact hovering about six inches above it.

The boy had never met a wizard but he knew all about them. Accordingly he smiled politely and walked a little bit faster. But the wizard looked at him, and he stopped.

"Hello, boy," said the wizard.

"Hello, wizard," said the boy. "Would you like to buy a jar of my grandmother's home-made nettle jam? It's very nice, apart from the chewy stringy bits."

The wizard frowned at him. "You can take your nettle jam," he said, "and you can shove it where the sun never shines." At that the boy knew the old man really was a wizard, because how else would he have known that the boy's grandmother always kept her jam in the cupboard under the stairs, where it was cool and dark? "Listen," the wizard went on, "how'd you like to do a job for me and earn yourself a few — something valuable?"

The boy's eyes opened wide. "Yes, please," he said. "What would you like me to do?"

The wizard stood up, or at least he hovered six inches above the ground instead of the stump. "You see that cave over there? Well, I want you to go into the cave, where you'll find a chair and a table. I want you to sit down at the table and wait until a magic voice asks you three questions. If you answer the questions correctly, I'll give you this." From his pocket, the wizard produced a little cloth bag. "In this bag," he said, "there's a magic nut. If you plant it in your garden, it'll grow into a great big tree and come midsummer it'll bear a huge crop of nuts, which you can take to the market and sell for money. Well? Is it a deal?"

The boy couldn't believe his luck. "Oh, yes please," he said. "That'd be wonderful and grandmother will be so pleased." Then a thought struck him and he was very sad.

"But what if I don't know the answer to the questions?" he said.

But the wizard just grinned and said, "You'll be just fine," so the boy went into the cave, and, sure enough, deep inside he found a chair and a table. On the table was a curious square white box, with a window in the side facing him. As soon as he sat down, the window lit up and started to glow, so the boy knew at once that it was a magic box, put there by the wizard to help him. Then almost at once the boy heard a voice, even though he was alone in the cave. "Hello," said the voice.

"Hello," said the boy.

"I can't get my broadband to work," said the voice. "I've got to where it says 'input source code and password' but I don't know what that means. What do I do?"

The boy had no idea what any of that meant, but straight away the magic box's glowing window flickered and some words appeared on it. The boy read out the words, and the voice said, "Right, I'll try that, hold on," and a moment later, the voice said, "It's saying *Error Message 344T*. What do I do now?"

The boy looked at the shiny window, and, sure enough, new words appeared there. He read them out, and the voice was quiet for a moment, and then it said, "Now it's saying do I want to open or save. Which one should I do?"

The shiny window flickered and the word *save* appeared. "Save," said the boy; and a moment later the voice said, "That's great, it's working now, thanks," and then there was a loud clunking noise, like a pair of boots being dropped on the floor, and the shiny window went dark, and the boy realised he'd just answered three questions. So he got up and went outside.

The wizard smiled at him and handed him the cloth bag. "That was very good," he said.

"Thank you," said the boy.

"In fact," the wizard went on, "it was so good that if you come back this time tomorrow and answer fifteen questions, I'll give you five of these magic nuts, which means by this time next year you'll have five more nut trees and your grand-mother'll be able to pack up jam-making for good. How about it?"

The boy was so happy he couldn't think of anything to say, so he just nodded six times, bowed respectfully to the wizard and ran all the way home; and when his grandmother heard the news she was so pleased she gave him a great big hug and opened a bottle of her special home-made nettle cider to celebrate.

Meanwhile, the wizard drew a magic sign on the ground with the end of his staff and vanished. He reappeared in another place entirely, entered a tall grey building, went to the seventeenth floor and knocked on a door.

"Well?" said the man he met there. "How did it go?"

The wizard sighed and sat down. "Pretty good," he said. "I found a place where we can outsource your technical support call centre to. They're reliable, they do as they're told, they want the work and you can get away with paying them peanuts."

The goshawk swooped down out of the sun, like inspiration into the mind of a poet. Prince Florizel watched it in rapt awe as it opened its wings, banked a little, soared straight past the little scrap of minced-up chicken held loosely between his gloved fingers, carried on for about a hundred yards and perched in a tall beech tree.

"Sod it," he said.

"That's a pity."

He hadn't seen or heard her approach, but that sort of thing didn't surprise him any more. He swung round and there she was, wearing the same red cloak-and-hood outfit as the last time they'd met. A sunburst of wild joy in his heart met a cold front of extreme irritation moving down from his brain, resulting in condensation in his larynx. He cleared his throat.

"Hello," he said.

"You shouldn't have let it pitch in a tree like that," she said. "Sometimes it's days before they come down. Or it could just fly away and not come back."

He realised he still didn't know her name. "Is that right?"

"Oh yes. And I bet it was really expensive."

She'd have won her bet, if she'd found anyone gullible

enough to take it. "It'll come down when it's hungry," he said confidently.

She looked at him. "Yeah, right. And then it'll fly off after a pigeon or something and you'll never see it again. You don't know a lot about hawks, do you?"

"Of course I do. I'm a prince."

"Ah. So you knew not to feed it for four hours before flying it."

But it had looked so hungry and sad, and he'd felt sorry for it. "That's the traditional approach," he said briskly. "In modern falconry—"

"Mphm."

The goshawk spread its wings and flew away. When it was an almost imperceptible dot on the skyline, Florizel said, "Was there something?"

"What?"

"Was there something you wanted to talk to me about?"

She looked at him, and he realised he was still holding a scrap of raw chicken in his uplifted left hand. In context, it didn't make him look good. He dropped it, took off the glove, remembered that there were no damn pockets in this stupid doublet thing, and stood there holding it, like a prune.

"Well?" he said.

"What? Oh, sorry. Yes. I wanted to talk to you," she said, "about the wizard."

He blinked. "Wizard?"

She nodded. "Because, well, you did say you wanted to know if there was anything you ought to be doing something about, and I think it's high time this whole wizard business—"

"There's a wizard?"

Inscrutability really wasn't one of her faults. "You don't know about the wizard."

"Um. No."

She sighed. "You really ought to get out and about more. All right. There's this wizard. Actually, he's probably the most important man in the whole kingdom." *Present company excepted*, she pointedly didn't say. "And *I* think that some of the stuff he's been getting up to is—"

He decided he could afford a patronising smile. "It's all right," he said.

"Is it?"

Make that a patronising grin. "Magic isn't real," he said. "It's just made up, like in stories. Make believe. So whatever this so-called wizard is doing—"

The look on her face would have made a handy-dandy diamond grinder. "He can disappear and reappear at will," she said. "And make things vanish. And turn water into beer. Not very good beer, but—"

Florizel frowned. "Illusion and sleight of hand," he said. "Your basic conjuring tricks."

"And change base metal into gold," she went on. "And make lightning shoot from his fingertips. Oh, and he can fly, too. And stuff."

Florizel bought time with a carefully crafted fake sneeze. "That's not actually *magic*," he said. "There's undoubtedly a perfectly simple non-magical explanation. It's a well-known anthropological law, any sufficiently advanced technology is indistinguishable from—"

"He can raise the dead."

"Um." Florizel thought for a moment. "Are you sure about that?"

"Seen him do it," she said casually. "We all have. Everybody around here knows the wizard. Except," she added politely, "you, apparently. And what I think is, some of the things he does, I don't think he ought to be allowed to get away with it. It's not right. It's destroying the foundations of a sustainable, ecologically responsible economy."

His eyebrow lifted. "Flying? Raising the dead?"

"Well, not that, specifically. I was thinking more of some of the other stuff. Like, he's got my dad and my uncles out there in the forest cutting down loads and loads of trees, and what's that doing to the ozone layer?"

Florizel cast his mind back. "Well," he said, "it's a huge forest."

"Yes, but—"

"If memory serves, it stretches from the Blue Hills right across the High Country as far as the Sair Calathorn."

"Carathorn."

"Sorry, yes, what you said. Anyhow, it's not like they've made any significant difference. In fact, if you compare the most up-to-date maps with the ordnance survey carried out fifty years ago, you'll see that the deforested area is basically the same now as it was then." He paused. Something he'd just said struck him as a bit weird, but never mind. "So really, I don't think there's any cause for—"

"Is that true?"

He nodded. "I think so," he said. "I mean, I was out that way the end of last week, and I got lo— I happened to have a map with me, and the clearings in the forest are pretty much as they're marked, and there's definitely no signs of danger-ously excessive deforestation, so honestly, I think you may be worrying about nothing. In fact," he went on, "I was thinking, maybe a programme of controlled felling and land reclama-tion might not be a bad idea, you know, diversify a bit away from the over-dominant forestry sector into agriculture and food production, because, I don't know if you've noticed this, there don't seem to be terribly many farmers around here, so how people get anything to eat is a bit of a mystery to me."

Something in her troubled eyes suggested that the same thought had crossed her mind once or twice. But; "All right," she said, "forget about cutting down the trees for the moment. What about the dwarves and the goblins? He's a bad influence on them, *I* think, and one of these days—"

"Dwarves."

A blank look. "Yes, you know, Drain son of Dror's lot, under the Mountain."

"*Goblins.*"

"King Mordak's people. *Surely* you know about the—"

"Yes, sure, of course I know about *them*," said Prince Florizel, making a mental note to say something really horrible and snarky to the Royal Remembrancer the moment he got back to the palace. "What about them?"

Before she could answer, the sky went dark as a cloud covered the sun. Except that it wasn't a cloud; it was a huge, fast-moving shape, a very long way up but still almost impossibly big; a bird, except that the wing shape, the long neck, the serpentine tail—

"What the hell," Florizel gasped, "is *that*?"

"What? Oh, it's just a dragon. Like I was saying, *I* don't think —"

"A *drag*—"

"Of course." She was staring at him; not contempt, genuine surprise. "Do you mean to say you've never seen a dragon before?"

The monster had banked and wheeled. It was coming towards them, and she was just standing there. "For crying out loud," he whimpered. "It's a dragon. We ought to—"

"Oh, it's all right," she said, "a knight'll kill it, they always do. Actually, that was another thing I wanted to talk to you about—"

But Florizel had had enough. Ignoring his tethered horse, he took to his heels and ran, not stopping until he'd reached the cover of a plausibly fireproof granite outcrop. He crawled under a jutting ledge as far as he could get and tried to catch his breath.

Dragons, he thought. *Dragons.* What in God's name have I let myself in for?

A blanket of darkness swept over him, faster than a man could run, and he heard the slow whop-whop of unimaginable wings. No, he told himself bitterly, this is not fun.

Which meant, he realised, that things weren't turning out a bit like he'd imagined. The idea was, a nice relaxing place he could slip away to, when the stress and aggravation of everyday life got to him; a place where he could escape from his troubles, his shortcomings, the disappointment of being himself—

Something warm and wet was trickling down his leg. He listened hard. The whop-whop sound was fading. No it wasn't. It was dopplering and coming back. Oh hell.

It had never occurred to him, even in his most wimpish, panic-stricken moments, that he might actually come to harm here, possibly even die; that his escape from real life might end in a premature rendezvous with real death. Of course not. Don't be so silly. It's perfectly safe, or they wouldn't have—

The shadow was back, but it wasn't moving so fast. In fact, it had stopped, and the wingbeat noise had turned into a monstrous puppy-dog snuffling. Do dragons hunt by scent rather than sight? he wondered; and then realised that he had no way of knowing, because there was no data, because dragons weren't *real* and therefore no scientist had studied them. On balance, though, it seemed likely (because dragons are presumably reptiles, and lizards have notoriously poor eyesight, and why in God's name was he trying to extrapolate biological information about an *entirely mythical* species?); and thanks to the right old state he'd got himself into, chances were he stank to high heaven of sweat and adrenalin and various other less honourable bodily odours, in which case his only hope was if the dragon had a really bad cold, in itself improbable in a natural fire-breather—

He heard something else; the whinny of a horse, the clank of metal. What on earth? A horse-drawn plough? An old-fashioned rag-and-bone man? Or – what was it she'd said, just before he so impressively ran away? A knight.

A deafening roaring noise blotted all thought from his mind. It seemed to go on for ever, and then it stopped. Silence; then a man's voice saying, "Sorry. Nothing personal."

Florizel realised he'd stopped breathing. Damn silly thing to do. He put that right with a deep, ragged gasp.

"Learn your destiny," said a voice that spoke ordinary words but definitely wasn't human. "You must ride to the forest of Evinardar—"

"Actually," said the man, "would it be all right if I stopped you there, because in actual fact I have no intention whatsoever of going to bloody Evinardar, it's a godawful place, the food's lousy, the women smell and the gross national product is less than the cost of the two sets of horseshoes I'd wear out getting there. So, if it's all the same to you—"

"Suit yourself," croaked the other voice; and then there was a ground-shaking thump, as though something very heavy had fallen over. About a minute later, Florizel heard the sound of a saw, and some out-of-tune whistling.

"Excuse me," he called out. "Hello?"

Pause. Then an upside-down face appeared just below the jutting ledge, "Hello," said the face. "You all right down there?"

"Is it dead?"

The face grinned. "As a doornail," it said. "You'll be the prince, then."

In spite of everything, Florizel couldn't help wondering – "How'd you know?"

"Come on." A mail-clad arm extended towards him. "Let's get you out of there, and then we can talk."

While he'd been under the ledge both of Florizel's feet had gone to sleep, a fact he only became aware of when he tried to stand on them. So he sat down instead, with his back to the rock. "I'm Prince Florizel," he said weakly. "How can I ever—?"

There was a slightly glazed look on the young man's face. "Oh, let's not bother with all that now," he said. "I'm Sir Turquine, by the way. Look, is there any chance of a cart and a dozen men?"

"Of course," Florizel said. "Anything else?"

"Rope," said Sir Turquine. "About two hundred square yards of muslin would be nice. And if you could possibly come up with half a ton of ice—"

Florizel nodded eagerly. "There's a sort of cave thing out in the back of the palace, full of the stuff. They use it for making sherbet, whatever that is. Help yourself."

The knight gave him a beautiful smile. "Look," he said, "about your daughter—"

"I haven't got a daughter."

"Sorry, silly me, your sister—"

"I'm an only child."

"You are? That's splendid." Sir Turquine looked genuinely pleased. "That's that sorted, then. Look, how far away are the ropes and the cart and stuff? Only, time's getting on and it's a warm day."

As best he could, Florizel gave him directions to the palace. "Ask for the Grand Steward," he said, "say I sent you. And if he gives you any trouble—"

He must have said something amusing, because the knight laughed. "He won't, trust me. Well, thanks ever so, and it was a pleasure doing business with you."

"No, thank *you*."

"Whatever. And if you get any more dragons, remember, Turquine's the name. Fast, efficient service, no supernatural monster too large or too small. Cheerio for now."

Turquine vaulted onto his horse, which sagged slightly; then he trotted away, making a sound like a panel-beating contest. When he was out of sight, Florizel slowly turned round and looked at the dragon.

For obvious reasons, it didn't look back at him. Its eyes were open, and there was dust on its eyeballs; its yard-long jaws were slightly open, and Florizel could see teeth as long and yellow as bananas, and a cushion-sized segment of pink tongue. In spite of its size it looked very, very real, and as sad as road kill. No, he thought, I'm definitely not having fun. In fact, why don't I just go back where I came from and get a real life?

This is real, said a little voice in his head. *And it's not right.*

Where did that come from, he wondered. No idea. No way in hell could the existence of real dragons be considered his *fault*; and if there are real dragons in or near a populated area, someone's got to deal with them, because otherwise they'd slaughter everything that moved. A predator this size, capable of flying and breathing fire, must use up an inconceivably high level of energy, which means it'd need to be feeding all the damn time. Obviously you'd have to control the creatures – control? Wipe them off the face of the Earth. Damn it, if the nice man in the iron knitting hadn't happened to be passing, I'd be toast—

A cart, twelve men, muslin and a lot of ice. Maybe that was what was wrong.

Not my problem, he assured himself. Yes, this is real; but it's not my fault, I'm a *tourist*, I came here under the misapprehension that it'd be a bit of fun, and now I'm going to go away and never come back—

Well, said the little voice. *Go on, then.*

He allowed himself a little groan. Oh, all right, he admitted to himself, maybe it is my fault, just a teeny-weeny bit; not anything *I've* done, of course, it's one of those transfer-of-undertakings things, like when you buy up a company and that makes you responsible for all its outstanding debts. I did choose to be the prince, didn't I?

For some reason, when his mind referred that one back to committee, he was rewarded with a fleeting mental picture of her, the annoying girl with all the difficult questions. No way, he protested, no way in hell. True, she was pretty – was she? Actually, he wasn't sure. All the girls here were pretty, just as all the men were handsome; like under-thirties in a daytime soap (because you don't progress far enough in the dramatic profession to be cast in one unless you meet a certain standard of physical appearance); accordingly, after the first week, a sort of snow-blindness had set in and he no longer registered beauty, except on the rare occasions when it wasn't there. So it wasn't that, he reassured himself, and if it's not that, for someone as shallow and superficial as me, what else could it possibly be—?

Suddenly, the earth shook. He staggered. It felt like standing up on a fast-moving train while drunk.

Earthquakes, for crying out loud. Somehow (probably thanks to all those trips he'd taken on fast-moving trains while drunk) he managed to keep his feet; then, when it was all over and the ground had stopped moving, he put his foot in a rabbit hole and fell flat on his face.

He discovered that he was eye to glassy, dusty eye with the dead dragon. He jumped up, swore, and ran back to the palace without looking round.

The slight tremor that so distressed prince Florizel was no bother at all to Yglaine as she made her way through the forest. Yglaine was an Elf, and Elves have a sort of special relationship with the ground; which is why they can walk over snowdrifts without sinking in, and why wellington boots aren't available in Elf foot sizes.

It made her frown, though. If the earth was shaking, it meant that the goblins, or the dwarves, or both of them were back to work in the mines. That was very bad. There was no need for it, they only did it to make *money* for their greedy, brutish leaders, and it was terribly bad for the trees and the environment and wildlife and stuff. She'd often wondered why they couldn't all get normal, sensible jobs, doing the sort of things Elves did for a living – abstract contemporary pottery, for instance, or sitting on committees, or writing amusingly snide reviews of each other's latest volume of collected essays.

She made an effort and shooed all such unpleasant thoughts from her mind. Today, after all, was going to be a special day, quite possibly the happiest day of her life, and it'd be such a pity if she let dwarves and goblins spoil it for her.

Suddenly there was an ominous disturbance in the bushes beside the road, and a fully grown wolf sprang out. It hesitated for a moment, its red eyes blazing, its tongue lolling out of the corner of its panting mouth. But then, before she'd had a chance to quote it the latest statistics about the decline in squirrel numbers or lecture it about the known risks of red meat, it tucked its tail between its legs and fled.

All her life, Yglaine had lived to make music; and now – she still couldn't quite believe it – here she was, on her way to her first performance with the Sylvan Elves' Youth Ensemble, the most prestigious orchestra in Elvenhome. As she ducked under an overhanging branch and took the left fork in the path that led to Harpers' Glade, she couldn't help wondering what the first piece she'd be called upon to play would be. Of course, she knew the entire repertoire, had done since she was six years old, but she rather hoped it'd be something that would allow her to shine; Tantuviel's Third, perhaps, or maybe Luvien's *Exquisite Teardrops* suite, or possibly even the overture to *Gloriel and Glorfandel*, with its thrillingly sustained G minor diminuendo in the ninth movement—

She'd arrived. In fact, she realised with horror, she was late, because the other members of the orchestra were all there, sitting or reclining gracefully on the mossy bank under the shade of the ancient *miramar* trees, drumming their fingers and looking irritable. She stammered an apology, which the conductor received in stony silence and handed her a score. She sat down, opened her violin case and glanced at the sheet of music she'd just been given.

The Four Seasons. Vivaldi. One; Spring.

Never heard of it. She ran her eye over the first few bars and thought, *what?* It wasn't Elven music, that was for sure. There were far too many notes, for one thing. Elven music tends to average two notes a minute. Also, this thing appeared to have a *tune*. As for Viv-whatever-it-said, that sounded suspiciously to her like a human name; at least, it wasn't dwarf or goblin, and it most definitely wasn't Elf, so what else could it be? Still, she was well aware of the Youth Ensemble's dedication to cultural diversity and showcasing the very best of the artistic traditions of inferior races; she'd just never imagined she'd have to play any of the stuff, that was all.

The conductor tapped his baton against his music stand, and the musicians came to attention. As he lifted the baton for the first weird sounding notes, Yglaine noticed out of the corner of her eye that there was a woman standing next to him, and she wasn't holding any sort of musical instrument. Odd; but maybe she was there to turn the maestro's pages for him. No time to speculate about that now, though. She touched catgut to catgut, and began to play.

Maybe she struggled just a little to begin with, what with the music being so unfamiliar and strange, not to mention the pressure of the occasion, but within a few dozen bars she'd managed to let go of all outside concerns and immerse herself soul-deep in her performance. The violin became a living thing in her hands, and the music – actually not so bad once you got used to it – unfolded before her, guiding her along enchanted paths of mathematical intervals and pro-gressions to its inevitable, cathartic conclusion. When the last note had died away, she sighed softly, laid down her violin and took the score from her music stand—

They were all looking at her. Sheepishly, trying desperately not to blush, she put it back.

A few moments of perfect quiet and stillness, and then the conductor tapped the stand and raised his baton. And then they played it all again.

Well, she told herself, obviously it wasn't right the first time, and after all, this is the Youth Ensemble, where perfec-tion is simply a starting point. She let the music envelop her, and before she was aware of any time having passed, they'd reached the end. This time, she didn't move. After a few moments of perfect quiet and stillness, the conductor tapped the stand and raised his baton, and they played it again. And again. And again—

At some point (the sixth, or maybe the seventh time), it occurred to her to wonder what the woman standing next to the conductor was actually there for. She didn't turn pages. She just stood. Also, what was the function of the large brown circular thing with a hole in the middle, like a wheel with an extremely fat rim and no spokes, that hung from the lowest branch of the nearest *miramar* tree? Not that it was her place to question anything, but—

A strident *brr-brr* noise, loud as a shout, cut across the music. Immediately, the conductor lifted his baton for silence. Yglaine froze in mid-note. *Brr-brr* again; then a click, and then the woman next to the conductor seemed to come to life. Her eyes opened, and, in the most beautiful voice Yglaine had ever heard, she said, "Thank you for calling Kawaguchiya Integrated Circuits. There's no one here to take your call right now, please hold." And then the conductor's baton came down with a swish, and everybody started playing again, exactly where they'd left off.

Just a moment, she thought.

The current of the music was still pulling her along, driving her aching hands (she'd never played so many notes in one day before), but her mind was floating free or, more accurately, drowning. What did it mean? Was it avant-garde and experimental? There was nothing in the score to indicate vocals—

That *brr-brr* again. The baton lifted and froze; dead silence. And the woman said, "Your call is important to us, please hold," and then they all carried on, this time right through to the end, after which they played it *again*. Exactly the same, or almost exactly; three interruptions this time, and in different places.

Ten hours later, numb-fingered, exhausted and horribly bewildered, Yglaine set off homewards through the darkling wood. The music was still playing – a night shift had taken over, though the woman with the beautiful voice had stayed at her post, grey-lipped with fatigue but motionless, like a mighty oak – and Yglaine could hear it in the distance for quite some time. Even when she could no longer distinguish the music from the soft sigh of the wind in the treetops, it seemed to be repeating over and over again in her head.

What did it mean? The second message wasn't so bad. You could interpret it as the composer's apostrophe to Lintuvuviel, Goddess of Music, the Arts and Literary Criticism; *your call, that fateful summons to join the lonely, exalted few, is important to us, please hold* – hold what? The line against the darkness of egalitarian barbarism, presumably, something like that. But the first message – *there's no one here to take your call right now*. It scanned, she noted, a perfect iambic pentameter, so maybe it was a quotation; a searing comment on the new philistinism rampant in Elvenhome, perhaps, ever since the High Council had slashed subsidies to the Arts down to a pitiful 86 per cent of GDP. Fair enough. But who *was* Kawaguchiya Integrated Circuits, and why had she never heard of Her before?

Still, she'd made her debut with the Youth Ensemble, and she'd done all right. That should have been enough, more than enough, the proudest day of her life; and here she was, fretting herself to death on account of some abstruse allusion that had gone over her head. And nobody had said, "Don't bother coming back tomorrow." So she'd definitely got the job; which meant security, tenure, a job for life. There wasn't a single Elf in the Forest who wouldn't give her ear-points for an outcome like that.

For life; and, since Elves are practically immortal, that was likely to be a long, long time. Would they be playing something different tomorrow? She sincerely hoped so, logic demanded that they would, but nobody had said anything, let alone handed her a score to read through overnight. What if – the very idea was absurd, but what if she was now committed to spending the rest of practically Eternity playing the first movement of Vivaldi's *Four Seasons* in an endless loop, interrupted only by the brr-brr noise and the motionless woman's beautiful voice?

Gosh, she thought. Lucky me. But—

Don't be silly, she rebuked herself. Think about it. After all, what purpose would endlessly repeating music possibly serve?

Quite.

There was another slight earthquake as she walked the last mile to her home in the high branches of the third *marshmallorn* tree from the left in Exquisite Row, but she ignored it.

There was a small ante-room just behind the Royal Throne in the great Hall of the palace, and Florizel had claimed it as his own. He'd had to fight like crazy. The Master of the Rolls had been using it to store Rolls in, and no sooner had Florizel won the long, savage battle to get him to put them somewhere else than the housekeeper swooped and filled it with buckets and mops. When, after a war that made the primordial strife of dwarf and goblin seem like a free and frank exchange of views, he'd got rid of all her clutter, the high priest had started carpet-bombing him with hints about what a nice little chancel it'd make, with its perfectly square proportions and north-facing windows. He'd finally resolved that by painting a sign reading DANGER – STRUC-TURALLY UNSOUND and hanging it on the doorknob. Endearingly, the inhabitants of the palace tended to believe what they read, so that was all right.

It had been worth all the aggravation, because Florizel *needed* that room. It was the only confined space in the whole thirty-acre complex with a door with a bolt on the inside.

Having shot the bolt, and wedged a chair under it just to be on the safe side, Florizel walked across the otherwise empty floor to the only piece of furniture in the room; a small, plain table, on which rested a small, plain wooden box. Its lid was fastened with a tiny silver padlock and hasp, and from his pocket Florizel drew a tiny silver key on a fine silver chain. The lock opened with a soft click, and he lifted the lid.

Inside was a doughnut.

The box was made of cedarwood, which is supposed to keep things fresh. It doesn't work with doughnuts. This particular example was so stale that if it got dropped on the floor, it would probably shatter like glass. But that was all right, because the doughnut wasn't for eating. It was the way home.

Also, strictly speaking, it didn't exist; at least, its existence in that quadrifurcated sub-version of reality (see under "multiverse theory", *passim*) was problematic, to say the least. It had come a very long way to end up in the cedarwood box. It had originally been baked in a factory on the outskirts of south London, and supplied to a catering outlet on the platform of Paddington station. The Royal Palace had a map-room two hundred yards square, on whose shelves you could find a copy of every map, chart and atlas ever drawn, but you wouldn't find Paddington or London marked on any of them. The doughnut, like Florizel himself, was from Somewhere Else.

He lifted it carefully out of the box, using only his fingertips. He wasn't sure what would happen if any harm came to it. He reassured himself with the thought that he could always cajole the royal kitchens into making him a replica – they had doughnuts over here, but only the solid kind, with jam, not the jamless hole-in-the-middle sort; still, how hard could it be? Even so, there lurked at the back of his mind the dreadful thought that a locally sourced version might not work, and then where would he be?

Answer; here. For ever and ever. Eek.

Carefully, therefore, he lifted the doughnut until it was more or less level with his nose. He took a moment to clear his mind of extraneous thoughts, then stared earnestly into the hole in the middle of the doughnut. For a split second, nothing happened; and then—

As Nietzsche would have put it; if you gaze too long into the hole in the middle of a doughnut, the hole in the middle of a doughnut gazes into you. He felt its single black eye upon him, looking past the outward show of his appearance, the transitory illusions of the flesh, deep into his soul, his inner being, that small part of him that was eternal and true. Ah, it seemed to say, there you are. And what are *you* doing *here*?

And then he wasn't; not there, at any rate. The bare stone walls of the ante-room vanished, and he found himself in another place, exactly the same but totally different. The room was square, the walls were bare stone, the only furniture was a table with a box on it and a chair, wedged against the bolted door. But he *knew* this room. It was the room above his Uncle Gordon's garage, and he was home.

He put the doughnut carefully down and glanced at his watch: seventeen minutes past eleven, on Friday 16 April. When he'd last looked into the doughnut – six months ago, his time-lagged brain shrieked at him, but he ignored the poor, sad thing – it had been fourteen minutes past eleven, on Friday 16 April. He frowned. He'd lost two minutes. That shouldn't have happened.

Ah well. He made a mental note to fret about it later. Meanwhile, he had other things to think about. Already, as he locked the doughnut away in the old tin deed-box and pocketed the key, the other place and being Florizel were evaporating from his mind like spilt petrol on a warm forecourt. He felt the urge to fight, to cling on, but it was no use; like trying to snatch a sodden piece of paper out of someone's hand. Besides, he decided, it probably wasn't healthy to hold on, now that he was back home. He'd had his fun. Duty called.

He clattered down the stairs out onto the lawn and remembered, just too late, that it was pouring with rain. He ran to the back door, shook rain out of his hair like a dog and scuttled into the living room. His revision notes were exactly where he'd left them, five minutes earlier. To judge from the respective sizes of the piles of notes, To Do and Done, he was making excellent progress and nicely on schedule. Unfortunately, he couldn't remember a damn thing about whatever it was he was supposed to be revising—

He looked at the nearest sheet of paper. Ah yes, physics; the branch of natural philosophy that deals with observed phenomena, as distinct from alchemy, which is mixing things together until they explode. Um. He had an idea that there was rather more to it than that.

He sat down and picked up a sheaf of paper. In two weeks, he'd be sitting his final exams at Uni, and right now, with his state of mind, he'd have difficulty getting his head around the notion that the Earth revolves around the Sun. So maybe using YouSpace as a means of mid-revision relaxation hadn't been such a good idea after all.

He blinked, and when he opened his eyes something was different. He looked at the notes. *Can the dual resonance model be used to explain strong interactions in particle physics? Discuss, with reference to Witten, Hawking, Maldacena and Suskind.* He smiled. Piece of cake. It was all coming back.

He yawned. He was hungry. Reasonably enough; he hadn't eaten anything since breakfast. More to the point, his body in this continuum hadn't eaten anything for six months. He took a moment to consider that, identified at least two paradoxes that he'd have to give some serious thought to when he had five minutes, and shrugged them away, as if slipping out of a soaking wet coat. First some food, then revision, and then maybe, if he still had the energy, he could think about stuff like that.

He wandered into the kitchen and opened the fridge. It's a curious thing about youth, the incredible resilience of its innate ability to suspend disbelief. Its natural credulity fades, but only gradually, and only where the harsh light of evidence and peer review manages to penetrate. Thus it was that, although it was now over ten years since he'd stopped believing in Santa Claus, the Tooth Fairy and the Easter Bunny, a part of him was still convinced that there was some supernatural agency responsible for keeping the fridge well stocked with nibbles, and that if he opened the door and found nothing in there except milk and lettuce, it was someone else's fault. True, it didn't help that he'd just spent the last six months/two minutes in a place where the buttery was always replete with Simnel cakes and cold roast partridge, but even so.

Eventually, after a certain amount of archaeology in the kitchen cupboards, he found a tin of Ambrosia rice pudding and, more eventually still, a tin-opener. Hardly what he'd become accustomed to, but it'd have to do. He went back to the living room, grabbed a fistful of notes, propped his feet up on the sofa and began to read.

Maybe it was because of his holiday; the break, the radical shift in perspective, the degree to which his mind's eye had become acclimatised to the light of a very different sun. Whatever it was, he quickly became aware that there was something wrong with his notes. They didn't make sense. A great deal of the stuff in them was simply untrue. He put the notes down, closed his eyes, counted to ten, looked at them again. No, still wrong. Take, for example, all this guff about E equalling mc^2. Or the inane witterings of the man Heisenberg – he checked his watch just to make sure, but there was no mistake; April Fool's had been fifteen days ago, so it couldn't be that. For crying out loud, he thought, as he considered the idiotic ramblings of Jordan, Hilbert and Bose, I could disprove the whole lot of this in two minutes with the back of an envelope and a pencil.

Three minutes later, he had. Then he sat and squinted at what he'd written. Um, he thought.

The thing of it is, equations can't lie. Unlike humans, with their complex and subtle structures of periphrasis and euphemism, they can't make you believe one thing while presenting something quite other as unassailable fact. X either equals Y or it doesn't. So; if his maths was right (and he checked it twice, and it was), no other conclusion was tenable but that everything he'd been taught over the past three years, everything that everyone else believed, everything he was about to be examined on in a fortnight's time was basically wrong. No nuances to pull over anyone's eyes, no comfy grey areas to hide in. Newton, Einstein and Hawking had got it wrong. They couldn't have been more deluded if they'd believed the world was a flat dish where babies are delivered by storks. And he could prove it. And—

But it was *true*.

Indeed. And whoever said *the truth shall set you free* had clearly never had a live, toxic, radioactive, ticking-with-the-pin-out truth dumped in his lap. Right now, the truth was an arm round his windpipe, pinning him to his chair, unable to move. In two weeks, he'd have to sit down in an examination hall and either scribble out a whole load of lies or demonstrate in a few cogent lines of calculus that the examiners were gullible idiots. And wouldn't they just love him for that. Oh yes.

Fine, he thought, I'll lie. After all, presidents and prime ministers do it, so it must be all right, mustn't it? And then, after I've got my bit of paper from the vice-chancellor, I'll tell the truth to the world, and everybody will say how clever I am. Meanwhile—

It was no good. He had to tell someone. The sheer magnitude of the discovery was so vast that unless he communicated it out of his head, it'd bust his skull open like a volcano. He ran through his various lecturers and tutors; brilliant men and women all of them, but open-minded and receptive to new ideas? Well, maybe not. All right, then, how about his friends? A much shorter list to consider; and besides, they wouldn't do, it had to be a grown-up or it wouldn't count. Put like that, the decision was simple. It'd have to be Uncle Gordon.

Oh well. He felt in his pocket for his phone, but it wasn't there. Strange. But he didn't have time to worry about that now. He used the land line, and dialled the number.

Uncle was a long time picking up; presumably he was in a business meeting or something. Some people have no consideration. Eventually, there was a click and a familiar voice said, "Yes?"

"Oh, hi, Uncle Gordon, it's me."

"Of course it is. What do you want?"

"Well, it's like this. I think I may have disproved the laws of thermodynamics."

Slight pause. "Say again."

"The laws of thermodynamics. Also the general theory of relativity, the law of conservation of matter-oblique-energy, Hooke's Law, Boyle's Law—"

"All right. I'll—"

"Bell's theorem, Ehrenfest's theorem, Dalton's law of partial pressure, Gauss's principle of least restraint—"

"All *right*. I'll be right there. Don't touch anything."

"Thanks, Uncle Gordon. Sorry. Was this a bad time?"

Click. He put the phone back. Uncle had sounded – well, yes, but that was only to be expected. He'd also sounded worried – no, more than that. Worried not so much in the usual how-much-is-this-going-to-cost-me sense, but *worried* worried. Almost as though he was afraid something bad might happen.

Don't touch anything, Uncle had said, so he daren't sit down. From where he was standing, he could just about read the top page of his revision notes. Well, he thought, I suppose I ought to crack on with it, even if it is all untrue. He closed his eyes and mumbled the five salient points about the wave-particle duality of energy and matter under his breath. One—

Yes, but it *isn't*. Never mind about that. Think about the *exam*.

He tried, *how* he tried, but he just couldn't. The thought of sitting down and cold-bloodedly writing out a whole bunch of lies revolted him. It would be *wrong*, on a level so fundamental as to constitute a breach in nature, an abomination, an act so terrible that it couldn't fail to have disastrous consequences; like shaking antimatter sprinkles over your cappuccino. I can't do it, he realised miserably. Which means I can't take the exam. Which means I can't finish my course. Which means—

He shivered. His fingertips and toes had gone cold. An unseen hand grabbed a fistful of his intestines and squeezed.

Which means I'll have to leave Uni and get a *job*.

He whimpered. It wasn't supposed to be like this. Oh no. It was supposed to be: graduate (with first-class honours), then three years' postgraduate, then another three years as a junior lecturer somewhere, then assistant professor, a fellowship, a nice cosy little corner of research into something so abstruse and obscure that nobody would know enough to tell him he was wrong, and *never having to go to work ever*. That had been the route map of his life for as long as he could remember, and now it was all slipping away from him like the torn scraps of a dream; like being Prince Florizel. All the cloud-capped mountains and lofty towers had sunk back into the ground with an unearthly shriek, leaving him alone in a desert of suits, ironing shirts, getting up at seven o'clock, buying sandwiches at the station to eat at his desk. Face it, he told himself, your life is *over*. And all because of the rotten, stinking, inconvenient truth.

How long he stood there he didn't know. Only Salvador Dalí could have designed a watch capable of monitoring the passage of time between the moment when he put the phone down and the click of Uncle's key in the door.

"All right, where are you?"

"In here."

One of our greatest failings as a species is our tendency to judge by appearance and first impressions. On that basis, Uncle Gordon didn't score very high. It was only—

"You bloody idiot," Uncle Gordon said. "What've you gone and done now?"

—when you'd known him a while, say nineteen years, that you came to understand that behind that forbidding exterior was a generous, warm-hearted, extremely patient man who just happened to shout a lot. "Sorry, Uncle," he said.

"Of course you're sorry, you're always sorry, and you know what? It *doesn't help*. Oh for God's sake, don't *loom* like that. Sit *down*."

"Sorry, Uncle. You said not to touch anything."

It was nobody's fault that Benny Gulbenkian was six foot four, and his uncle was five foot three and twice his weight. For some reason, though, Uncle had always taken the height thing as a personal affront, as though Benny was doing it to be cheeky. It hadn't helped when one of Uncle's oldest friends, seeing the two of them standing next to each other with Benny wearing a scarf on a windy day, had said they looked just like a quaver. Or that Uncle hadn't known what a quaver was until Benny told him.

"Now then," Uncle said, drawing a deep breath as Benny folded himself into a chair, "tell me what you've done."

"Well." Benny took a moment to compose his thoughts. "I was revising my notes for the exam, and suddenly I realised, loads of this stuff doesn't work. I mean, it isn't right."

"This stuff being—"

"The laws of physics. So I sat down and did the maths, and it turns out I was right. Look, I can show you if you want."

Uncle's eyes were like two tiny portholes onto the abyss. "No, that's fine. Look, are you *sure*?"

"Oh yes. I double-checked."

"Christ Almighty."

Later, it occurred to Benny that Uncle hadn't doubted for one moment that his calculations had been right. Odd, that. In so many other aspects of his life, Uncle assumed as an article of faith that his nephew was an idiot; not unreasonably, it had to be said (and Uncle had said it, eloquently and at length) This time, though, there was no *don't be stupid, you've got it all wrong, as usual.* He'd accepted the statement at face value and moved straight on.

"Have you told anyone about this?"

"Yes."

"Oh God."

"You," Benny clarified. "But that's all. Really."

Uncle blinked twice at him and counted to ten under his breath. He did that a lot. "Just me. Nobody else."

"No. I promise."

"That's all right, then." The words came gushing out, like air from a suddenly depressurised cabin. "No harm done. We'll just forget all about it and I can get back to my meeting and you can get on with your revision, and—"

"Um."

Uncle Gordon had that way of freezing, as if he'd just walked into an invisible wall. "Um?"

"I don't think there's any point me revising any more, Uncle. I don't think I can take the exam."

And now the still, small voice. "Why not?"

"Because I can't answer the questions if I know they're wrong. Can I?"

And now the very sad voice. "Why not?"

"Well, it'd be wrong. It'd be lying."

"Benny." There were times, usually just before he threw things at the wall, when you could hear the love under all the anger and contempt. "I don't know who you've been listening to lately, but lying isn't actually all that bad. People do it all the time. Lying is the lubricant without which the machinery of society would seize up and crash. It's no big deal, really."

"Yes, but—"

A long sigh, mostly of resignation. "Oh, come on," Uncle said. "You've worked really hard these last three years, Benny, you've really knuckled down and got on with it, and for the first time in your otherwise unsatisfactory life you're on the verge of *achieving* something. And now you're going to throw it all away just because of some *technicality*. Now, take me."

"Uncle—"

"*I* never got the chance to go to university. *I* had to leave school when I was sixteen because my dad needed me in the shop, dicing the kidneys, cleaning out the sheep's heads. When I think what I could've been if I'd had the advantages you've had—"

Benny pursed his lips. Once, when Uncle had made this speech, he'd pointed out that if Uncle had gone to college and got a degree, he'd probably have got a proper job and ended up in the Civil Service or something, instead of starting his own business and making his first million before he was thirty. For some reason it hadn't gone down well, so he decided not to say it now. Instead, he sat perfectly still and let the speech flow over him. The interval gave him time to think – he knew he'd be safe until I-promised-your-poor-mother – and it occurred to him to wonder, not for the first time, what it was that Uncle Gordon actually did. Business, yes, he'd sort of grasped that over the years. But when he'd asked the straight question, the reaction was always a barrage of covering fire, masking an orderly retreat to prepared positions. Now, however, it might well be kind of relevant, because fairly soon they'd be getting on to what-are-you-going-to-*do*-with your life, and—

"Well," Benny interrupted, "I thought, maybe I could come and work for you."

Benny was, above all, a peaceful sort of person. Violence alarmed him. He winced at the sound of fireworks, and *The A-Team* gave him nightmares. On this one occasion, however, only military imagery would do. Imagine a tank, barging its way through walls and squashing cars flat under its tracks. That'd be Uncle, in full swing. Now imagine that tank driving over a mine.

"Say what?"

"Come and work for you," Benny repeated. "By the way, what exactly is it—?"

"You wouldn't like it," Uncle said quickly.

"Oh, I don't know. I suppose it depends what it is."

"Accountancy."

"Oh, *maths*. I like maths."

"Not the mathsy sort of accountancy," Uncle Gordon said, and his voice had got slightly higher. "More like management consultancy. Very dry and boring. Lots of meetings. You'd have to wear a suit."

Benny hesitated, just long enough to make Uncle think he'd won. "That wouldn't be so bad."

"And a tie."

"Ties are all right."

"Early starts most days. Lots of breakfast meetings."

Benny did his eager-beaver smile. "I'm sure I could get used to that. And it sounds really interesting."

"Does it?" Uncle's eyes widened into perfectly round black holes, reminding Benny awkwardly of something he'd seen once, in a doughnut somewhere. "Dear God. You know, I had no idea you thought this way."

"Joining the family business? You bet. I'm up for that. I mean, you and me working together—"

Little beads of sweat were forming on Uncle's forehead. "You'd have to start at the bottom, of course."

"Naturally."

"But I promised your mother—" Uncle stopped dead, as if he'd suddenly been unplugged. He's *scared*, Benny suddenly realised; then, *does not compute*, because Uncle Gordon wasn't afraid of anything. Then Uncle took a deep breath, and it was as though that strange, aberrant moment had never happened. "Believe me," he said, "you'd hate it, you really would. Besides, I haven't spent a small fortune in tuition fees so you can flush it all down the toilet in a fit of wild integrity."

Even so; he couldn't forget that moment of raw terror. "You think I should take the exam."

"*Yes*. And you can keep your fingers crossed under the desk while you're writing, if it'll make you feel any better."

"It might," Benny said, and then realised it was meant as a joke. "But I don't know, Uncle Gordon. I've got this funny feeling that if I pretend like that, it'll make things very bad. Very bad indeed."

"Listen." It was the serious face. "I only want what's best for you, got that? And I know, if you pack in Uni now and wind up in some dead-end boring job, like accountancy or management consulting, you'll be unhappy and miserable, and I'll have let you down. But if you pull yourself together, get stuck in and get a good degree, you can carry on and do what you want to do, and everything will be just fine. And when you're a professor somewhere, and people will actually listen to what you've got to say, *then* you can go blowing up the foundations of modern science and they'll probably give you the Nobel Prize for it. You go shooting your mouth off now, they'll think you're just some wacko kid and you'll be finished, you hear me? So, you do the exam, you finish your course, you don't drop out, you don't go disproving *anything* until *I* tell you it's the right time. Got that? Well?"

For a split second, Benny wondered if he ought to tell Uncle Gordon about the YouSpace thing. Because maybe there are such things as coincidences, but if so, this was a pretty monumentally, visible-from-orbit huge one, so it could well have a bearing on the situation, so Uncle ought to know about it so he could factor it into his advice. But the thought of what Uncle would say if Benny confessed he'd been skipping in and out of alternate realities when he should've been revising simply didn't bear thinking about. "Yes, Uncle," he said.

"Promise?"

"Promise."

"Good boy." Quite unexpectedly, Uncle Gordon smiled. It wasn't something that happened very often, roughly on a par with a total solar eclipse; unlike an eclipse, it made the world a very bright place. "I don't know, you're a bright kid, Benny, really, *really* bright, but there are times when you can be really, *really* stupid."

Benny grinned back. "I know," he said. "Sorry."

Uncle Gordon sighed deeply and glanced at his watch. "Hellfire," he said. "I've got to go. I've got sixteen South Korean venture capitalists sitting round a table drumming their fingers waiting for me. I told them I was just nipping out for a piss. See you later, all right?"

Uncle departed in a flurry of clomping feet and mislaid car keys, leaving the usual empty silence behind him; when he left a room, it tended to be far emptier than it had been before he arrived, as if his exit had drained all the energy from it. But stillness, peace and quiet are what you need when you're revising, and Benny was (he noticed with a degree of mild surprise) doing just that. At least, he was reading the notes and uploading data into his medium-term memory; but it was coming in hermetically sealed and labelled WARNING – UNRELIABLE, with one of those toxic-waste symbols stencilled on each package. He really wasn't sure he wanted stuff like that in his head, in case it leaked out and got into something important. So he sealed off the bit of his brain he thought with from the warehouse space, and occupied it with thoughts like—

Well, he was very good about it, really.

Yes, except—

What?

I'm still not entirely sure what he was being very good *about*.

Excuse me?

I mean, it's not like I'd done anything wrong—

Whoa there, cowboy. You disproved the laws of thermodynamics, for crying out loud.

Yes? So? I mean, if they're wrong, they're wrong.

Sure. That's like saying, Stoke-on-Trent is a pretty horrible place, so let's burn it to the ground. You can't do that. People *live* there. At the very least, you've got to give them time to get their things and move out. Same with trashing the foundations of accepted knowledge. You can't just light the fuse and run away. Well, can you?

Actually, I quite like Stoke-on-Trent.

Bull. You've never even been there.

I so have. On a train.

Passing through. Looking out the window. That doesn't count.

All right, fine. But he wasn't just being nice about that, he was being nice about me wanting to drop out of Uni.

Didn't let you, though.

No, because it wasn't the right thing for me to do. He explained that.

You agreed with him.

Well, yes. He was right.

I put it to you, he only wants you to stay on and do your exams so you won't make him give you a job at his work. Because he doesn't want you there.

He said, it wasn't the sort of thing I'd enjoy doing.

Because he *doesn't like you.*

No, I can't accept that. Just look at everything he's done for me.

Yes, because he promised your mum.

You're just trying to make trouble. He likes me. I'm his nephew. When he's gone, all this will be mine. He said so. And I live here. If he couldn't stand the sight of me—

He'd have packed you off to boarding school when you were twelve. Oh, wait, yes, he did. And then straight to college. You hardly had time to unpack.

I'm here now.

Now *look.* One, none of that is true. Two, it's beside the point. All I was saying was, he could've been really upset and angry, shouting, throwing stuff. And he wasn't. All right?

Yes, and isn't that just a teeny bit suspicious?

Oh come *on.* You can't have it both ways.

No, you come on. You saw how he reacted when you asked him what he actually does for a living.

And he answered the question, didn't he? Accountancy. Management consulting.

Mphm.

All right, what?

No, it's fine. You seem perfectly satisfied with that answer. Far be it from me to go stirring up trouble.

Look—

It just occurs to me and my nasty, suspicious mind, if that's really want he does, why did the question stop him dead in his tracks—

Ah yes. The crass militaristic tank metaphor.

Actually, I thought it was rather good.

You would.

Anyway. Sorry, where was I? Oh yes. So, two things for you to think about. One. All right, I'll concede, he's fond of you, to some extent. But he goes to a lot of trouble and expense to get you out of the house and a long way away. Two. Questions about how he makes his money stop him dead like a bear trap. Now, then. Exercise that fine analytical brain of yours. Don't you think there may be something just a little bit—?

He'd had enough. Damned if he was going to sit still and listen to himself saying horrid things about Uncle Gordon, when he'd been so nice. He needed to get away, go somewhere he could clear his head; somewhere the insidious little voice couldn't follow.

The garage. Or, to be precise, somewhere over the garage, way up high, to wish upon a doughnut. He wasn't quite sure how, but he knew that the voice couldn't get at him there. Maybe – his memory was oddly unclear on the point – that was why he'd gone there the last time.

Tin box. Doughnut. Here goes nothing—

And into nothing he went; and stepped out into bright sunshine under a clear blue sky. No change there, then. Amazing they ever managed to grow anything in a place with so little rainfall. He reached for a pocket to stow the doughnut in, but the stupid tunic thing he was wearing didn't have one. He wasn't entirely sure where he was; inside the palace grounds, but that's like saying you're not lost because you know you're somewhere in Europe. He looked round, but for once the place wasn't seething with courtiers and guards and gardeners with wheelbarrows. And that was another thing. Where did the money come from to pay all those people? Taxes? Excise duties? A 4 per cent levy on traditional narrative tropes? He made a note to ask the Chancellor, first chance he got—

Something swooped down at him out of the sun. He barely had time to drop into an instinctive terrified cringe when a hawk shot past him, its wingtips brushing his face, snatched the doughnut from his hand, and swung away, two feet or so above the lavender bushes, and vanished from sight.

The small part of him that really was Prince Florizel felt quite smug about that; told you it'd come back when it was hungry, assuming it's the same hawk, but then, there can't be an infinite number of goshawks in these parts, assuming it was a goshawk. The rest of him, outnumbering the Florizel bit by several hundred to one, froze in horror. The doughnut. The way home.

He sat down on the gravel, too shocked to stand or move. His mind was racing, trying to remember the rules of the YouSpace device. For your convenience and ease of use, YouSpace can be accessed through the hole in the middle of any doughnut, fried onion ring or bagel; so, wherever you are, in practically any alternative reality in the multiverse, you're never far from a handy, reliable portal back to your default universe. Fine. He remembered sitting on his bed, on the day when he'd first found the stupid thing, reading the book of instructions and drawing a glowing yellow line through the word *practically* with a highlighter pen. Practically every universe; in other words, there are universes (how couldn't there be, in an infinite multiverse?) where there aren't doughnuts with holes in them, fried onion rings or even bagels. That was why, on that fateful day, he'd stuffed the instructions back in their envelope, put the envelope back in the box, and shoved it away under his bed as far as his arm could reach. Too risky, he'd told himself. Find yourself in a doughnut-free continuum, you'd be screwed; stuck for ever, unable to get home. Then, later, when the tedium of revision had begun to gnaw his brain and he'd resolved to give the thing a try, he'd promised himself that he'd pay very, very close attention to safeguarding at least one doughnut at all times, to be on the safe side, to be *sure*. And now—

Don't panic, cried his inner Lance Corporal Jones. Well, indeed. All was very far from lost. All he had to do was go to the kitchens, find the cook and demand a doughnut. He was entitled to do that, being supreme ruler of the kingdom. And even if they couldn't do doughnuts, they ought to be capable of a simple bagel. And if they couldn't do bagels, any bloody fool can batter a bit of onion.

Finding the kitchen turned out to be a challenge in itself. He knew it was in a separate building, because of the risk of fire. That narrowed it down to a choice of thirty-five. Thirty-fifth time lucky; he knocked on the door, waited for several minutes while nobody answered, remembered that he was the prince, damn it, opened the door and went in. Two dozen men and women stopped what they were doing and turned to stare at him.

"Hello," he said, in his best Florizel voice. "Which one of you's the cook?"

It was one of those I-am-Spartacus moments, and it went some way to explaining why the soup was always lousy. "Fine," he said, selecting one at random. "I want you to make me some doughnuts. Please," he added, before Florizel could stop him.

The man, a huge creature with hair in his ears, looked at him. "Doughwhats?"

Oh Christ. "They're a sort of—" He hesitated. A sort of what, for crying out loud? Bread? Pastry? Now he came to think of it, he had no idea what was in a doughnut, or how you went about creating one. Flour, presumably. Maybe eggs. That was the total extent of his knowledge. Might as well show a builder a pile of stone blocks and expect to get a perfect replica of the Parthenon.

"Bagels?"

"You what?"

"All right," he said, trying to fight down the surge of panic in his insides. "How about a nice fried onion ring?"

He'd said the wrong thing, apparently. The cook went white as a sheet, made a complicated sign with his fingers across his forehead, and started to back away, mumbling something under his breath. "Sorry," Benny said quickly, "I didn't mean to upset anyone, I didn't—"

The stares of the kitchen staff pierced him like arrows. Well, of course. He might not be expected to know that onions, or fried onions, were anathema and abomination in these parts, but Prince Florizel would know, of course he would. He cleared his throat and smiled. "Very good," he said, "just testing. Carry on." Then he left the kitchen, very fast.

Practically every reality. Oh boy. He leaned against a handy wall and caught his breath. This is hopeless, he thought. No doughnuts, no bagels and especially no fried onion rings, not if you don't want to end up with your head stuck on a pike somewhere. How am I going to get *home*? This is *terrible*.

Think, he ordered himself.

Look, it's cooking. How hard can it be? Flour, eggs, water, a source of heat, a flat pan, butter. Any bloody fool can fry an onion.

Amend that to *practically* any bloody fool, because he could think of one prime example of bloody stupidity who couldn't, and he was wearing his shoes. It's all very well to speak airily of rustling up a quick plate of doughnuts and a side of onion rings, but he knew his culinary limitations, and he was in enough trouble as it was without adding arson to the equation. Not me, then; someone else. There's got to be someone in this kingdom who'd be prepared to cook me something with a hole in the middle without feeling the need to send for the Witchfinder General.

Then it occurred to him that he didn't actually know a lot of people in his kingdom; certainly not on could-you-do-me-a-small-favour terms. Most of the people he did know were court functionaries of one kind or another, politicians, precisely the sort of person who couldn't be relied on to keep their minds open and their mouths shut if His Majesty came and asked them to do something unspeakably weird to an onion. Which left – well, two or three of the gardeners were all right, and the man who looked after the dogs, and the odd-job man. At least, he'd smiled at them a couple of times and said hello, and they'd smiled back instead of doing all that awful bowing and bobbing about. One of the women who did the laundry looked like she might be quite nice, except that she was stone deaf and just grinned when he spoke to her. Apart from that—

Come *on*, he told himself (and he created a mental image of Uncle Gordon to say the words, to give them immediacy and impact), cooking is cooking, you're a *quantum physicist*. If you can extrapolate the existence of the Higgs boson from observing the simulated collision of two protons, you can probably make a functional doughnut. Provided, of course, that you have a recipe—

Of course. All he needed to do was Google "donut recipe" on his phone. He'd already established that, although he couldn't make or receive real-life calls in this universe, he could access the internet, give or take a few inconsequential anomalies – all the semicolons became dollar signs, for instance, and any reference to Australia made it crash, but he could live with that, just about. A simple recipe, and he could—

He'd lost his phone. He remembered realising that, back at Uncle's house. He closed his eyes and cursed silently; and then it occurred to him that, although he'd discovered the loss back in real life, it must actually have taken place *here*, on this side. In which case, his phone had to be around here somewhere, and if he could only find it, assuming it hadn't got trodden on by unicorns and the battery hadn't gone flat, he could get the recipe, pay some poor old peasant woman a million gold coins to cook him one and get the hell out of here, back to where he belonged. If only.

Right. A certain degree of confidence returned, because looking for misplaced articles was something he knew all about, from a lifetime's bitter experience. He knew, better than anyone, that the Great Primordial Question, the starting point of every journey and the fountainhead of all wisdom, is *where did you have it last?* Now, then—

The girl. The irritatingly bright girl who asked questions. He'd been using it, the time before last that he'd met her. She'd been interrogating him about something or other, and he'd said something to annoy her, and she'd deliberately stamped on his foot—

Forget about that. The phone. He'd had it when he met

her, and he couldn't remember seeing it or using it after that. He tried to picture in his mind the spot where the meeting had taken place; in the forest somewhere, well, that's a great help. No, wait. There had been a funny-looking tree—

A funny-looking tree. In a forest. Well.

Yes, but it was something, a tiny scrap of straw to cling to. *If* he could find the tree, and *if* his phone was still there, and *if* it was still working, he stood a reasonable chance of getting home. If not, he'd be stranded here for ever and ever. Put like that, he didn't have much choice. Funny-looking tree, here I come.

"That's a five and a three makes eight," said King Mordak, sliding his counter across the squares with his foreclaw, "which means I pass Go, collect two hundred gobbos, thank you, and, yes, I think I'll buy that. How much is it?"

The first goblin-dwarf summit in three thousand years was at a crucial moment. King Drain opened his eyes, closed them again, wiped beer out of them and blinked. "Three hundred and fifty."

"That's fine," Mordak said. "Now, that means I've got all the black ones, so I think I'll build three dungeons on Arak-Zigar and a Dark Tower on Arathloom."

"Snot."

Drain was taking it pretty well, all things considered, given that things weren't exactly going his way. After forty-six hours of play, Mordak had all the green ones, the blue ones, the red ones, the yellow ones and now the black ones, while Drain had the Sewers of Snoria and the Waterworks. Still, as Mordak kept reminding him, there was still everything to play for.

"My go." Drain glugged a big mouthful of beer and shook the dice. "Two anna one. Bollocks."

Mordak counted on his claws. "All right," he said. "That's the Enchanted Groves of Plorien with three dungeons and a tower, so that's one thousand, three hundred gobbos."

Drain hiccuped and fumbled with his money. "I only got nine hundred."

"Doesn't matter," Mordak said, "I'll take the Sewers of Snoria and your return-unexpectedly-from-the-dead-free card, and we'll call it quits."

"Righto," said Drain. "Your go."

Mordak left the dice where they lay. "Let me get you another drink," he said.

"Yeah, sure. Great beer, this."

"It should be," Mordak said pleasantly, filling his cup. "It's from the plunder we took when we stormed your fortress at Gorm's Deep and slaughtered the entire garrison."

"Ah," said Drain. "That'd explain it."

"And that cup," Mordak went on, "is the garrison commander's head. Right, here we go, oh look, double six."

Three moves later, Drain's head slid forward onto his beard-cushioned chest, and he began to make a noise like the death of hemp sacking. Mordak waited a little while, then carefully tugged on the string around the dwarf's neck, on which hung the Great Seal. Mordak melted a little sealing wax by breathing on it, blobbed it at the foot of a long, densely written scroll of parchment, then applied the seal. Job done.

Having put everything back where it should be, Mordak leaned back in his chair (the ribcages of his enemies creaked ominously under the strain) and sighed deeply. No doubt about it, war was easier. That, presumably, was why nobody had bothered trying peace for a thousand years. War, however, didn't work. Whether peace would be any better was anybody's guess, but it had to be worth a try.

To pass the time, he read through the treaty that Drain had just unconsciously put his seal to. There was going to be hell to pay when the terms were announced, from both sides. When he'd first come up with this plan, he'd intended to screw the dwarves to the floor and give nothing in return; fortunately, wiser counsels had prevailed. Instead, he'd put in six key concessions on the goblin side, the sort of things he'd have resisted fang and claw if they'd done real negotiations. Nobody on either side would believe for one moment that Mordak would've included anything like that in a *forgery*. Besides, Drain would have to be able to tell his people he'd won something, or they'd shred him and crown someone else. The four really *key* key concessions, on the dwarf side, were all that really mattered; everything else he could live with. And so, he reflected with pride, could about thirty thousand goblins, ditto dwarves, who otherwise wouldn't have had the option.

Even so. All this not-fighting made his skin crawl and his scalp itch. It wasn't right. Or, rather, it wasn't natural (and it was that distinction, so recently recognised, that kept him awake at night) and he couldn't help wondering what had got into him lately. Thoughts seemed to explode inside his head, suddenly and devastatingly; they took his mind hostage and dragged it away to strange places where everything was bewilderingly different, and when at last they let it go and it wandered home, there was still that lingering doubt – St'k'hm syndrome, the head-shrinkers called it, the phenomenon whereby the hostage becomes emotionally attached to and dependent on his captors. Well, maybe. Goblins weren't in the habit of hearing voices inside their heads – other people's heads, yes, because a suitably adapted enemy's skull makes a super-duper loudspeaker – and there were times when he wondered if he wasn't going, you know, a bit *odd*. But he'd secretly consulted a leading Elf nerve specialist, who'd told him that he was perfectly normal, for a goblin (the question he'd asked was, *Am I sane or am I crazy?*, and the Elf had grinned as he replied; but that, of course, was perfectly normal for an Elf); so that was all right.

Drain's snoring turned into a sequence of grunts, which culminated in a ferocious snort, which woke him up. Mordak quickly rolled up the treaty and tucked it away under his chair out of sight, then grabbed the beer jug. "Refill?" he said.

Drain squinted at him through bleary red eyes. "What?"

"More beer?"

Drain frowned, and winced. "Maybe not," he said, and reached a shaking hand towards the dice. "Whose go is it?"

Mordak shook his head. "Game's over."

"It is?"

"Yup. You won, remember?"

"Did I?" Drain rubbed his eyes with two peach-stone knuckles. "Course I did. Right."

"And we've sealed the treaty," Mordak went on, "and had a nice drink, and it's probably time you were getting back, before your lot start to fret."

Drain nodded. "Load of bloody worrywarts is what they are," he said. Then he pulled a doubtful sort of face. "Did we seal the treaty?"

"Oh yes." Mordak produced it from under his chair. "There you are, look. Your seal, right next to mine."

Drain groped under his breastplate for his glasses and stuck them on his nose. "So it is," he said. "Right. Good. Glad that's settled. Um, did I—?"

"Drive a hard bargain? I should bloody well say so." Mordak did his best synthetic scowl. "I'm going to be in so much trouble when my lot get wind of this. Still, so long as you and I understand each other, what can they do?"

Drain shrugged. "Kill you, I guess."

"Well, yes, there's that." He closed his hand tight around the scroll. "Maybe this wasn't such a good idea."

Drain snatched the scroll from him and put it on the table, next to the game board. "Don't you dare," he growled. "Don't even think about backing out now." Then he hiccuped, and sat back in his chair, holding his head in his hands.

"All right," Mordak said, "if that's the way you feel, I guess I'll just have to deal with the consequences and to hell with it. I'll see to it you get your copy in the morning."

Drain groaned, stood up and sat down again. "You'd better," he whimpered. "And keep the bloody room still, can't you? How's a dwarf supposed to stand up if the stupid room keeps wobbling about?"

"It'll stop in a minute," Mordak replied. "It's just minor seismic activity. Earthquake," he translated.

"Oh, one of those. Fair enough." Drain closed his eyes for a moment. "Good game, that. Where'd you get it?"

"It's a human game originally, I think," Mordak said. "I had my people tinker with it a bit, but basically—"

"Clever bastards, the humans," Drain growled. "You know what? Once we've done the Elves, we ought to do the humans, too. I don't trust clever bastards."

Indeed. And there, Mordak reflected, in a nutshell is the problem with this whole coalition. The dwarves are savages and their leader is an idiot. On the other hand, the legacy of centuries of free collective bargaining between the dwarf miners' union and the mine owners was the best trained, equipped and experienced army in the whole of the known world. So the choice was; have these people as your enemies, or make them your friends and stab them in the back later. The humans had a word for it: *politics*.

"Splendid idea," Mordak said, "I'll make a note of it."

"Good man." The dwarf straightened his knees and rose

slowly but surely to his feet. "Good man. And no hard feelings, eh?"

"No hard feelings."

"That's the spirit. Good game, too." He staggered a few steps towards the door, swayed, stopped, looked back. "Here, Mordak."

"Hmm?"

"You sure I won?"

"Would I lie to you about a thing like that?"

When he'd finally gone, Mordak unrolled the treaty scroll on the table, smoothed it out and read it from beginning to end. He winced five times, and closed his eyes twice. How can it be, he asked himself, that you can have something that nobody wants, that makes everybody on both sides very angry, but which is quite obviously the right thing to do? The world can't possibly work like that, can it?

His left hand was itching like mad; he rubbed it, but it didn't seem to help. There was a small red swelling in the web of skin at the base of the sixth and seventh claw. He knew what that was all about; another one about to come through. No big deal, except that goblins tend to get their blood claws in early adolescence, and Mordak was a hundred and six. Still, late claw development was by no means unheard of. He put some sulphur-paste-and-mercury cream on it to take the swelling down, and forgot about it.

11

"Let me stop you there," Buttercup said firmly, lifting the cloth off the top of her basket. "Now, we both know you're not really a little old lady, in fact you're a horrible, smelly, incurably stupid wolf, and this can only turn out one way. Unless," she added brightly, "we find a way to break the mould, overcome the limitations of our stereotypes and work together to resolve this situation so it doesn't end in blood on the grass. So," she went on, as the wolf made a faint whimpering noise, "in this basket I've got a bouncy yellow ball, a rawhide bone, a soft toy that goes squeak when you chew it and a generous helping of Doggybix Chicken Crunch. And," she added, "a hatchet. So, it's up to you. Which is it going to be?"

"Um," said the wolf helplessly. "All the better to see you with, my—"

"Oh come *on*," Buttercup snapped, grabbing the bouncy yellow ball and throwing it at the wolf, who ducked. "Don't you understand? You *don't have to say it*. We can—"

"Yes I do," mumbled the wolf.

"—dawn of a new era in human/wolf, sorry, what did you just say?"

"I got to," said the wolf. "Not up to me, see? Got to do as I'm told or it's—"

"Yes? What?"

Painfully and carefully, the wolf mimed a ferocious human scowl. "*Bad*," it said, in a voice two octaves deeper than usual. "*Bad boy*."

Buttercup looked at it. "If you don't say the words, someone will be *cross* with you?"

The wolf nodded eagerly. "Very cross. Bad boy. All the better to hug you with, my dear. Wrf."

"Who'll be cross with you?"

The wolf backed away, shaking its head. "Can't tell. Mustn't tell. Very bad."

"Look, you stupid creature, I'm trying to *help*—" Too late. She must've got too close and triggered some instinctive reflex; the wolf sprang, missed her as she swerved out of the way, and landed in a heap on the ground with Buttercup's axe head socket-deep between its eyes.

"*Dammit*," Buttercup yelled, and gave the dead wolf a kick in the ribs with her dainty little foot. Then she discovered that a tear had somehow found its way onto her cheek. She wiped it off with her sleeve. "Damn," she said, and put the stuff back in her basket.

Quite a good haul from the cottage, including a fine electroplate teapot and five spoons, a set of lace doilies and a wooden carving of a pig inscribed *A Present from Innsbruck*. She dumped them in her basket and slammed the door behind her.

"Buttercup? Are you all—?"

"Not now, William. Just not now, all right?"

The woodcutter's head drooped. "Sure," he said. "I was just passing, and I thought—"

"Go away."

He looked so sad as he plodded away, trailing his axe behind him through the leaf mould, that she called him back. He bounced towards her like a happy dog. "Yes?"

"Here."

His eyes shone. "For me?"

"Well, yes."

"Hey. Um. What is it?"

Buttercup forced a smile. "If you squeeze its little tummy," she said, "it makes a squeaking noise."

"Hey. Oh, wow, so it does. This is so cool."

"That's fine, William. You enjoy it. Somewhere else, please."

"Thanks, Buttercup, you're the greatest."

She waited until he'd gone, and the squeaking noises had been subsumed into the gentle murmur of the forest. Then, from the bottom of her basket, she took a small grey rectangular object, like a thick, undersized roof tile. *You*, she thought, *it's all your fault*.

Quite why she was so sure, she had no idea. But it was so obvious. Something was wrong, so very wrong; the world can't possibly work like this, it's insane. And the grey tile thing clearly wasn't from around here, she had no idea what it was for or even what it was made of – not wood, not metal, not clay or bone or anything like that – but, equally clearly, it was for *something*, because a hell of a lot of work had gone into making it, not to mention a hell of a lot of cleverness—

Too much cleverness, in her opinion. She hadn't shown it to anyone, needless to say. She knew exactly what the reaction would be. That's a wizard thing, it must belong to Him, don't touch it, you've got to give it back. Fair enough; except she happened to know that it didn't belong to the wizard. It belonged to the prince, the handsome but incredibly irritating young man who, in his spare time, when he wasn't hunting, practising falconry and chatting up gormless young peasant girls, *ran the country*. Was, not to put too fine a point on it, the Government. Was therefore at least nominally responsible for how things were run around here. Whose fault, therefore—

She shook her head. Much as she'd like to believe it, she couldn't. He just didn't look the type, somehow. Not that she had the first idea what The Type was supposed to look like; just not *that*.

In the distance she could hear music; the Elves, most likely, doing whatever it was Elves did. Nobody knew, far less cared. That, of course, was a large part of the problem. Nobody gave a damn, so long as things went on more or less the same way as they always had – her father and uncles, planing down trees into forty-foot planks; the woodcutters, felling lumber and killing wolves; the Elves, floating around being ethereal and snarky. Spring flowers all year round. The occasional earthquake. The way things had always been, as long as anyone could remember. The way things should be. Maybe.

Behind her, she could hear the sound of galloping hooves. She frowned, and started to count under her breath. Seven, eight, nine, *thump*. She nodded, turned round and walked back along the path.

"Ah," she said. "I've been looking for you."

He was lying on his back, directly underneath the overhanging branch that everyone else who rode through the forest knew all about. Close nearby, a milk-white horse was nibbling primrose leaves.

"Ooh," he moaned. "My head."

"Should've looked where you were going," she said crisply. "Now then, about the balance of payments deficit—"

"Help me up," he said pitifully. "Please."

She grabbed his hand and yanked him upright. He winced and flexed his arm. "Thanks," he said.

"Don't let your horse eat that, it'll get colic. I've been thinking, and though every single wolf I've killed in the last six months has had a teapot and a big box full of tea, nobody around here grows the stuff, the climate is completely wrong, so presumably it's all imported. Which in turn implies—"

"Tea?"

"Yes, you know, *tea*. Just add boiling water and serve. Except, if you're a wolf, how can you drink the stuff? Can't hold the cup, can't get a claw through that little itsy-bitsy handle. So why—?"

"You've got tea in this godforsaken country?"

"I just said so, didn't I?"

The prince looked stunned. "I asked the palace kitchens, and they looked at me as if I was mad."

"Ah," said Buttercup, "but you're not a wolf, are you? That's my *point*. My dad and my uncles don't use the stuff, the woodcutters don't drink it, and neither do the little old women gathering firewood, the poor but honest shoemakers, the Elves, the goblins or the dwarves. And that's about it, there isn't anybody else."

"Yes, there is—" the prince started to say; then a thoughtful look passed over his face and he fell silent.

"So," Buttercup went on, "obviously it's worth someone's while to freight in tea all the way from Mysterious Cathay or wherever the hell it comes from, just for the wolf market. And, since the wolves don't make anything or perform any useful services they can provide to the tea importers by way of exchange, presumably they pay for the tea in hard currency. Which means, " she went on, after a quick, deep breath, "you've got large amounts of cash leaving the country but no significant exports, which must mean that any day now you're going to have one mother of an exchange rate crisis, leading to massive devaluation of the florin, galloping inflation and fiscal collapse. Well? Are you listening to me?"

"The wolves have tea?" the prince said. "Do you think they'd sell me some?"

Buttercup grabbed him by the ear and pulled his head down until they were nose to nose. "*Yes*," she said. "The *wolves* have *tea*. And it's *wrong*."

"Um." He tried pulling away gently, but she had a thumb and forefinger of iron. "Look, would you mind not—? Thank you. Ow." He straightened up and took a long step back. "No one told me," he said. "I'm sorry."

"You're supposed to be in charge. You ought to—"

"Yes," he said gently. "I know. And I'm *trying*."

The anger seeped out of her like oil from a Land Rover. "Try harder," she said, but her voice was practically the coo of a dove. "And if you want tea, I've got some."

"You have?"

"Plenty."

"Good God. Would you possibly consider—?"

"Two florins a pound."

"Done."

She blinked twice. *Two florins*. She believed in the existence of two florins in the same way as she believed in the sea: never seen it, never expected to, just sort of took it on trust that it was out there somewhere. "Um, all right. How about a nice teapot?"

"Excuse me?"

"To make the tea in. Tea's not much use without a teapot, is it?"

"Er, no, I suppose not. You've got a—"

With a shy smile she threw the cloth off her basket. "There you go," she said. "Solid, um, silver, not a mark on it, five shillings and I'll throw in the spoons. Well?"

He shrugged. "Fine," he said. "Um, thank you." His hand was feeling for a pocket that wasn't there. Then he remembered, and took the purse from his belt. "Now, just a—"

"The florins are the thin shiny yellow ones," Buttercup said helpfully.

"Ah, yes, right. I knew that."

"Of course you did. The shillings are the slightly thicker silvery ones with the thistle on the back." And your face on the front, she didn't add. "So, five of those ones and two of those ones, all right?"

"Sure. There you go. Sorry, you were saying."

"Was I?"

"About the wolves. And the balance of payments deficit."

"So I was. Um."

"And the answer to your question," the prince went on, his hand tightening around the box with the tea in it like a vice, "is that we get large amounts of hard currency from the wizard in exchange for, well, *stuff*, so although there are localised imbalances in some sectors, overall there's a slight net foreign exchange surplus which we're applying towards regearing our sovereign debt position vis-à-vis King Mordak and the dwarves. Or at least," he added ruefully, "that's what they keep telling me. OK?"

She nodded. "Yes, fine."

There was a yearning look on his face that would've melted a heart of stone. "You wouldn't possibly have any coffee, would you?"

"Any what?"

"Ah. Never mind," he said bravely, "tea's just fine. All they've got up at the palace is either wine or beer, and I don't really like any of that stuff. Gives me a headache."

"The woodcutters make a sort of posset out of fermented birch sap," Buttercup heard herself say. "Mind you, it's not very nice."

"It sounds horrible."

"It is." A long moment passed, silent apart from the distant violins of the Elves. "You said you were looking for me."

"What? Oh yes." He stopped and frowned. "What's that awful noise?"

"Excuse me?"

"Over there somewhere. Sounds like—" He stopped dead and didn't finish the sentence.

"Oh, that's the Elves. They do that."

"Really? Why?"

"We don't like to ask."

"Ah. Do they do it a lot?"

She nodded. "All day and all night. They do shifts. It's cultural or something."

She had a horrible feeling she was blushing, which was something she simply didn't do. But then again, she'd never met anybody quite like him before, someone with money. It spoke to something deep inside her, and its voice couldn't be stilled. One day her prince would come; she'd known that all along, resigned herself to it, built her entire life alongside it, like the people who build villages on the lips of dormant volcanoes. But, of all the things she'd expected or dreaded her prince would be, she never thought he'd be *rich*. Princes tended not to be, in these universally threadbare parts; probably because of the screwed-up economy and kingdoms dividing because of dragon slayers, and all that. You could tell them apart from the woodcutters by their white horses and the fact that their hand-me-down clothes were brighter colours and embroidered with frayed gold thread. This one, however, had a purse practically bursting with florins. That put a completely different complexion on it. She smiled.

"You wanted to see me about something," she prompted.

"Yes, right." The smile seemed to be causing difficulties with his speech, so she switched it off. "I was wondering."

"Yes?"

"Can you cook?"

It took a moment for her mental spin doctors to swing into action. Then they assured her that honesty and down-to-earth practicality were refreshingly different, tending to reinforce the view that this prince wasn't like the others. Which was a good thing. Even so. "Yes," she said.

"Great. Can you do doughnuts?"

"Whatnuts?"

His face fell. "Bagels?"

"What's a bagel?"

"Fried onion rings?"

A moment later, her hand hurt; a sort of stinging, burning sensation. She imagined it was worse for him, but she didn't care. At least he'd shaved recently. Must be hell to slap stubble. "Ow," he said. "Sorry."

I just whacked my handsome prince across the face, she thought. My *rich* handsome prince. But there are limits. He was babbling apologies, something to do with not being from around here and not realising how strongly people felt. For pity's sake, she thought; as though mere geography could make any difference. She grabbed her basket and was about to storm off when one of those annoying thoughts dropped into her mind, and she hesitated. She turned and looked at him.

"You don't know, do you?" she said.

"Excuse me?"

"You don't *know*. About—" She had to nerve herself to say it. "The O-R things."

"Well, no. That's what I just said. Clearly, I'm woefully out of touch with regional sensibilities."

She made herself focus on the dear little gold discs in his purse, and took a deep breath. "Just so you won't make the same mistake again," she said. "We're a pretty broad-minded lot around here, but food with a hole in the middle is *out*. Forbidden. Not something we even talk about. What's the word I'm looking for? Taboo. OK?"

He looked curiously desolate, as if he'd just found out

that the pile of brown stuff he'd just stuck his finger in wasn't chocolate blancmange. "Any sort of food with a—?"

She nodded quickly. "Yes," she said. "It's anathema and an abomination and all sorts of other really nasty things beginning with A, and if you don't want to have a thoroughly unpleasant encounter with a pitchfork, you won't mention it again, ever. Got that?"

He nodded sadly. "Yup."

"That's all right, then." It wasn't, of course, but still. "So, cooking. Yes, though I say so myself, I'm not bad at it. Roasts, stews, good strengthening soups—"

"No, that's fine," he said, turning away. "Sorry to have bothered you."

"Scrambled eggs on toast?"

"Really." He fumbled for his horse's reins. "And I didn't mean to upset you like that. See you around."

His foot was in the stirrup. The thought of all that money, on the point of riding out of her life for ever, tore her heart like rotten cloth. "I do a stonking bread and butter pudding," she called out, but he was already too far away to hear.

Fool, she thought; and then, *meaning him, or me?* Both, she decided. Him, well, because he was one. Her, because she'd just belted a man with *all that money* and driven him away because of some arbitrary old taboo that made no sense at all when you came to think about it dispassionately—

Food with a hole in it. Yuck.

She made a massive effort and stopped the squirm in its tracks roughly halfway down her spine. Why, she asked herself, *why* does the very idea of food with a – let's not go there – make me want to throw up and then scrub every inch of my skin with sandpaper? And was it possible that somewhere, in a faraway land of which she knew nothing, there were people who didn't see it that way?

She felt something in her left hand and opened it; two

gold coins, five silver ones. Her running-away fund. For years, with every passing day, every slaughtered wolf, she'd dreamed about it, the moment when she'd have saved up enough money to leave, go away, go as far as she could get. Two florins; was there enough distance in the whole world to use up two florins? I can do it, she thought, I can go now.

And there was that voice again, nattering away in the vacant lot between her eyes and her ears; yes, but where? And what if you got there – Ultima Fule or Far-Distant Cathay – and it was *just like here*? Screwed up; weird; wrong. In Far-Distant Cathay, she had good reason to believe, there were great plantations where they grew tea for wolves, and where was the sense in that? And there seemed to be places – he came from one – where they did food with holes in, which was just gross. What if simply being somewhere else (being somewhere else without her two lovely florins, because she'd have spent them getting there) made no difference? That's the problem with running away, said the little voice. No matter where you go, you have to take yourself with you; and if yourself is constitutionally incapable of leaving well alone and not worrying if the rest of the world is weirder than ferret ragout, where the hell is the point?

Get stuffed, little voice. You've done nothing but make trouble ever since I first heard you, and I'm not going to listen. I've worked really hard for this, and anywhere's got to be better than here, and—

If anything could possibly be more annoying than the little voice talking, it was the little voice staying smugly silent. Inevitably, when that happened, she found herself making its case for it. Yes, all right, supposing I stay here instead, what do you suggest I do, marry a woodcutter? Well, no, not with two florins, I think we can safely say we're way past wood-cutters at this point. So, yes, just possibly, though it makes my skin crawl just thinking about it, I could marry my handsome prince and help him spend *all that money*, and maybe, just possibly, nag and shame and force him into doing something about all the stuff that's wrong around here; which he, apparently, might just possibly be capable of doing, since he's not quite like all the other princes you hear about, like he might just possibly have slightly more in his brain than his trousers—

She counted on her fingers. Four just-possiblys. Make that five, because the handsome prince might just possibly want to marry *her*. But only if—

Doing *that*. With an *onion*. Oh my God.

And those other things he'd talked about, the ones she'd never even heard of. If he was into even weirder stuff than onion rings, she really didn't want to know. You wouldn't think it to look at him, butter wouldn't melt, which only went to show that appearances deceive. Not a bad appearance, at that, or at least you wouldn't mind terribly much having it around the house. Um. But that didn't really count for anything as against the, er, culinary issues.

Purely out of interest, how *would* you go about frying a—?

She shuddered. How could anyone even think of it? But you don't know, do you, what goes on behind the kitchen curtains. And where he came from—

Where *did* he come from?

She remembered the grey rectangular tile. It was his box, so it stood to reason it came from where he did. She resisted the temptation to take it out and look at it again, because you never knew who might be watching. The box. The first time she'd seen it, he'd been prodding at it with his fingertips; in a very methodical fashion, now she thought of it, so not just random poking. It had reminded her just a little bit of the time she'd snuck through the undergrowth to watch the Elven orchestra. But it wasn't a musical instrument, because it hadn't made a noise. Unless it was a *silent* musical instrument, which didn't make a whole lot of sense, but she was getting close to the point where nothing would surprise her about what people did ever again.

Whatever it was, there was a strong possibility that he'd like it back. Might even pay money for it; a florin? Two? She paused until her head stopped spinning and thought, Yes, but if we're in this for the long game, that box could be worth a hell of a lot more than two florins. If only I knew what it *did*.

Her hand had stopped hurting at last. Two florins; two and two makes four, with four florins Dad could build a huge sawmill with a waterwheel and a buzz-saw, he could hire practically every able-bodied man in the district, they'd be rich inside a year. Or she could buy a farm, grow crops, raise livestock, and then the woodcutters wouldn't have to buy their bread and cheese in the market, and *she'd* be rich inside a year. Or she could—

Me again, said the voice. You know perfectly well it's not going to happen. Dad wouldn't want to run a big sawmill, and if he did he'd be hopeless at it, and all the money would be gone. And the farm idea's a non-starter, because who the hell around here knows about ploughing and harrowing and drilling and the three-field system and how to cure mastitis? Face it; you might as well drill holes in your pretty gold florins and hang them round your neck for all the good they're going to do you. Things don't change. They just don't.

Something was different. The music had stopped. Odd, though by no means unwelcome. She shrugged, and started to walk home. She hadn't gone far, though, when she was frozen in her tracks by a horrible scream and the noise of breaking branches. Before she knew it, she'd taken the hatchet from her basket and started to run.

Just a minute, she thought. I'm heading in the wrong

direction. I should be running *away*, not towards. This is all—

Something roared.

Oh hell, she thought, that's not good. She stopped dead in her tracks, which proved to be a good choice, since a fraction of a second later she heard the distinctive cracking noise you learn to recognise if you live in a forest, and a tall maiden beech tree toppled and fell, hitting the ground with a soft, earth-shaking thump more or less exactly where she'd have got to if she hadn't stopped.

Eek, she thought. Then she thought; it's got very dark all of a sudden. Then she looked up.

She'd never seen a giant before, though of course her grandmother's stories had been full of the things. Even without her rich cultural database to draw on, however, she wouldn't have had any trouble making the connection. In a sense, he was perfectly ordinary; a middle-aged man, running slightly to fat, wearing the usual woodcutter's ensemble of checked shirt, breeches, grubby red scarf and hobnailed boots. The only real difference was that he was *huge*. Also, she observed, he appeared to have taken the old saying about two heads being better than one just a bit too literally.

On the plus side, he didn't seem to have noticed her. All his attention was focused on a slender oak tree about fifteen yards away, behind which a knight in shining armour was trying to hide, with indifferent success. He didn't look very happy, maybe because he seemed to have lost all his weapons, and his helmet had jammed against his gorget at an angle of roughly fifteen degrees. As a result, he was having to peer round the side of it, and the tip of his nose stuck out.

He's not going to make it, she thought. The giant's already seen him, and all it's got to do is push over that tree, and the knight'll be squashed. Which would be a shame.

She took a long stride forward and deliberately trod on a twig. It didn't snap. One of those days.

"Hey, you," she shouted.

The giant straightened up a little. One of its heads craned round to look at her, studied her for a moment, dismissed her as a threat and went back to considering the geometry of falling trees.

She resented that. Not a threat, huh? Go tell that to any wolf between here and the Blue Hills, and see what they say. "Hey," she yelled. "I'm talking to you."

The giant made a grumpy noise in its throat. Rough translation: not now, I'm busy. A red veil seemed to come down over her eyes; *how dare you*, she thought, and somehow the hatchet was in her hand. The old familiar feel (the weight balanced forward, but not too far; the comfortable anchor of the hart's foot on the end of the handle against the base of her thumb) sent messages to her brain that she would have found irresistible, had she been in any mood to resist them. Patronise me, would you, you bastard? I've been patronised by *Elves*. You're nothing.

She couldn't even see its heads, they were so high up. But, as the woodsmen knew so well, if you're going to cut down a tree, the lower you cut, the harder they fall. She was dimly conscious of taking the swing, and then there was a deep, chunky sound and a shock that ran up through her wrist into the tendon of her elbow.

The giant hadn't been expecting anything like that. It yelped, a weird, ear-splitting, high-pitched noise that startled the pigeons out of the trees all the way to Cair Danathros, and slewed round, neglecting to notice the stately old ash tree right beside it. The thunk as its nearside forehead hit the tree trunk made the ground shake, bringing dirt and small clumps of rock down on the heads of the goblins in Shaft 3/72. The giant swayed and wobbled, tried to restore balance by moving its feet, lodged a toe against the trunk of the recently fallen beech, tripped and went over. A small stand of holly saplings broke its fall to a certain limited extent, but its offside head caught a fearful glancing blow from a hollow oak, which dissolved into dust and crumbs. As panic-stricken goblins rushed to evacuate the entire upper gallery on Level 2, and teacups rattled off occasional tables and smashed on the flagstones of a dozen derelict wolves' cottages all across the Forest, the giant hit the ground and lay motionless, never to move again.

Buttercup stood quite still, the hatchet hanging forgotten from her hand. "Oh," she said.

A creaking noise made her look round, and she saw that the knight had managed to wrestle the helmet off his head. His shoulder-length golden hair—

"You stupid bloody woman," he roared. "What the hell do you think you're playing at?"

"**Y**ou poor darling," said Yglaine's mother, without looking up. "It must have been awful."

"It was," Yglaine replied to the back of her head. "It just suddenly appeared sort of out of nowhere and started trampling on people. It's a miracle nobody was killed."

"Mphm." Mummy crossed out a word and wrote something in over the top. "How dreadful."

"And it trod on my violin," Yglaine said. "And it's ruined."

"What? Oh damn. Well," Mummy went on, tucking a stray lock of hair behind her needle-pointed ear, "we'll have to see about that. I'll definitely say something about it in my column."

Mummy was a columnist for *Sarcasm Now* (circulation 37,596), one of the top 30,000 most widely read lifestyle magazines in Elvenhome (population 37,602). "That's wonderful, Mummy," Yglaine said. "Um, what am I supposed to do about my violin? Only I need it for work, you see, and—"

Mummy frowned. "I suppose you'd better sue somebody," she said. "Go and talk to your Uncle Glorion, he'll know what to do."

"Yes, but till then—"

"I don't know, do I?" Mummy snapped. "You'll have to buy a new one, or borrow one from somewhere. Now *please* go away, you're ruining my concentration."

So she went and asked her father, but he was busy with tomorrow's lead editorial for *Sneer* and waved her away without speaking. She went and sat in her room for a while, but the empty violin case seemed to watch her every move, till she couldn't stand it any longer. So she went to Uncle Glorion's office, on the seventy-fifth platform on the tallest *miramar* tree in the Grove.

"He's not here," said the receptionist, looking past her as though she wasn't there. "He's in court, huge intellectual property case. He might be able to window you in six weeks' time, but don't hold your breath."

"Oh. Is there anyone else I could see?"

"Without paying? No." The receptionist gave her a bleak smile, then went back to correcting the proofs of her latest collection of essays. Yglaine gathered up the bits of her ruined violin and headed for the ladder, but her way was blocked by someone coming up. She stepped aside to let him pass, and suddenly caught her breath.

Round ears.

Don't stare, she ordered herself. The young man – young *human* – gave her a nice smile, and she remembered hearing something about Uncle's firm taking on a human trainee, as part of the Inferior Species Encouragement Initiative. She looked at him; he was short, quite stout, hair already starting to get a bit thin on top, and his ears were entirely pointless. He tried to ease past her – she was blocking the top of the ladder – and, in doing so, knocked the broken violin out of her hands onto the floor.

"Sorry," he said, and stooped to pick it up.

Yglaine froze. What she should have done, would have done if he'd been just another Elf, was make a disdainful clicking noise with her tongue, snatch the violin and sweep past without a word. But there was something about the way he'd apologised – there was a word for it, began with S; *sincerity* – and she was afraid she'd hurt his feelings—

Hello? Get a *grip*.

"That's a really nice violin," he was saying. "What on earth happened to it?"

"A giant trod on it."

"Dear God." He looked genuinely shocked. "Where?"

"In the forest, just now. We were just sitting there as usual, playing *Four Seasons*, and it just sort of loomed up at us out of nowhere."

"That's awful. You must have been terrified."

Another abstruse concept beginning with S. Sympathy. It was supposed to be a sign of weakness and moral decadence, but she found she rather liked it. "I was, a bit," she said. "It stamped on all the violins and cellos, then crashed off into the trees. I suppose it's still out there somewhere."

He frowned and pursed his lips. "You ought to sue somebody," he said.

"Yes, but Uncle's busy and I can't afford to pay anyone, so—"

A faint blue light seemed to glow in the young human's eyes. "Come through to my office," he said.

"Really?"

"Definitely. Just out of interest, have you ever come across the concept of the contingency fee?"

"The what?"

He smiled as he opened the door for her. "I'm sorry," he said. "I didn't quite catch your name."

It was the strangest lawyer's office she'd ever been in. On the bookshelves, instead of double-banked rows of authors' copies, there were law books with titles like *Irfangyl's Personal Injury* and *Theory & Practice of Creative Billing*. The desk was covered with blue, green and yellow folders, not galley proofs. There was a bit of wood with his name on – John the Lawyer – and also a little picture frame, with a black and white silhouette of a woman with a big nose. For some reason, she didn't like that.

He must have seen her looking at it. "My mother," he said, with a grin. "Please, sit down."

That one began with a P. On the tip of her tongue. Politeness. Talk about your collector's items. "Um, thanks," she said. The chair was lovely and comfortable, and had little wheels instead of feet. "So, do you really think you can get me a new violin?"

John smiled. On the wall she noticed a little framed sign: *More Flies with Honey.* "No problem."

"And I don't have to pay any money?"

"That's the sheer joy of it, you don't. Whoever we end up suing pays the bill. Assuming we win, of course."

"You think you'll—"

"I always win." His smile beamed, like sunlight reflected on polished armour.

She remembered how to sneer. "Really?"

"Oh yes." He hadn't noticed, or he was sneerproof. "Always. Partly because I only take cases I can't lose, partly because I'm really rather good, but mostly because I'm human." He paused, to let her say something. She didn't. "Really," John said. "It's the most wonderful advantage. Elven judges always let me win because it makes them look liberal and caring about inferior species. And because I'm the only human lawyer in Elvenhome. While there's just one of me, I'm chic. As soon as humans start pouring in and taking all the jobs, they'll be down on us like a ton of bricks. But by then I'll be rich and I'll have retired. So," he went on, his big puppy-dog smile revealing all his teeth, "I can give you a one hundred per cent guarantee of success. I love Elvenhome," he added happily. "Provided you've got a skin as thick as dragonhide, it's a wonderful place to practise law. You're so litigious, and your Elven lawyers are too busy reviewing each's books other to prepare their cases properly. Now, then. You were playing your violin in the forest."

So she told him all about it, while he made notes on a little yellow pad. When she'd finished, he didn't speak for a while, just sat there looking thoughtful.

"Well?" she said. "Do you think I've got a case?"

"What? Oh, sorry. Yes, most definitely. In fact, the only problem's deciding who we sue first."

"Oh."

John nodded vigorously. "I mean," he said, "do we kick off with Prince Florizel, for breach of his statutory duty to maintain a safe, giant-free environment, or do we go after the orchestra, for multiple health and safety violations, or the Elvenhome Parks and Forestry Authority, or the Royal Highways Commission, or what? We're so spoilt for choice, you wouldn't believe it. I guess it all comes down to who's got the most money."

She frowned. It was all a bit hard to follow. "But I only want a new violin."

He gave her a smile that was almost Elvish. "No, you don't," he said. "You want exemplary damages for mental trauma, anguish, personal injury, loss of earnings—"

"The orchestra doesn't *pay* me."

"Doesn't it? Excellent, we'll hit them for breach of implied duty to remunerate while we're at it. All in, I'm looking at a minimum ballpark figure of twenty million florins. And a shilling and fourpence," he added, "for the violin."

She pursed her lips. "I don't think Prince Florizel's got twenty million florins," she said. "Or any of those others you mentioned. I don't think there's that much money in the whole—"

But John was nodding. "Exactly," he said. "So we need to bring in King Mordak, and probably the dwarves as well. Maybe even," he added, with a slightly dreamy note in his voice, "the wizard. Um, let me think. You know what, I'm no expert, but I'd be prepared to wager good money that the only reason the giant was roaming around loose in the forest was because it had been driven from its natural mountain habitat by environmental disruption caused by ecologically irresponsible mining operations. What d'you think?"

At last he'd said something she could relate to. Mummy and Daddy were always writing articles about how the mines were threatening the environment. It was the one issue that united the entire Elven Fourth Estate, and a topic they never seemed to tire of. In fact, when Mordak opened the new gallery under Dol Umfroth, the woodcutters had had to fell all the pines on the Frif escarpment to provide enough wood pulp for the special editions. "Can we sue the goblins?" she asked doubtfully. "They might not like it."

He looked confused. "I'm a lawyer," he said, "I can sue anybody. Besides, they'll settle, they always do."

"Even the wizard?"

A strange, faraway look glowed in his pale blue eyes. "As far as I know," he said, "nobody's started a lawsuit against the wizard before. Which is odd," he went on, with a slight frown, "but absolutely no reason why we shouldn't try. In fact, I think we should make him our number one target."

"Do you?"

"Oh, I think so. After all, he's got the most money." He lifted his head and smiled sweetly. "For now, anyway," he said. "Because if we can establish liability for your giant, I can confidently predict this is going to be *huge*. I don't know if you're familiar with the term 'opening the floodgates', but that's what we'll be doing. We can make everything that happens round here his fault. And then we take him for every penny he's got."

He looked so happy and bouncy that she caught herself looking round for a ball to throw for him. "Really? You think you could do that?"

"Absolutely. Everybody hates him. Well, maybe not the people who work for him, the miners and the woodcutters and all the other people who get money from him. But everybody else, the commentators and columnists and people on committees, the overwhelming majority of right-thinking people everywhere, they hate his guts. That's what matters." His smile broadened so much it was in danger of unzipping his face. "I'm so glad you happened to stop by, Ms Yglaine, because this is the start of something truly wonderful." He clasped his hands together with a damp smack. "It's going to be such an adventure, you'll see."

She could feel it, too. It was almost as though music was playing.

"Oh yes," he said. "We're off to sue the wizard. What could possibly be better than that?"

(13)

"**N**o offence," Mordak said, "but you don't look much like mercenaries."

The old man didn't look offended; far from it. He grinned, revealing a wide space where teeth had once been. "'Scuse me," he said, "but that's a laugh. If my old platoon heard that, they'd bust a gut."

The young man, his companion, was eating a slice of Simnel cake. "Your *old* platoon," Mordak said. "Isn't that the point?"

"Forty years we was together," the old man went on, "and never a cross word. They were good lads, bless 'em. Forty years in the trade, Your Highness, sir. You can't put a price on experience."

"Mm," Mordak said. "What about him?"

The old man smiled happily. "Young Art, you mean, sir? He's a good boy. Learning the business, just like me at his age. Very promising, though I do say so myself. He's got the feel for it, see, the bloodlust. If you ain't got the bloodlust, I always say, you might as well not bother."

The young man swallowed the last of the cake and started to unwrap an individual pork pie. "Does he ever stop eating?" Mordak said.

"Got to keep his strength up," the old man said. "Very important, at his age. Strong as an ox, he is, mind. Worth ten men in a tight spot."

Well, Mordak thought, there's enough of him, at least in the *y* axis. Even sitting down, he had his head practically on his chest, to keep from bashing it on the ceiling. Impressive, but maybe not the physique for agility in confined spaces. Or (he considered the young man's twiglike arms) anything involving heavy lifting. "Well," Mordak said, "I've got to admit, these references couldn't be better. King Rience of Gath calls you his twin gods of war."

The old man beamed. "Good old King Rience," he said. "Proper gentleman, he was. We put down a rebellion for him, in the southern provinces."

Mordak raised all three eyebrows. "Is that right?" he said. "You and whose army?"

"Oh, no army, sir. Just us."

Well, Mordak thought, rubbing his chin-spikes with his claw-tips, you shouldn't judge by appearances. Even so. "And the Dark Lord of the Snif reckons you two are, and I quote, Death, the destroyer of worlds, unquote. That's—"

"He's too kind," said the old man, wiping away a tear. "But that's so like him, bless him. We helped him out with storming the impregnable citadel of Karttun. Five-minute job, nothing to it really, but he was so pleased."

"The impregnable—"

"Oh, they had to call it that, because of the insurance, you see. Turned out it was dead pregnable once you set your mind to it. We do a lot of jobs like that."

"No army?"

"No, sir, just us. Why keep a dog and bark yourself, I always say."

Then the old man must've breathed in the wrong way, because he broke into a fit of coughing, which shook him like a rag doll until Mordak gave him a skull of water. "Thank you so much," the old man said, "very good of you, sorry to be a bother. I get like that sometimes, but it's perfectly all right. Now then, how can we oblige?"

"What?"

"What would you like us to do for you, sir?"

Mordak looked at him, then down at the four-inch-thick wad of references, then back at young Art, who was eating an egg mayonnaise sandwich. Appearances, he told himself. "Well," he said, "you may have heard, I've recently made peace with King Drain and the dwarves."

"Ah, yes, sir. We like to keep up with current affairs, Art and me."

"You may be wondering," Mordak went on, "why someone who's just signed a peace treaty needs the best hired swords money can buy."

"Oh, we never wonder, bless you, sir. None of our business."

"Make an exception," Mordak growled. The old man shrank back a little, and young Art stopped chewing, for a second.

"Well, let's see," the old man said. "Pound to a penny, I'll bet you're thinking that maybe the wizard won't like you making peace with King Drain, on account of so long as there was a war, he could play you two off against each other and force down prices on them glowing rocks he has off you. But if you and the dwarves are at peace, you can present what's known as a united front and force the price up. Would that be sort of in the right area, Your Majesty?"

"Not bad," Mordak said. "So?"

"So you realise, no disrespect, that your goblins and Drain's dwarves, wonderful fighters, sir, nothing but the deepest admiration, you wouldn't last five minutes if you was up against *magic*. So if the wizard got it into his head to break up the peace, like, there's not a lot you could do about it."

"Go on."

The old man nodded, and the peak of his ancient cap flopped down over his eyes. He thumbed it back into position and went on, "But then I guess you heard about how we got a certain reputation in certain circles, if I can put it that way, specially with us not being from around here originally, don't know if you knew that, sir, but it's true. And you thought, if anyone can turn the tide and hold the line against the growing darkness from the east, it'd be W & A Military Services. That's me and the boy, sir. I'm W and he's A. Is that what you was thinking, Your Majesty?"

Mordak closed his mouth, which had dropped open. "Close enough for manslaughter," he said. "Yes, that's more or less it. So, you think you can handle the wizard."

The old man pursed his lips, while Art bit into an Eccles cake. "Don't see why not, sir," the old man said, and Mordak realised he'd been holding his breath while he waited for the answer. "We got a few tricks up our sleeves, Art and me, like, you pick up a wrinkle or two when you been in the business as long as I have. Not saying it'll be easy, mind, but we could have a stab at it, if you'd like us to."

"That's—" Mordak's head was beginning to hurt. Also, watching young Art had made him feel so very hungry. "You really think you can defend my kingdom against magic. Only—" He stopped, and peered down at young Art's shoes. He'd never seen anything like them before. Instead of black leather they were made of some sort of white, shiny material, and they had blue and red lines drawn on them, and a label: *Dead Man Walking, from Aberzombie & Witch*. He lifted his head and, for the first time, really looked at the two strangers sitting opposite.

"Who *are* you?" he asked.

The old man looked right back at him, and then Mordak turned away his head, his mouth suddenly dry. "Right you are, then, sir," said the old man. "When would you like us to start? We can do Tuesday, if that'd suit you."

"That's fine," Mordak said, in a little tiny voice. "It's great having you on the, er, team. Just for the record, how do I reach you?"

"Oh, don't worry about that, sir. We'll contact you. Thank you so much for you time. Come along, Art. *Art!*"

The young man sat up suddenly, swallowed the last bit of his Bakewell slice, and rose to his feet. Crumbs dropped from him like the last desolate leaves of autumn. He nodded vaguely at Mordak, and followed the old man out of the room.

After they'd gone, Mordak sat for a long time, waiting, because it wouldn't do for the goblins to see him like that. It was universally accepted through the goblin kingdom that there wasn't a single living thing on Earth that King Mordak was afraid of. He had a shrewd, uncomfortable feeling that that was still true. When at last he'd got the shakes under control, he reached under the desk, grabbed a skull and a bottle, and poured himself a drink that would've poisoned a large city. It helped, but not much. Then it occurred to him that the one thing they hadn't got around to discussing was how much his two new helpers expected to be paid, or what form that payment would take. Not, Mordak decided gloomily, that it mattered all that much. There was no doubt in his mind that, when the time came, he'd find out. No doubt whatsoever.

"**Y**ou stupid bloody woman," roared the knight. "What the hell do you think you're playing at?"

Buttercup gave him a long, steady look, then stooped, picked her hatchet up off the ground, turned on her heel and walked away. She'd gone about five yards when a clanking noise behind her made her stop.

"I'm talking to you," yelled an angry voice. "How *dare* you kill my giant? What in God's name were you—?"

It proved to be a deep, mellow sound, like a gong. Probably, she decided later, when she'd had time to think about it, that was because she'd turned the hatchet round and hit him with the flat bit on the back rather than the cutting edge, which would most likely have produced a duller, tinnier noise. "*Ow*," the knight yelped, taking two quick steps back and nearly falling over. "Have you gone mad or something?"

Buttercup wasn't smiling. "Not yet," she said. "Give me time."

His visor, she noticed, had dropped down over his face when she hit him, but it must've got twisted or something during the fight with the giant, because it didn't close properly. It made him look ridiculous, which calmed her down slightly. It took him several tries to wrench it open again, and even then it stuck halfway.

"You're welcome," she said.

"You what?"

"For saving your life. When you were about to be squashed flat just now. If you can remember that far back."

"What do you mean, saved my life? I had the situation completely under – no, don't do that."

Now she smiled. "Why not?"

"You'll dent my bloody helmet is why not. You know how much it costs raising dents in carbon steel? You can't just whack 'em out over a sandbag, the whole thing's got to be annealed and then re-heat-treated, it's specialist work." He stopped, and glared at her. "You just don't care, do you?"

"No."

"Look, will you put that thing *away*, you stupid girl. You could do someone an injury."

"Gosh, do you really think so?"

He was breathing hard through his nose, and she didn't really want to have to hit him again, so she decided to forgive him. "Look," she said, "I'm sorry I bashed you just for being an ungrateful pig, and I'm sorry I humiliated you by rescuing you instead of leaving you to be squashed like you deserve, and I promise faithfully I won't make the same mistake again. All right? And if you want your stupid helmet fixed, try John Smith down the bottom of the valley, third farmhouse on the left after the old mill. He's not very good but he's cheap. Say Buttercup sent you."

He peered at her for a moment. "Old mill?"

She nodded. "Go back the way you came about a mile, at the crossroads take a left. Carry on about half a mile, past fourteen derelict cottages, you'll come to a bridge. Follow the river upstream about six hundred yards, that's the old mill. Have you got that, or would you like me to draw you a map?"

"Buttercup?"

"It happens to be my name."

"Good heavens." He took his helmet off and examined the dent. "You would have to go and bash it right on the bloody seam," he said. "Even if this bloke of yours can fix it, it's never going to be *right*. Two shillings I paid for this helmet, and now it's—"

"Oh, for crying out loud." She dug furiously in the fold of her sleeve and found two of the coins she'd had from Prince Florizel. "There. There you are, two shillings. Buy yourself a new helmet. Only, for God's sake, stop *whining*."

He looked at her, then at the coins, then at her again. "Whining?"

"*And stop repeating every damn thing I say.* Yes, whining. Well, you were."

The knight frowned. Then he extended his hand and turned it palm upwards. The coins fell into it and chinked together. "Thanks," he said.

"That's all right."

"My name's Turquine, by the way. Sir Turquine Le Coeur Hardi of Outremer."

"And that's better than Buttercup how, exactly?"

"Excuse me?"

"Nothing." She looked at him. "And I shouldn't have hit you, even if you did provoke me beyond endurance."

His hand closed tight around the coins. "That's all right," he said, "I shouldn't have yelled at you like that. Truth is, I'm having a really bad day. Was having. Anyhow, that doesn't excuse bad manners. I'm sorry."

She shrugged. She couldn't think of anything to say, and that was unfortunate. "The giant."

"God, yes. Ain't that the way? First day off I've had in

months, and how do I get to spend it? Fighting monsters. For free," he added bitterly. "Unpaid voluntary work. Not my scene."

"He who fights monsters must take care lest he becomes a monster himself," she said. "And if you stare into the abyss—"

"You what?"

"Sorry. Just something I read."

He looked startled. "In a book?"

"Yes."

"You read books?"

"Well, sometimes the wolves have them in their cottages – yes," she said. "So?"

He raised both eyebrows, then shrugged. "You get a lot of them around here? Giants."

"Not many, no. Wolves, yes. The occasional troll."

"Dragons?"

"One or two."

"I kill dragons. It's what I do."

"That must be an interesting job."

She'd offended him. "It's not a *job*," he said. "I'm a knight, I don't have a *job*. It's a vocation."

"A paid vocation."

He shrugged. Rivets creaked. "Used not to be," he said. "When I was a kid, it was just something you did occasionally, to keep the village sheep from getting eaten. Now, though, there's dragons everywhere. Just as well there's money in killing them, or the place would be overrun."

She frowned. "Let me guess," she said. "The wizard."

He nodded. "Cash on the nail, I'll say that for him. Really, it's transformed my life. I'm making more in a week than I used to get in a year just from rents and tithes and stuff. Of course, I'm saving every penny I can," he added quickly, and the knuckles of the hand gripping the coins showed white under his tan. "After all, you just don't know how long this dragon thing's going to last."

"Or wolves," she said without thinking.

"Sorry?"

"Wolves," she said. "You do dragons, I do wolves."

"My God."

"Oh, it's no bother. Of course, I'm not as, well, not as organised as you. I don't go looking for them, or anything like that. Don't have to," she added bitterly. "But when they're dead, if they've got any stuff worth having, well, why not?"

"Quite. Waste not, I always say."

"Like, tea, for example. They've all got it, and if there's people willing to pay silly money, then where's the harm in that?" She looked down at her hands, for some reason, and wished they weren't quite so big and red. "Will you be able to get a helmet for two shillings?"

"Should be able to."

She shook her head. "Not round here. Unless you don't mind second-hand, of course. You could try in the town, Honest John's House of Plunder. Third on the left as you go past the Guildhall, second floor, over the apothecary."

"Oh, used is fine, saves you the bother of breaking it in. Beats me why anybody ever buys new, actually. First time you do up the chin strap, that's ninepence down the pan for a start."

And she caught herself asking herself; is it possible to fall in love twice in one day? Not that she had, of course, but still; two men quite unlike anyone else she'd ever met before, both so different from all the foresters and woodcutters that they might as well belong to a different species; both of them so unthinkably similar to herself; one who actually seemed to understand about money, and one who had so much of it. "Like shoes," she said, in a voice like the breeze in the sycamores.

"Shoes? Don't talk to me about shoes," he replied, and his passion startled her, but in such a good way. "Pair of half-decent boots, steel toecaps, in the market at Beal Regard, one and fourpence."

She gazed at him. "You didn't pay that, did you?"

"Did I hell as like. See these?" He lifted the hem of his chain-mail chausses. "Goblin government surplus," he said. "Sixpence. And a damn good boot, if you're not fussed about the space for the sixth toe. Just pack it out with a bit of old rag, and there you go."

Things he'd said a moment ago – I'm saving every penny I can, more in a week than I used to get in a year from tithes and stuff – floated into her mind on a fluffy pink cloud. "Honest John does really good thick winter shirts," said her voice, seeming to come from far away, "penny-halfpenny, and some of them haven't got bloodstains."

He was looking at her as though she was a two-for-one offer on Holy Grails. "This Honest John," he said, in a slightly strangled voice. "Does he do a loyalty card?"

She shook her head, because nothing is entirely perfect. Some things, though, and some moments come pretty damn close. But there was one thing she had to ask, before she let her heart fly away. "Food," she said.

"What? Oh, yes, good idea, I'm starved. Do you know anywhere round here that's good and not too—?"

"You don't like *strange* food, do you?" she asked.

"Strange like how, exactly?"

She fought the blush and the blush won. "Sort of, oh I don't know, unusual things with onions?"

He frowned, then shook his head. "I'm more a bread-cheese-and-porridge sort of man myself," he said. "Of course, you eat what you can get when you're on the road all the time."

That was enough. She gave him a smile you could've

sunbathed in and tucked her arm round his. "The Blue Boar, in the village," she said decisively, "and it's Wednesday, so it's buy-one-get-one-free on pease pottage with bits of leftover sausage." She looked up into his eyes. "Show you the way there if you like."

Walk a mile in another man's shoes, the saying goes, and you'll understand him. Not true. If it was, Benny reflected sadly as his fingers combed the leaf mould, I'd understand Uncle Gordon better than anyone, and I don't.

Benny had walked many a mile in his uncle's footwear, mostly because he and Uncle happened to take the same shoe size, and Benny didn't really care about what he put on his feet so long as they didn't hurt and he didn't have to pay money for them. Besides, Uncle had dozens of pairs of shoes, many of which he'd only ever worn once. You wouldn't think to look at him that Uncle Gordon was a shoe addict, but he was; not in the Imelda Marcos league, perhaps, but not a hell of a long way short of it. Benny had no idea why, though maybe it was because Uncle was a short man with huge feet. In any event, it was a useful eccentricity, most of the time.

His fingers closed on something; about the right size, and sort of rectangular. He scrabbled like a dog and came up with a flat, squareish stone. He swore and threw it into the bushes.

Maybe, Benny reflected sourly, it's all God's way of punishing me for borrowing Uncle's shoes without asking; because it was in a shoe box, wedged in along with all the others at the bottom of a wardrobe, that Benny had found the YouSpace stuff. And if he hadn't been snooping where he had no business to be, he wouldn't be stuck here now.

The contents of the box, jammed into the far corner of his uncle's closet, couldn't have been more unpromising if they'd tried. An empty beer bottle, and a wodge of printouts stapled together in the top right-hand corner, and that was all—

Congratulations!

He could so easily have put the lid back on the box and the box back where he'd found it, and gone on to lead a normal, happy life. But it hadn't worked out like that. He'd happened to catch sight of a familiar name on the first page of the printout; Professor Pieter van Goyen, the greatest particle physicist since Meitner, Bethe and Hahn, who'd vanished in unexplained circumstances a few years ago. Van Goyen was one of his heroes, and seeing his name on a sheet of paper found in a shoebox had snagged his curiosity, so he'd read on.

Congratulations! You're now the proud, incredibly privileged owner of the YouSpace XP3000 personal multiverse interface and home entertainment centre. Your new YouSpace XP3000 will unlock the gateway to an infinity of impossibly exciting and stimulating experiences. The only limit is your imagination.

Yes. Well.

The YouSpace XP3000, designed by Professor Pieter van Goyen of Leiden,

Ah.

. . . is an omniphasic Multiverse portal, capable of transporting you to any or all of the alternate realities that make up the Multiverse. Intuitive targeting software and state-of-the-art Heisenberg compensators mean that all you have to do is think of where you'd like to go, and you're instantly there. It's as simple as that.

All you'll need to operate your YouSpace XP3000 personal multiverse interface is a dream – and a doughnut.

Oink?

Simply lift the doughnut (which in this context acts as a Sonderberg phase-base converter/condenser lens) flat side on, until you're looking straight through the hole in the middle. Visualise, as precisely as possible, the alternate universe you would like to visit. Before you know it, you'll be there!

The YouSpace XP3000 isn't a virtual reality experience – it's real reality. When you arrive at your chosen destination, you'll actually be there, in a guaranteed 100% genuine functional alternate universe, every bit as real as the one you've just come from. That's what makes the YouSpace experience so intense and so unique. Real goblins; real space aliens; real fairy princesses. It's the best possible way to discover the real you. By crossing through the hyperdimensional interface between the infinite number of potential spatio-temporal divergency streams, your dreams really will come true. And remember; in an infinite multiverse, **everything** is possible!

WARNING—

He'd skipped that bit, because everyone knows that the stuff headed WARNING in users' manuals is just a load of guff put in there by the lawyers – always wear safety glasses, consult your doctor, don't drive or operate heavy machinery, may contain traces of carbon/silicon/hydrogen/oxygen/nuts, never attempt to use this hammer to drive in nails, the surgeon general has determined that decapitation may be injurious to health, all that garbage. He carried on reading the next section, headed *Where Would YOU Like To Go?*; and that, no question about it, had been his undoing.

Even now, he wasn't entirely sure that the YouSpace device was Van Goyen's invention, as the brochure had claimed. On the one hand, the concept behind it bore all the hallmarks of Van Goyen's anarchic, chaotic, lightning-bolt genius. On the other hand, if it really had been a Van Goyen artefact, he couldn't help thinking it would've worked a bit better—

No, be fair. It worked perfectly. Once you'd charged up the bottle with a static supersymmetric dark matter field (simple-to-follow instructions on pages 3 and 4 of the printout) and popped into the baker's for a doughnut, the YouSpace 2.1 Home Entertainment Center did exactly what it promised to do. Simply hold the doughnut up to your eye and look through it, and the YouSpace effect would transport you to the alternative reality of your choice, where you could relax and engage in a wide range of invigorating leisure activities before doughnutting back in exactly the same way you'd arrived, to find that while you'd been away, real time had stood still. Thus, you could spend a year as the only male in a universe of gullible, short-sighted nymphomaniacs and be back before the kettle you put on just before you left had had a chance to boil. Or, if you were just the right sort of idiot, you could escape into a universe of myth and magic, to act out your fantasies and make your wildest dreams come true—

And get stuck there. Oh boy.

Not for the first time, he cursed himself for not taking better precautions beforehand. Whoever designed YouSpace

2.1 had chosen doughnuts, bagels, Cheerios, fried onion rings and other perforated foodstuffs as transdimensional portals because they were omnicultural; go wherever and whenever you choose in the Multiverse and the one thing you can rely on getting hold of easily and without fuss, in practically every permutation of reality, is food with a hole in it. It's a fundamental law of sociophysics, apparently, holding true in 99.969 per cent of environments capable of supporting carbon-based, oxygen-breathing life. You'd have to be *really, really unlucky*—

Yes. Well.

He looked up, and the branches of the odd-shaped tree cast dappled shadows on his face. This was quite definitely the place where he'd dropped his phone, and he'd searched it with infinite care. Therefore, if the phone wasn't still here, it had to be because someone (or some*thing*; remember where you are) had picked it up. And if it hadn't been the girl—

Unless she *had* picked it up and not made the connection in her mind between the alien object and the man she'd been talking to; in which case, she must have it somewhere, unless she'd simply thrown it away, or sold it in the market as a curio. There was nothing for it. He'd have to find her again and ask her, straight out; and if she came out swinging, at least this time he'd be prepared, and could try and get out of the way.

99.969 per cent. There, now.

He stood up and brushed decomposing leaves off his trouser knees. There remained the question of what the fateful shoebox had been doing in Uncle Gordon's wardrobe in the first place. He'd given it a fair amount of thought, and had formed various hypotheses, not all of them equally satisfactory. For example, there was straightforward statistical analysis. Such a large proportion of the world's shoeboxes had made their way to Uncle's closet, so why not this one?

Answer, because it didn't contain shoes. Uncle had acquired the YouSpace device, and hidden it away where nobody, no sane person, would go looking for it. But – Uncle Gordon day-tripping in Fantasyland? The other one, when pulled, is a campanological delight. Someone had put it there *as a trap* – some enemy, wishing to harm Uncle Gordon and unwilling, on ethical or legal grounds, to use a simple bomb. But who'd want to hurt Uncle? Someone had hidden it there, one shoebox among so very many, intending to return and collect it later. But the perimeter of Uncle's house was better alarmed and fortified than the White House, so that wasn't very likely. Finally; Uncle had bought the horrible thing as a present for Benny's birthday. It was the most likely explanation, and if true, it had been a sweet thought, but on balance, he'd have preferred socks. You can't have too many socks, and a sock, if used responsibly, is unlikely to strand you in an existential no-man's-land with no hope of escape.

Something rustled in the bushes nearby, and he whimpered. The narrative-dynamic operating system that ran this place could easily have decided that this would be a good time for Prince Florizel to have a thrilling adventure with a terrifying mythical beast, whose head he could cut off and bear home in triumph to impress the chicks with. That was the way it thought, apparently, and he was sick of it. His hand crept unwillingly to the hilt of the sword that dangled from his waist, undrawn, ever since he'd got here; it was a bloody nuisance, banging against his ankle and tripping him up, and for two pins he'd have binned it long ago, if there were any bins in this godforsaken place, which there weren't. Now, he reflected wretchedly, it might well be the only thing between him and an untimely death. In which case, he was probably screwed—

The bushes parted, and out trotted a unicorn.

They aren't really horses. Genetically, they are in fact

considerably closer to zebras, as goblin scientists discovered as part of their enquiries into the recent processed meat scandal, following on from the discovery of unicorn DNA in products branded as 100 per cent horse. But they're pure white, and they have a golden horn sticking out of their noses, and they're almost unbearably cute, and almost Elflike in their pickiness about who they condescend to associate with. This one had little blue eyes under ridiculously long eyelashes, and was chewing a nettle. It looked at Benny, ears back, then ears forward. It swished its tail appealingly, and its jaws worked in that characteristic rotary motion. It didn't seem the least bit frightened.

Benny looked at it and decided that it was probably not going to attack, although that didn't mean there was no cause for concern. One careless move with that big golden spike and he'd be kebabbed beyond medical help. "There now," he said, in a strained talking-to-kids-and-animals voice. "Nice, um."

The unicorn took a few dainty steps towards him, then sat down, carefully folding its knees, and rolled over onto its side, the epitome of love and trust. That reminded Benny of one of the things everybody knows about unicorns, and he thought; yes, thank you, no need to rub it in, and in any case it's none of your damn—

A twig cracked. The unicorn lifted its head, but stayed where it was, curled up at Benny's feet. Three men dressed all in green came out onto the road. Two had spears, and one was carrying a crossbow. They looked at the unicorn, then at Benny.

"Oops," said the crossbowman. "Sorry, didn't see you there, Your Highness."

They were grinning. One of them sniggered. "That's perfectly all right," Benny said, with all the dignity he could muster. "You're, um, huntsmen, right?"

"Yes, Your Highness."

"That must be a very interesting job."

"Has its moments, Your Highness." And this, to judge by the smirks on their faces, was one of them. Benny breathed out hard through his nose and forced a smile. "Well, don't let me hinder you," he said. "I'm sure you've got lots to do, somewhere else."

"Yes, Your Highness," said the huntsman, backing away. "Come on, lads, nothing to see here." He bowed, then stepped back into the undergrowth, followed by his two companions. A little later, Benny heard one of them say, "But that means he must be a—", followed by the cracking of a large twig.

Benny looked at the unicorn. Then he picked up a stone and threw it. He missed. The unicorn gazed at him adoringly. He swore, and sat down on the ground with his head in his hands. Act out your wildest fantasies. Yeah, right.

99.969 per cent. Someone up there must really hate me.

Or – the thought hit him like a meteorite, digging a huge crater in his world view and exterminating the dinosaurs of certainty – someone up there must really like me a lot; enough to want to keep me here, possibly for ever and ever. Enough to go to all the trouble and expense of inculcating into the heads of the locals a superstitious dread of food with a hole in the middle. He thought about that. How, unless it had been deliberately introduced, would a taboo like that get started in the first place? But as a snare, or a security measure— He suddenly thought about the hawk that had snatched his precious doughnut. Did hawks usually do stuff like that? Seagulls, yes, and dogs, and some cats. But hawks? If only he had his phone, Wikipedia would tell him in a flash. As it was—

He shook his head, as if trying to dislodge the idea out through his ear. Impossible. For one thing, that sort of manipulation takes time, you'd need generations to implant a superstition that deeply. True, but to a YouSpace user, time spent Somewhere Else doesn't pass back home; you could doughnut in, spend a thousand years building a culture and a civilisation from scratch, and be back where you started from before your coffee went cold. Yes, but who would bother? Who might possibly have that much of a vested interest in—?

The unicorn stood up. It was looking at him out of those great big gormless blue eyes. "Not now," he snapped, "I'm thinking," but the unicorn continued to stare, making rational thought impossible. He sighed, turned to face it and said, "What?"

The unicorn fluttered its ridiculous eyelashes. Then, with the tip of its delicate hoof, it pawed at the ground.

"What?" Benny demanded. "You want to go toilet?"

The unicorn pawed again; and this time, Benny could see that it had traced a pattern in the leaf mould. A circle; no, two concentric circles, a big one with a little one inside. The shape of a—

"Oh come *on*," Benny said. The unicorn tossed its head, so that for a moment its mane floated like sea spray; then it shuffled over a bit to a fresh patch of leaf mould and started again; first a big circle, then a smaller one inside. It gave the impression that it was prepared to go on doing it all day, if necessary.

I should be excited, Benny thought. I should be filled with fragile hope and wild joy. Instead – he ran a quick analysis protocol, and the result came back; *insulted*. Yes, quite. On the other hand, it wasn't as though he was awash with alternative courses of action. He cleared his throat.

"Hello, unicorn," he said.

Flutter, flutter, went the eyelashes. Bat, bat.

He pointed at the circles in the mould. "Doughnut."

Bat, bat, flutter. Dear God, he thought. No wonder Barbie loves these creatures. "You know where I can find a dough-nut."

Flutter, flutter, bat, flutter. "Got you. Right, can you take me there?"

Flutter. Bat.

"Is that a yes or a no?"

Flut.

Shouting won't help, he told himself. There's no need to shout. "*Hey!*" he shouted. The unicorn opened its eyes wide and backed away a step or two; and that's me told, Benny reflected. "Nice unicorn," he said, and tried to find a smile from somewhere. That made the unicorn back away further, and he could see its point. "*Nice* unicorn. Take me to your doughnut. Please?"

The unicorn tossed its mane again, and swished its tail. It was deciding whether to forgive him, which was so *unfair*. Never mind. If it took him to a doughnut, and the doughnut took him home, none of it would matter; he could get on with his revision, take his exam, tell the necessary lies and get his first-class honours degree, and never have to think about Prince Florizel or unicorns or anything of the sort ever again. So: "Nice unicorn. I'm sorry I shouted, and I think your mane looks really pretty, and *please* can you show me where the doughnut is? Please?"

Slowly the unicorn arched its neck, then solemnly lowered its head in an unmistakable nod. *Yes!*, Danny thought, and took a slow step forward—

Which was just as well, because if he'd stayed where he was, the arrow that snaked through the air and buried itself up to the socket in a tree would have hit him, and that would have been that. As it was, he felt a blast of air like you get from one of those pocket electric fans, and found himself staring at a quivering arrowshaft, about four inches from his nose. By the time he'd snapped out of it, the unicorn had bolted.

"*Hey!*" he yelled, and was about to run after it when the bushes rustled and out jumped six goblins. He froze.

"Oops," grunted the lead goblin, in the act of nocking an arrow on his bowstring. "Sorry, squire, didn't see you there."

The goblin was about five feet tall, hunchbacked, NFL-shouldered, its huge head attached to its massive chest by the shortest neck ever. It had curly tusks at the corners of its mouth, ears like fried eggs and no perceptible nose; and the old joke, *so how does it smell? Terrible*, was no more than a statement of fact. Benny tried to say something, but his jaw had gone numb.

"Didn't think, see?" the goblin went on. "Like, you don't worry about hitting anyone when you shoot at unicorns, cos they won't let people get near. Not unless they're—" He stopped and grinned. "Anyhow," he added, "no harm done. Come on, lads, we can head it off by the waterfall." It grinned again, revealing a mouth containing far too many teeth, all pointed. "I expect you just haven't met the right girl yet," it said. "See you around."

The goblins loped away up the road, chuckling hoarsely. Benny sat down without intending to, and kept perfectly still until his heart had stopped trying to bash its way out of his ribcage. Goblins. The orcward squad. It just gets better and better.

Eventually he found the strength to start walking; and as he walked, he thought; come on, how hard can it be? You get flour, water or milk, probably an egg, you whisk them all up together to make a sort of paste, roll it into a string and join the ends, then you warm it over a heat source and there you go. Food with a hole in the middle. I can do this.

So he trudge back to the castle with a stone in his shoe, and stormed into the kitchen yelling, "Everybody out!"

When he'd shooed away the last of the kitchen staff and had the place to himself, he nosed around until he'd found flour, eggs, milk, a slab of evil-looking white lard and a frying pan. He'd remembered at the last minute that you deep-fried the things. He emptied two scuttles of coal onto the fire and blew it with the bellows until it was roaring cheerfully away. Now then, he said to himself. Let the dog see the rabbit.

Evicted by royalty in person, the kitchen staff fled in all directions, then crept back and reconvened on the archery lawn, grouped around the old well. Fortuitous; because when first black smoke and then long, curling tongues of flame started billowing out of the kitchen window, they were only a couple of dozen yard away and were able to swing into action immediately, filling buckets from the stable yard and forming a human chain. An hour and a half later, the fire was under control; and, apart from the thatch having to be dragged off the haybarn as a precaution, damage to the adjoining build-ings was minimal. Most important of all, the prince came through the ordeal with hardly a scratch, thanks to prompt action by a junior kitchen maid, who kicked down the door and carried him out over her shoulder. A good night's sleep worked wonders, and the doctor was able to assure the assembled court that, provided he got plenty of rest, His Highness would be up and about again in a day or two and no harm done.

The last part was something of an overstatement, because the kitchen block itself was a total ruin. The appropriate brave face was jammed on the situation by the Lord High Chamberlain, who arranged for emergency bread and cheese to be freighted in by fast (fastish) cart from the outlying vil-lages; until it arrived, he announced, there was plenty of celery in the walled garden, and nice fresh watercress, and some delicious crab apples from the tree opposite the south gatehouse, and they could all muck in together, no standing on ceremony, and it'd be fun. His words were received in respectful, stony silence by the hundred and sixteen men and women who worked in the palace and got their meals as part of their pay, though they were rather less taciturn later on, apparently. Anyway, nobody had been killed, that was the main thing, and any impromptu cookery session you can walk away from is a success. Even so—

"What were you thinking of, Your Highness?" the chamberlain said, not for the first time. "With all due respect, leaving the purely physical damage to one side for a moment, the political fallout—"

"I just wanted to cook something, all right?" Benny groaned. "For crying out loud, it's my kitchen—"

"Was your kitchen. Also, Your Highness, that's not strictly true. Under the doctrine of separation of powers embodied in the fifth schedule to the third amendment to the constitution, you as Prince represent the executive arm of the State, whereas the everyday routine functions of government, including the smooth operation of the palace complex, are properly speaking the prerogative of the administrative arm, as represented by myself and the Lord Chief Equerry of the Bedchamber. So, to be nit-pickingly pedantic—"

"It's your kitchen."

"I like to think of it as *our* kitchen," the chamberlain said smoothly. "Once it's rebuilt, of course, which I have to say isn't going to be any day soon. Apparently the slates for the roof have to come from Beal Regard, which is a two-week trip by river barge or three weeks by pack horse, because you can't get a cart across the Whitewater before July at the earliest—"

"Um," Benny said wretchedly. "I'm being a real nuisance, aren't I?"

"You're the prince," the chamberlain replied, his tone of voice making it quite clear that that wasn't to be construed as an answer to the question. "So, naturally, your word is law and your actions are above reproach. However—"

"Quite."

"Indeed. So, if it's entirely convenient to Your Highness, and not wanting to check or hinder your unfettered executive powers in any way, if you could possibly see your way to staying out of the kitchen when it's rebuilt—"

Benny sighed. "All right."

"If at all possible, never ever setting foot in that part of the castle campus ever again—"

"All *right*. Fine. Why is it some people find it so hard to take yes for an answer?"

"And furthermore," the chamberlain ground on, "if Your Highness could possibly be good enough to give a binding undertaking not to interfere or concern himself in any way in matters relating to food preparation— Only," he went on, lowering his voice, "there's been a quite ridiculous rumour going the rounds lately, obviously no basis to it whatsoever, but associating Your Highness with, let's say, some highly unsavoury food-related practices; and rather than have the rumourmongers rounded up and beheaded, which we really don't want to have to do if we can possibly avoid it, maybe it'd be better if the whole issue just died quietly away and was forgotten about, which isn't going to happen if Your Highness goes around the place making, well, *suggestions*—"

"Ah."

"Yes. So, if you could please just eat what's put in front of you and leave everything else to us, it'd make my life so much easier, and probably rather longer as well. If it pleases Your Highness, of course."

When the chamberlain and the other courtiers eventually went away and left him in peace, Benny lay back in the darkness and reflected that, if he really was being controlled by an unseen power rather than simply being a replay on Life's pinball table, the unseen power was winning hands down. Not only was he stuck here; every avenue of escape he'd so far identified had been methodically blocked. That was probably just his paranoia talking (other people have parrots), because at each step there was a perfectly reasonable alternative view. A falcon had stolen his doughnut; well, birds do that sort of thing, and tame falcons are trained to snatch food from the hand. The people here didn't know about doughnuts; well, so what? They didn't know about Scotch eggs or tiramisu either; that's not evidence of a supernatural conspiracy. The food-with-holes-in thing looked a bit mean, but every society has its taboos, like not eating with the left hand or not walking through the streets with no clothes on – weird to outsiders, as inherent as breathing to those who believe in them. The fire was just the sort of thing that happens when inflammable materials and a culinary kludge come together in a confined space. Break the sequence of events down into its component parts and examine each part, and you're left with a collection of the sort of Stuff that Happens. So there you go. Who's a clever boy, then, croaked his paranoia.

Fine. Now for a plan of action. Um.

He sent for the chamberlain. "I want you to organise a hunt," he said.

The chamberlain relaxed. This was more his idea of proper prince stuff. "Of course, Your Highness. So good to see you're yourself again."

If only, Benny thought. "A unicorn hunt."

The chamberlain's eyes narrowed slightly. "Do you think that's altogether wise?"

"Yup," Benny said crisply. "Let's say tomorrow morning, shall we?"

"The association in the public mind; you and unicorns—"

"Nice early start, I think. They say it's going to be sunny."

"Apropos of nothing at all," the chamberlain said, "the King of Lyonesse's daughter comes of age in three weeks, and they say she's a very nice girl, once you get to know her. You could do worse."

"Say about half ten? We'll need hounds and beaters and all that sort of thing."

"Or there's the Grand Duchess of Beal Regard," the chamberlain said. "Sweet nature, very artistic, by all accounts. She makes wind chimes out of old gate hinges."

"I shall want the unicorn taken alive, of course," Benny said firmly. "After all, they're quite rare, and it'd be nice to have a tame one in the palace garden."

"Or there's the new barmaid at the Red Lion."

"That's all for now," Benny said. "Thank you so much."

John the Lawyer – people had trouble with his name; they tended to elide the -aw sound into an I – enjoyed working with Elves. It suited him perfectly, particularly when it came to his relationship with his co-workers. For John, revenge wasn't just a dish best served cold; it was a delicacy to be savoured, with infinite care taken over its preparation, to produce the ultimate banquet. To start with, a delicate resentment soufflé, garnished with insults and disdain *rechaufée aux fines herbes*, followed by a bloody steak of deviousness with sides of highly spiced retribution on a bed of bruised feelings, followed by a chocolate and vanilla gloat, coffee and biscuits. So; every time an Elf looked down its nose at him, or pretended not to have heard what he said, or explained a simple concept very slowly and carefully for his benefit, John smiled, bided his time and added another course to his dream menu.

In the meantime, however, he had a living to earn, targets to meet and surpass; which could have been awkward, since the partners never gave him anything to do, arguing that although they themselves were wonderfully liberal and advanced and had no problems about humans whatsoever, they couldn't expect their clients to share such enlightened attitudes. No problem; John was perfectly content to fend for himself, preferred it that way, in fact, since it gave him so much more scope to be creative as far as the niceties of professional ethics were concerned. The invention of the contingency fee had been a stroke of genius, though he did say so himself. And now, with the case of *Yglaine vs the Universe*, he had the perfect springboard, the chance of a lifetime; a shot at the wizard himself.

If you're going to undermine the very foundations of society, you have to dig deep. So John started with newspaper clippings. He needed to know where the wizard had come from, how long he'd been here, how he'd started; basic, obvious facts that nobody, when they came to think about it, actually knew. Fortunately, the archives of *Sneer* and *Superior on Sunday* went back a thousand years, though the older material had been transcribed onto gossamer some time ago and was a real bitch to read.

His initial findings surprised him, though in a good way. A thousand years ago, the wizard was already well established and occupying roughly the same pivotal position in the society and economy of the Known World as he was today. Splendid: the deeper the roots, the bigger the hole you make when you drag the tree out with chains. He turned his attention to the media collection of the Elvenhome University library, department of Classical Journalism.

In order to house its vast archive, the department rented a network of disused mineshafts from King Mordak. It wasn't terribly nice down there: cold, damp and an uncomfortable whiff of goblin, with the possibility of a cave-in ever-present at the back of one's mind. As is so often the case, however, the best treasure is buried deepest. It was in a three thousand year-old edition of *Supercilious!*, classified-ads section, that John found what he'd been looking for:

WANTED: musicians to play the same piece of music over and over and over again. Apply with detailed CV to—

And then a name he couldn't begin to pronounce, and a box number. Fortunately he'd brought with him his copy of the official authorised history of the Sylvan Elves Youth Ensemble, so it only took him a moment to glance at the index and discover that the SEYE was founded three thousand years ago; a fortnight, in fact, after the newspaper ad first appeared.

He grinned, made a note of the file reference, brushed dust out of his hair and trimmed the wick of his lamp. He had a date, a starting point, and – he thought lovingly of the absence of a statute of limitations in Elvish law – three thousand years' worth of potential class actions. Furthermore, he could be fairly safe in assuming that this wonderful resource was his and his alone. The thought of Elven lawyers getting up off their bony arses, huddling down here in the cold and the dark, actually doing some work for a change, was laughable. The other side wouldn't know what hit them.

A 2750-year-old edition of *Snark* yielded up the next gold nugget. In an editorial white-hot with self-righteous fury, the environmental-affairs correspondent fulminated against the dwarves for their criminally reckless plans to expand their mining operations under the Forest, with all the concomitant threats of pollution, water contamination, subsidence, seismic instability and property values meltdown that went with them. In his final paragraph, the writer spared a teaspoonful of venom for the shadowy figure behind it all, the secretive and reclusive buyer known only as the wizard, whose insatiable appetite for shining yellow rocks had prompted this appalling violation of natural resources. When will the dwarves finally realise that their short-sighted pursuit of mere profit will one day quite literally cost them the earth, etc, etc.

An extra point of interest snagged his attention; loads of ripe stuff about the dwarves, but not a single mention of the goblins. Now he came to think about it, how long had the goblins been involved in the mining caper? Goblin history was very much the Cinderella of academic enquiry – the horrid things have a history? Who cares? – so there wasn't a handy reference book he could turn to. He made a note to find out more about it, and ploughed on. The roof of the tunnel shook and a small cloud of dust floated down, coating the backs of his hands. Not that there was anything to worry about. The goblin Mine Safety Commission had inspected these tunnels and certified them Moderately Safe.

A paragraph in a 2200-year-old *Beautiful Yellow Face* caught his eye. It was the lead story in the paper's Human News section (you had to know where to look – sandwiched in between the gardening column and the wine reviews). The headline was; *Human Prince Torn Apart By Mob,* and it told the story of how Prince Valentine (twenty-one) had been killed by his own subjects for gross breaches of human food taboos. Reliable sources stated that Valentine had previously burned down the palace kitchen in the course of his bizarre and twisted experiments into illegal food, and only his exalted rank had saved him from prosecution after he'd made explicit advances to local women, trying to make them his accomplices in acts of food perforation. Pursued through the town by a furious mob armed with pitchforks, Valentine had reportedly sought sanctuary from the wizard, who barred the doors against him. Unconfirmed reports added that Valentine's last words, as he cowered against the bronze gates of the wizard's sinister compound, were *It's all his fault, he—*

The final paragraph was just the usual Elven moralising and demands for immediate action on pitchfork control;

nothing new there. By the look of it, he decided, this Prince Valentine had deserved everything he'd got. Even so— Maybe it was just one of those royal things, he thought; maybe all that waving and smiling and opening village fêtes eventually gets to you, and you find yourself compelled by some dark urge to do things to pastry. He didn't know much about young Florizel, but if what he'd heard was true, he was headed in the same direction; in which case, there was bound to be a lawsuit in it somewhere. Watch this space.

But that was all just side salad and croutons in the great scheme of things. The important bit was how the doomed Prince Valentine had gone running to the wizard, and those absolutely fascinating interrupted last words. It's all his fault. He—

He what?

Infuriatingly, the *Face* was the only paper back then that bothered with human stories, unless they had an Elven interest angle, so there weren't any other accounts to compare this one with. But humans kept records, too, particularly where royalty was concerned. The problem was getting at them. Somewhere in the palace archives there'd be an autopsy report, the conclusions of an internal security review, something of the sort; witness statements, possibly with a slightly fuller version of those tantalising last words. It's all his fault, he— *what?* He made me do it? He left me no choice? He said he'd cover it up for me? Of course, there was the danger that the full, true account might turn out to be relatively innocent; he never told me, or, he warned me but I didn't listen. Sometimes a tantalising fragment is so much more effective than the full text, because even juries have imaginations, and everyone loves to think the worst. Looked at from that perspective, *it's all his fault, he—* was about as good as it gets. After all, he reflected, when I saw it I conclusion-jumped faster and further than a New Year Games athlete, and I'm used to this stuff, and I'm human. An Elf juror, simply crying out to have his preconceptions about humans graphically confirmed, is going to leave me eating slipstream.

He grinned; but the smile froze on his face. The roof wasn't just shaking, it was visibly moving, up and down like somebody's chest when they breathe. Thick clouds of dust and grit filled the air, and when he jumped to his feet, the ground sort of wriggled under him, nearly pitching him flat on his face. There was no time to think; he ran, and kept running until the stitch in his side was bad enough to override the blind terror and make him stop and drop to his knees. Fortunately, he'd come far enough; he was out of the side shaft and back in the main gallery, which appeared to be behaving itself. By the time he was able to breathe again, the tremors had stopped. He sat with his back to a wall for a long time, content to concentrate on being alive. Odd how you take that for granted, when it's such a remarkable thing.

It was a long time before he could bring himself to stand up and walk the dozen yards or so to the end of the gallery, and look back at the tunnel he'd come running out of. About fifteen yards down, he could see a great pile of rocks, completely blocking the passageway. He closed his eyes, trying at all costs to avoid the enormous fact that he could so easily be under all that weight, if he'd been just a tad slower, or if he'd tripped over and fallen. One little slip and he'd have been the flattest man in the world; John, the human crêpe. Oh boy.

Then he thought: Moderately Safe? I'm going to sue those bastards for every penny they've got.

And then he thought; the records. All that data. All that *evidence*. And it was there, I *saw* it, and now it's gone and I can't prove anything. That is just so—

Fortuitous?

He looked up. All he could see was roof, but he knew that above and beyond it was earth, blue sky, a world he'd always believed was comfortingly random, chaotic and meaningless. Stuff just happens, he'd always taken that absolutely on trust, and manifest destinies and grand designs are just things people make up in order to manipulate the gullible. There's no rhyme or reason, there's no need for anything like that. Goblin-built tunnels collapse; of course they do, the real wonder is that they stay up at all. And giants wander down from the mountains from time to time, and idiotic princes get caught with their fingers in the batter, and that's just the crumblings of the primordial cookie, it doesn't *mean* anything. Which is fine; because if for one moment you thought it was somehow planned, prearranged, that someone somewhere was doing all this shit to you *on purpose*, you'd get so mad you couldn't stand it a moment longer—

A deep rumble suggested that this wasn't really the time or the place for an internal debate on the nature of the universe. He retreated to the stairwell, then paused to take one last long look. We'll call it an accident for now, he silently announced. But if I find out that it was deliberate, I'm warning you—

A pebble the size of a grape dropped from the roof and bounced off his head. With a squeal like a startled pig, he scampered up the stairs and didn't stop until he was outside in the light.

The receptionist at the Slam Corporation offices gave Uncle Gordon a production-line smile, issued him with a plastic pass with his name and a photograph that looked worryingly like Lee Harvey Oswald in a sandstorm and asked him to walk through the arch. Needless to say, it bleeped like crazy. They always did. He sighed, froze and waited for Security.

"They don't like me," he explained. "Scanners. They always give me a hard time."

Security was prodding him with a sort of squawky wand. This took some time. Eventually, Security assured him that he was clean, and apologised for any inconvenience. "That's quite all right," Gordon replied, smiling sadly. "I'm used to it."

A flying glass box, designed to scare you to death by making you believe you're standing on thin air, lifted him a hundred feet off the ground and stopped. A man was waiting for him. "Hi," the man said, and leaned forward to read the badge. "You're Gordon Penn."

Which was true. "Hi," Gordon replied. "And you're Leo Greenlander."

The man smiled brightly. "Follow me."

Mr Greenlander was obviously a man of great importance, because he had an office with non-transparent walls. There was a framed photo of a generic wife, child and dog; the human touch. The offer of coffee was probably quite sincere, though Gordon declined it. "Right, then," Mr Greenlander said. "What's the deal?"

Gordon settled himself happily in his chair. It was time for The Speech.

The Speech tended to go on a bit, because once he'd settled in to it and forgotten he was trying to persuade a perfect stranger to part with serious money, Gordon rather enjoyed giving it. He liked the way the other guy's expression went from doubt to bewilderment to sudden understanding and belief, followed by wild longing and deep, deep greed. The Speech was, in fact, the thing he liked most about the thing he did for a living, so he could be forgiven for making the most of it.

Boiled down a bit, The Speech was—

What's the biggest overhead [Uncle Gordon was wont to say], the most frequent source of aggravation, the least reliable and most expensive aspect of doing business in the modern world? Got it in one, it's people. Trouble is, unless you're prepared to do everything yourself (which, in the case of a trillion-dollar multinational, probably isn't possible) you need people, to do all the things that need doing. Bummer. Now, the problem can't be solved, but it can be made a whole lot less costly and stressful if you have the *right* people. Defined as—

Reliable. Motivated. Responsible. Efficient. Undemanding. Dedicated. Passionate about what they do. And, most important of all, very, very cheap.

Unfortunately, thanks to vote-grubbing populist politicians and wishy-washy liberal views of the dignity of labour, people like that are nearly impossible to find in the affluent industrialised nations. There's only so far you can go with mechanisation, so unless you're prepared to cave in to the incessant demands of your workforce, if you want your business to survive and flourish you really have no choice these days but to outsource. Trouble with that is, even remote, primitive tribes in faraway places get spoilt rotten after a while. They start demanding more money, shorter working hours, time off to be sick, give birth or die; so, before you know it, it's time to uproot the whole operation and go off in search of even remoter, more primitive tribes who haven't yet caught the Western disease of thinking they're almost as good as you. And, sooner or later, the Earth being small and largely covered in water, sooner or later the supply is going to run out entirely, and then where will we go to get our widgets made and our phones answered?

Fortunately [here Gordon pauses, smiles, relaxes visibly; he knows he has the attention of his audience], there's an alternative. There is a place where amenable, cheap people can still be found. It's inconceivably far away, but you can get there in a couple of seconds. They speak English; better still, they *understand* English – also French, Spanish, Chinese, classical Sanskrit, any language you care to mention, they're perfectly at home in it. They work cheerfully and diligently for extremely long hours and next to no money. And, best of all, they'll go on doing so indefinitely, for the foreseeable future, because they're spoilproof. Yes, really. No danger at all that five or ten years down the line they're going to come at you whining for health plans and maternity leave and flexible working arrangements and lots and lots and *lots* more money. And, even better than best of all, the supply of them is practically unlimited.

At this point in The Speech, Gordon likes to pause, maybe stretch his legs out, stifle a yawn, drink coffee or tea if available, anything to break the flow and tweak up the suspense. He knows he's at the point at which the audience was starting to be torn between the comfort of *there's bound to be a catch* and the tantalising hope of *but maybe there* isn't *a catch*. It's a good point to hold them at, just for ten seconds or so, before proceeding to mess with their heads and prise open their wallets.

The difficulty is— Actually, there is no difficulty.

You'd be forgiven for thinking there might be a difficulty, because these people, these hard-working, wealth-indifferent people, don't exist in precisely the same way you and I do. Oh, they're real all right. I can pick up that phone there right now and dial a number, and you can talk to one, and he'll tell you how to get a great deal on your car insurance or fix your computer. It's not that they don't exist. It's just that they exist *differently*.

Mister [your-client's-name-here], you were young once. You were a kid. You read story books and watched Disney films, maybe you had an imaginary friend. Back then, before you grew up and got wise and had to start paying for things, you had no trouble at all believing in the story-book people living in fairy-tale-land, where there's dragons and talking animals and magic that really works. Well; you're older now and wiser and you've got kids of your own to tell fairy stories to, but you're essentially the same person. Well, aren't you? Your DNA is unchanged, your fingerprints, your blood group. All that's happened to you is that a bunch of the cells you were born with have been replaced by other cells that do exactly the same thing, and maybe not all the trousers in your wardrobe fit quite as well as they used to. No big deal. You haven't changed that much. You can still believe, if you want to. And if I can make it worth your while, I promise you, you'll believe.

Let me cut to the chase, Mr [your-client's-name-here]. The company I have the honour to represent can arrange for you to outsource your manufacturing, shipping, customer support, admin, the whole goddamn shooting match – apart from your job, of course, which is completely safe because you're absolutely irreplaceable – to the other side of the crystal portal; to a land where magic is real, where the seventh sons of seventh sons find genies in bottles, where wild animals talk (and can answer telephones, for a trivial sum), where the rules are just different enough to allow a man with your qualities of perception, mental clarity and vision to make an absolute fortune and get away with it. I'm not asking you to believe right now or take my word for it. All I'm asking you to do is come with me and see for yourself.

Well?

The speech had gone down well. Mr Greenlander was looking at Gordon as though he had just bludgeoned him over the head with a million dollars. Gordon knew that look; not there yet, but well on the way. Here was a man who might very well come to believe.

"Well?" he repeated.

Mr Greenlander was breathing heavily through his nose. "What exactly do you mean," he said, "come and see for myself?"

"Just that." Gordon snapped open the catches of his brief-case. "Won't take very long, and we won't have to leave this office."

"But you said—"

"Ah." From the briefcase, Gordon removed a square gold box with elaborate catches. He snapped them open, care-fully lifted the lid and took out a doughnut. "Ready?"

Mr Greenlander was looking at him with raw fear in his eyes. "What've I got to do?"

"Just keep perfectly still, and when I say breathe in, breathe in and hold it. No air in the interface, OK? Right then, here goes nothing."

The clock on Mr Greenlander's office wall read 2:47 and thirteen seconds. He checked to make sure Mr Greenlander was motionless and holding his breath, then he reached out and held the doughnut perfectly equidistant between them. Through the hole, their eyes met. And then—

"What the hell?" Mr Greenlander said

He was sitting on a tree stump – at least, he was in the same sitting position he'd been in a moment ago, but his trousers weren't actually in contact with the wood. He was, in fact, floating just above it. His left trouser leg was embar-rassingly wet, and a huge three-headed dog was standing over him, sniffing his crotch.

Gordon stood up and the dog bolted. "Don't mind him," Gordon said. "He's quite harmless. Actually, I've got seven hundred and forty more like him answering phones for a leading airline. Come on," he added with a smile, reaching out a hand and hauling Mr Greenlander to his feet. "Time's a-wasting."

Gordon didn't look quite the same. Instead of his charcoal-grey lounge suit, so nondescript you had to make a conscious effort to notice it, he was wearing a long powder-blue robe with the signs of the zodiac embroidered on it in gold thread, and a blue hat like an upturned ice-cream cone. "Right," he said, looking around and nodding. "We've landed on the edge of the Idyllic Pastures, so Peaceful Village ought to be about three minutes' walk that way. I thought we might check out the monastery, and then the stirrer plant."

The grass was green, short and weed-free, like a lawn. Birds sang, impossibly loud and clear; and they weren't just making tweet-whistle sounds, they were *singing*. The sun was a white ball in a cloudless blue sky, and at regular intervals (every five yards or so) there was either a rose bush in full bloom or a cute, floppy-eared rabbit. In spite of himself, Mr Greenlander felt the anxiety and bewilderment fade from his mind like breath on glass. He inhaled the sweet, pure air and caught himself thinking, *I know this place, I've been here before.* Which was nonsense, since he'd been born in Pittsburgh and hadn't seen an acre of grass that didn't have baseball players on it until he was fifteen years old. In spite of that, a voice inside him was telling him that he was finally back home, in the place he belonged, which he ought never to have left—

"Our preliminary survey suggests that directly under where we are now there's a vast deposit of premium-grade bauxite," Gordon said. "Just perfect for open-cast strip mining. Soon as I find a buyer, someone's going to get seriously rich."

Mr Greenlander shuddered, but didn't say anything. A squirrel with a fat, fluffy tail scampered in front of him, stopped, turned back, smiled at him and flolloped away. "What did you say we're going to see?" he asked.

"The monastery," Gordon replied. "See that glade over there? That's where we're headed."

They walked in silence for a while – it was hard to gauge exactly how long; time seemed different here, measured in moments rather than seconds, minutes and hours, and the length of a moment (Mr Greenlander suspected) would depend on how long you *wanted* it to last. A perfect moment could be practically forever. Mr Greenlander thought about that. This moment (the sunshine, the sweet air, the green grass, the wildlife, the absence of people yelling at him down telephones) maybe wasn't quite perfect, but it was very nearly close enough for jazz. It occurred to him that if it was any more perfect, perhaps it really would last forever, in which case he'd be stuck here, unable to get home, for all eternity. The thought made him whimper, at which Gordon turned and smiled at him. "Yes," he said.

"What?"

"Sorry, I was reading your mind. Bad habit of mine. Over here, you see," he explained, "I'm a wizard, I can do that kind of stuff. Don't ask," he added, as Mr Greenlander opened his mouth, "it's complicated, and you don't need to know. But you're quite right about the time thing. It's vitally important while you're over here not to let the moment get too perfect. There's always got to be something spoiling it. So you'll be just fine," he added cheerfully, "so long as you're with me."

Mr Greenlander decided he didn't want any of that stuff in his mind, so he shooed it out and said, "The monastery?"

"You'll see," Gordon said brightly. "Ah, we're here. Now, before we go any further, you'll need to put this on." He opened his briefcase and produced something that looked like a silver net curtain. "Invisibility cloak," he explained.

"You what?"

"Makes you invisible," Gordon translated helpfully. "The

thing of it is, the locals are used to me, but seeing you might freak them out a bit. There you are, it goes on over your head like *this*, and—"

Mr Greenlander had leaned his head forward so the cloak could go over it; he'd been looking at his feet. But they weren't there any more.

"Yes they are," Uncle Gordon said cheerfully. "And they still work and everything. You just can't see them, is all."

"You bastard," Mr Greenlander wailed. "What have you done—?"

"Shh," Gordon said. "Quiet as a little mouse from now on, OK?"

A glade of weeping willows, which quite definitely hadn't been there a moment ago, reared up at them out of the short grass. Mr Greenlander could just make out the faint echo of plainsong. "One of my best ideas," Gordon was saying, "though I do say so myself. There, look."

So well hidden among the trees that Mr Greenlander had to look twice to see it was a high stone wall, surrounding a large rectangular building with a domed green copper roof. The music, a low hum like bees, was definitely coming from there. "Come on," Gordon said, "there's nothing to be scared of. If we're lucky, we'll be just in time for Evensong."

Before long they'd joined a well-trodden path that snaked between the trees to a low, small door in the wall. Above it hung a tarnished brass bell, with a bit of string dangling down. Gordon yanked the string a couple of times, and after a while a panel in the door shot back, and a beady blue eye peered at him for a moment. Then the door opened.

"Bless you, my son," said Gordon. "Just a social call."

The monk (shaven head, brown habit, rope belt, sandals,

no socks) who'd opened the door stepped aside to let him pass. He was mumbling under his breath, with the fierce concentration of the reluctant multi-tasker. Mr Greenlander couldn't quite make out what he was saying; it sounded curiously like *one zero zero zero one zero*, or words to that effect.

They followed the monk along an ancient cloister, the pale yellow stone of the pavement worn smooth by the passage of countless sandalled feet. The walls were plain and bare, but the roof timbers were beautifully carved with a repeating dot-dash motif that was both strikingly simple and enticingly sophisticated. At the end of the cloister, a great grey oak door, unimaginably old, stood in a high wall. The monk, still mumbling, opened it for them, and they went through.

"Oh—" Mr Greenlander started to say, but Gordon trod on his foot and he cut the expression of wonder off short and contented himself with gazing, upwards, side to side. Mr Greenlander loved to travel, and at one time or another he'd visited all the great cathedrals of the world, but he'd never seen anything like this. It made St Mark's in Venice look like a gas station.

It was also packed. From where they were standing, they could see thousands, possibly tens of thousands, of brown-habited monks kneeling in prayer. The soft purr of their chanting rolled and echoed off the gloriously frescoed walls and around the vaulted hammer-beam roof, creating swirls and eddies of sound that made Mr Greenlander's head swim. It was only when he followed Gordon down the main central aisle towards the high altar (a disappointing plain black rectangular box, though mounted on a stunning cruciform pedestal carved from a single block of rose alabaster) that he realised there was something very strange about the chanting. The monks weren't all reciting the same words. In fact – he had to concentrate and strain his hearing to differentiate – he could have sworn that each monk was saying something different. Some of them seemed to be reciting scientific or historical tracts, some of them were mumbling about special two-for-one internet-only deals, most of them were just repeating sequences of ones and zeros. From a distance, the sound had blended into a tranquil blur. Close up, it was the stuff of nightmares.

Gordon stopped and made a perfunctory nod towards the black box, then turned and went back the way he'd come. When they were back in the cloister and the great door had shut behind them, Mr Greenlander could bear it no longer. "What *was* that?" he hissed.

"Ssh," Gordon replied. "Tell you in a minute."

Three monks were walking towards them, heads lowered, hands in sleeves, chanting softly. Then, quite suddenly, one of them dropped to the ground. The other two walked on, as though nothing had happened, while the fallen monk writhed and twisted on the ground for perhaps three seconds, and then lay perfectly still—

"*No,*" Gordon hissed under his breath, before Mr Greenlander could move. "Leave it."

"But—"

"*Shh.*"

They had to step over the fallen monk. He was lying on his back, his eyes and mouth wide open, absolutely motionless. Mr Greenlander tried to stop, but Gordon held his arm in a grip like a mole-wrench and hustled him towards the small door they'd come in through.

Once they were outside, back in the forest glade, Mr Greenlander tugged the invisibility cloak off over his head and threw it on the ground. "That monk—"

"It's fine," Gordon snapped at him, "don't worry about it. Now put the cloak back on right now, or I won't be responsible for the consequences."

He said it so grimly that Mr Greenlander reluctantly

obeyed. "Look," he whimpered as his head disappeared, "what *is* that place? It's—"

"It's a computer server," Gordon said. "Come on, this way. I know a short cut to the stirrer plant."

He set off walking so briskly that Mr Greenlander had to trot to keep up. "A what?"

Gordon smiled. "Think about it," he said. "What's the biggest headache of the IT revolution? Servers, right? You need a huge great building full of really expensive, temperamental machinery, which pumps out kilowatts and kilowatts of heat, so you've got to spend a fortune on sophisticated ventilation systems; the capacity is never enough and the electricity bill's a killer. Result; overheads so far over your head they're halfway to Alpha Centauri."

Mr Greenlander couldn't help wincing; sore subject. "Yes, but—"

"So instead," Gordon went on, "why not adopt an organic approach? Instead of all that technology, simply download all those bits and megabytes of information into the brains of a bunch of monks?" He smiled proudly. "You don't need me to remind you about the staggering storage and retrieval capabilities of the human brain. I've got twelve thousand monks in there, that's all, and between them they can handle the entire output of five major home shopping networks, a leading search engine and a Latin American government. And," he added, his voice close to breaking from emotion, "it doesn't cost me a nickel."

"It – what did you just say?"

Gordon shrugged. "They do it for free," he said. "They think the voices in their heads are the word of God, they don't want *paying*. And the pious locals give them food and stuff, so that's all covered. Which means I can undercut the competition out of existence and still get a quite satisfactory return. It's perfect. I've got ninety-six more like this one scattered about, and I'm planning on building another two hundred by this time next year."

Mr Greenlander could no longer feel his fingers and toes. "That's—"

"Yes," Gordon said simply. "Isn't it?"

"But that monk, the one we saw—"

"Oh, he just crashed, it happens all the time." Gordon dismissed him with a vague gesture. "They overload, they freeze solid for a while, and then they're right as rain. Usually it's just a touch of software incompatibility, it doesn't hurt them. Humans are amazingly resilient, you know. But when that happens to a *machine*, you've got outages that last for hours, and all the traffic lights go crazy in seventeen states."

"Yes, but—" Mr Greenlander's mouth opened and closed, but no words came out. Sure, it didn't *seem* right. But he'd seen it for himself, the monks had seemed genuinely serene and happy, and the cathedral was a place of beauty and joy. And all *absolutely free*—

"That's the key thing you have to understand about out-sourcing," Gordon went on. "It may look like ruthless exploitation from our decadent liberal *sklavenmoral* perspective, but to these people it's great. It gives meaning to their lives, not to mention a higher standard of living than most of them have even dreamed of. And from the point of view of the hard-pressed businessman in today's no-nonsense marketplace environment—"

"Really and truly," Mr Greenlander croaked hoarsely. "You don't pay them *anything*?"

"Not a cent. Well, no, I tell a lie." Gordon frowned. "Twice a year I give them a dollar fifty, for their benevolent fund. They use the money for good causes in the local community. But that's purely *ex gratia*, a goodwill gesture. Great for PR. I guess I'm just an old-fashioned philanthropist at heart."

"A buck fifty."

"Goes a *very* long way in these parts," Gordon said. "Without getting too technical or giving away how this whole thing works, let's say exchange rates are definitely in my favour. It's all to do with gold in this reality having a negative atomic number. Right then, this way to the stirrer plant."

They walked on through dappled woods, silent apart from the faint distant piping of songbirds, occasionally passing broad clearings, where heaped bonfires of cut brash sent straight lines of smoke up into the breezeless sky, and from time to time a few derelict cottages, their thatch smothered in creeping honeysuckle. After they'd been walking for an hour, Mr Greenlander said, "So how big is this place?"

"I told you," Gordon replied. "As big as it needs to be. Ah, we're here. I promise you, you're going to love this."

A dense stand of ancient oaks had somehow appeared; it must have crept up on them while they were preoccupied. The trees were forty-foot fingers groping blindly for the sun, which glittered in ribbons between the softly swaying branches. Directly ahead of them, a roe deer froze, stared and bolted, her hooves barely stirring the leaf mould. In the middle distance there was a sun-dappled clearing, in which stood a long, low building, its thatched roof carpeted with red and gold autumn leaves.

"In there," Gordon said.

The door was open and they walked in. It took Mr Greenlander a moment to get used to the light; then he saw a long workbench, and four white-haired old men in clean, worn overalls. One of them was slowly sawing lengthways through a forty-foot log with a handsaw, working by eye, but cutting a perfect straight line; he looked up and nodded respectfully at Gordon, then went back to work. Next to him, another man was planing a long plank until it was perfectly flat and smooth. The third man was painstakingly rounding off the corners of an already planed plank with a drawknife and a rasp. The fourth held a paintbrush; he was decorating a finished plank with the distinctive logo of a leading fast-food franchise. Leaning against the shed wall were about a thousand finished planks. The floor was ankle-deep in shavings and the air was heavy with the rich scents of newly cut wood and linseed oil.

"Coffee stirrers," Gordon said quietly.

Mr Greenlander blinked. "What?"

"Coffee stirrers," Gordon repeated. "You know, the little wooden stick things? You twiddle them round in your latte, then dump them in the trash."

Did not compute. "They're forty feet long," Mr Greenlander pointed out.

"Perspective differential," Gordon replied. "In our terms, these guys are an inch tall. Over here, though, size really doesn't matter. I guess," he added with a grin, "it's one of the reasons I like it so much."

The old man with the plane paused, crouched down beside the plank he'd been working on and examined it carefully, using the light from the shed's one narrow window to identify any rough or uneven spots he'd missed. After about thirty seconds, he reached out his hand, marked a place with a stub of pencil, stood up and took a gentle, light cut. A paper-thin shaving curled upwards from his plane and floated to the floor. Then he stooped again, to satisfy himself that the surface was now perfect.

"Good work," Gordon said cheerfully. "Carry on."

The four men turned and smiled at him, and he and Mr Greenlander quietly withdrew.

"*Coffee stirrers?*"

"That's right," Gordon said. "Of course, they can churn them out on a machine in Jiangxi province in China, but the cheapest they can do it for is eighty-seven cents a thousand. These guys, sixty-two cents a thousand, and that's using sustainable hardwoods."

Mr Greenlander swallowed. "But they're doing it all by hand," he said. "However long does it take?"

Gordon shrugged. "On a good day, they can turn out three, maybe four. Lucky for us, though, time is relative here. Also, there's a lot of these people."

"How many?"

"As many as it takes," Gordon replied airily. "That's how it works."

As many as it takes. Well. "And you pay them—" Mr Greenlander's brain nearly boiled with the strain of doing the maths. "Nought-point-zero-zero-zero-zero-one cent an hour?"

Gordon smiled. "Actually, we don't pay them anything," he replied. "All we have to cover is the shipping cost from the interface to the container depot. And we're looking very closely at shaving that."

Mr Greenlander made gurgling noises for a moment, until he finally managed to say, "So why are they—?"

"Doing it?" Gordon grinned. "Sorry, but that's what you might call restricted information. The point is, we're supplying a worldwide fast-food outlet with coffee stirrers for significantly less than the competition. Isn't that all that matters?"

For some reason, Mr Greenlander couldn't bring himself to answer that. "Can we go now, please?" he said. "This place gives me the—"

"Me, too," Gordon said. "But you get used to it." He glanced at his watch. Mr Greenlander couldn't see any hands. "One more, and then we're done. Now this one's going to blow you away."

Mr Greenlander shot him a pleading look. "Couldn't we just—?"

"No."

They walked in dead silence for quite a while, leaving the forest and climbing the lower slopes of a great white-capped mountain. About a third of the way up, Gordon pointed out the mouth of a cave. "You don't have a problem with confined spaces, do you, anything like that?"

"Well, as it happens—"

"Splendid, splendid. Follow me."

The cave led into a long, dark tunnel. Gordon muttered something under his breath, and a ball of bright blue light appeared, hanging in midair. "A flashlight would do just as well," Gordon said, "but they don't work around here. Do try and keep up."

Mr Greenlander didn't need to be told. The further down they went, the more obvious it became that the tunnel wasn't a natural occurrence. The rock walls bore the marks of steel tools, and the floor was quite smooth. "The call centre business," Gordon said (his voice echoed eerily in the soft-edged darkness), "is worth billions of dollars a year, and what do you actually need? A phone line, and people at the other end. That's all, really. Of course, to create a really great call centre, you need a special kind of staff. Fortunately—"

They turned a corner, and found themselves in a vast natural cavern. The roof was too high up to see, but Mr Greenlander was distressingly aware of great rippling sheets and curtains of needle-pointed stalactites and stalagmites, reciprocating like teeth in the jaws of a huge carnivore. He touched something with his foot; lighter than a rock, it dislodged easily and rolled away. He caught sight of it as it crossed the border between the circle of blue light and the sea of shadows. It looked horribly like a human skull. He grabbed Gordon's arm. "Look—" he said.

The sound of his voice had disturbed something; something very large indeed, which had been sleeping in the silent darkness. Slowly it lifted itself off its side onto its haunches, and sat up.

Maybe the size of a young Indian elephant; it had the body and tail of a lion, the wings of an eagle and the head of a beautiful woman. It blinked two hubcap-sized eyes, and yawned.

"Keep perfectly still," Gordon hissed. "We shouldn't have to wait very long."

"That's a sphinx," Mr Greenlander whispered, in a tiny, bewildered voice. "There was a picture of one in my myths and legends book, when I was a—"

"Shh."

The sphinx turned its head just a little, and Mr Greenlander realised with utter horror that it was looking straight at him. The pupils of its eyes were daffodil-yellow. He shivered. Then he remembered he was wearing the invisibility cloak, so presumably it couldn't actually see him.

"Don't count on it," Gordon whispered. "She knows exactly where you are, for sure."

That didn't make Mr Greenlander feel any better at all. "Can we go now, please?" he said. "I mean, I'm deeply, genuinely impressed, but I really, really need a—"

"*Shh.*"

Then Mr Greenlander heard what was unmistakably a dialling tone, amplified to just below the point where it would have been painful to listen to. It rang three times, and then there was a click. The sphinx's head shifted back, almost mechanically, to where it had been before, staring straight ahead. It closed its eyes and said, in a high, flat voice; "Hello, you're through to FirstServe Internet Banking, how may I help you?"

Um. Mr Greenlander felt rather than heard the voice; it wasn't coming from anywhere, or, more precisely, it came from everywhere at once. *Yes, hello, I'd like to move some money from my, um, deposit account to my current account, please. Hello?*

The sphinx opened its eyes. "Certainly, madam," it said. "First, please state your account number, sort code and four digit PIN."

The sphinx's eyes closed again while the voice mumbled a bunch of numbers. Then the eyes snapped open again, and the sphinx said, "And how long have you lived at your current address?"

What? Oh, um, I'm not, let's think, four years, no, sorry, make that five, because it was February when Tony had his operation. Five years.

"Thank you," said the sphinx. "Now, what is the name of your favourite pet?"

I haven't got a pet.

"I need you to tell me the name of your favourite pet."

I don't, oh hang on, I remember. Arthur. My niece's cat.

"Thank you," said the sphinx. "Now, I need you to tell me the third letter of the first name of your first teacher at primary school."

What? Blimey. Oh, hold on, I've got a pencil somewhere. I. It's I.

"Thank you." The tip of the sphinx's tail twitched just a little. "Now I need you to tell me what's the fastest fish on three wheels?"

Long, long pause. *What did you say?*

"I need you," the sphinx repeated, "to tell me what's the fastest fish on three wheels? Otherwise I cannot access your account."

I – I'm sorry, I don't know that one. My mum's maiden name was Moore, if that's any good.

"I'm sorry," said the sphinx, "but that is not the correct answer. You are only allowed two attempts. If you give another incorrect answer you will be locked out of your account, funds held in your account will be forfeited, and I will hunt you down to the ends of the earth and kill you. Now, can you please tell me what's the fastest fish on three wheels?"

Um.

"I'm sorry, could you repeat that, please?"

I, oh God, this is like a riddle or something, right?

"I'm sorry, I'm not authorised to disclose additional information or provide hints. Now, if you value your life, can you please tell the name of the fastest fish on three wheels? You have five seconds. Four. Three."

I, oh hell, I don't, no, hang on. It's a motorpike.

"A motorpike with a—"

Sidecarp?

"Correct," said the sphinx; its face didn't move, but its tail twitched again. "Now, I need you to tell me the colour of the scarf worn by the woman who trod on your foot at the bottom of the escalator at Oxford Circus Underground station on the afternoon of 6 July 1997."

You what?

"The colour of the scarf worn by the woman who trod on your foot—"

I don't know. I don't remember. I don't think I've ever been to Oxford Street Tube station.

"Sorry, that's not the right answer," the sphinx said in a sing-song voice. "I'm afraid I shall have to put a block on your account and confiscate the funds held therein. Also, kindly prepare to die. If you haven't yet made a will, perhaps you'd like to hear details of our expert and confidential will-

writing and estate planning service, operated by fully quali-
fied staff and regulated by the Financial Services Authority."

Green. It was green.

"Correct." The sphinx's tail swished, backwards and for-
wards, three times. "You may now access your account. How
may I help you?"

*What? Oh God, I don't know. Um, I'd like to move fifty-seven
pounds forty from deposit to current.*

"Doing that for you now. Done. Transaction complete.
Thank you for calling FirstServe Internet Banking. Have a
nice day."

There was a loud click. The sphinx closed its eyes for
about five seconds, then opened them again. Its tail suddenly thrashed, and a low growl made the floor of the cavern
shake.

"Oops," Gordon said, grabbing Mr Greenlander by the
arm, "time to go. I'd run if I were you."

They ran. They didn't stop running until they reached
the mouth of the cave and stumbled out into the light. They
dropped to their knees and knelt gasping for breath for quite
some time. Then Gordon said, "Actually, she's quite nice
once you get to know her. Well, no, I tell a lie. But she's
damned good at her job."

"I gathered that."

"Anyway." Gordon stood up, made a big deal out of
brushing dust off his knees. "That's just a few examples of
the sort of thing we can do for your company. Unless there's
anything else in particular you'd like to see, I suggest we go
back to your office. OK?"

Mr Greenlander nodded dumbly, and Gordon reached
inside a fold of his robe, took out the golden box and
looked around carefully – up, down, three-sixty-degrees all
around – before opening it and taking out the doughnut.
"Ready?"

"Oh God, yes."

This time, it was like being inside a flashbulb when the picture gets taken. Mr Greenlander opened his mouth to scream, and found he was sitting in his chair in his office, looking straight at the clock on the wall, which read 2:37:14. Gordon was putting the gold box carefully away in his brief-case.

Mr Greenlander realised his face was wet; sweat, rapidly cooling. Gordon handed him a Kleenex, and he dabbed his forehead with it. "What the hell," he asked, "just happened?"

Gordon steepled his fingers and looked at him steadily. "What do you think just happened?"

"I—" Mr Greenlander hesitated. Yes, he knew what he'd just seen. He'd been there, and there was absolutely no doubt in his mind. The trouble was, everything he'd seen and heard, in an experience which, according to his office clock, had taken no time at all, was impossible. Gordon was watching him keenly, like a cat guarding a mousehole. "Yes?"

"We visited some places," Mr Greenlander said. "A computer server. A place where they make little wooden sticks. A—"

"Call centre?"

"Thank you, yes, a call centre. It was all—" He paused. Gordon's eyes were fixed on him, like the tiny red dot on your forehead that tells you the sniper's looking straight at you. "It was all very interesting."

"Indeed." Gordon closed his briefcase with a snap. "Well, you were curious to find out how we can undercut our competitors on the goods and services your company needs. Now you know. Unless you've got any questions?"

Questions, yes; many, many questions, the answers to which he really didn't want to hear, not if it meant having to live with them for the rest of his life. "No, no, that's fine. It all seems, you know, perfectly fine."

"And ethical? You don't have any issues on that score?"

"Absolutely not. And your prices are—"

"Yes?"

"Competitive. Extremely competitive."

"I'm sure your shareholders will think so," Gordon said smoothly. He leaned back in his chair, which creaked ever so slightly. "So," he said, "what can we do for you?"

Buttercup had never felt this way before.

The trouble was, she couldn't be sure whether the strange floating sensation, the breathlessness, the burning, was love or indigestion. She'd never been troubled with either, and from what she'd been able to gather, from elderly female relatives and eavesdropping, the symptoms were so similar that it was a job to tell them apart. Usually, she'd come to the conclusion, you could figure out which was which from context; but she'd just spent an hour having a heavy meal with an undeniably attractive man. So—

Split the difference, she decided. A bit of both.

Turquine was gazing longingly at her, or at least in her direction. "You want the rest of that bread roll?" he asked.

"Yes."

"Oh. Fine." The slightly strained expression on his noble face (particularly good in profile) suggested that he might possibly have a touch of indigestion, too. Or the other thing. "Pudding," he said.

"Yes?"

"Do you fancy some pudding," he said. "Only I saw some-one over there getting apple pie, and if there's one thing—"

"It's tuppence."

"Oh."

A wave of indigestion swept through her, and she smiled. "Go on," she said, "I'll treat you."

"What?" He frowned, then smiled back. "I keep forgetting, you've got all that money. All right, then, thanks. That'd be nice."

She chewed a mouthful of bread roll thoughtfully. If he was in love or indigestion with her – if his heart burned for her, would it matter if it was because she had a pocket jingling with florins and shillings? Probably, she decided, not. What, after all, is love? A largely irrational attraction, generally focused on some superficial attribute of the beloved, the value of which the lover tends to exaggerate out of all proportion. As far as men were concerned, in her limited and circumscribed experience, the attribute tended to be a body part – cornflower-blue eyes, or mammary glands of a certain size, profile and ogive. She'd always reckoned that was a pretty silly way of going about things, though she was prepared to concede that women's approach was scarcely more rational. Well; if you can love someone for their eyes or their boobs, why not for their money? And why shouldn't that love (or indigestion) be every bit as pure, ardent and holy? Beauty, after all, inevitably fades, but money only dissipates if you're foolish enough to spend it.

Indeed. But fourpence for two slices of apple pie could be regarded in the circumstances as a perfectly sound investment. She waved to the innkeeper, and placed the order.

"Would you like clotted cream with that?"

"Is it extra?"

"No, same price."

"Yes, please."

Besides, she reflected, around here everyone's nice-looking; for some reason, we just don't seem to get ugly people (why *was* that?) so the traditional criteria for choosing a life partner were frustratingly difficult to apply. A really sensible, down-to-earth attitude to personal finances, on the other hand, was distinctly rare. She'd known Bill the wood-cutter spend his last farthing on a bit of ribbon to tie up his true love's hair, and where the hell was the sense in that? And all those idiots who bought wood from the woodcutters in the marketplace, when you could go fifty yards further down the road with a wheelbarrow and simply help yourself— No, she knew, she could never love any of the men around here. But Turquine (she caught a glimpse of a neatly darned hole on the elbow of his otherwise perfectly good shirt, and her heart melted) was different.

"It's funny," he was saying. "I move around a lot in my line of work, but I don't think I've been in these parts before."

She shrugged. "One sleepy little market town's the same as any other, surely."

"You'd have thought so. Actually, most of them are. Dumps. This one, though—"

"Different?"

"Yes. Bloody sight more expensive, for one thing."

She tried not to blush, but she had an idea that that was her doing. After nearly a decade of selling the personal effects of dead wolves, she had an uncomfortable feeling that she'd stimulated the local economy rather more than was good for it. People liked to buy nice teapots and cushions and place-mats and matching sets of silver-plated spoons, but it did mean they had to put up the price of their firewood to com-pensate, and she had an idea that that in turn had led to food and other thing costing more, though since the fire-wood buyers didn't seem to mind paying the higher prices (why? *Why?*) it didn't actually appear to matter all that much; they had enough money, wherever it was they got it from, and the net result seemed to be that life went on exactly as it always had, except that a considerable number of people now had teapots and teaspoons, which they put carefully away in cupboards for best and never used. And why not?

"You know," he went on, and there was a distant, faraway look in his eyes that gave her indigestion something rotten, "I figure that if you bought a whole load of stuff in one of the other villages, where everything's cheaper, and stuck it in a cart and brought it here and sold it, where everything's much dearer, you could make out like a bandit."

She caught her breath. "You think that?"

"Well, yes."

"Me, too," she said shyly. Further down the street, some-one had just started playing a soupy sweet tune on a violin. At any other time, she'd have been annoyed.

"But you never—"

She shrugged. "It's different," she said quietly, "when you're a girl. You ask people how much to hire a cart for three days, and they just look at you, or they laugh."

"That's stupid."

Sharps and arpeggios. "You think so?"

"Of course. If I had a cart I wasn't using and some woman came and offered me money to borrow it for a day or so, I'd take her hand off at the wrist. I mean," he added, "money's money, no two ways about it."

"We could—" She stopped. It was too soon. She barely knew him.

"What?"

"We could get a cart," she whispered. "You and me. I know where there's a good, big six-wheeler, hardly been used, just sits there in a barn all week. You could get a lot of stuff in it."

He smiled. "Yes, why not? Tell you what, it's got to be better than killing bloody dragons. And that's another thing. Actually killing them's only about, what, ten per cent of the time. The rest of it's lugging carcasses about the place, in carts. So really, it'd be more or less what I'm doing right now, only I'd get more money. Not to mention not being flamed at by nasty great big lizards."

Her eyes were shining. "You don't like being a dragon-slayer?"

"It's *silly*." The vehemence of his outburst seemed to have startled him; he had that it-just-came-away-in-my-hand look on his face. "Well, it is," he said. "I mean, for one thing, there never used to be all these dragons about. But the more we kill the stupid things, the more of them there are. And all this stuff, carting them to the wizard's house; what the hell does he want with thousands of tons of dragon meat? What possible use could it be to anyone?"

Her brow furrowed in thought. "Maybe," she said, "he's got a deal on with a butcher, or someone who makes pies or sausages or whatever."

"Dragon pies? Who'd buy them?"

"Maybe they don't let on that they're dragon. Maybe they mix the dragon in with a load of proper pie meat – horse, dog, rat, you know – in such small proportions that people don't know what it is they're actually eating. If dragon's a whole lot cheaper than rat or horse, you could make a fortune."

Turquine frowned. "Surely not. I mean, who'd be dumb enough to fall for that?"

She shrugged. "Just a thought."

"I mean, great idea," he added quickly, so as not to offend her, "if you could get away with it. But my guess is, it's something magical, something special wizards need dragon for. Making potions, that sort of thing."

"You're probably right," she said. "Anyway, I think it sounds like a horrible way to make a living."

"You're so right. For one thing, there's all the princesses."

She sat up a bit. "Princesses?"

"God, yes. Half my kingdom and my daughter's hand in marriage. It's so *embarrassing* having to say thanks-but-no-thanks all the time. They look at you out of their great big sheep eyes."

"How unpleasant for you," she said, a trifle coldly. "Time you got into another line of work, if you ask me."

"Couldn't agree with you more. So, where is this cart, exactly?"

And could it be more perfect than this, she asked herself; and yes, obviously it could, but this was appreciably better than staying home and washing her hair. She thought of Prince Florizel, a man with so much money that he'd paid two florins for a bit of old tea without a second thought. No, she could never feel love, or even a slightly upset tummy, for a man like that, no matter how loaded he might be. No good having it if you don't value it. Take away his wealth (and there'd be so many clever people out there trying to do just that) and he was just another Bill the woodcutter, all purchasing power and no trousers. Besides, she guessed she'd already reached a decision, or else why did the thought of the sheep-eyed princesses make her want to reach for her hatchet?

She told him some more about the cart, and where they could get a team of horses really cheap; and he said, hang on, what about oats and hay and so forth, which was so sweet of him, and when she mentioned how she knew where they could get a deal on a load of perfectly good hay, some slight water damage but nothing to worry about, he gave her a look that turned her knees to jelly. And then she realised that they were the only customers left in the taproom, and the innkeeper was putting the chairs up on the tables.

"Let's do it," Turquine said suddenly. "Let's do it now."

"All right," she said softly. He took her hand, and together they left the inn and crossed the town square to the livery stables; and if hens clucked instead of bluebirds singing, she wouldn't have had it any other way.

The old man who'd been playing the violin in a doorway opposite the inn watched them go. He was frowning. As the door of the livery stable closed behind them, he put his fiddle and bow back in its battered case, scooped the handful of coppers out of his hat and dropped them in a pocket without counting them, and walked briskly up the street in the direction of the forest. He carried on for several miles, choosing the left-hand fork at the crossroads and following the old cart track that led to the mountains. It was a long, slow climb and he kept stopping, but eventually he cleared the tree line and came out into bright sunlight. Then he looked around until he found a narrow path, scarcely more than a suggestion of a path in the sparse heather, which went straight up the steep incline towards the summit of Nol Cuithin. He didn't pause until he reached the outcrop-fringed hollow known locally as the Wizard's Chair; there, he put down his violin case and looked carefully round, as if making sure there was no one watching him. The Chair was, of course, the perfect place for seeing and not being seen. It also had other virtues, though the townsfolk wouldn't have understood them even if they'd known.

Two ravens swooped down out of the clear sky, circled him twice and pitched a yard or so away. He stooped and picked up a stone; they lifted and flew off, complaining bitterly. He let the stone fall from his hand, then reached inside his frayed old coat, took out his LoganBerry and keyed in a number.

The royal hounds – greyhounds, lymers, alaunts, brachets, harriers and a small liver and white spaniel – were snuffling about in the trash out the back of the disused stable block that now served as a temporary palace kitchen. There had been an awful lot of noise at one point, but since then they'd found a chicken carcass and half a dozen vintage fish-heads, so they were happy.

John the Huntsman, by contrast, wasn't happy at all. He didn't hold with unicorn hunting, which he thought was silly, and the prince's express instructions that the unicorn was to be taken alive and unhurt was the icing on the cake. All his life he'd been a staunch royalist, in much the same way as he'd been an air breather. The monarch, he'd been brought up to believe, can do no wrong. He'd had no trouble with that right through the old king's reign, but this new chap was different. Not that John believed all those rumours about, well, food and stuff, not even when the kitchen burned down; and the unicorn thing was funny, he'd had a good old laugh about it with the lads, but when he'd stopped and thought, it was funny in the other sense of the word. After all, princes; spending all day flouncing round the place on a white horse, every possible opportunity to meet girls, it's practically expected of them. And now, with half the palace staff having real trouble keeping a straight face when they bumped into him in corridors, His Highness was actively arranging a unicorn hunt and proposing to go on it himself. It wasn't right, somehow. There is, after all, a world of difference between stepping on a bit of apple peel and ending up flat on your face, and shipping in specially waxy skinned varieties of apple from the ends of the earth and sitting up all night carefully greasing the soles of your boots with lanolin. And, now he came to think of it, why was the prince the prince? There didn't seem to be a father or an uncle anywhere, so why wasn't he the king? Made no sense.

For the first time, therefore, in his thirty-six years' service to the royal household, John had to make an effort to bob, smile and generally act respectful when his employer came out into the courtyard.

"Hello," said the prince. "You're, um—"

"Yes, Your Highness."

"Everything ready?"

"Oh yes, Your Highness."

The prince lowered his voice. "You managed to find a, um—?"

"Yes, Your Highness. My daughter Rosebud. She's waiting in the stables, with the horses."

"Fine, thanks, yes. Well, let's get on with it, then."

(And it'd be a long time, John reflected gloomily, before he heard the last of that. The way she'd rolled her eyes and said, *"Dad!"* when he'd asked her a perfectly civil question—)

"Yes, Your Highness. We'll be under way in just a couple of shakes."

The prince wandered away, and John shook his head sadly. A prince setting off on a hunt, even a stupid unicorn hunt, should have a spring in his step and a twinkle in his eye. He should also have made an effort, rather than crawling into the first clothes that happened to meet him on his way from the bed to the wardrobe. Court fashions were, of course, a complete mystery to John, so maybe the clearly-dead-for-some-time look was in, and soon everyone would be drooping about looking like that. John hoped not. It'd make it so difficult to tell the nobility apart from drunks and scare-crows (and when you came right down to it, apart from clothes, what else was there to go by?)

He marched down to the stables and gave the assembled beaters and whippers-in their orders for the day. There were raised eyebrows and audible grumbles when he told them they'd be catching the unicorn alive; he didn't say anything, because he knew exactly how they felt. That done, he went back to round up the gentry, gently prise their stirrup cups out of their hands, and finally get things moving. Daft way to make a living, he thought—

And stopped dead, in the narrow paved alley between the stables and the tack shed, and asked himself; where the hell did *that* come from? I'm a huntsman. My father was a hunts-man, so was his dad before him, it's what we do. And if the boss wants the unicorn caught alive, or he wants to go hunt-ing wearing nothing but a full-face helmet and a quart of fruit salad, that's really none of my concern. Damn it, a thought like the ones I've just been having would never have entered Dad's head, it wouldn't have fitted in there, and if it had somehow managed to squeeze its way in, it'd have been stoned to death by the mob in two seconds flat. What's going on around here? What's *happening* to me?

He made himself walk on, though he was having a bit of trouble steering and bumped into a gatepost and the corner of a barn before he made it into the main courtyard. It's not just me, he reflected; he called to mind what people had been saying about his sister's girl, that Buttercup; she was always going around saying daft things these days, so maybe it was catching. Of course, it didn't help that the prince was, well, you know, sort of— But come on, think about it, we've had some real lulus on the throne over the years and people haven't suddenly started thinking *thoughts*. Must be more to it than that.

A little voice in his head said, *I blame the goblins*, and he felt a little better. Of course; pound to a penny the goblins were involved, if something wasn't right. Pretty well everything in that line turned out to be because of the goblins, when you got right down to it. Probably they'd been digging in some new place and something nasty was seeping out into the drinking water, turning everyone funny. The thought made him feel hot with anger; it's time we did something about those buggers, he snarled to himself, sorted them out once and for all.

"There you are." The prince was looking stressed out. "Where the hell did you wander off to? I said ten sharp, and it's five past already."

"Sorry, Your Highness. All ready now, you just give the word, and—"

"Yes, all right, whatever. Can we please get on with it?"

"Your Highness." John bobbed a little noddy bow and dashed back the way he'd just come. When he reached the stable yard, he yelled, "Come on, you useless bloody lot, they're all waiting," even though he knew he'd told them to wait there till he came for them, and sprinted off again before they could say anything. Not right, he was thinking, not right at all. Usually stuff just gets done at its own pace, and nobody gets worked up about it. If we all start carrying on like this, we'll be at each other's throats in no time.

The whole place is falling apart, he thought wildly. Damn those goblins!

After that, things just kept getting worse. The hounds

went dashing off after what turned out to be a little old lady living alone in a cottage; by the time the hunting party caught up with them, they'd got the house surrounded and were baying and scrabbling at the door; terrifying, no doubt, for the poor old woman and really bad for the hunt's reputation. It had taken him an hour to get the stupid animals back under control, by which time it had started to rain, and John had hoped that the prince might call it a day and let them all go home. No chance. They drove the rest of the east end of the forest, but no unicorns – deer, wild boar, hares, bears, all manner of warrantable game, but His Highness plainly wasn't interested and got quite upset when John suggested they might try and salvage something from the day by changing tack. So they plodded on, across the middle and over into the west end, where the hounds stumbled across a sleeping dragon and nearly got them all fried. Fortunately, something must've been wrong with it, indigestion maybe, because after taking a long, calculating look at the members of the hunting party, it simply spread its wings and flew away. By this point most of the attendant nobles had had enough and were dropping hints like falling meteorites about going home now, but they glanced off His Highness, who just looked bleakly at them and gave the order to carry on. Eventually, mid-afternoon, with the hounds and horses worn out and the beaters limping and moaning about having missed lunch, they struck unicorn tracks.

John was proud of the way the hounds worked the scent in spite of their obvious fatigue. But it soon became obvious that there was something wrong about the unicorn. Thinking about it later, it was pretty clear what had happened; the unicorn must've been drinking from the river, which flowed down off the mountain into the town aqueduct, so whatever the goblins had done to the water had turned it funny, too. How else could you account for the fact that it had taken one look at Rosebud and run like hell? After that, they'd had the devil's own job finding it again. By the time they picked up the scent, it was getting dark, and any sensible hunter would've given it up as a bad job and gone home. Not Prince Florizel. He'd been determined to carry on, even though he didn't seem to have enjoyed the day one little bit, John had seen merrier faces in the stocks, with a buy-one-get-one-free offer on frost-damaged turnips down at the feed store.

So, what with Rosebud quietly sobbing, the dogs whin-netting, the beaters muttering about time and a half and the prince snarling haven't-you-found-it-yet every two minutes, it hadn't been a cheerful last hour, and he'd been mightily relieved when, finally, they'd caught sight of a milk-white tail vanishing into a clump of briars at the overgrown mouth of what John knew for a fact was a blind canyon; no way out unless you could scale cliffs, for which purpose a unicorn is woefully overlegged. Gotcha, John whispered under his breath, and started placing the beaters for the final drive.

And then, just to put the gilded and intricately niello-inlaid tin lid on it, the prince had come stomping across with a map in his hand, and said, "Right, you and your bunch of jokers just clear off and leave it to me, you've done enough damage for one day" – which, coupled with the extremely nasty look he'd given poor Rosebud, had almost been enough to convert John to republicanism on the spot.

Still, what can you do? "Right you are, sir," he'd chirped through gritted teeth. "All right, lads, you heard the gentle-man, last one down the Blue Boar gets them in." And, with that in mind, he'd taken the long way back into town, hoping against hope that he'd be able to reclaim the cost of the round from petty cash at some point in a pretty bleak future.

When he was sure they'd all gone, Benny walked into the mouth of the canyon.

At first he did his best not to make any noise, but by the time he was five yards in, he was so hopelessly tangled up in briars and brambles that he gave up stealth entirely and concentrated his efforts on trying to force his way through, which meant that, a minute or so later, he was wedged solid, and the only part of his body he could move with any degree of freedom was his eyelids.

Sod this, he thought. "Help!" he yelled.

After a long interval, he saw something moving in front of him; something white. He could also hear a sound, something like a blend of distant train noises and an old man sucking a boiled sweet. "Hello?" he said.

The white shape kept on coming, slowly, relentlessly, until what he could see of it through the very narrow gaps between swatches of bramble gradually began to suggest the shape of a horse. The sound grew clearer; munching. At this point, Benny remembered that he hadn't had anything to eat since breakfast.

"Unicorn?" he said. "Is that you?"

More munching sounds, and the creak of bramble stems

under pressure. "I'm here," Benny said. "Just in case you hadn't noticed, I mean. Hello?"

A silver horn slid through the briar tangle about a foot to the left of his head. It was about two feet long and very sharp. Then a head, equine but distinctly different from your ordinary workaday horse, smaller and with a pointier nose. Its jaws were chewing a monstrous portion of bramble. "You clown," it said.

"I'm stuck."

"Yes," said the unicorn, "aren't you? Hold still, I'll see what I can do."

Slowly and methodically, the unicorn gnawed him free. "You're so lucky," it said with its mouth full, "that I happen to like brambles. If you'd got yourself stuck in thistles, you'd be on your own."

"Thank you." Benny tugged his sleeves free of the last residual thorns. He felt like one enormous consolidated scratch. "I came looking for you."

"I sort of gathered that," the unicorn said. "You and your nasty friends. Gave me the fright of my life, till I saw you there."

Benny blushed. "I didn't know how else to find you," he said.

"Fine. That's like saying, how do I go about defrosting a chicken? I know, I'll burn the house down. There's ways and ways, you know."

Defrosting? "I'm sorry."

"Yes, well. You're here now. Next time, just hang around in a clearing somewhere, and I'll find you."

He had to ask. "Defrosting a chicken?"

The unicorn nodded. "That's right."

"As in frozen—?"

"Well, yes. Highly recommended, unless you want to break teeth."

"You *know* about—"

"Ah, right, I see. Yes, I know about defrosting frozen chickens and other similar concepts, alien to this environment but familiar in the one you originally came from. Me, too, actually."

Benny waited, then asked, "You too what?"

The unicorn swished its tail. "I too am not from around here. Originally. I, however, have made some sort of an effort to blend in, which you palpably haven't. Did you see the way those people were looking at you? They think you're *weird*."

That, from a talking unicorn. "I don't give a damn," Benny said. "I just want to get out of here and never come back. And you—"He hesitated. "You're the same unicorn I saw the other day, right?"

He'd said the wrong thing. "Because of course we all look the same to you, I suppose."

"Sorry, I didn't—"

The unicorn gave him a look. "You're sorry. And now you're going to tell me you're not a bigot, some of your best friends are unicorns. Fine. You know, I think you're right. The sooner you go back where you came from, the better." Its lips curved in what, in human terms, would've been a grin. "We don't need your sort round here."

"Fine, we're agreed. And you know how I can get back."

The unicorn fluttered its ridiculously long eyelashes. "Yes," it said, "I do."

"Doughnuts."

The unicorn shied, as though someone had just prodded it with a stick. "Keep your voice down, for God's sake," it hissed. "Haven't you got it into your thick skull yet? We don't use the D-word."

"They don't know what it means."

"Don't you believe it." The unicorn's voice was low and urgent. "Oh, most of them don't, granted; not the woodcutters and the peasants and the rest of those idiots. But *he* knows. *His people* know, just fine. And you never know who might be listening."

"Right, sorry, sorry," Benny said quickly. "Out of interest, who's *he*?"

"Oh, for crying out loud."

"*Sorry*. Look, forget all that, it really doesn't matter. Just tell me where I can get a you-know-what, and I'll be out of here so fast I'll just be a blur. OK?"

The unicorn chewed at him for a moment. "It's not as simple as that," it said.

Benny made a whimpering noise; quiet, restrained, almost dignified. "Oh come *on*," the unicorn said. "Don't be such a *girl*. You weren't honestly expecting to be handed the way home on a plate, were you?"

"Well, yes. Literally."

The unicorn's upper lip curled slightly, and it nipped off a tender young bramble shoot with its front teeth. "You should know by now," it said, "things just don't work like that here. You need to remember who and where you are."

"Oh, but I do. I'm Benny Gulbenkian, third-year physics student from Orpington, Kent. I've got my final exams in just under a week. I need to get out of here and revise."

"No." The unicorn shook its head, narrowly avoiding inscribing the mark of Zorro on Benny's forehead with its needle-sharp horn tip. "You couldn't be more wrong. You're Prince Florizel, and this is your kingdom. Things are expected of you, and you have as much free will as a cue ball. If you want the D-thing, you're going to have to play by the local rules. Sorry, but that's how it is."

Benny sagged a little, then said, "All right, if you insist. What have I got to do?"

"Ah." The unicorn tossed its mane. No doubt there was a mirror hidden somewhere in the forest where it practised for hours on end. "In order to fulfil your quest—"

"Would you *please* not use that word? It's so Robert E. Howard."

"Fine. Your mission, should you choose to accept it, is to travel to the far ends of the Earth . . . "

"What? In these shoes? You must be joking."

"Crossing arid deserts and steaming jungles," the unicorn continued grimly, "fording mighty rivers and climbing snow-capped mountains—"

"I take it scheduled public transport isn't an option."

"Until you reach the Cradle of All Goblins, interrupt just once more and I wash my hooves of you, where you will encounter three trials. You must uncover the great truth that was hidden, you must right the ancestral wrong, and you must throw the fire into the ring of power. Only when you have done that—"

"Excuse me—"

"I warned you. Only when you have done that will you—"

"Excuse me," Benny said firmly, "but I think you may have got the last one a bit turned round. Surely it should be throw the *ring*—"

"Right," the unicorn snapped, "that does it. If you insist on interrupting all the damn time—"

"*Sorry*," Benny shouted. "But this is all too much. I can't possibly do all this hero stuff. Look, all I want is a dough—a one-of-those. There's got to be another way."

"Well." The unicorn gave him a look that turned his blood to sorbet. "Yes, there is."

"Really?"

"Oh yes. Just find your phone, Google a recipe and make one yourself. Piece of, no pun intended—"

"And that'd work, would it?"

"Sure." The unicorn pawed gently at the ground. "Why not?"

"And my phone still exists, and it's working?"

"Indeed."

"And that'd do just as well as finding the Goblins' Cradle—"

"Cradle of All Goblins. The Goblins' Cradle is a wool shop in Num Casamar. Yes, it would. But I thought you'd prefer to do this the easy way." The unicorn took a step back. "Still, if you relish a challenge, by all means go the phone route. After all, glorious failure does have a certain picaresque charm."

"Oh, come on. Finding my phone—"

But the unicorn was backing away. "Your choice," it said. "I've told you everything I can, and now it's up to you. I strongly advise you not to come looking for me again. Oh, and if I were you, I'd find myself a girlfriend. As a matter of urgency. Go in peace, Benny Gulbenkian. I hope you make your way home. Who knows, one day we may meet there, on the far side. But not," it added, "if I see you first. Farewell."

"Hey," Benny yelled, but it was too late; the unicorn had gone, and there was no way through the brambles that he could follow. "Bugger," he wailed, and sank down on the ground.

21

Thirty-four thousand eyes in the heads of twenty thousand goblins followed him as he walked slowly up the long, porphyry-paved aisle of the Grand Chamber of the Big Shouting Place. Mordak wasn't easily intimidated. He'd won the throne in single combat with his predecessor, a mighty warrior who'd devoted his life to disproving the old saying that the quickest way to a goblin's heart is through his stomach. He'd fought dwarves, Elves, humans, cave-trolls, dragons and his first wife's cousins. He prided himself on his brash confidence. If there's one thing goblins admire more than a leader who wears his heart on his sleeve, it's a leader who wears his enemies' livers on his epaulettes, and who do you think started that fashion? But that walk from the door to the rostrum was the closest he'd ever come to feeling over-awed, and for his money it was plenty close enough. Apart from the click of his claws on the polished floor, there was no sound whatsoever. On the rare occasions when goblins do solemn, they do it well.

Why am I doing this? he asked himself, not for the first time. The answer, etched into his brain, was curiously hollow and alien, as though it had been put there: to improve the lot of goblinkind, to raise the sun on a glorious new dawn and to strike a blow for a new tomorrow. He thought; I don't talk like that, so why should I suddenly go all pompous and shit-faced when I think? This just so isn't me.

He caught sight of his reflection in the polished breastplate of a deputy chamberlain. Yes it bloody well is me, he told himself. That's the problem.

Directly ahead of him was the podium and the royal throne, flanked by the royal arms (goblins came late and distressingly literal-minded to heraldry), and he saw two incongruous figures among the cordon of palace guards; two humans, one short and old, one young, tall, thin, eating a chicken sandwich. If things got really bad, at least he had someone he could rely on. He looked at them again and thought, oh *God*.

Seven trumpeters blew a fanfare. The echoes bounced around in the roof space for what seemed like a very long time, then died away. Absolute silence. Oh well, Mordak thought, here goes nothing. He turned, faced his assembled people and cleared his throat.

"My fellow goblins—"

His tongue appeared to have seized up. Though as a rule goblins aren't the quickest on the uptake of the Three Races, they seemed to have sensed that what they were about to hear wasn't going to be the usual run-of-the-mill State of the Pandemonium message, full of comfortable stuff about war victories, increased mine output, foiled conspiracies and the relentless drive towards perfect orthodoxy in political thought. They knew something was coming, the way rats can smell stormy weather. For the first time ever, they were *listening*.

Better give them something to listen to, then. "My fellow goblins," Mordak said. "Together we stand on the threshold of a new dawn. Together we stand ready to set our hands to a new path. Together, we can achieve the change, the real change, that our society has been crying out for."

He paused for the usual standing ovation; three minutes precisely. He had an idea that some of them at least were beginning to relax; this was, after all, exactly the way all royal speeches had begun for over two thousand years. Sorry, lads, he thought, but I can do no other, God help me.

When he looked at them, he said, what did he see? He saw a strong people, united in their common goals of remorseless progress, legendary brutality and total victory. And yet (immediately the assembly froze) how long was it since any one of them had stopped to consider the best way of achieving those goals, unanimously shared as they were by the entire goblin people? Excellent though their traditional way undoubtedly was, might there not just possibly be a better one?

In the second row back, a senior goblin official was slowly grinding his jaws, whetting his tusks together with an audible slop-slop noise. Oh hell, Mordak thought. Still, on we go.

As long as there have been goblins, he said, goblins had been miners; brave, bright-eyed, dedicated heroes of labour who'd hewn the living rock in search of the shining stone prized above all other minerals. To defend what was rightfully theirs, generations of goblins had fought the dwarves for possession of those mines, and that conflict had shaped the goblin people, as the hammer and the anvil shape the red steel. What were the proudest battle cries of their race? *Our shafts, for ever*, and *Mines, not yours*; and that shared heritage of valour and sacrifice was the very core of goblinkind, a heritage that would endure as long as a single goblin waddled on earth. And that was, of course, exactly how it should be.

However—

Mordak swallowed hard and went on. However, he said, although the miners' heart, the miners' courage, the miners' ruthless determination, the miners' very soul were indispensable parts of being goblin, maybe mining itself didn't have to be. He would like them to consider a few hard facts. Although output of shining rocks had risen steadily by at least 10 per cent every year for over a century, net income from shining rock sales had remained absolutely constant. Deaths from mining accidents had also risen, year on year; likewise, casualties in the dwarf wars. More goblins than ever were dying to produce more shining rocks than ever before, but they, the hard-working families of the United Hordes of Goblindom, weren't seeing the benefit. Now, he asked them, who was to blame for that?

Dead silence; but, he dared to hope, not the sort of silence that immediately precedes the first shout of *Get him!* Call it a miracle, but they were still listening.

Naturally, he went on, we blame the dwarves. Dwarvish aggression started the war, dwarvish greed kept it going, generation after weary generation. But there was peace now. Finally, Drain's people had been dragged to the negotiating table and forced to see sense. From now on, not one more goblin need fall to the murderous axes of the ancient enemy.

Pause. On their faces he saw that sullen, resentful, salad-is-good-for you look that told him he still had a very long way to go. In which case, he told himself, onwards –

We have shown the world, he said, that goblins aren't afraid to break the mould. We have shown all those who sneer at us and mock us that goblins have the courage, the faith, to do what it takes for a better tomorrow. (The human book he'd cribbed that last bit from had said a better, *brighter* tomorrow, but he'd had the sense to realise that, in front of an audience of cave-dwellers, it probably wouldn't play too well.) It was time, he told them, to summon up all that courage, all that determination and sheer goblin grit, and go for real change, real progress. It was time, he told them, to leave the mines.

Maybe they were just too stunned to move. He looked at

them and figured he had fifteen seconds, twenty at the most. He drew a very deep breath and went on.

The mines, he said, are holding us back. We work, we sweat, we die, but who gets all the profits? The wizard. We increase output; do we get paid more? No, we do not. We fight off a dwarf invasion of our galleries, but do we reap the benefits? No, the wizard does. And there's absolutely nothing we can do about that, because only the wizard wants the shining stones; and, so long as he can get them from the dwarves as well as us, he's in a perfect position to tell us how much he wants to pay for them.

So, he went on, we have two choices. We can exterminate every last dwarf under the mountain and so gain a monopoly, or we can leave the mines and find another way to earn a living. I know that every fibre of your being is shouting for the first option. I have to tell you, it can't be done. Stop, I beseech you, and think for a moment. We've never lost a war with the dwarves, but – you know this yourselves – we've never really won one, either. We can wipe them out, but we'll be wiped out, too. And for whose benefit? The wizard's. Is that what we really want? Don't let's give him the satisfaction.

Mordak paused, partly for rhetorical effect, partly to make sure that his pre-planned escape route was still open. He didn't dare glance over his shoulder, but the reflection in his carefully placed gauntlet showed him that the way was clear as far as the back of the hall, where his two trusty mercenaries would hold them off while he lifted the trapdoor down to Gallery Six. Once he was down there, it'd be a straight run to the border and Drain's solemn promise of political asylum; a term which, he couldn't help thinking, perfectly described the assembly facing him right now.

Here we go, he thought.

There is, he said, a better way. It's a way that leads us out of the mines. A way of prosperity, of security, of independence, of freedom for ever from the greed and oppression of the wizard. It's the way, the only way, that goblins can be free and still be, to the very roots of their souls, *goblins*. It's the way of basket-weaving.

Thirty-four thousand eyes blinked simultaneously. If he'd been in a better frame of mind to appreciate it, he'd have thought it was a wonderful thing to behold.

Basket-weaving, he told them. He, their king, had thought long and hard, wrestling with the problem day in and day out, and finally the solution had come to him. After all, people the world over need baskets. They've always needed baskets, they always *will* need baskets. And what occupation could possibly be more suited to the unique talents and traditions of the goblin people? To weave a basket, you first *hack* down a young sapling. Then you *tear* it lengthways until it *splits*; then you *twist* the riven split with your *bare hands* and *force* it into *contorted* shapes, while *piercing* holes in the growing lattice with a bare, *sharp* bodkin. Then, when you've done that, you *slice* off the sticking-out ends with a *big knife*, and, lo and behold, there's your basket. My friends (said King Mordak), don't you agree, isn't that precisely the sort of work that we goblins were born to do?

And so, he said, I offer you two choices. One leads to the glorious but inevitable extermination of our race. The other leads to wealth, fulfilment, happiness and power. It's not an easy choice, but since when did goblins relish the easy way, the soft way, the coward's way? My fellow goblins, I have nothing to offer you but bark, sap, sawdust, toil and sweat. I know you will make the right choice, not just for yourselves, not just for your broodspawn, but for your broodspawn's broodspawn. Thank you.

It was the deepest, heaviest silence he'd ever known, but what was most remarkable about it was that he couldn't read it – he, King Mordak, born and raised in the dark, silent mines. For all his shrewdness and insight into the narrow, bony heads of his people, he simply had no idea what the twenty thousand goblins facing him were going to do next.

And then they began to shout.

It started with a few barks at the back of the hall, grew into a clattering, like heavy raindrops on a tin roof, and swelled into a roar that shook the walls. They were all bellowing at the tops of their voices, and what they were shouting was: *Mordak! Mordak! Mordak!*

So that was all right.

He let them rip for a minute, then raised his claw for silence and got it. My fellow goblins, he said, let us now go forth. Let us leave slavery and the mines and go into the forest. In the forest, we'll hack and split and twist and stab and slice ourselves a golden future, until every basket, every basket in the whole world, is made by *us*. Of course (he said, and paused, and they all paused with him), there may be some people who don't like it. There may be some who don't want us to take over the fat basket-weaving monopoly they've enjoyed for so long. They may not want us to swarm out like lava over the willow coppices, cutting a swathe so wide it'll be visible from the highest mountain. They may not like it at all. But I tell you this, my brothers. If the Elves don't like it, if they come for us, with their poison arrows, their spears, their sneers and their ears, we'll teach them a lesson they'll never forget.

It's always a good idea, Mordak reflected as they carried him shoulder-high from the chamber, to leave the best bit till last. Even so, it had been a hell of a gamble, and he'd risked it, and he'd won. *I* won, he thought. I did it. All alone, against the odds, I *did* it.

And then he thought; what the hell did I just do?

"**S**o," Yglaine said, after a pause, "you haven't actually done anything, then."

John the Lawyer blinked twice, then smiled. "On the contrary," he said. "Like I just told you, I've been researching the origins of the wizard, and I have to say, it's quite—"

"About getting me a new violin. You haven't done anything at all."

Elves, he thought. With ears like that, you'd think they'd listen just occasionally. "Like I told you," he said pleasantly, "I've been researching the origins of the wizard, who I believe is at the very heart of a chain of causalities whose roots go deep—"

"It wasn't the wizard who broke my violin, it was a giant. I thought you'd grasped that."

John sighed. "Yes, it was a giant, but—"

"Right. So what are you wasting time chasing after the wizard for?"

"Point one, the giant is dead and can't be sued, point two, even if it was still alive it wouldn't have any money. The wizard, by contrast, is still very much with us, and he's so ridiculously wealthy he could afford to buy you a thousand million violins, and if we can establish a direct causal link—"

"I don't want a thousand million violins, where on earth would I *put* them all, I just want one. And you're not doing anything to get it for me."

Don't shout, he ordered himself. Shouting at an Elf would get him deported; and though on one level nothing would please him more, it'd be such a shame to get thrown out now, with possibly the biggest score in legal history practically within his grasp. "You're quite right," he said. "I'm sorry, I was being, um, human. You know what we're like. Butterfly minds. The wood from the trees, that sort of thing. That's why I'm so glad I've had this opportunity to work with Elves, the chance to learn intellectual discipline and the ability to focus."

Maybe her cold blue dead-fish eyes softened a little. "That's all right, then," she said. "Now, get on with getting me a new violin, and we'll say no more about it."

"Of course."

She waited a moment or so. "Well? What are you going to *do*?"

He nodded eagerly. "Probably the best thing, if you agree, would be if I issue proceedings. I thought maybe if I apply for a writ of *certiorari* in the Chancery division, leading to an interlocutory hearing to establish due cause, coupled with an application for a Treluviel injunction, pleading *res ipsa loquitur*, I could then move to join further multiple defendants on an ad hoc basis once we reach the exchange of pleadings stage, without prejudice to other causes further or in the alternative that might emerge in the light of secondary documentary evidence becoming available during the discovery process. Or do you think I'm barking up the wrong tree entirely?"

She looked at him as though he'd just turned into a fish. "No," she said, "no, that sounds pretty good to me. I mean, that's what I'd do, if it was me."

"Absolutely. And if the counter-pleadings give rise to counterclaims requiring issue of further interlocutory proceedings before the deputy registrar, we can always register an intent to proceed, with reservation of evidence in chief pending resolution of the primary claim at first instance, subject to appeal in chambers on any relevant points of law."

"Well of course we can. That's just basic common sense, really."

"Of course it is. Although, while we're on the subject, if we get hit with a Glorfangel interdiction during arguments *in camera*, do you think we should move for dismissal or lodge a payment into court subject to order, with an associated petition for exemplary costs?"

She opened her mouth and closed it a couple of times, but no words came out. He counted up to five in his head, then added, "You're quite right, it's best to play that sort of thing by ear when the time comes. I mean, that's what people like me are for, so that the real decision-makers don't get bogged down in *de minimis* trivia." He smiled. "Like I said, that's what's so good about working with Elves. They see things so clearly."

Well, that was phase one, Shutting Up The Client, successfully completed; now on with phase two. Once she'd gone, John sat down in his comfortable chair next to the window and reached for the huge wad of documents he'd gone to so much trouble to squeeze out of the miserable pointy-eared bastards down at Consolidated Records.

Elves, as is universally acknowledged, make the best civil servants in the known world. Only Elves truly understand that the real function of the official archivist is to preserve everything while at the same time making it impossible to find; that way, the information is protected from officials, and the officials are protected from the information, and everybody can sleep easy in their beds, or their office chairs if they're in one of the higher administrative grades. Since the passing of the Freedom of Information Acts, over a thousand years ago, anyone could go down to the archive and look at anything he liked; the proviso, which made all the difference, was that the archive staff were under no obligation to help him find what he was looking for. Since the lives of 99.967 per cent of Elves are dominated by copy deadlines, the school run and the need to dress for dinner parties, nobody had the time to go rummaging about in dusty old boxes for the stuff that might actually mean something. No Elf, anyway.

John the Lawyer squinted, and held a page up to the light. He'd had to copy all this stuff himself, and since he was a lawyer his handwriting at its best looked like other people's crossings-out. Never mind; he remembered this bit so clearly he didn't really need the transcript. It was the wizard's original application, made three thousand and four years ago, for planning and zoning permission to build the Wizard's House at Sair Carathorn, the seat of his power.

Three thousand years ago, of course, slap bang in the middle of the Second Age, the mountainous deserts around Sair Carathorn were still impenetrable forest, part of the realm and under the jurisdiction of the Elvenhome Sylvan District Council. Back then, when dwarves, goblins and men still wore animal skins and hunted with flint spears, and even the Elves were only just coming to terms with the three great pillars of civilisation – movable type, classified advertisements and the Sunday colour supplement – the power of the Elven bureaucrats had not yet waned into the pale shadow of itself that had survived into the late Third Age. Wielding the might of the Three Rings (like the One Ring but, inevitably in context, in triplicate), the officers of the ESDC had held sway from the Blue Mountains right across the plains to the Sea; and every castle, fortress, township, manor house, cottage, pigsty, woodshed and hayrick had needed planning consent from the Elder Folk before anyone could do so much as dig a hole in the ground or hammer in a gatepost. Such was their authority that even the wizard, lately arrived from the Shining Lands, had bowed low before them and filled out Form 188C (Residential); a copy of which, transcribed by the light of a guttering candle stub, now lay on John's knee as he struggled to decipher his own lamentably obscure squiggles.

Most of it – pages 1 through 677 – were just the usual official stuff; but at the back, where he'd known it would be, was the building regulations inspector's report, with a full specification and plans and elevations in the approved format. As he read, occasionally stopping to leaf through the pages of his Old Middle High Elvish dictionary, John's face slowly changed; from a smile to a hungry grin, from a grin to a worried frown. And then he stopped, as though turned to stone, and sat staring at the drawings for a long, long time.

Surely not, he thought. It can't be.

While he'd been copying it, his mind had been on other things; the cold, the rats, the inordinately long interval between meals. Now, when he came to consider it carefully, with the bright light of a summer afternoon blazing in through the unshuttered window, he didn't just suspect, he knew. That shape; that set of two concentric circles surrounding a hollow void; the section between the two circles raised into high relief and contoured into a continuous semicircle. He'd seen it before, once long ago, and in the most unlikely place he could possibly imagine—

"Oh come *on*," he said aloud. Then, as if suddenly conscious of what he held in his hands, he covered the page with a bit of scrap paper and put it down on the floor.

No. Surely not.

It took him a long time to nerve himself to take another look. This time he concentrated on the text, in particular the annotations and explanatory notes. The concentric circles surrounded a hole in the back wall of the main storehouse in the deepest vault below Sair Carathorn. It was described in the report simply as *access port*, which could mean anything. Reading between the lines, the building inspector seemed to have assumed it was part of the plumbing, a subject which Elves find quite distasteful and prefer not to dwell on. A sinkhole, sump or soakaway, the inspector appeared to have thought, and was content to leave it at that.

But he'd been wrong, because, according to the geological survey annexed to the environmental impact report, the hole in the middle of the two circles was bored into the solid basalt of the mountain; no way in hell anything could soak away into that, except just possibly concentrated nitric acid. So, what was it, if it wasn't the outflow of the wizard's personal toilet? A hole (circular, twenty feet in diameter, for crying out loud) drilled into the living rock in the roots of the mountain; not a mine, because there was nothing worth having over that way; if there had been, goblin and dwarf prospectors would've been all over it centuries before the wizard arrived. Storage? But there was plenty of that already without drilling into rock. Some kind of safe, maybe? Yes, but there was no door.

Door, he thought, *door*. No, it's just a hole. Not a door. When is a door not—?

He could feel his brains beginning to delaminate inside his skull; two more minutes of this and the finest mind in the legal profession would be fit for nothing but a goblin readymeal. Let's just recap, he told himself. We have this hole, this *big* hole drilled into solid basalt, down in the bottom cellar of the wizard's castle. Not only that, but it really does look exactly like a—

And there, of course, was the problem; because, when all is said and done, it's no earthly use knowing a fact if you simply daren't tell it to anyone else, and if you did, ten to one they wouldn't understand what you were talking about until you explained it to them, whereupon they'd immediately have you arrested. Frustrating didn't begin to describe it.

His eye fell on a section headed *Materials Used*; he read it and his jaw dropped open. Mortar, sand quicklime, aggregate, cement, yes, fine; but flour, eggs, milk, butter—

Oh my God, John thought. It is. It really is.

He felt like he wanted to scream; and yet, at the same time, also oddly justified. He wasn't exactly ashamed of his vices; they were part of him, they'd gone towards making him what he was, every bit as much as his virtues had done, and the end result was by and large sufficiently to his satisfaction. Even so, there had been times over the years when he'd felt a certain degree of guilt about his penchant for, let's say, dubious literature concerned with certain rather unorthodox aspects of the culinary arts. Keeping his collection in a locked trunk under his bed was no more than a perfectly reasonable security precaution. The locked compartment in his mind was another matter; but no, in the final analysis he was fine about it, so long as it stayed locked away and nobody ever found out. Which, he had every reason to suppose, they never would.

Unless he told them. Which, of course, he'd have to do, at the very least indirectly, if he wanted to make any use at all of the blinding, earth-shattering discovery he'd just made—

Namely, that deep in the cellars under Sair Carathorn, the wizard had built a giant, twenty-foot-high—

Doughnut.

There; he'd allowed himself to think the word, and now it was out in the open and he could look at it in daylight. A giant, twenty-foot-high doughnut. God, but there are some sick bastards out there. *Twenty feet*, for crying out loud. The biggest one he'd heard of (*in my extensive experience*, he heard himself telling the judge, and whimpered) was no more than five inches. What would anyone, no matter how twisted, want with one so goddamn *big*?

He realised he was trembling.

Not that he was, well, *into* that sort of thing, not in any serious way; for him it was mostly just curiosity, all right, a slight thrill, a certain shiver down the spine at the thought of food with, you know, holes – but nothing heavy, nothing really soft-centred, like some of the freaks and weirdos out there. He knew he could give it up any time he liked without a second thought, or at any rate without a fifth thought, it was nothing he couldn't handle. Compare and contrast the sort of deviant who installs a *twenty-foot* specimen in his basement. You really would have to be seriously weird—

And this seriously weird person was the single most powerful entity in the known world.

Um, he thought.

"**W**hat we need," Buttercup said thoughtfully, "is a name."

"You what?" replied Sir Turquine through a mouthful of nails.

Buttercup balanced a turnip on top of the pile, turning it slightly so that its best side was facing the street. "For the stall," she said. "It needs a name. A distinctive identity."

"What it needs—" Turquine paused to hammer in a nail; which he did, eventually, after hammering other things in the process, his thumb included. "What it needs is a roof, in case it rains. Here, pass me that bit of wood. No, not that one, the other one."

Buttercup, daughter, niece, granddaughter, great-great-granddaughter and so on back to an infinite succession of expert carpenters and cabinetmakers, didn't say anything. Instead, she smiled. Turquine bent a couple of nails in the crossbar, which then peeled off sideways and hit him on the head. He said some words that knights probably weren't supposed to know, and started again. She liked him for that. Ninety-nine knights out of a hundred at this point would've vindicated their honour by reducing the stall to matchwood with a battle-axe.

"Something people can remember," Buttercup said. "That way, you foster customer loyalty and ensure sustainable market share. It's essential."

Turquine looked at her in amazement for a moment, then shrugged. "Whatever," he said. "Call it Turquine and Buttercup's. Or Buttercup and Turquine's, if you think that's—"

"Oh no." She shook her head. "Where's the hook in that? Where's the *je ne sais quoi*?"

"You what?"

She frowned. She'd never heard the words before, but she knew. "It means: I don't know what."

"You don't know what?"

"That's right."

"Sorry, I'm getting confused here. What don't you know?"

She sighed. "*I* don't know, do I? It's just an expression. It means—"

"You don't know what it means?"

"*It's an expression.*" She took a deep breath, and the bluebirds, which had ducked for cover under the eaves of a nearby house, crept back out and carried on singing. "Just our names won't make a very good name for the stall. We need a *word*."

Pause. "Names are words."

She drew in a breath, but forbore to use it, and a thought struck her. Maybe, she thought, this is what happy-ever-after actually is; in real life, if it's capable of existing there at all. Maybe happy-ever-after means not always seeing eye to eye, now and then letting slip a less than kind word, maybe even once in a while wanting to throttle the other half of one's very soul with one's bare hands; all that, but it doesn't really *matter*, because even so, in spite of that and his occasional annoying turns of phrase and the fact he can't even knock a nail in straight; even so—

Um. Even so what? Oh, *je ne* bloody *sais quoi*. It doesn't *matter*, that's all. And that's happy-ever-after, not the simpering, cow-eyed adoration, the hands-over-the-eyes-guess-who soppiness she'd been brought up on and never quite managed to believe in. And belief was everything, wasn't it?

"All right," Turquine said suddenly. "How about Turquine's Excellent Stall?"

She turned and stared at him. "Actually," she said, "that's not bad."

"Well, it's a bit long."

"Oh, that's all right, people'll shorten it. Probably right down to the first letters of each word."

He mouthed the initials silently under his breath. "You know—" he said.

"And we need to make it sound a bit more – well, *bigger*, if you know what I mean. Like, it's different from all the other stalls, it's not just two buckets, a sheet and some planks of wood, it's a *thing*. With an *identity*."

"Okay." He thought for a moment. "How about The Turquine's Excellent Stall *Company*? That's like more sort of—"

"Corporate," she said. "Yes, you're right, that's brilliant."

"I'm not sure," he said doubtfully. "It's rather a mouthful, isn't it?"

"Not when people shorten it down, like I said." She took a step back to admire her work. "How much did we pay for these swedes?"

"Fourpence a ton."

"Perfect. We can charge a farthing a pound, undercut the competition by fifty per cent, and still make out like bandits." She wrote in a number on a scrap of plywood and perched it on top of the pile. "This is such a good idea," she said. "What amazes me is that nobody's—"

He was squinting at the piece of plywood. "What does 'organic' mean?"

"Oh, that. It means it was grown entirely free from chemical fertilisers or pesticides. Which means you can charge double, at least."

"Ah." He frowned. "But nobody round here uses that stuff."

"Yes, but—"

"Nobody can afford to, it costs an arm and a leg. That's why the yields are rubbish."

"Yes, all right, but it's still *true*. All our produce is hundred per cent organic. So, if it's true, why not say so?"

"Because nobody knows what organic means?"

She smiled. "They will," she said. "Trust me, they will."

Turquine drove the last nail into the canopy frame. This time, he managed to catch it before it hit him. "It's not going to rain," he said briskly. "We don't need a canopy." He threw the hammer into the toolbox and sat down on an upturned bucket. "What's sustainable market share?" he said.

"What? Oh, that's when people keep coming back to your stall rather than anyone else's. We need that. Good for business."

"Fine. Only, I never heard it called that before."

"Nor me," Buttercup admitted. "The words were suddenly just there in my head, and I understood them. It happens quite a lot, actually."

"Is that right?" Turquine looked at her a bit sideways.

"Yes. A lot more often just lately, mind."

Turquine put down the sack of carrots he was carrying. "I knew a girl once who suddenly got words in her head," he said. "Trouble was, the words were stuff like *drive the Elves out of Tarn Gethemir*, and when the Elves got to hear about it, I have to say, things did not go well for her. Yours aren't anything like that, are they?"

"Certainly not," Buttercup said sharply. "Mostly it's stuff

like *macroeconomic climate* and *exchange rate mechanism*, and what's really strange about it is, I know what they mean."

"Really?"

"Yes. No." She scowled. "I know that price-to-cash-flow ratio is calculated by dividing share price by cash flow per share to find the number of years of free cash flow required to recoup the initial purchase price, but—"

"Yes?"

"I don't know what *that* means. It's just there, in my head. It's like I learned it by heart years ago and then forgot I'd ever seen it before. I mean, what's a share, for crying out loud?"

"I know that," Turquine said. "It's the steel bit on a plough. I heard somewhere you make them out of swords or something."

"Oh. Yes, but cash doesn't *flow*. It sort of rolls and bounces."

Turquine thought hard. "I think it must be magic," he said. "Wizard stuff."

"I'd sort of gathered that. But what does it—?"

"It's a spell," Turquine said. "For farmers and black-smiths. You pour the money it takes to buy a plough over the blade thing, and it tells you – no, that doesn't work. You can't have heard it quite right, in your head."

She sighed. Well, at least he hadn't told her she was imagining things, and not to be so silly. And maybe he couldn't knock a nail in straight, but if she wanted nails driven in properly, she could hire a man to do that, she didn't have to marry one. Happy-ever-after; realist's shorthand for *not too miserable quite a lot of the time*. She looked round the market-place, at the apple-cheeked countryfolk, the cheerful woodcutters, the laughing children, the shoppers with their baskets over their arms, chatting with the jovial stallholders. That's happy-ever-after, she thought – also happy before and happy during, always happy, nothing but happy, and why? Because they were being *fooled*, was why.

"Buttercup? Are you all right?"

Sweet of him to be concerned. "I'm fine."

"No you aren't. You've gone a funny colour and you're shaking."

"Oh, I just realised something, that's all."

He looked closely at her. "More words in your head?"

"No." She closed her eyes for a moment while she thought. "It's like – it's like I've had a particular bit of knowledge for a long time without realising, and I've just tripped over it and noticed it's there." She reached out and grabbed his arm. "Turquine," she said, "what exactly do you know about the wizard?"

He frowned. "Well, he's magical."

"Yes. Apart from that."

"Um. Well, he pays good money for dragon carcasses, and the dwarves and the goblins sell him shining yellow rocks—"

"And my family make planks for him."

"And he's a whatsisname, philanthropist and patron of the arts, because it was the wizard who originally endowed the Sylvan Youth Orchestra, or so someone told me. Why?"

She pushed him gently away. "Just a minute," she said. "I need time to think."

He looked at her sideways. "Suit yourself," he said. "I'll just finish setting out the broccoli."

She sat down on a wall and tried to make sense of the ideas swirling round inside her head. Take love, for example; her own mother and father, thirty years and never a cross word. Or the bashful, smiling woodcutters, forever popping up out of the bushes holding bunches of flowers. It was hard for her, because her own experience was so limited, but it stood to reason; you can't really love someone for thirty years without yelling at them occasionally, it can't be done. And if there's a form of relationship that can endure that long with-out blazing rows, slammed doors and flying crockery, it's something else, it isn't *love*. It's love in the same way that a firewood-and-wolf-plunder based economy is an economy. It wouldn't work for five minutes unless someone was *messing around with it*; someone playing dolls with a whole world.

And who, she asked herself, might that possibly be? Rhetorical question.

She got up and walked over to the stall, where Turquine had somehow managed to get the canopy to stay up. True, it looked a bit like a heavily pregnant flag, but it's the thought that counts. "Turquine," she said, "would you mind terribly much if we put the stall on hold for a little while and went and did something else for a bit?"

He looked at her, and his nose twitched. "Such as?"

"I want to go and ask the wizard something," she said. "And if he won't give me a straight answer, I want you to hit him until he does. Would that be all right?"

"Oh." For a moment he seemed almost disappointed, but then he frowned, as if to indicate that, actually, he wouldn't mind doing that at all. "Sure," he said. "Only—"

"Yes?"

"You do realise we've paid for the pitch in advance? And I don't think they'll give us our money back."

"Turquine," she said solemnly. "There are some things in this life that are more important than money."

"Um."

"Not many of them. In fact, amazingly few. Maybe three. But this is one of them. All right?"

The clear, bright light of trust shining in his eyes was her sun, her stars. "Fair enough," he said. "Let's do it."

"*Splendid*. Right, get the horses and we'll be off. Oh and Turquine—"

"Yes?"

She bit her lip. "Better bring your sword and your armour and stuff. Just to be on the safe side. You never know."

He thought for a moment, and she realised; he's really quite brave, which is a good thing. Very brave wouldn't be good, because the dividing line between very brave and fatally stupid is on the thin side, but quite brave is actually *useful*. She turned away, but he called her back. "Buttercup."

"Yes?"

"What are the other two things?"

"Get the horses."

"Right you are." He stopped dead. "Buttercup."

"Yes?"

"Your basket." He was staring at it. "Why's it making that funny noise?"

"What funny—?" And then she heard it too. Like singing. Like the distant sound of the Elves in the forest, but definitely coming from the basket. Instinctively she reached for her hatchet, but, of course, it was where it always was, in the—

"It's asking me," Turquine said quietly, "to help me make it through the night."

They looked at each other. "Make what through the night?"

Turquine shrugged. "It, apparently. I don't know, do I? It's your basket, you ask it."

And then she had one of those little lurches of intuition, the sort she was starting to get used to, the same way you get used to a loved one's snoring, and she reached down into the basket, groped around until she found Florizel's strange grey slate, and pulled it out. The noise, the little tinny voice, was indisputably coming from inside it.

"What the hell," Turquine said, "is that?"

"No idea," Buttercup said. "But I think it belongs to Florizel. I think he dropped it in the—"

At the word "dropped" she fumbled her grip on the thing – it was smooth and slippery, like glass – and it nearly slipped through her hand. She grabbed it just in time to stop it falling, but the pressure of her fingertips seemed to wake it up, because suddenly it was glowing with lights and strange symbols. "Hellfire," Turquine whispered, but she shushed him, because the tinny singing had stopped.

"Buttercup, I don't think you should—"

"*Shh*. It's saying something."

She waited. It said it again. It said, "Hello?"

Turquine's hand flew to the dagger hanging from his belt, but Buttercup gave him a furious look and he froze. "Hello?" said the voice. "Benny?"

Buttercup and Turquine looked at each other, eyes wide. "Should it be doing that?" Turquine whispered.

"How should I—?"

"Well, it's your pencil case."

"Hello? Benny? Are you there? Stop pissing around and pick up."

Before she could stop him, Turquine had snatched the slate from her hand. "Hello," he said.

"Benny?"

"Yes," Turquine said, in a loud, slightly high voice. "Reveal yourself."

Dead silence; but somehow Buttercup knew the voice was still in there somewhere. And then words came bursting into her head; she grabbed back the slate and said, "Benny's not available right now, can I take a message?"

Another pause; then, "Who the hell are you?"

Buttercup's lips were shaping the first syllable of her name, but Turquine clapped his hand over her mouth. "No," he hissed, "don't tell it, you mustn't," and she knew immediately that he was right. She nodded, and he took his hand away. "Who shall I say called, please?" she said.

An even longer pause; then the voice said, "Oh hell," and there was a buzzing noise, then silence. They waited, and the lights on the slate went out.

Buttercup looked up at Turquine, who'd gone white as snow. "That was close," she said. "Just as well you had the sense to—"

He shrugged. "Anyway," he said, "I think we got away with it. Now, first chance we get, that thing goes down a very deep well."

"I guess." She looked at him again. "It could be useful."

"Really? What the hell for?"

"Well, it's got to be something to do with the wizard, right? *I* think that was his voice, just then. Coming out of the slate."

"He talks through a little glass-fronted box? Surely not." Turquine shook his head. "Why would anyone want to do that?"

"I think," Buttercup said, "he uses that thing to talk to people from a long way away. I think Florizel had it because he talks to the wizard with it. And that's why he's been acting so weird." She frowned, striving to remember. "I saw him talking to it. I think the wizard uses the box to make Florizel do really weird stuff." She lowered her voice. "You know, with *food*."

Turquine shuddered. "Then we'd better make it a very, very deep well, hadn't we? I don't know about you, but my life's complicated enough already without that bastard grooming me into doing pervy stuff with egg whites."

Buttercup was still and quiet for a moment. Then she said, "No, we'll keep it. It's got to be useful. We can use it to get to the wizard. After all, if it's a special magic thing and he's lost it, he's going to want it back."

"You said Florizel lost it."

"Stop being so *logical*, I can't think when you do that. All right, we go to Florizel, we say, you can have your box back if you take us to the wizard. There," she added firmly, "that's settled. Well?"

Turquine looked at her, and she could see the little wheels going round and round. "Yes," he said, "why not? But I'm warning you, one cheep out of that thing about six ounces of plain flour, and it's getting a swimming lesson." He paused, and took a deep breath. "Buttercup."

"Yes?"

"What *are* the other two things?"

She gave him a look of exasperated affection. "Well," she said, "one of them's health."

"*Health?*"

"Exactly. If you haven't got your health, what have you got? That's what I always say."

"Oh for crying out—"

"Come *on*."

Gordon looked at the phone in his hand, then put it back in his pocket. Well now, he thought.

A man's voice, slightly half-witted; *reveal yourself!* Actually, amend that; he wasn't half-witted, he was scared. There's a difference. Then a generic phone-answering female who'd said the name, *Benny*. That shot a hole in his initial hypothesis – that Benny had dropped his phone in the street and some druggie had picked it up; unless the druggie had a quick-thinking girlfriend who worked in a call centre. But why answer it at all, in that case?

Hypothesizing in the absence of data, he rebuked himself. He took his phone out again, and selected the nasty little app he'd had put on Benny's phone without telling him, the one that allowed him to track where Benny was, to within five feet. It came up blank. So; no reception – except that couldn't be right, could it, because he's just called Benny's phone and had a response. That made no sense.

No, worse than that, far worse. It did make sense, in one very particular context.

Gordon winced and closed his eyes. The *idiot*.

Allow that possibility into the frame of reference, and a plausible hypothesis was much easier to come by. If Benny was where he thought he might be, and he'd dropped his phone and a perfect stranger had picked it up, then it was entirely likely that it could fall into the hands of (a) someone who'd never seen or heard of a phone before (b) someone who spent her life answering phones; and they could be standing right next to each other. Entirely possible.

The idiot. The clown.

He got up and went to his bedroom, where, among the shoeboxes in his closet, one special shoebox was carefully hidden-in-plain-sight. He opened it. Empty.

"You *moron*," he roared, and drop-kicked the empty box across the room.

Then, with a *plunk* and a soft tinkle as it rolled round on its rim for a moment or so, the penny dropped. Benny and the laws of Newtonian physics. Of course. You'd have to be blind not to see it straight away—

—Because someone who's been spending time in another reality, a universe very different from our own (see multiverse theory), would inevitably be changed by the experience right down to the subatomic level. Just as people going abroad can get stomach upsets from funny food or foreign water, the laws of alien physics can get into your bloodstream, right down into the areas of the brain that process mathematics. It's a bit like suddenly switching from base ten to base eight without realising it; the same sums give different answers, and the new answers are just as right as the old ones were. That would explain why Benny could do the same calculations as all the scientists at Harvard and MIT combined, get a radically different answer and still be *right*. It was a phenomenon that Gordon was well aware of; more than that, it made him a great deal of money, because if you did the sums a certain way, identical ten-gram pure gold coins worth $400 over here were worth a thousand times that over there; so he had no excuse, he should've picked up on it straight away. Even so. The *idiot*.

Suddenly, Gordon felt very tired. There comes a point where the hassle outweighs the buzz, where the money stops mattering and just becomes a way of keeping score, where you realise that you aren't running the business, the business is running you, like a dog on one of those extending leads. It wasn't the first time he'd felt like this, but always he'd told himself: I can't stop now, there's people out there, on both sides of the line, depending on me – people who need their coffee stirrers, whole societies who've grown to be entirely dependent on me, and I can't just abandon them or there'd be chaos— He'd said it so many times he wasn't sure any more whether he believed it, or whether he'd taught himself to believe it; when he stopped and looked at it objectively, he realised he didn't have the faintest idea what would happen if the wizard simply disappeared and left them all to get on with it. For him, it had been five years; for them, close to four thousand, and any society that stays basically the same for four thousand years must be functional, at the very least, and if you arbitrarily rip away its support mechanisms, surely there'd be Armageddon . . . and then the exam-question proviso: *would your answer be different if you weren't making a fortune out of it?* Hypothetical question, because what possible incentive did he have for stopping?

Answer: because his idiot nephew had strayed over there, and Benny wasn't fit to be let out on his own in Orpington, let alone in a realm where dragons were real and goblin recipe books had whole sections headed *1001Mouthwatering New Ways With Human*. Not only that; given that the mechanisms that drove economy and society over there had all been carefully socio-engineered over centuries (local time), what would the effect on them be of a gormless halfwit with good intentions and a spanner?

Oh hell, Gordon thought. And it's big over there; world-size, in fact. Just for fun, he'd calculated its circumference once, based on astronomical observation and magically obtained geostatistical data, and had been mildly stunned to find it was a third again bigger than real-life Earth. And the stupid boy could be *anywhere*.

He flicked his phone into organiser mode and considered his schedule; then he laughed at himself, because time over there isn't real time. He could spend as long as it took, and still be back punctually for his 3:46 meeting with the Shark Corporation. Then he reached into his other coat pocket, and took out a doughnut.

Someone was waiting for him as he stepped through the portal on the other side.

"Areweth," he said. "Talk to me."

The tall, silver-haired Elf opened the large leather-bound book she was carrying. "Messengers from King Drain," she said. "He wants to talk to you, urgent."

He headed off down the corridor. Arweth followed, her dagger-pointed heels clicking on the marble floor. "Also," she went on, "there's a letter from King Mordak you'll want to read ASAP."

"I doubt it," Gordon replied, without turning his head. "And?"

"Human trouble. Rumours of a *coup d'état* brewing against Prince Florizel, they say he's been dabbling in the unspeakable arts. Also, there's a renegade knight and some village girl trying to set up a free-market economy."

That made him stop dead. "Say that again."

She turned two pages and found the place. "They've bought a large quantity of groceries in one village and they're proposing to sell them in another village where prices are dearer."

"A male and a female? In *business*?"

"According to our sources, yes."

"Together? Equal partners?"

"It would appear so. Also note the rank disparity between a knight and a commoner."

He didn't have time for this. Even so: "What's a knight doing fooling around with cabbages and stuff? He should be out slaying dragons."

"My thoughts precisely," Areweth said. "Hence the need to draw it to your attention. Also, a human lawyer working for an old-established mumble law firm is investigating your origins, with particular reference to the ground plans of this facility."

"Dear God." He frowned, then asked, "An old-established *what* law firm?"

"Elven," Areweth said, loud and clear. "Regrettably I have to say, the partners in the firm are of the Elder Race. The lawyer in question is, however, entirely human."

"And what was that about a coup?"

"So far, only at the disgruntled muttering in taverns stage. However, any form of treasonable activity is so rare that I felt it necessary—"

"Yes, quite." He turned his back and looked at her. "Bloody hell. I'm away for two minutes—"

"You have in fact been absent for several days."

"—And the whole place goes to hell in a handcart. Don't any of you people know the meaning of the word initiative?"

"Initiative," she repeated. "A term used in human politics to denote a brief burst of undirected activity designed to give the illusion of decisive and substantive action. Would you like us to do that? I'm sure it can be arranged."

Elves, he thought. "No," he said. "I want you to get off your bony arse and deal with it. Find this knight and feed him to something. Same goes for the lawyer."

"Understood. And Prince Florizel?"

"Get rid of him. Replace— No, hang on." Gordon frowned. "What did you say he's supposed to have been doing?"

"Obscene things with food," Areweth replied. "Also, his ability to talk to unicorns has given rise to a certain amount of ribald humour, but that's not the primary—"

"Unicorns. He's been talking to unicorns."

"Allegedly."

"And the unspeakable food thing." Gordon was talking to himself. "That means with holes in the middle."

"Apparently he burned down the palace kitchen trying to cook something disgusting. Given the nature of human cuisine, I'd have said that was par for the course, but—"

"Get me his file," Gordon snapped. "Meanwhile, don't do anything about him until I say so, understood?"

"Perfectly. There's no need to—"

"And get on with those other two, the knight and the lawyer. I want them jumped on hard, but don't be obvious about it."

"Of course."

She clip-clopped away, and Gordon stumped up the stairs of the North Tower to his office. Prince Florizel, he thought; talking to unicorns and trying to make a doughnut. Well, at least the idiot hadn't made himself hard to find.

He remembered something about a letter, and found it on his desk. Easy to tell which one was from King Mordak. Other species made their parchment from sheepskin. Among goblins, however, the saying about reading someone like a book is distressingly non-metaphorical.

King Mordak to the wizard; greetings.
Please accept this letter as formal notice of revocation of the contract between us regarding the supply of shining

yellow stones. The United Goblin Federation has ceased mining operations and will henceforth be exploring new opportunities in other sectors. Hoping this finds you well.
M. R.

Gordon stared at the letter for a minute and a half, his mouth moving soundlessly. Then he grabbed the little silver bell and shook it ferociously until the clapper flew out and bounced off the wall. An Elf appeared, looking smug.

"Get me the goblin ambassador," Gordon yelled. "Right now."

The Elf cleared his throat. "The goblins have closed their embassy and withdrawn their diplomatic staff. If you look in your in-tray, you'll find a full report—"

"Go away."

"With pleasure."

Gordon sank back in his chair and caught his breath. No wonder Drain wanted to see him, now that he reckoned he had a monopoly of supply. Over my, no, let's be sensible, over *his* dead body. But Mordak, suddenly quitting the mining business; what the hell was all that about? Why was everything suddenly falling to pieces all around him? What could possibly . . . ?

One thing about having a nephew like Benny; if something goes wrong, you never have to stop and wonder who's to blame. What exactly Benny had done this time he wasn't yet sure; that he'd done it, there could be no doubt.He picked up the silver bell and shook it, then remembered that it wasn't working any more. One damn thing after another.

"Elf!" he yelled, and, sure enough, an Elf appeared. "Was there something?"

"Get me Prince Florizel."

The Elf frowned. "By *get*," he said, "do you mean invite him to make an appointment to call on you, demand his attendance or abduct him by force?"

"Yes," Gordon said. "Quickly."

The Elf said nothing. Elves saying nothing are the most eloquent entities in the Multiverse. When he'd gone, Gordon threw a stapler at the door he'd just closed, but it just wasn't the same.

25

Here be dragons. Well, yes, Benny thought, rolling up the map and reaching for another. Tell me something I don't know.

The next one was hardly more helpful. Apart from *here be dragons*, it was depressingly short on useful information: place names, geographical features, that sort of thing. The artwork was superb, needless to say. The margins were richly decorated with gorgeously gilded and illuminated drawings of weird and wonderful creatures (drawn, Benny was quite sure, from the life), and the mountains were little mountains rather than brown fried-egg shapes, and the forests were thousands of beautifully drawn little trees, no two the same, and such settlements as were shown consisted of a dozen or so dear little houses, with proper roofs and tiny wisps of smoke coming out of the chimneys – GPS, Benny remembered with a pang of unbearable nostalgia, what I wouldn't give right now for a functional satnav. Or, come to that, my phone.

The royal map room was famous throughout the known world for the size and quality of its collection. In practice, that meant it had nine maps, two of them almost but not quite identical, all of them exquisite, all of them *useless*.

Number six, for example, had the mountains of Nawn sweeping down to the sea, whereas number five had them in the middle of the Very Big Desert – you could just make them out, if you were paying close attention – peeping out from under the tail of a particularly fine dragon. None of them had a scale, let alone a gazetteer; if you didn't know where the place you were looking for was, there was no point trying to look for it, which Benny couldn't help but feel was missing the point; unless these maps were like the aerial photographs of their houses that people buy to hang on the wall, to remind themselves *You Are Here* in moments of existential doubt. Of the Cradle of All Goblins, there was no trace. Well, duh. He wanted to find out where something was and he'd tried looking on a *map*. How dumb is that?

Lateral thinking, he told himself. In a society where the last place you'd look for geographical information is a map, where *would* you look?

Five minutes later, he found what he'd been looking for: a street urchin, standard issue, wearing a too-big hand-me-down jacket and ragged trousers, munching an apple he'd just stolen from a market stall. Perfect.

"Excuse me," Benny said. The boy didn't seem to have heard him. Well, of course not. You don't hear polite if you're a street urchin. "Hey, you."

The half-eaten apple vanished up the boy's sleeve so fast it looked as though it had been teleported away. "Guvnor."

"Here's a shilling." Benny held it up so the light would glint off it. Obligingly, it glinted. "Yours if you take a letter to the Cradle of All Goblins."

The boy hesitated. Not a good sign.

"You know where that is," Benny said.

"Course I do. But me mam says—"

Benny smiled. "You don't look to me like the sort of boy who does what his mother tells him to."

236 • TOM HOLT

"Course I ain't. But—" The boy looked genuinely scared. "There's *goblins* there, see? They eat you."

Fair point, and one that had crossed Benny's mind once or twice since he'd parted from the unicorn. But what choice did he have? "Tell you what," he said. "You show me how to get there, and you can have the shilling. How's that?"

"Deal," the boy said quickly. "All right. From here, you go straight up Main Street far as the watering trough, take a left, down Cow Street till you're outta town, follow your nose till you're at the crossroads, take a right, follow the course of the road, next crossroads left, two miles, next crossroads right then sharp left, follow the road and take the second left then the second right, keeping the river to your left and bearing south-south-west until you reach the third derelict cottage on the right—"

Benny produced a scrap of parchment and a stick of charcoal. "Why don't you," he said, "draw me a map?"

Piece of cake, Benny said to himself, as the boy ran off. That was getting there taken care of. That just left the problems connected to being there, which were harder to shrug off. By now he'd got used to wandering around the place with a stupid great big sword dangling from his belt; he hardly ever tripped over it any more, and when he wasn't wearing it he felt strangely lopsided, as though one leg was slightly shorter than the other. But he hadn't ever drawn it, in case it was sharp and cut his fingers. *You'll be fine,* the boy had told him, *you gotta sword.* Yes, but having something and being able to use it are two very different things, as witness the very fine Fender Blacktop Jaguar currently sitting unplayed in his wardrobe at home.

Home, he thought, oh God. He tried to picture it, and realised that, slowly but surely, he was starting not to believe in Home, just as not believing in Santa Claus comes on you slowly, over time, without you really noticing. Could there really be such an improbable place as his bedroom, with its battery of home electronics, its comfortable bed, its familiar piles of discarded clothes and unwashed plates? He'd been certain of it once, just as he'd been certain of Elves and talking animals and schools of wizardry, but you can't go on just *believing* for ever; belief is a garment to clothe the soul, and it doesn't take much spiritual growth before the cuffs are up around your elbows. Did I really live there, he asked himself, once upon a time, or was it just my imagination? And can it really still be there, somewhere over the doughnut? Bless him, he still believes in reality, that's so *sweet*.

Meanwhile, there were very real goblins in his immediate future, and all he had to defend himself with was a stupid *sword*. According to the Captain of the Guard, its name was Tyrving, and it had been forged in dragonfire from meteorite iron by Weyland the Smith and tempered in the blood of his mortal enemy; thirty-seven properly accredited heroes had wielded it over the centuries, and the ruby set into its hilt had once been the eye of Mogroth. And, Benny knew for sure, if he tried to open so much as a tin of baked beans with it, he'd cut himself to the bone.

Well, he told himself, if I see a goblin I'll just have to hide behind something till it goes away. He studied the map carefully, folded it and put it away. Then, feeling even more helpless than usual, he turned to face east and started to walk.

Mercifully, the roads were deserted, and he didn't see a living soul until eventually he stood in the shadow of the Great Mountain, gateway to the goblin-mines. The road led right up to a cliff-face, and stopped dead. He gazed at the blank, featureless rock and thought, *Oh come on*.

There was a soft creaking noise. A fine line appeared in the stone and quickly thickened out into the outline of a vertically aligned rectangle, about five feet high. The sun was setting behind him, and the last red rays fell on a series of grooves cut into the rock, which proved to be letters, which read *Please Use Other Door*. Thank you so fucking much.

It was nearly dark when he stumbled across the gateway. Flanked with really quite revolting twice-life-size carvings of goblin warriors, it framed two massive bronze gates, weathered to a soothing green. Just for kicks Benny gave the left-hand gate a gentle shove, and it swung open until it hit something and clanged dully. Oh well, Benny thought, and walked in.

He hadn't got a torch, of course; not even one of those sticks with pitch-soaked hemp tied round the top, that light up better than halogen and last for practically ever— But it didn't matter, because someone had thoughtfully cut long, narrow shafts diagonally through the side of the mountain just to illuminate this corridor, and the last dregs of sunlight bathed the tunnel in a rosy-red blaze. About two hundred yards down the tunnel was a left-hand turn, and after that there was no more red light; instead, he found he could see perfectly well by the soft golden glow of fist-sized chunks of rock, set in alcoves in the walls about twelve feet up. He remembered that the goblins and the dwarves mined shining rocks, and was impressed; at last, he'd found something that people did in this awful place that was actually *useful*.

He walked on about half a mile down the same dead straight tunnel. The air was slightly damp and musty, but apart from that it was fine, and the only sound was the faint echo of his feet on the polished stone slabs. This is way, way too easy, he thought, and where are all the goblins?

Where indeed? He reached a crossroads and had to stop for a moment, blinded by the glare coming from the side galleries. There he saw wagons piled high with shining rock, with pickaxes, crowbars, hammers and shovels stacked neatly next to them; as if the day shift had clocked off and the night shift hadn't yet taken their place. From what little he knew of goblins, that didn't seem likely. A few small bones on the ground suggested that someone had waited here for a short while, enjoying a well-earned snack. There was no dust to speak of, on the floor or the wagon rails. Weird, Benny thought, but I'm not complaining.

It occurred to him that he hadn't the faintest idea where his phone was likely to be. For some reason he hadn't expected it would be an issue; getting there, yes; not being eaten, most definitely. But locating something small in a huge network of tunnels— He realised, with shame, that he'd started to think like a hero – because heroes don't spend their time and earn their everlasting glory *looking for things*. They expect all that sort of stuff to have been taken care of before they arrive.

Then he thought; yes, but heroism is predictable. It obeys certain laws, like any sequence of events involving objects in motion. One such law is that the task is tailored to the hero. It has to be, so that only so-and-so, by virtue of some unique attribute or ability, can perform it. Now, here's me, down this tunnel; I think it's safe to assume that hero rules are in effect. I've been brought here to perform a task, which *only I can achieve*. Because—

He smiled. Put like that, it was simple. The task wasn't abseiling or dragon-slaying or orc-slaughtering, which any damn fool in these parts could do standing on his head. The task is *looking for something*, in a sensible, methodical fashion; something that no glorious muscle-head hero would have the patience for. But something at which Benny Gulbenkian, inveterate loser of things and proprietor of one of the five untidiest bedrooms in Europe, had a lifetime of hard-won experience. Put a knight or a warrior down here and tell him to look for something, small, grey plastic, about yay long and wide; ten minutes later, he'd be bashing the walls with his balled fists out of sheer frustration. Whereas Benny Gulbenkian would be going through the procedures he'd spent a substantial part of his life perfecting – no, not under the bed, maybe it's in the wardrobe; no, not in there, maybe it's in my coat pocket, and so on, for hours if needs be, until he'd found it.

The thought hit him like a golden arrow. Maybe I am a hero, after all. Maybe *that's* why I'm here. Maybe the YouSpace device is programmed to take you to the one and only reality in the Multiverse where you really can be what you yearn to be, deep in your unconscious soul. In my case; a magic realm where you can be Theseus and Siegfried and Frodo and all that, just by virtue of having spent your life making your immediate environment into a pig-heap.

Wow.

Filled with hope and something not entirely unlike joy, he quickened his pace and bustled on down the tunnel. How far he went he had no idea, but he stopped three times to explore side tunnels that proved to be dead ends, terminating in chipped and rough-hewn rock faces. He felt no trace of weariness, because heroes don't; and when he scuffed his knuckles on a sharp flint and drew blood, he never felt a thing. Instead, he hurried on, his keen eye scanning every inch of the way for possible nooks and crevices where a phone might lurk, until suddenly he came to a closed door, dead ahead of him.

Closed doors, he told himself, yeah right, we know exactly what to do about closed doors. We *open* them, no shit. He gave the door a sharp biff with the heel of his hand, and it swung open noiselessly on well-oiled hinges. Take that, door, and let it be a lesson to you. He grinned and walked through.

He found himself in the corner of a huge room, white, with a high ceiling and brilliantly lit, so that his eyes, accustomed to the discreet glow of the yellow stones, blanked out and began to hurt. He closed them for a moment, and got a private firework display that took several seconds to die down. When he opened them again, he found he was looking down at someone.

"Can I help you?" she said.

The ears were pure Elf, but the smile couldn't have been more different; also, Elves tended to be tall and thin, not short and enticingly curved, though, all things considered, the green smock thing wasn't her best friend ever. Over the top of her head he could see hundreds, maybe even thousands, more like her; they were sitting at long workbenches, busy at a variety of intricate-looking tasks. Jolly music of the sort that Benny associated with shops in winter played over some sort of unseen PA system. It was almost like being home.

"Um, yes," he said. "You haven't seen a phone, have you?"

The elf-girl grinned at him. "Often," she said.

"Um, this particular phone. It's a LoganBerry XPXX3000—"

"Ooh, nice."

"Dark grey casing, with this and that and the other."

"Cool."

"It's mine," Benny said. "I dropped it."

She gave him such a sad smile. "Sorry," she said, "haven't seen one of those. Give me your number, and if it turns up, we'll call you."

"That's the point, I *haven't got a phone* – Sorry," he added, "I really didn't mean to shout, I've been having a bad day."

She nodded. "I hate those. Email address?"

"Just a minute." He looked deep into her silver-grey eyes. "You know about technology and stuff."

She laughed; silver bells and tinkling waterfalls. "Of course we do, silly. It's our business."

His heart stopped still. "Really?"

She half turned and pointed at the benches. "Precision electronic engineering," she said. "It's what we do."

A little light came on in his head. Elves, but small and friendly. The music. The green smocks. Consumer electronics. "I know who you are," he said. "You're Santa's little—"

"Please," she said, and the pure silver of her eyes clouded just a little, but then she forgave him. "That's a common misconception. We are, in fact, independent contractors, and for many years we did work almost exclusively for a client commonly associated with lists and reindeer."

"But not any more?"

She shook her head. "Dreadfully sorry about your phone," she said. "If it turns up, I'll have them put it somewhere safe. Goodbye."

Suddenly he wasn't quite so welcome. Never mind. "Fine," he said, "and thank you, that'd be really kind. Meanwhile—"

Her eyes were getting colder by the second. "Yes?"

"I was just wondering," he said. "You know, kids nowadays, you must've made *zillions* of phones and laptops and tablets and things, you know, for the SC person."

"We might have done."

"Great. Um, you wouldn't happen to have one left over I could buy off you, by any chance? Expense no object. I have gold."

She shook her head. "Terribly sorry," she said, in a voice that suggested she wasn't sorry at all. "But under the terms of our agreement with our new exclusive client, we aren't allowed to sell anything to anybody else. Have a nice day, now. That's the door, over there."

"New client?"

Her eyes narrowed. "You're the press, aren't you? A journalist."

"Me? Good God, no. Promise. Cross my heart. Look, this client. He's got technology?"

"Oh yes."

"Phones?"

"Undoubtedly." She hesitated, and a hint of her earlier tone crept back into her voice. "But that's not what we're making now."

"You don't suppose your client would sell me a phone?"

She laughed, but this time it wasn't silver bells. "I don't think so, no. Not unless you're a major government."

"Allow me to introduce myself," Benny said. "I'm Prince Florizel. Around here, they don't come much majorer than me."

"Um." Her eyes narrowed. "That might be different. I'd have to ask the wizard, of course. But—"

"The wizard. That's who you work for."

"Of course, who else? But I happen to know he's looking to expand his activities in this sector, so I can ask him, if you're interested. Of course, there's minimum-order requirements, end user certificates, that sort of thing. Still, there's ways round everything."

"Hold on," Benny said. "End user certificates. Isn't that just for—?"

"Well, yes. We're making guidance systems for long-range intercontinental ballistic missiles." She smiled confidingly. "It's a bit of a step up from Xboxes and PlayStations, but that's the direction the industry's going in, so we reckoned we'd better keep up or get left behind. And when the wizard offered us such a good deal, which was so much better than what Mister Shave-Those-Margins-Ho-Ho-Ho used to pay us, we thought, heck, why not? After all, microcircuitry's microcircuitry, and who gives a damn what it's eventually used for?"

Benny was suddenly rather short of breath. "Just to clarify," he said. "You used to make toys for kiddies and now the wizard's got you making missile parts."

"Yes. So?"

"Well." He took a deep breath. "It's not very Christmassy, is it?"

She looked at him, and he knew that, yes, she was an elf all right. "So?"

He smiled. It came out all wrong. "Very sorry to have bothered you," he said. "I think I'd better go now."

She shook her head. "Security," she called out. "Get him."

Security were Elves, too, but with a distinct goblinish look. They stood maybe five feet in their iron-shod boots, but height isn't everything. They advanced. Benny took a long step backwards, and stopped. The wall was in the way. Oh, he thought. Then, feeling incredibly self-conscious, he drew his sword.

Later, he rationalised that they weren't to know he was the world's foremost fencing klutz, and maybe the sword Tyrving was as famous as the guard captain had told him it was. In any event, Security stopped dead in their tracks and stared longingly at him, like a dog on a lead watching a cat. He edged along the wall until he could feel the door handle in the small of his back. "Sorry," he said, then he turned the handle with his left hand, darted through the door and slammed it hard behind him.

Preoccupied as he was for the next three minutes with running down tunnels and being terrified, Benny neverthe-less found spare capacity in his brain for a fierce burn of indignation. Missile guidance systems, for crying out loud. Really, there's no call for that. Whoever this wizard was, evi-dently he was a nasty piece of work, and if only he could spare the time from doughnut-hunting he'd be inclined to send in the palace guard and have him arrested. And then he thought; really, so you'd pick a fight with someone with magical powers, who would appear to have access to the sort of technology you need to get home. Besides, missile guidance systems aren't all that bad. At least, if they're any good, they stop the bombs falling in the wrong place. Practically humanitarian.

A sharp stitch in his chest made him stop for breath; he listened, and could hear no pursuing footsteps. Jurisdictional issues, presumably, goblins and Elves not being known for working and playing well together. Talking of goblins; in his headlong flight, he'd noticed several more apparently abandoned ore carts and neat stacks of tools, but not a single goblin. Which was, of course, delightful, but he couldn't help wondering where they'd all got to. Another thing he hadn't seen was any sign of his phone, though he hadn't been searching quite as diligently as he'd have wished. So much for heroism.

His feet were sore from running, but he trudged on down the tunnel, gazing keenly into the shadows as if to make up for his earlier casual attitude, until he came to a three-way junction. His heart sank. Still, if he was right about why he was there at all, this was exactly the sort of challenge he ought to expect, a trial of diligence and perseverance. He called to mind the time he'd spent a whole day searching for a phone-jack adapter, when he could've gone online and ordered a replacement for the price of a slice of cheesecake. I can do this, he told himself, and took the left-hand fork.

Another long, arrow-straight tunnel, goblin-free and adequately lit. He walked down it for about three minutes, and came to a door. He tried it. Locked.

He turned away and was about to go back the way he'd come when he heard graunching noises, as of a key being turned in a rusty old lock. The door had opened a crack, and a nose was sticking out.

"Hello?" said the nose.

"Um," Benny said.

The door opened enough to reveal the nose's face. It was old, bald apart from a few wisps of white hair that really shouldn't have bothered, and decorated with a pair of spectacles with the thickest lenses Benny had ever seen. "Yes?"

"What?"

"Does he want something?"

"Excuse me?"

"Does he want something?"

Ah, Benny thought, one of those conversations. He was about to back away when a vestigial remnant of his inner hero nudged him sharply and said, *go on, ask him*. "Actually, yes," he said. "You wouldn't happen to have found a phone, would you?"

A blink, grotesquely magnified. "What's a foan?"

Shucks. "Small grey sort of box thing, about so long and so wide, glass on one side."

"Like a picture frame."

"I guess so, a bit. Why, have you found one?"

"No," said the bald man. "He'd better come inside."

Benny was about to point out that he was actually rather busy and in a hurry, but a stick-thin arm shot out and grabbed his wrist in a surprisingly strong grip, and he found himself being hauled through the door before he could resist. He heard a clang, and a repeat of the graunching noise. "This way," the bald man said, and vanished into the shadows.

"Um, excuse me," Benny called out, but all he could hear was footsteps pattering away into the distance. He examined the door; locked, and the key not in the keyhole. Damn, he thought, and plunged into pitch darkness.

He went quite some distance, with nothing but the ring of his own footsteps for company, until he collided with an invisible barrier. He groped for it and found it was another door, this time unlocked. He opened it and went through into the blinding glare of a single candle, stuck in the mouth of an empty beer bottle.

"Welcome," the bald man said.

He was sitting in a chair, the only one in the huge chamber. Behind him, on all four walls, were huge floor-to-ceiling highly polished brass plates, which amplified the candle's flicker into a blazing light show; and on the plates, so small he could barely read them, were hundreds of thousands of names. He squinted and read the closest ones. He recognised them at once—

Stardollars Coffee

Orinoco.com

Fleabay

Anglo-Latvian Petroleum plc

Booble inc

"Welcome," the bald man repeated, "to the registered office. We," he added, after a short pause, "are the Chairman. We can spare him two minutes."

"Um, thank you," Benny said. "But really, I ought to be—"

"Would he," the bald man said, leaning forward and peering at him so hard that Benny was afraid the glare through those lenses would set him on fire, "like a job?"

"Um."

"Of course he would," the Chairman said. "Well, let's see, we think we'll start him off as CEO of Booble Holdings inc. It's a nice straightforward job, nothing much to it."

"Excuse me," Benny said gently, "but I think you'll find Booble's already got one."

"Oh no." The Chairman shook his head. "Trust us, we know. We're the Chairman."

"Um, really," Benny said, backing away a pace or two. "I mean, they're the biggest dot-com company in the world,

I don't see how they'd manage without someone running things."

"Ah." The Chairman laughed, revealing four teeth. "He's thinking of Booble inc. We're talking about Booble *Holdings* inc. The shell company."

Benny wasn't quite sure why he was arguing the toss with a man who looked like the Before photo in an advert for resurrection. But he said, "That's the same thing, surely."

"Oh no." The Chairman shook his head, dislodging a carefully placed wisp of hair, which floated off and hung down over one ear. "Completely separate. Chinese walls. Got to be. Otherwise—" he stopped and looked carefully round. "Otherwise, *they* could get through, see?"

"No, not really."

"Got to be separate," the Chairman went on, rubbing his bony hands together. "All of them, all of our companies, all separate, all safe. Safe, in here, with us. This is the registered office."

Benny took a deep breath. "You're sure you haven't seen a phone? It's a LoganBerry XP—"

"*He* brought them all here," the Chairman went on, sucking the tips of three fingers. "For us to keep them safe, from *them*, safe, separate, all our beautiful companies. They're all ours, of course," he added, suddenly throwing his arms wide. "All our companies, safe, in here, separate, with us."

Benny looked at him. "It's a tax thing, isn't it?"

The Chairman let out a screech that went through Benny's head like an ice pick. "No," the Chairman yelled, scampering round and round in a tight circle, "mustn't say it, not the T word, *they'll* hear, it's not safe. He mustn't say the T word, not ever. Now then." The Chairman seemed about to go from hysterical to calm in a heartbeat. He straightened up and went back to his chair. "We think we'll also make him CEO of Orinoco Holdings and United Amalgamated

Tobacco (2013) inc. Too much for us to do on our own, see, not as young as we were, got to look after them, got to keep them *safe*. Can he start straight away? There's a handsome remuneration package, and benefits."

"Really," Benny said, "it's terribly kind of you, but I do have to get out of here and find my phone." He stopped. It was worth a try. "Benefits?"

"Oh, yes. Lovely benefits. He can have all the benefits he wants."

"Private jet? Penthouse suite?"

"Naturally. Nothing too good for the CEO of Orinoco Holdings."

"Expense account lunches?"

"Well, of course."

"With maybe a, um, doughnut to follow?"

The Chairman started to cackle wildly. "Of course," he screeched, "of course. All the doughnuts he can eat, of course he can. So long as he does as he's told. So long as he keeps them separate, keeps them *safe*, he can stuff his face all day long, bless him."

"Ah." Benny managed to find a smile from somewhere. "Actually, I could really do with a doughnut right now, if you've got one handy."

The Chairman turned his head sharply and gave him a grave stare. "Not *now*," he said. "He can't have his benefits *now*, what can he be thinking of? Only when *He* comes, when the wizard comes, to settle the accounts for the Great Reckoning. Then he can have his doughnuts, the horrible greedy creature, then he can have all his benefits, and *they* won't be able to touch them, they'll be *deductible*. When the wizard comes, he can have a *bonus*. But not till then."

"Ah. Well, in that case—"

The Chairman was running his fingers over the names inscribed in the great brass plates. "He can start immediately," he said. "And if he's thinking of escaping, he can't, because the door's locked and we've got the key. Must keep the door locked, or *they'll* get in."

Bugger, Benny thought. Really don't want to have to do this, but it doesn't look like I've got a choice. He put his hand to the hilt of his sword and said, "Look, it's not that I don't appreciate the offer and it's really nice of you, but I think I'll go now, so if you'd be very kind and just unlock the door—"

The Chairman looked at him, then looked away again. If he'd noticed the hand on the sword hilt, he gave no sign of it. Damn, Benny thought, and he drew the sword.

"I'm sorry," he said, "but I'm going to have to – *ow*, that *hurt*."

The Chairman had moved so fast, Benny hadn't really seen what he'd done; a punch, a kick, something of the sort. In any event, the sword was lying on the floor with the Chairman's foot firmly on the blade, and Benny's hand felt like he'd just caught it in a car door.

The Chairman's bright, horribly amplified eyes were staring at him. "So," the Chairman said, "he's one of *them*, after all. We should have known, he said the T word, of course he's one of *them*. So, what are we going to do with him? Can't let him go, he knows where to find us, it wouldn't be safe, it wouldn't be separate, no Chinese walls, nothing. Can't let him go and bring *them* here, not to the registered office. So what *will* we do with him? What indeed?"

The Chairman rose from his chair and started walking towards him. Benny backed away as far as he could go, which wasn't terribly far, and then said, "Just kidding."

The Chairman kept on coming. "What did he say?"

"Actually, it was a test. The wizard sent me. To test your security. To make sure you're keeping them safe. And separate, of course."

The Chairman stopped. "The wizard?"

Benny nodded. "The wizard," he replied. "My friend." He turned up his smile to maximum beam. "Be— Florizel, he said to me, I'd like you to trot along down to the registered office and make sure everything down there's safe and secure. And separate," he added quickly. "I mean, he said, I'm sure there's not a problem, I'd trust the Chairman with my life, but when it comes to keeping them safe, you can't be too careful. Well, can you?"

The Chairman peered up at him out of his bug-like eyes. "Prove it," he hissed. "He must prove it. Or we'll eat him."

"Um, there's a bit of a problem with that," Benny said frantically, "on account of, how am I supposed to prove what was said in a private conversation in a secure environment with absolutely nobody else present? Love to help, can't be done. Looks like you're just going to have to take my word for it."

The extraordinary hissing noise suggested that the Chairman didn't think much of that. "We'll know," he said, and started creeping forward again. "We'll know when we smell him, oh yes. We'll know if he's been with the wizard any time in the last month, we always know. And if he's been telling the truth we'll let him go, and if he hasn't, we'll gobble him up, maybe with artichoke hearts, baby new potatoes and a dry Chablis." He stopped; his nose was an inch from Benny's chin. Snff, snff, like one of those dogs at airports.

"Look," Benny said, "about the job offer. On mature reflection—"

"Ah." The Chairman smiled, and wiped his nose on the back of his hand. "We apologise. We are so sorry to have doubted him. We hope he will forgive us and let the wizard know that everything is in order here."

"Oh yes," Benny said, having a little trouble with his throat. "Really separate and safe. I'll be sure to tell him."

"How very kind."

"Please, don't mention it."

"We'll unlock the door now," the Chairman said, "and he can go back and tell the wizard, and maybe the wizard will be pleased and send us more companies to keep safe."

"You know, I'm almost certain he will."

"More and more companies," the Chairman purred. "To keep them safe from *them*. Until one day, who knows, all the little companies will be here, all the dear little companies, and we will watch over them and keep them separate, and the T word will have no dominion. One day," he said, moving his glasses to wipe away a tear. "Perhaps."

"Entirely possible," Benny said, stepping round him to retrieve the sword. "Now, if you could just get the key."

A moment later he was on the threshold. He stepped out into the cold, quiet tunnel, and the door started to close behind him. Then it stopped, and the Chairman's nose appeared once more.

"You know," he said, in a higher, marginally saner voice than before, "you remind me of him a little. You have the same ears. Goodbye."

The door slammed shut, and there was that graunching noise again, and Benny was alone in the tunnel. He looked back at the door for some considerable time, because it wasn't the first time he'd heard that last assertion; then he walked back up the way he'd come to the triple fork.

The pale amber beams of the Horrible Yellow Face slanted down through the high branches of the willow grove, blazing a lattice of golden light on the red and brown leaf mould. The glow reminded Mordak of the shining stones, which only yesterday had been the whole *raison d'être* of his people, and which he'd deliberately turned away from. He grunted, swung his billhook and took his doubts and fears out on a sapling.

Leading from the front is the goblin way, and there had been no question in his mind – they could do this. If a bunch of supercilious high-cheekboned ponces could do it, the Children of Groth could do it better, faster and with infinitely more style. You cut off a bit of twig, you split it and twist the strips into a basket. Piece of ear.

Unfortunately, it wasn't turning out quite the way he'd anticipated. The sapling was ridiculously springy; you hit it with the billhook and it sort of bounced out of the way, then bounced back and smacked you in the face. When eventually you'd managed to chomp your way through it, assuming the hook hadn't sprung off and cut deep into your ankle, when you came to split it, the result was usually shredded bark and splinters. So far, the Children of Groth had levelled two acres of coppice, and nothing to show for it apart from blisters, a couple of dozen severed digits that'd take *days* to grow back, and a certain amount of ill humour.

I will persevere, Mordak told himself through gritted teeth. I'll do this if it kills me.

Pause for thought and a surreptitious look round at his subjects. I'll do this, and one of them'll kill me, he amended; unless I can get the hang of it and show them, and I really need to do that quite soon, or else there's going to be—

"'Scuse me, sir."

He froze his slash in mid-swing and looked up, and saw the old human bodyguard, who was watching him with a look on his face. Mordak bared his fangs. "What?"

"Do please excuse the liberty, sir, and I really don't mean to criticise, but there's, um, there's an *even better* way of doing that, sir, if you'll just allow me to show you."

Another furtive survey; nobody was watching. "Be my guest," Mordak grunted, and handed him the billhook.

The old man smiled, took the hook and proceeded to harvest an armful of neatly severed saplings in the time it'd take Mordak to eat a pickled nose. "Sort of like that, sir," the old man said, straightening his back with a grimace. "More a sort of diagonal motion, if you follow me, and as close to the ground as you can make it. You try it, sir, see how you get on."

Amazing. Goblins have a proverb; the worst thing a king can say is, I never expected that. Mordak had never thought he'd see the day when he learned something useful from a human. True, forty-eight hours before he never thought he'd see the day when goblins made baskets, except for the purely decorative kind woven from the ribs of their enemies. "Yes, that's much better," Mordak said. "Um, thank you."

"'Scuse me, sir? Bit deaf in this ear."

"*Thank you.*"

The old man smiled, and Mordak got the distinct impression that he'd just passed some kind of test. "My pleasure, sir. Well, I'll leave you to it, don't want to get in the way of the good work." He paused for a moment, then said, "Again not wanting to sound cheeky and push myself forward where I'm not wanted, but purely out of interest, there's a slightly different way of doing the splitting, too."

"You don't say."

"Oh yes, sir, believe it or not. I could show you some time, maybe, when you can spare five minutes."

"It just so happens I have five minutes right now," Mordak said. "So, what've you got?"

Once the lesson was over and he was absolutely sure he'd learned it, Mordak spent an hour practising, to make perfect, after which his back ached like never before and his right arm felt as though he'd been holding up the cavern roof with it. Never mind. He took a long, satisfied look at the neat pile of willow strips he'd built up, then stomped across to the middle of the glade, climbed up onto a fallen tree and yelled "Listen up!"

The goblins stopped work and looked at him. He put on his most terrifying royal scowl, counted to five under his breath, puffed out his chest like a frog and addressed his people.

They were all, he told them, useless. A bunch of globs straight out of the spawning vat could do better; damn it, *dwarves* could do better, blindfold in the dark with clamshell gauntlets on. It made him sick to his stomachs to watch them. Well, he couldn't bear it any longer, so he'd better show them how to do it. First, you hold your billhook in your right hand like *this*—

Much later, when they were gathering up the split withies and loading them on carts, Mordak reflected on greatness. So far, five goblin kings had been accorded the honour of being called The Great; Mog, Uzak, Blung, Azmak and Groon. Mog had started the war with the dwarves, and his bleached skull still decorated the guest bathroom in Drain's winter palace at Hazad-Gloom. Uzak had slaughtered the Elves at the battle of Hoon, and all they'd ever found of him was one tattered sock. Blung had won a civil war; so, subsequently, had Azmak; Azmak's successor Groon had had their skulls made into a condiment set – Blung was salt, Azmak was pepper, and in due course Groon joined them as salad dressing. That sort of thing, in goblin eyes, constituted greatness. If anyone remembered the name Mordak in a hundred years' time, assuming there were any goblins left by then, it'd be as Mordak the Basket-Weaver, or Mordak the Big Girl's Blouse. And quite right, too, he reflected. The purpose of goblins is to fight, hurt people and die. Surviving, prospering, being happy; a simple case of the wrong tool for the wrong job, like trying to drive in a nail with a rose.

So, he thought, what *has* got into me?

They'd finished loading the carts, and now they were sitting round a roaring campfire of minced-up brash, roasting squirrel kebabs and passing round a big jug of malted milk. They seem happy, Mordak said to himself; and the voice inside him said, exactly, that's the point, goblins aren't *meant* to be happy, any more than the sky is meant to be green. A green sky or a happy goblin may have a certain superficial attractiveness, but they're both inherently wrong. Goblins can't function on contentment, it's lacking in certain essential vitamins absolutely required to sustain goblinity. A bit like celery; you can eat celery all day every day and still die of starvation. Goblins need *protein*.

Mordak frowned. Half a dozen of his personal guard were playing darts, each taking it in turn to be the dartboard. They were smiling and laughing, but there was no war. No war, and they were happy . . .

The old joke: I'd just taught my donkey to survive without food and it went and died on me. Well, Mordak thought. Sod it. I shall teach the Children of Groth to survive without protein, and let's see how far we get.

He heard a twig snap behind him. "Look at them," he said, without turning his head. "They seem to have got the hang of it."

"Yes, sir. All credit to you, sir, if I may say so. Quite a transformation, don't you think?"

Mordak grunted. "The Elves are always banging on about Change," he said. "Like it's a good thing. Not that they ever do anything about it, of course, but that's Elves for you. If they didn't have anything to whine about, they'd pine away and die." He shifted round a little and gave the old man a long, hard stare. "Me, I'm not a great fan of change. Why mess with something when it's been working pretty well for a thousand years? And even if it hasn't, you're just as likely to replace it with something worse, so why go asking for trouble?" He shook his head. "And now look at me. Mordak the bloody Innovator. Makes me wonder if someone's been putting something in the drinking water."

"You mean, apart from the main sewer outflowing into the rainwater tank?"

"We happen to like it that way," Mordak said coldly. "Really, I'm starting to wonder. All this." He waved a vague claw. "Why me, for Groth's sake? Why did it have to be *me*?"

The old man shrugged. "There's an old human saying, sir. Only Nixon could go to China."

"Who?"

"Doesn't matter, sir. Just a saying. I'll let you get on now, sir. Young Art will be wanting his dinner."

Mordak nodded, and the old man wandered away and soon vanished among the trees. Mordak sighed, opened a packet of candied fingers and started to chew. Only who could go to where? Bloody cryptic humans.

A loud shout, followed by a crash, made him spin round.

His guards, one of them with a dart sticking out of his forehead exactly between his second and third eye (double top to start, presumably), came hurrying up, axes at the ready. Another crash, then a dazzling flash of light, then a distinct howl of pain.

"Dwarves," someone growled, but Mordak told him to be quiet. Dwarves didn't make lightning flashes; that was someone else's trademark. Oh, Mordak thought. Oh well. "All right," he said to the guard captain, "take six men, find out what that's all about."

The captain didn't look happy at all. "Right away, Your Majesty," he said, and then, "Now then, you, you lot and you, with me." But suddenly there was no need for that. The old man and his nephew were walking up the track. The nephew held a hooded, muffled figure dangling by its collar in one hand, a bacon sandwich in the other. As they approached, Mordak could smell sulphur.

"All right, gentlemen," the old man was saying, "it's all over, nothing to see here, move along now, please, let the boy through. Excuse me, sir, but could you spare us a moment?"

Mordak dismissed the guard, and the nephew dumped his prisoner at Mordak's feet. The hood fell back, revealing a pair of pointy ears. "He's out cold, sir," the old man said, "sorry about that, young Art doesn't know his own strength sometimes. Be all right in a minute, I should think."

Mordak frowned at the stunned Elf, then looked at the old man. "Just now," he said. "There was a sort of bright—"

"That's right, sir. Magic, sir. Silly sod tried to blast us out of the way with fireballs. I'm afraid we don't take kindly to that sort of thing, do we, Art?" The young man shook his head and ate a cheese and onion slice. "So I'm afraid we were a bit sort of brusque with him, sir, so he won't be available for questioning for an hour or two. Still, we know who sent him, so that's all right."

Mordak looked at him. "Do we?"

"Oh, I think we do, sir. The wizard. Who else?"

Who else indeed. The old man had a solemn look on his face, incongruous as an undertaker in a nightclub. "Do you reckon it's war, then?" Mordak asked.

"I should think so, sir, yes. I don't think he's too happy about you giving the dwarves a monopoly on them yellow stones. Take you out of the picture, so to speak, and probably your people will go back down the mines. Sort of makes sense, sir, from where he's standing."

Mordak suddenly felt very cold. He'd faced death every day of his life, that's what being a goblin *is*, and he'd lived accordingly; only for the moment, but with a view to living for ever in the hearts and minds of brood as yet unspawned. Now, for some reason, it was different. The thought of dying, of not being here tomorrow to see what happened next, terrified him. Quite deliberately, he transmuted the fear into cold rage. Goblin alchemy.

"Do me a favour?" he said.

"Course, sir. What would you like me to do?"

"Take a message to King Drain," Mordak said. "After all, why the hell should we have all the fun? Tell him what just happened, and that if I go he'll be next. Make him understand that, you hear me? Tell him, if we're united, goblins and dwarves together, we can beat the wizard."

The old man raised an eyebrow. "You want me to lie to him, sir? Not that I got any problem with that, just checking I got your meaning right."

"It'd be a lie, would it?"

"Oh yes, sir. But that's all right. I'm a very good liar, though I say so myself as shouldn't. Not like young Art, sir. Couldn't tell a lie to save his life, bless him, just like his poor mother."

Mordak looked at the old man, but he couldn't make out

anything at all; just wrinkles, and a pair of very deep pale blue eyes. "Who the hell are you, anyway?" he said.

"I'm Art's uncle," the old man said, "and he's my nephew. I'll be getting along now, sir. Art'll look after you while I'm gone."

Mordak glanced at the stunned Elf, and nodded. "Right," he said. "So long as he doesn't mistake me for a cheese and onion slice, I'll be just fine."

"Not much chance of that, sir," the old man said, not unkindly. "Well, cheerio for now." He started to hobble away, then turned back. "Almost forgot, sir. When we done the Elf, this fell out of his pocket. You might find it useful."

He handed Mordak a small, flat, rectangular thing, smooth and black with a sheet of glass on one side, a bit like a picture frame. "What's that?" Mordak said.

"Magic stuff," the old man told him. "It's how the wizard talks to his henchmen. You press this here, see, and a light comes on. Oops, careful, sir, they don't work too good if you drop them. Then you press here and here, and a little list comes up, and then you choose an option and go like that, and you can talk to people a long way away. It does other stuff, too, but I wouldn't worry about that right now, sir, if you get my meaning."

It was resting on Mordak's palm, colourful and glowing like one of the yellow stones. Very slowly, keeping his hand dead level, he lowered it until the back of his hand was flat on the ground. Then, with a clawtip, he gently nudged it off his palm and quickly snatched his hand away. He was sure he could feel it tingling. "Keep that disgusting thing away from me," he growled, in a voice that brought goblins running from all over the glade. "Get rid of it, for crying out loud. It's —"

"Useful, sir," the old man said reproachfully. "But not to worry. Young Art'll look after it for you, he's used to them, spends all his time playing with the bloody things, sir, pardon my Elvish. You can even play chess on 'em, sir. Wonderful what they think of nowadays."

"Don't be stupid, how can that thing play chess, it hasn't got any arms." Mordak looked up, terrified. "It hasn't, has it?"

"Not in that price range, sir. Here, Art, look after this phone for the gentleman. And don't go using up all his battery, neither." The young man stuffed his sandwich in his mouth to free his hands, picked the box up carefully and put it away in an inside pocket. "Well, I'll be off. Look after His Majesty, Art. Be seeing you."

Maybe the word was finally starting to get around, because the wolf looked like it really, really didn't want to have to do this. But it was making an effort to smile, in spite of the way its teeth were chattering. It was enough to break your heart.

"Listen, wolf," Buttercup interrupted. "You don't know it, but this is your lucky day."

"All the better to see you with, my— what?"

With the sort of fluent efficiency, bordering on grace, that only comes with long practice, Buttercup reached out and twisted the wolf's ear round her hand. The other hand held the edge of the hatchet blade to its scrawny throat. "It just so happens," she said, "that I don't need any clocks or spoons, I'm all right for tea and I've just had lunch, so I don't want any cucumber sandwiches. Also, my friend's there behind that bush, having a pee, and he thinks girls disembowelling wolves is unfeminine. So, I'm going to count to three. One. Two. You're still here."

"You're holding my ear," the wolf pointed out.

"What? Oh, right." Buttercup looked into its eyes, and saw nothing but stupidity. "If I let you go," she said, "you're going to try and jump me, and then I'll have to kill you."

"Um."

"I could wait for my friend and get him to hit you over the head with a rock, but your skulls are so damn thin on top, I don't suppose he can get away with just stunning you." She thought for a moment. "There wouldn't be any rope in your cottage, would there?"

"Sorry."

"Oh damn. Look, could you *try* not to jump me, just this once? I won't tell anyone if you don't."

The wolf looked really sad. "Sorry," it said.

"Me, too." Buttercup braced herself for the long slice across the jugular vein, then hesitated. "Turquine," she called out.

Sir Turquine appeared from the bushes, adjusting his breeches. He took one look at the wolf and drew his sword. "Hang on, I'm—"

"It's all right," Buttercup said wearily, "everything's under control. Look, I want you to do something for me."

"Sure."

She looked back at the wolf. "Right," she said. "I'm only the poor defenceless little country girl, but that over there is the fortuitously arriving knight. With me so far?"

"Wrff."

"Splendid. Now, obviously, you've got to do your damnedest to eat up the little country girl, I understand that. In a way, I sort of respect you for it. But clearly, if the fortu- itously arriving knight has fortuitously arrived, you're no longer under any obligation to attack me, and you can run away and save your miserable skin. Agreed?"

The wolf narrowed its eyes in thought. "A knight."

"Most definitely."

"Not a woodcutter."

Hell, she thought. She'd so hoped it wouldn't pick up on that. "Think of him as a sort of honorary woodcutter."

"Hey," Turquine objected. "And besides, in actual fact I'm not a *practising* knight any more, I'm in retail groceries."

The confusion in the wolf's eyes would've touched a heart of stone. "He's a grocer?"

"With a sword. Big, sharp sword. He kills dragons with it."

"This is all wrong," the wolf protested. "It's not *fair*. Grocers aren't allowed."

Buttercup stopped grinding her teeth long enough to say, "Turquine, be a love and just chop down that sapling there, would you?"

"What, this one?"

"That's fine. *Now*," she went on, "you saw that, he cut wood. Therefore, he's a woodcutter. All right, in just a second I'm going to let go of your ear, and you're going to— Oh bugger."

"Never mind," Turquine said kindly, as she wiped blood out of her eye, "you did everything you could. I thought that woodcutting thing was really smart. Did you just think of that, or—?"

"Not now, Turquine," Buttercup said, as the dead body slumped into an untidy heap on the ground. Always so messy, legs in a tangle, head impossibly sideways. "Oh, damn and blast the stupid thing. What did it have to go and do that for?"

Turquine was frowning. "It wasn't your fault. Not the wolf's fault, either. It's the system."

"Oh, of course. Society is to blame. That's so very profound."

"You heard what it said," Turquine replied quietly. "It's not right, it said. I think I have to agree. Same with the dragons. Something is so not right around here."

Buttercup shrugged, wiped her hatchet on the grass and put it away in her basket, on top of Florizel's nasty talking box. "No argument from me on that score. Come on, we might as well check out the cottage. Well, it'd be a shame to let it go to waste."

They found the usual stuff inside the cottage: scatter cushions, a nice clock, a carved wood tea caddy and a rather fine bone-china tea service, the milk jug slightly chipped. Buttercup shovelled them into her basket, out of force of habit. There wasn't quite enough room, so she had to squash them down a bit to get the cover back on. "This is really strange," Turquine said, examining one of the chairs. "All this stuff. We never had anything as good as this back at the castle, and my dad's a baron. How can a *wolf*—?"

He froze. Buttercup's basket was playing music again. "Oh hell," he said.

Buttercup tumbled all the wolf-plunder out onto the floor. The slate thing was glowing, and the music was definitely coming out of it. "I must've woken it up somehow," Buttercup said.

"That does it." Turquine picked up Buttercup's hatchet. "I'm going to kill it, right now."

"No, don't." He lowered his arm. "I'm going to talk to it."

"Are you sure that's—?"

"No," Buttercup said, "but what the hell." She picked it up, held it at arm's length and said, "Hello?"

It carried on playing music. "It can't hear you," Turquine said.

"I think you have to squeeze it in a special place."

"Ick."

The glass plate, she observed, was decorated with bizarre symbols. She prodded one at random with her fingernail. "Hello? *Hello.*"

"Hello?"

She dropped the slate, but managed to catch it before it hit the ground. "Yes, hello. Are you the wizard?"

"Who is this?"

She looked at Turquine, then said, "If you're the wizard, we've got your talking shiny slate thing."

Pause. "Well, of course you have, otherwise we wouldn't be having this conversation. Is Sir Turquine there, by any chance?"

Buttercup stared at the slate, then turned and held it out. "It's for you."

"No way." Turquine shook his head ferociously. "For all I know, it'll suck my soul out through my nose. And anyway, how the hell does it know my—?"

"*Talk to it.*"

Turquine shrugged, then took the slate from her, pinching it warily between thumb and middle forefinger. "Yes," he said, "I'm Sir Turquine. What about it?"

"This is the wizard. Thank you for finding my magic box."

"Ah, so it *is*—"

"If you'd be kind enough to bring it to the front gate of Sair Carathorn, I'll give you fifty gold florins. Hello? Are you there?"

It was talking to Turquine's foot, because at the words *fifty gold florins* he'd dropped it and frozen stiff, like a mammoth in a glacier. Buttercup swept down, grabbed it and stuffed it back in his hand, then kicked him on the shin.

"Ah, right, yes," Turquine said. He seemed to be having trouble with his lower jaw. "Fifty florins, well, that's fair, I guess. See you soon."

"Splendid. Thank you."

"You're welcome. Um, what do I do now?"

"Just put the magic box in your pocket, it'll be fine. Goodbye."

Turquine shrugged and pocketed the slate. His mouth formed the words *fifty gold florins*, but no sound came out.

"Turquine."

Probably because 90 per cent of the women he'd met

over the last five years had been princesses he didn't want to marry, Turquine was no expert on female psychology, as he'd have been the first to admit. Interpreting the tone of Buttercup's voice, however, was hardly rocket science. "*Fifty gold—*"

"He doesn't mean it. It's a trap."

"Oh come on," Turquine pleaded. "We've got his box. He wants it back. He's got *loads* of money. Why the hell has it got to be a trap?"

"He's the wizard. And we're on our way to do him over. Or had you forgotten?"

Turquine made a faint whimpering noise. "All right," he said. "No problem. We'll punish him by making him pay us fifty gold florins if he wants his box back. How much more harsh do you want to be?"

"It's a trap," Buttercup said firmly. "Trust me. There are no fifty florins. And we aren't going to walk up to the gate of Sair Carathorn and ring the bell. Got that?"

Turquine winced, then nodded sadly. "You're right, of course," he said. "Too good to be true and all that sort of thing. Pity, though. Fifty gold florins, for crying out loud. Have you any idea how much cheese we could've bought for that?"

"Cheese?"

"For the stall. I was thinking. Vegetables are all right as far as they go, but cheese is where the real money is. I was in a tavern in Atramar the other day, one miserable little corner of stale cheese, a penny farthing. We could make out like *bandits*."

She couldn't resist. Before she knew what she was doing, she was in his arms. "Ouch," he said. "You're squashing the hilt of my dagger into my solar plexus."

"Turquine."

"Yes?"

"Stop *talking*."

Which he did, for nearly two minutes. It was probably the happiest moment in both of their lives so far, and it was a pity it had to be spoilt by a loud voice calling out, "Armed Elves, we have the cottage surrounded—"

"Damn," Buttercup said.

"—Throw out your weapons and come out with your hands on your heads. I repeat—"

Turquine wiped his mouth on his sleeve. "Elves?"

"Better go and see what they want."

"Bastards. Oh well." He unbuckled his sword belt and threw it through the window. "What could we have done to piss off the Elves?" he said.

"Well, we're grocers now. Maybe we misused an apostrophe."

They walked through the door together, and found themselves in the middle of a ring of black-clad pointy-eared bowmen, all aiming straight at them. If Buttercup had been on her own, she'd have ducked and let them shoot each other, but with Turquine along she didn't want to take the risk. "You," ordered an Elf. "Step away from the basket. I say again—"

"I heard you the first time." Buttercup put the basket down. "Who are you? That's not Elf Service uniform, you're not policemen. You can't just—"

But it turned out that they could, and they did. Buttercup and Turquine were cuffed, blindfolded and loaded into a windowless cart. When they were aboard and the doors had been bolted and padlocked shut, the cart and its escort moved off down the road, in the direction of Sair Carathorn.

If, as he'd hypothesised, heroism for Benny Gulbenkian consisted of patience and thoroughness in the face of dispiriting frustration, he'd overtaken Beowulf some time ago and was catching up fast on Robin Hood and Luke Skywalker. He had no idea how many miles of identical paved, surprisingly well-swept tunnel he'd walked down, how many side turnings and cul-de-sacs he'd explored, all to no result. His feet were hurting, he was starving hungry and he needed a pee, and the thought of Perseus and Captain Kirk choking on his dust was no longer quite enough to keep him motivated. The afterburn from the adrenalin rush he'd got from escaping from the Chairman was about all that was keeping him going, though he wasn't entirely sure that what he was feeling was that and not heartburn. All he needed was toothache, and his wretchedness loyalty card would be all filled up.

Toothache or goblins; but he still hadn't seen one, which was very strange. The deeper into the mountain he went, the more evidence he'd encountered that goblins had been here once, from half-gnawed bones on the floor to goblin graffiti on the walls (rather an anti-climax; mostly it was stuff like *Victory to King Mordak and the seven-year plan!* or

Productivity is the sinews of war, with just the occasional *Thrag was here*, and the pinnacle of goblin humour, *See other wall*). The neatly stacked pickaxes suggested they hadn't left in a hurry or a panic; they'd just gone. Maybe it was a goblin holiday; or maybe, more likely, they'd all gone off to fight the dwarves. In which case, they could be back at any moment, probably feeling jovial and boisterous. He shivered, and quickened his pace.

He turned a corner and entered a long, high-roofed gallery, in use until quite recently; the walls were bare rock, and here and there they sparkled with tiny knobs of the same shiny yellow stone that lit the tunnels. A worked-out seam, presumably. Benny didn't like the loud noise his feet made on the sheet-metal floor. He was trying to decide whether to spend a long time shuffling across it as quietly as possible, or march across it quick and noisy and get it over with, when he realised there was something breathing behind him.

Mental geometry, coupled with best-guess estimates of the time it'd take him to run the length of the gallery, compared and contrasted with the best time of a notional goblin warrior. The results of his calculations weren't encouraging, so he turned to face the breather.

"Oh," he said. "You again."

"Hello," the unicorn said. "You found it all right, then."

"Have I?"

"Oh yes." The unicorn nodded, setting its milk-white mane dancing in a revolting display of gratuitous prettiness. "This is Gallery One, more usually known as the Cradle of All Goblins. Just think, it was on this very spot, two thousand years ago, that the first Ecumenical Goblin Council met and voted that they were a species."

"Fancy," Benny said. "All right, then. Where is it?"

"Where's what? Oh, you mean—"

"Yes," Benny said. "You told me, if I went to this Cradle place, I'd find a doughnut."

"That's not what I actually said."

"Sure." Benny laughed scornfully. "Here it comes, you're going to weasel out of it, aren't you? Because there isn't a doughnut, is there?"

"No," said the unicorn.

"Ha! I should have known."

"No doughnut," the unicorn repeated. "Just a phone."

Instantly, it had Benny's full and undivided attention. "What? A real phone?"

"Mphm. Here, look. I'm resting my hoof on it."

And so it was. There was only a corner visible, but enough for Benny to identify it as a sixth-generation Kawaguchiya Integrated Circuits ZX5000 InTouch, quite possibly the coolest phone in the multiverse. It was glowing faintly, which meant it was fully charged and working, and if the unicorn shifted its weight just a tiny bit in the wrong direction it would go *crunch* and be completely useless. "That phone," Benny said.

"Yes."

"Look, would you mind awfully keeping *very, very still*, because—"

"Oh, don't worry about that," the unicorn said pleasantly. "I'm not going to tread on it and crush it *accidentally*. Anyway, where was I? Oh yes. I promised you, didn't I, that if you made your way to the Cradle of All Goblins, you'd find what you need to get out of here and go back to where you came from. And here we are, and here it is. Another prophesy fulfilled, on schedule and under budget."

"Did you just bring it here?"

"Well, yes. It didn't walk here on its own."

"So you had it all along."

"Yes."

"So you could've given it to me back in the forest."

"No," the unicorn said, "because back then you hadn't earned it. But now you have. And here it is, available for you to take and use. Except," it added quickly, "termsandconditionsapply."

Disappointment can be quite relaxing. "Of course they do," Benny said wearily. "All right, what's the deal?"

The unicorn swished its tail. "In order to gain possession of this phone—"

It paused. A cue. "Yes?" Benny obliged.

"This entirely functional KIC ZX5000 InTouch, capable of receiving a signal *anywhere*. Including here."

"Yes."

"And capable, therefore, of enabling you to Google a foolproof doughnut recipe that even you will be capable of following without loss of life or excessive damage to property—"

"*Yes?*"

"All you have to do," the unicorn said, "is take it. You indicate to me that you want it, I step back, you pick it up, it's yours. That's it. That's the deal."

Benny looked at the unicorn. "That's it."

"Absolutely. Everything I've just told you is true."

"Yeah, right. What about the devious little catch you've neglected to mention?"

"I have left out nothing of importance."

Benny blinked twice. "I say, move away from the phone, and then you move away and it's mine and it works?"

"That's right."

"So all I have to do to get it is want it?"

"Concisely, accurately and elegantly put," the unicorn said. "All you have to do is want it."

The unicorn's eyes were as deep as wells. "It's a trap," Benny said. "Isn't it?"

"Of course it's a *trap*, silly. But everything I've told you is true, and I haven't left anything out."

Benny sighed. "You'll have to excuse me," he said, "I'm being a bit thick today. If everything you've said is true et bloody cetera, how's it a trap?"

"Ah." The unicorn looked smug. "If you take the phone, you can never go home."

That feeling of stepping on a missing stair. "But you said it's working."

"Yes."

"And if I take it, I can Google doughnut recipes and make a doughnut and escape."

"Yes."

"Right back to where I came from, a fraction of a second after I left."

"Exactly so. I guarantee it. You can get on with your revision for your exams. What fun."

Benny craned his neck for a better view. Yes, beyond question a KIC ZX5000. He could just about remember a time (three days ago, from one perspective) when a KIC InTouch was the one thing he wanted most of all in the entire universe. Now it was a plastic box you could do something useful with, just a way of getting what he really wanted. And also, apparently, a trap. "I'm sorry," he said, "I still don't get it. Would it absolutely kill you to explain?"

"Of course not," the unicorn said brightly. "My apologies, I'd assumed you'd already figured it out, a smart boy like you. If you take this phone, you will escape from this world and never return. With me so far?"

"You bet."

"You may have noticed," the unicorn went on, "that there's quite a lot wrong with this world. Put crudely, it doesn't work."

"I'd sort of noticed."

"That's because it's been messed around with by an unscrupulous character from your own reality, the individual known over here as the wizard. Sooner or later, if things go on as they are, the wizard will control and exploit every living thing in this world, and it won't be a very happy place. In fact, it'll be utterly wretched."

Benny winced. "And how is that my fault exactly?"

"Not at all. Not your fault, not your problem. However, you are the only person in the multiverse – you know about multiverse theory? Oh good. You are the only person in the multiverse capable of stopping the wizard, setting these people free, undoing the harm the wizard's done and making it all happy-ever-after. Only you. But you don't have to."

"Um."

"You're perfectly at liberty to pick up this phone, find out how to make doughnuts, make one and leave this world for ever, go back to your old life and carry on exactly where you left off. Just say the word. You don't have to do that, even. Just nod. Ready? Or would you like me to count you down from three or something?"

Then Benny remembered something. "Just a minute," he said. "You're forgetting something. Back in the forest, there was all that stuff about three tasks."

"That's right."

"The great truth that was hidden, right the ancestral wrong, and throw the fire into the ring of power. Only when I've done all that—"

The unicorn gave him a sweet smile. "I think we may be at cross purposes here," it said. "The three tasks were if you wanted to go home. If you want to escape back where you came from, just take the phone. Now, are you ready? Three—"

Benny shook his head. "All right," he said, "hold on a second. If I go away, things will be very bad."

"For everyone here, yes. Not for you personally. You'll be just fine."

"Things will be very bad, for everyone."

"Everyone *here*, that's right, yes. But what do you care? You're not even from this reality. After all, back in the reality you came from, things aren't exactly super-wonderful. There's starvation, disease, your economy's stupendously buggered without even the excuse of supernatural intervention. You never seemed particularly concerned about any of that stuff when you were there, so it's not like you're one of those bleeding-heart types who can't sleep at night for thinking of the plight of the ring-tailed lemur."

Benny realised his fists were clenched. Silly. But human. "There was nothing I could do."

"Of course not," the unicorn said soothingly, "I forgot, sorry. That doesn't alter the point, though, does it? The bad stuff there wasn't your fault, and neither is the bad stuff here. So why not take the phone and depart in peace?" It lowered its voice into a soft whisper. "Nobody will ever know."

Benny took a deep breath. "Fine," he said. "Step away from the phone."

"Ah!" the unicorn's eyes gleamed, but it backed delicately away. And there was the ZX5000, glowing soft as the dawn, all the colours of the enhanced rainbow. Benny looked at it for about four seconds, rather a long time in context. Then he took a long stride forward, placed his heel on the phone and ground it into the iron plating of the floor, until he could feel its screen go *crunch*.

"Indeed," the unicorn said. "What is life without the occasional grand gesture? Well done."

"Don't you patronise me, you Disneyfied bloody mule." He stepped back, and there were little popping noises where he trod on tiny shards of broken glass. "That wasn't fair. Because it's *not* my fault, and I shouldn't have to sort out other people's messes. And what the hell do you mean, I couldn't have gone home?"

The unicorn suddenly went blank. "Sorry," it said, "this unit is not programmed to resolve fundamental metaphysical issues. Sayonara, Florizel. Have a great day."

Benny stooped to grab the wreckage of the phone, but, by the time he'd straightened up with his arm cocked to throw, the unicorn had vanished.

"**Y**ou've got it?" asked John the Lawyer breathlessly.

The Elf scowled at him, then made a slight beckoning gesture with her head. He followed her, out of the newsroom, down some stairs, out through a window onto a broad, tapering branch. John suddenly realised he was a hundred and twenty feet off the ground, standing on a tree branch, in the rain. "Well?" he said.

"It's all in here." The Elf tapped a brown manila envelope. "Everything you asked for. Though what you want with that stuff I really can't begin to guess. It's *disgusting*."

"Let me see."

The Elf gave him a shrivelling look. "We are the Elder Folk," she said. "Logically, therefore, it follows that we weren't born yesterday. You first." A strange pale light suddenly glowed in her harsh grey eyes. "Have *you* got it?"

A hundred and twenty feet up a tree is solitude enough for most purposes. On this occasion, however, John felt the need to look carefully all round, up and finally down (*oooh!*) before reaching into his pocket and bringing out a small iron box. "Of course."

"Let me—"

"Ah-ha," John rebuked her, lifting the box out of her

reach, "no grabbing. You have no idea how much aggravation it cost me, getting you this."

"So what?" The Elf edged an inch or two closer, and it occurred to him that humans aren't nearly as comfortable in trees as Elves are, and nobody would be in the least surprised if a human fell to his death off a slippery branch, in spite of a nearby Elf's valiant efforts to save him. Well, they might not believe the second part, but the inquest would accept the first bit without question. "Give it to me. *Now*."

"Just a moment," John squeaked. He held the box out at arm's length. Directly underneath the tree, he'd noticed, was a dense patch of brambles. Elves despise getting scratched. "Let's just both calm down a bit, shall we? You'll get your box when I get my file."

"Humans," snarled the Elf. "Can't wipe their arses without *melodrama*."

"Your box," John said. "My file. Give me the file and I'll give you the box. Simple as that."

The Elf gave him a look that would've liquefied nitrogen. "Here," she said, and held out the envelope. At the last moment, she snatched it clear of his closing fingers. "Box."

He looked at her. He didn't trust her one little bit. Just as well, then, that he was smart. "Here you go." He held out the box and she snatched it. "It's locked, of course."

She froze. "Bastard."

"I'm a lawyer," John replied. "Now give me the envelope."

He could see her doing calculations in her head; assessing probabilities, risk factors; a wooden box she could smash open with a stone, but an iron box takes specialist tools, appropriate to trades that Elves don't sully their hands with. She could try bashing it open with a *big* rock, but what would that do to the contents? *I'm smarter than you*, he thought, and the revelation filled him with a special kind of dark joy.

"Fine," the Elf spat, and thrust the envelope into his hands. "Now, *give me the key.*"

"Well obviously it's not *here*," John said sweetly. "I'd have to be really stupid to have it on me, so you could take it from my dead body after you've pushed me off this tree. It's down below, hidden under something. Now, let's have a look in here."

He opened the envelope and saw the crest of the Elf & Safety Executive. His heart leapt, and he nearly lost his balance. "Looks all right," he said, trying in vain to be casual. "Right, down you go. I'll meet you at the bottom."

Five minutes later, they both stood at the foot of the mighty *marshmellorn* tree that housed the offices of *Sneer!* magazine. By now she was literally trembling with rage; by contrast, oddly enough, John had never felt more serene in his life. He'd tucked the envelope deep down inside his shirt, under his woolly vest. Three Elves went past, on their way back from lunch. He was safe.

"*The key.*"

He smiled at her. "Actually, it's not locked. I was lying."

With a snarl like tearing cloth, she scrabbled at the lid of the box, found the catch, pressed it and flipped the lid open. Inside, she saw, nestling in red velvet, a single Cheerio. She gasped, and slammed the box shut.

"Well?" John asked.

"It'll do," she whispered. "Are there – any more?"

He grinned. "Yes," he said. "Five. But nothing on earth would induce me to get them for you." He edged away just a little. "Well, I think we're all done. I'd like to say what a pleasure it's been—"

Her eyes were filled with hate and yearning. "Please," she said. "Just one—"

"—But I'm not such a big liar as all that, so I'll just say *ciao* for now and thank you. Goodbye."

As soon as he was out of her sight he started to run, and he didn't stop until he was safely back at the mouth of the cave where he lived. There he paused, to make sure the leaf he'd wedged in the doorframe when he'd left home that morning was still there. Yes, it was; same leaf, too (he'd pricked six holes in it with a pin) He fished out his key, let himself in, lit the candle and triple-bolted the door. The room was too small to hide an intruder, but he checked anyway. Only then did he haul out the envelope and drop it on the table.

He didn't open it straight away. Instead, he kicked off his shoes and sprawled in the chair, suddenly realising how utterly drained and exhausted he was, and how much he disliked Elves. Other species terrified him – dwarves, goblins, trolls – but at least their horribleness was a secondary function, ancillary to their main purpose of staying alive and reproducing. For Elves, by contrast, being thoroughly unpleasant was their prime imperative. Survival of the snarkiest. Hell of a way to run a species.

Now, to business. He picked up the envelope, turned it over in his hands a couple of times. Opening it, he knew, was likely to prove to be one of those axes, or should that be fulcra, around which the world turns, or balances, or loses its balance and goes crashing down. It seemed ludicrous to him that it was in his power to delay such a moment, at whim; but he could. He could put the envelope down, go and fix himself a drink and a cheese and tomato sandwich – such arrogant power, he thought, of the kind ascribed to gods by people whose intensity of faith verges on blasphemy. Shouldn't be that way. History should turn on battles, riots, assassinations, peace treaties, coronations. It shouldn't wait patiently while a trivial, scruffy individual has lunch.

And it won't have to, John decided, because I'm going to open this envelope *now*, and the hell with the consequences.

Amend that, slightly; hooray for the consequences, because while the world crashes in ruins (see above) and all our pre-conceptions come plunging down around our ears, I shall be filing the biggest damages claim ever, and that's all I care about.

Pause. Is it?

John hesitated, peered right down into the very deepest recesses of his soul and decided that yes, it was. So that was all right. He stuck a finger behind the flap, flipped it out, and slid a sheaf of papers into his hand.

A report from the Elf & Safety Executive; sworn affidavits from the Elvenhome Genealogical Institute, the Academy of Science, the College of Heralds; copies of original manuscripts from the Central Intelligence Archive, certified and notarised; other certified copies of translations of diplomatic documents and records, some of them translated from Goblin and Dwarvish. He read them. Then he put them carefully on the table in a neat stack and sat back in his chair, paralysed.

Oh my God, he thought. Oh my *God.*

I was right, though.

And small comfort he found it. There's an infinity of difference between suspecting and knowing, something of the order of magnitude of the difference between sleep and death. He suddenly realised that, all along, he'd been expecting to be proved wrong. *What have I done?* he asked himself, but the question didn't need to be asked. He'd changed everything, was what he'd done. Well. It had seemed like a good idea at the time.

A thought struck him, and he jumped up. His table looked like it was just a few planks scrounged from broken-up pallets and nailed together, just the sort of thing you'd expect to find in a human dwelling in Elvenhome. But he knelt down and by feel alone located a couple of hidden catches; the table top came loose and he lifted it away to reveal a shallow rectangular recess, a good size and shape for storing documents. He put the papers back in the envelope, put the envelope in the slot and replaced the table top, pressing firmly until the catches clicked. In the country of the half-witted, the paranoid man is king, or, even better, still alive tomorrow.

As if on cue, the door flew open – the bolts held but the hinges didn't – and at least a dozen armed Elves, all in black, burst into the room. John froze. At least 70 per cent of his recurring nightmares featured a scene like this, proving that wishing upon a star isn't obligatory. They hauled him up out of his chair, searched and handcuffed him, and then the boss Elf said, "Where is it?"

"Ah." John said. "Presumably you mean you want the toilet. Out the way you came, on your left there's a little wooden shed—"

That got him a punch in the stomach. It's a very odd feeling, having your body completely drained of air.

"Funny human," said the boss Elf. "Where is it?"

You can't do smartass convincingly if you haven't got any breath. "Where's what?" John gasped.

Oddly enough, it didn't hurt quite so much the second time. "Where is it?" asked the Elf.

"I have no idea what you're talking about."

"Fine," the Elf snapped. "Search the place."

Which they did; and the methods they employed made the expression *search and destroy* into a tautology. The only thing they didn't smash into little bits, in fact, was the table.

"Oh come *on*," the Elf said wearily. "All right, if you insist. We're taking you in."

Three Elves grabbed him and John started to move, though his feet were still. "Just a second," he said. "Aren't you forgetting something?"

"I don't think so."

"What about, I have the right to remain silent—"

"Yes, that's true, you do. And if I were you I'd exercise it, all the way to the interrogation centre. Oh, while we're on the subject, you have the right to a lawyer." He grinned. "A *real* one, not just some uppity human. Right, move it out, we're on the clock here."

As his heels bumped across the floor, John suddenly realised what was wrong. The uniforms. No lapels on the jackets, and *suede shoes*.

"Hey," he yelled, as they dragged him through the door. "You aren't real policemen."

"Never said we were," replied the Elf, and hit him over the head.

30

Gordon was taking a call.

"Absolutely," he said, wedging the phone between his cheek and his collarbone so he could use his hands. "I guarantee it. Whatever you're paying right now for disposing of contaminated dental waste, I'll halve it. The same quality of service, fifty per cent less cost to you. Yes, I'm serious. Yes, that's right. Well, yes, there is what you might loosely call an extra-natural or transnatural element involved, but, I promise you, there'll be no impact at your end, honestly, you won't know the difference ... Well, yes, actually the Tooth Fairy, but I can assure you, there's no danger whatsoever of anyone ever finding out, and even if they did, who the hell would ever— Yes, we can issue a safe disposal certificate, we're fully registered and compliant ... Well, yes, he was, rather, but I bought him a bloody good lunch afterwards and he quickly came to see it my way, it's amazing how sensible people can be sometimes, when something's so obviously in everybody's interests. Yes, well, if the Romanians can beat my price, you go ahead and sign up with them, but I don't think that's going to happen, do you? I mean, fair play to them, but they're only human ... All right then, you have your people draft something and we'll take it from there. Yes, a pleasure doing business with you, too. Bye now."

He killed the call and leaned back in his chair. Bloody cheapskates, he thought. You give them fifty per cent off, and still they want to haggle. Tyre-kickers, the lot of them. Sometimes he wondered why he bothered.

A soft cough made him look up, and he saw a tall, gaunt Elf with a folder under her arm. "Nioreth," he said. "Talk to me."

"Latest figures from the dragonmeat plant," she said, handing him a sheet of parchment. "Production up six per cent."

He frowned. "Is that all?"

She shrugged. "We can't process it if the knights don't bring it in," she said.

"Well, quite." Honestly, unless you spoon-fed these people every minute of the day. "So what you do is, you get out there, you kick some steel-plated arse, you get those knights out of the taverns and into the woods, killing dragons. That's if you want to carry on working for me." He grinned at her. "You do, don't you?"

She didn't actually yawn. "Indeed," she said. "Very well, I'll see to it."

Oh dear. "No." he shook his head. "Don't *see to it*. Get out there and *do it yourself*, got that? I don't know, you people and delegation. You'd get someone to do your breathing for you if you could."

Actually, he mused, examining the figures in detail after she'd gone, six per cent wasn't bad, considering the volume they were already doing. But it wasn't enough. His keen commercial instincts told him that dragonmeat was going to get very big quite soon, especially since government laboratories didn't test for the DNA of entirely mythical creatures. It'd come, of course, nothing good lasts for ever. But until then, the sun was shining on the hay meadow and every-thing was good—

He remembered and frowned. Almost everything.

He sighed, and rang the bell. Another Elf.

"Get me Glubfangel."

Sorry, Glubfangel's at lunch. Well, that's good, it'll make him easy to find. *Go.*

Ten minutes later, Gordon's chief of security appeared in the doorway, looking decidedly put out. "You wanted to see me?"

Gordon nodded. "Why haven't you found Prince Florizel yet?"

Shrug. "Because we haven't found him."

"But you are looking?"

"Oh yes."

"No you bloody well aren't. Either you're proofreading your latest slim volume or you're at lunch. Here's some back-ground data for you, it might help. Prince Florizel is not a typographical error. Nor is he likely to be hiding under a sprig of rocket on a bed of wild bloody rice."

Absolutely no effect. Might as well try putting out the Sun by pissing on it. "My people are looking for him," the Elf said. "I am coordinating."

"Of course you are." Gordon sighed. The truly sad thing was, Glubfangel stood head and shoulders above all the other Elves of his generation for dedication, single-mindedness and tireless effort. "What about that lawyer and that rogue knight, Turquine?"

"Both in custody," Glubfangel replied. "And we expect to pick up King Mordak within the hour. I've sent a full tactical unit."

Alarm bells. "Now hold on a second." Gordon frowned. "I thought I told you, I don't want you sending a bunch of your precious bloody hothouse flowers to pick a fight with the goblins. I thought we agreed you'd use a specialist."

The Elf nodded. "We did. But that didn't work, so I *used my initiative* and committed two platoons of elite forces. As I said, I expect them to report in any minute now."

"Elite forces," Gordon repeated. Then the penny dropped. "Oh, you mean—"

"Yes."

Gordon's first instinct was to be angry. Dragons' teeth didn't grow on trees. Worse still, they grew on dragons, which meant they were expensive to procure and extremely limited in supply. On the other hand, there was a distinct element of two birds, one stone; before he launched what could prove to be his most profitable line yet on the real-world market, it made a lot of sense to ensure they were properly field-tested and debugged first. Instant mercenary soldiers, smart, ruthless and entirely expendable – sow and forget – could prove to be his iPod moment, but if the product was unreliable in some way, it could do a great deal of damage, possibly prove to be his Deepwater Horizon. Looked at from that perspective, trying out a few jawfuls against King Mordak's goblins wasn't a bad idea at all. "Fine," he said. "And I want a full report on how they perform."

"Thought you would," Glubfangel replied, not quite smirking. "Meanwhile, I'll double the search parties for Florizel. All right?"

Gordon sighed. "Fine," he said. "Carry on."

Glubfangel nodded, clicked his heels – "Please don't do that," Gordon said – and withdrew, leaving Gordon alone with the last person in the multiverse he wanted to have a conversation with at that particular moment. He picked up the latest cost efficiency analysis on the Orinoco shipping and distribution centre – as he'd thought, efficiency was up 9 per cent, ever since he'd broken them of the habit of floating customers' orders downstream, lashed together to form a rudimentary raft – but his mind couldn't get any traction. Instead, all he could think of was his sister's mild, annoying voice, bleating *You will look after Benny for me, won't you?*

Well, he'd done that. God only knew, he'd done that. Anyone else in his shoes would probably have buried the problem under a pile of money – sent the boy away to boarding school, then built some distant university a new library on condition that they kept him amused and entertained for the rest of his life. But that, to Gordon's mind, wasn't looking after, not in the sense his sister had intended it. In that context, *look after* was a dialect form of *love*, which was something quite other. And somehow, against all the odds, he'd done it, after a fashion, give or take a bit, close enough for jazz – he'd let the annoying, common-sense deficient, ludicrously over-tall waste of oxygen crawl in through the cat flap of his affection and curl up in front of the radiator of his priorities. Ever since then the argument had run; Benny is gormless – more than that, he's a black hole into which gorm falls and is utterly consumed – so he'll never be able to cope after I'm gone unless he's cushioned from reality by lots and lots and *lots* of money. Therefore, in order to fulfil my sacred obligations, I must go forth and make lots and lots and *lots* of money, by any means necessary.

So he'd done that; and now, when everything was going, if not swimmingly, then not actively drowningly, Benny goes and buggers it all up. Retrieving him and sending him back Realside would not, he trusted, pose an insurmountable problem. He had people for that, even if their ears were sharper than he'd have liked. Dealing with Benny on his return, by contrast, would almost certainly be an unmitigated pain. There'd be questions, objections, moral qualms, the whinings of his tender little conscience – sorry, but I'm a busy man, I haven't got *time* for all that. Yes, but if you're doing it all for Benny, shouldn't he have a say in how it's done, no matter how fatuous? In other words, what if Benny were to decide to hate him? That wouldn't be good at all.

Not for the first time, Gordon wished he'd been an only child. Too late, though, for that. The Elves would scoop Benny up and shoot him through the doughnut portal back to Orpington; and the joy of it was, thanks to the real-time discrepancy effect, he'd be able to stay this side long enough to sort out these tedious issues and resolve on a plan of action, no matter how long it took, and still be back on the other side a fraction of a second behind Benny.

Put like that, it wasn't such a daunting prospect after all, and he offered a few silent words of thanksgiving to the late professor Van Goyen, inventor of the YouSpace device, for loading it with such eminently practical features. Anybody else, he reckoned, would've made do with a stopwatch, FM radio and a camera, but Van Goyen had clearly been the sort of man who thinks things through. My sort of guy, Gordon thought. Maybe he'd had a nephew.

Meanwhile, some good, solid R & D to look forward to. Someone once said that the only bits of a dragon that are wasted are the wing sheaths, the flame and the squeal; that was what made it the ideal form of livestock for the small to medium producer. Let's see, he thought, an average of ninety-six teeth per jaw, two jaws per dragon, so if these figures aren't just a blip in the curve, we could be in serious production pretty soon, and then we can follow up the contacts we've already made and do some serious marketing. An image of himself giving the spiel to assorted generals and heads of state flashed across his mind, and he wondered: will they really go for it? Well, of course they would. That was what was so wonderful about this business. Strip away the more unorthodox aspects, and it all came down to money, like everything in this life. And when it came down to money, he was always going to win. Simple as that.

Then he thought; if Benny finds out about the soldiers, he's not going to like it.

Well, he thought, we'll cross that bridge when we come to it. He yawned. Even thinking about Benny made him feel tired.

His phone rang. He picked it up, heard a familiar voice, smiled. "Mr President," he said. "I was just thinking about you."

For ever, there had been only darkness, silence, emptiness and the dreams.

Ah, the dreams. Gushing torrents of fire; engulfing floods of water; the methodical destruction of torn flesh and crushed bone. To exist only in one's own dreams is bad enough. That they should also be nightmares—

The last dream was the darkest of them all. Fire, so much fire; then the objectively observed experience of death, and then the bewilderment of being torn out of context, suddenly and impossibly separate from the whole; dreams of being scooped and heaped up, confined in darkness, alone, inert—

And then the dreams had stopped, and there was nothing.

That was the worst time, and after it came the best of all things; a dazzling blaze of light, a single second of falling, the touch of the earth, the sudden terrifying joy of realisation; *this is not a dream—*

He opened his eyes.

A voice, somewhere close. "Platoon. Atten-*shun!*"

The first he knew about his arms and legs was when he moved them. The legs came together, the arms slammed down plumb-line-straight at the sides, the head – one of those, too – tilted back on the amazingly engineered spine, chests out, chins in, just what do you think you're supposed to be, you pathetic excuse for a soldier? Well, what are you? Pathetic excuse for a soldier, Sarn't Major, *sah*!

And then he thought: Ah. So *that's* what I am.

"Platoon. At – *ayse*!"

It was as though his feet had been prised apart, and his hands – *hands!* – clasped each other passionately behind his back. He thought; I'm a soldier, or at least a pathetic excuse for one. And you know what that means, don't you. I am a soldier, therefore I *am*.

"Platoon." He identified the speaker. A mammalian biped, with pink hands and face and shiny black feet, the rest of him sort of runny green and brown. God, presumably. "By the left, quick *march*!"

Why God felt it necessary to shout quite so much, he wasn't quite sure; but He did, and beyond question, He knew best, so that was fine. Meanwhile, there was the sheer ecstasy of walking (first one foot, then the other, isn't it really fortunate I have two of them, or this would be really difficult), followed by the sublime bliss of stopping, standing at attention, standing at ease, right wheel, left wheel, then more walking, then more stopping, oh brave new world. With each lungful of air, he seemed to absorb terabytes of new, exhilarating information, about himself, about the world, about being a soldier, *everything*. Within an hour (time; oh, don't get me started about *time*, isn't it just the greatest?) he found it almost impossible to remember what it had been like before, in the dreams, before, when he'd been—

Oh, *ick*!

—When he'd been a *tooth*, for crying out loud. (With the tip of his tongue he explored the insides of his mouth. *One of these days you'll have teeth of your own, and then you'll understand.* Well, quite.) If it hadn't been for the overriding need to maintain discipline in the ranks, he'd have laughed, for the sheer glorious triumph of evolution, of the ascent. *I teach you the Supertooth. Teeth are something to be overcome.*

Then they went into a sort of cave thing, where a lot of very kind people gave them things; clothes (green and brown runny, just like God's), a bottle for water and a handy penknife and boots for their feet (they didn't fit very well but never mind, the Lord giveth) and a steel bucket thing to keep their heads safe, and a thing called a rifle, the purpose of which was to be explained later, and then they were marched into another cave, where 90 per cent of their hair was cut off, and then back outside again for more marching and wheeling and standing at attention, doing God's work, trembling at His wrath and basking in His approval. He thought; this is *life*! Oh, wouldn't it be grand if it were to last for ever and ever.

Then God spoke to them and told them what their purpose was to be; and he listened carefully, and when the general idea had sunk in, he thought, oh well, can't have everything. But what the heck, it's still a million million times better than being a tooth; and if God wants me to go out there and get those goblins, that's good enough for me. As for this King Mordak, whoever he was – well, wouldn't want to be in his shoes.

God called them to attention one last time, and then they were off. The excitement, the anticipation, the sense of purpose were almost more than he could bear. He concentrated hard on making sure he kept in step – apparently God set great store by everybody moving their feet at the same time; he wasn't entirely sure what was so great about that, but it had to be vitally important, or why had God spent so long teaching them how to do it? The sound of his boots on the rock floor of the tunnel was so different from the sounds he'd heard in dreams. He could *feel* it, right up into his skull.

I don't ever want to be a tooth again, he thought.

Abruptly, the tunnel turned to the left, opening into a wide chamber, and in front of him he saw a great chasm, at least fifty yards across, spanned by an impossibly narrow stone bridge. On the exact middle of the bridge stood a man. He was tiny and very old; he wore a brown warehouse coat, he was holding something in his left hand, and on his head was a cap. Behind him, on the far side of the bridge, stood a tall young man eating a veal and ham pie.

"Sorry, lads," the old man said. "You cannot pass."

"Two ranks," roared God, and they lined up on the edge of the chasm. "Present *arms*!"

The old man looked very sad, but he stayed where he was. "Front rank kneel," God thundered. "Take aim."

He knew all about that, thanks to God. On the far end of the rifle was a little pointy bit that stuck up. You looked at it through a hole in a thing on the near end. Then you lined up the sticky-up bit with what you wanted to kill.

"Sorry," the old man repeated. "But you cannot pass. More than my job's worth if you do."

"Ten rounds rapid," yelled God; and the young man at the other end of the bridge ducked behind a rock and ate a Snickers bar. "*Fire!*"

The noise boomed and rattled off the walls and the high roof of the cavern, surged down into the abyss and came welling back up again. The echoes chased each other round for a while and died away. The old man was still there.

"Now then, lads," he said. "There's no call for that sort of thing."

God was staring at him, then back at the Dragon's Teeth, then back at the old man, as if He couldn't believe what He saw. He shook his head; then, with a roar that seemed to fill the whole cavern, He grabbed a rifle from one of the Teeth and charged out onto the bridge, yelling, "I'll get you, you horrible little—" The old man raised his hand, and God stopped dead. "What?" God bellowed.

"Sorry, sir, but that's far enough. Can't let you go any further, I'm afraid. Orders, see. I'm sure you understand, being a military man yourself. Thirty years in the service I was, you know, service corps, digging latrines, mostly. Sorry, sir."

God hesitated, His eyes fixed on the old man's upraised hand. It was agony to watch Him. It was as though an invisible hand of incredible power was pushing Him against an invisible wall. Eventually, with a great twist and wriggle of his shoulders, He drew his bayonet, fixed it to the muzzle of his rifle and took a great stride forward. The old man stayed exactly where he was, and did something with the small grey box in his right hand. There was a deafening boom; the bridge cracked and gave way precisely where God was standing, and fell away into the abyss. For a split second God seemed to hang in the air; then, with a great cry of *Oh shi*— he fell.

The Teeth watched Him fall in dead silence. If you stare long enough into the abyss, a wise man once said, sooner or later the abyss stares back into you. Maybe, just this once, it winked.

The old man was having trouble keeping his balance. He danced a couple of little steps one way, then wobbled, then danced back again, his arms flailing; he toppled backwards, lost his footing, lashed out with his arms and managed to hook one hand over the edge. "Art!" he shouted. "Run for it, Art!" And then he lost his grip, and was gone.

The young man emerged from behind his rock, walked slowly across the bridge to the point at which it had broken away, and stood for a long time, looking down. Then he ate a macaroon.

They took the bag off John the Lawyer's head, and he blinked.

Much to his surprise and disappointment (because he'd always taken pride in despising machismo and shallow heroics) he wasn't scared at all. He wanted to be, because he'd long ago figured out that fear is a beautifully designed, magnificently efficient function of the survival instinct; but he couldn't do it. An overriding curiosity overwhelmed him, as soon as he saw the short, wide man sitting in the chair in front of him. Imagine how Richard Dawkins will feel on the Day of Judgement, when he stands before God; something like that.

"You're the wizard," he said.

A businesslike nod of acknowledgement. "And you're the nosy bloody lawyer asking all the inconvenient questions."

To extend the analogy, think how Professor Dawkins will feel when an archangel steps forward and presents him with his Best Atheist award. "Thank you," John said. "And if you wouldn't mind having that carved on my tombstone, as far as I'm concerned that's quits and no hard feelings."

The wizard looked at him for a moment, then grinned.

"You're a smart boy," he said. "You don't belong in a dump like this, working for Elves. What if I were to tell you that somewhere, over the rainbow, there's a better place, where a man like you could really fulfil his true potential?"

Suddenly, John realised why he wasn't scared. Not an execution; an *interview*. "Where you come from, you mean."

The wizard nodded very slightly. "Go on."

"The place where you send all the things they get and make for you over here. The wooden planks, the dragon-meat. The shining rocks."

"Go on."

"The place," John continued – the water was getting shallow, but he knew he had to keep swimming – "on the other side of your magic portal, the one that looks like a doughnut."

The wizard shook his head. "*Is* a doughnut. Well?"

"Which," John said, "was rather a smart move. You inculcated into these people a superstition about food with holes in, so they'd avoid it like the plague. Even the thought of it makes them feel sick and panicky, apart from a few perverts, but there's always one or two, isn't there? Anyway, it means there's practically no chance of anybody going through your magic portal by accident, finding out about the other place and giving the game away."

The wizard looked like he was doing mental arithmetic. "You figured all that out for yourself."

"Yes. With a bit of help from the Elvenhome archives."

"Not really." The ghost of a smile. Of course, you only tend to get ghosts where something has died. "Oh, the Elves have all the data to figure it out, they've been sitting on it for thousands of years, but it'd never occur to them to *read* any of it. Records are for keeping, that's all. Dwarves and goblins are too stupid – well, maybe not this King Mordak, I get the impression he's nobody's fool, shame really, but in any event he's not the sort to go nosing about in dusty old files. And humans – well, I've worked damned hard to make the humans around here what they are today. Of course, I didn't expect anything like you."

John decided to risk it. "Thank you."

"You're welcome. I should think what tipped the balance was when the Elves gave you a job. It got you away from the peasants and the jolly woodcutters, put you somewhere where you had to use your head for something more than just a hat rest, and at the same time installed a chip on your shoulder the size of a medium mountain. Yes, put like that, I guess I should've predicted that someone like you was bound to happen, sooner or later." He stopped; something was bothering him. "What do you mean, a few perverts?"

"Sorry? Oh, right. Yes, but there aren't many of them. A couple of dozen, here and there."

"With doughnuts?"

"And bagels and sort of breakfast-cereal things. Obviously they keep very, very quiet about it."

"You know about them."

"I'm a lawyer," John said proudly. "It's my job to know that sort of stuff."

"I want names," the wizard snapped. "Names, addresses, everything."

John smiled. "No problem," he said. "Always delighted to cooperate with the authorities." He hesitated. The words *and in return* seemed to hang in the air between them, daring one of them to be the first to say them.

"And in return," the wizard said. "Well?"

"Let's see. First, you don't have me killed."

"And?"

"Oh, I don't know. Money? Or how about a job?"

The wizard smiled. "I thought the idea was to sue me for every penny I've got."

"Plan A, yes," John replied. "But that was before I knew you might be hiring. Also, it never occurred to me, I must confess, that I'd have a bargaining chip. I assumed you knew about the doughnut underground and the fried onion ring."

The wizard may have growled softly. "Well, there you go," he said. "You'd like to come and work for me, then?"

"Oh, I should say so. Sounds to me like this over-the-rainbow place of yours has got a lot to offer, if it's where you come from."

The wizard raised an eyebrow. "Flattery?"

"Always. But what I meant was, it sounds a bit less, well, *provincial* than here, if you follow me. I figure there's two sorts of places, ones which export raw materials and ones which import them. I wouldn't know anything about the latter, never having been to one, but I'm prepared to bet they're a lot more fun. For someone like me, at any rate."

"You have good instincts," the wizard said. "Yes, I know, you're a lawyer. But there's a lot of lawyers over here, and none of the rest of them have ever made difficulties for me."

"They're Elves."

"True." The wizard frowned thoughtfully. "So how am I supposed to know if I can trust you?"

John shrugged. "Do you seriously expect me to try and answer that question?"

"Correct answer. All right, I suppose I could use you."

"I gather that's what you're best at."

"Careful. Well, it's that or have your throat cut, and then what good would you be to anyone? When can you start?"

John thought for a moment. "Now," he said.

"Splendid. In that case, welcome to the team." The wizard opened a drawer of his desk, took out a hat, and threw it to

John, who caught it awkwardly in his left hand. It was a strange hat; its brim didn't go all the way round, but stuck out in front, like a tongue. The letter W was embroidered on the front in gold thread. "You can begin by doing a little job for me."

"That's nineteen," Buttercup said, "plus five for going no trumps on a triple star, plus fifteen for the eight of cups rebated, doubled for going out blind, and ten for the rubicon makes eighty-eight, which makes—" She paused to do the sums in her head. "Forty-six thousand nine hundred and fifteen to me and twenty-six to you. Play again?"

Turquine shrugged. "Why not?"

The spider, which had spent the last five hours trying to climb the opposite wall, gave up and went to sleep. Buttercup shuffled the pack. She'd found it in the last wolf's cottage but six and tucked it away in a deep pocket in her pinafore, where the Elf who searched her had neglected to find it. "Right," she said, having dealt nine cards each. "I call trumps, so we'll have swords, fives and eights are wild, threes reverse the order, sevens and twos mean miss a go, fours and nines reversed, tens count as fives. My lead."

Turquine examined his cards. "What did you say this game was called?"

"Easy-Peasy," Buttercup replied. "I used to play it a lot with my gran when I was a kid."

There were, she had to admit, worse places than the wizard's dungeons. They were dry, clean and sweeter smelling than any of the inns and taverns in the area, and the food was remarkably good if you liked dragon (Buttercup had decided she did, especially the dragon and onion pie with chives and coriander). On the other hand it was still a dungeon.

Turquine played the six of coins. "Hatstand!" Buttercup said, laying out her cards. "Sixes and fours over nines. So let's see, I make that twenty-seven, doubled because we're in Sagittarius—"

"I know," Turquine said. "Let's jump the guard."

"'Scuse me?"

"Let's lure the guard in here under false pretences, bash him silly and escape."

She smiled at him. It had taken long enough, heaven only knew, but no man worthy of the name can put up with being taken apart at cards by a girl indefinitely. "That's a good idea," she said. "How do you go about that, exactly?"

Actually, the guard was quite nice, for an Elf. He seemed genuinely concerned when Buttercup yelled out that Turquine was having some kind of seizure.

"I'm a medical student, as it happens," he said, peering in through the bars without getting quite close enough. "I'm just doing this to pay my tuition. What are the symptoms?"

"He's twitching a lot and making funny noises, and he's not breathing."

"You don't say." The guard squinted. "Hold on, I've got my textbooks in my bag upstairs. Twitching *and* not breathing, you say?"

"And he's gone very pale."

"Really? He looks quite normal to me."

"Pale compared with how he usually is."

"Ah, right. Won't be two shakes. Watch him carefully, if you wouldn't mind. This could be one for the journals."

"This isn't going to work," Turquine muttered from the floor. "He's an Elf. They don't give a damn."

"Ssh, he's coming back. Well?" she asked. "Any ideas?"

"Could be Flimbromel's Syndrome," the Elf said, turning a page. "Only then he'd be starting to go blue around the lips. Any sign of that?"

"I don't think so. But he's stopped twitching."

"Heavy sweat? Traces of foam dripping from the nostrils?"

"Not as such."

"Well, it can't be Ydrail's palsy then. Temperature?"

Buttercup laid a hand on Turquine's forehead. "Ooh, he's burning up."

"What? Oh *sod*, that rules out Elroon's Disease." He frowned. "You sure there's no foam? Just one or two flecks would be enough."

"Sorry, no foam. Oh look, he's started twitching again." She nudged Turquine savagely in the ribs, and he twitched a couple of times. "Is that good?"

"Not sure." The Elf was running his finger down a column of index entries. "Twitching *might* mean it's acraural dyslepsia, except humans don't get that. Otherwise, we're left with goblin fever, and if it was that he'd be dead by now. Unless he's been eating garlic recently."

"No, no garlic." She looked up at the Elf. "Maybe it's something that's not in your book."

"Unlikely, it's the ninth edition. Unless—" Suddenly his eyes lit up. "He's a knight, right?"

"Yes."

"Been in contact with dragons lately?"

"Yes."

"My God, it could be dragonpox. Twitching, high temperature, pale, not breathing. Hold on, pages 3,667 to 3,671. Ah, here we are. Dragonpox."

"That sounds bad."

"Couldn't be better, actually. Everyone says it's bound to come up in the exam this year. Here, would you mind moving away from the door a bit, I can't quite—"

Turquine's boot got him on the point of the chin, and he fell just right, with the keys on his belt in easy reach. "Bastard," Turquine said, lugging him into the cell and locking the door. "I could've been dying in there."

"Yes, but at least we got him before he could bill you. Come on, I think it's this way."

The greatest test of love, as everyone knows, is navigation. If you still love someone after you've debated itineraries with them – left here, no, right, I told you we should've gone left, oh look, we're going round in circles, no, *you've* got the map – it's a pretty good chance it's the real thing and for ever. On that score, Turquine was amazing, the best she'd ever got lost with. He just nodded and said "OK", and when they arrived at the same junction for the third time, he appeared not to have noticed. Can't help lovin' that man of mine, she thought. "Left," she said.

"OK." They went left. About forty yards down the tunnel, he asked, "Where is it we're heading for, exactly?"

"The wizard's secret lair, obviously."

"Ah, right. And you know where that is."

"In the heart of the mountain. Stands to reason."

"Ah."

In fact, the further they went, the less sure she became. The corridors and tunnels went on for ever, straight as arrows and beautifully tiled in white ceramic; clearly someone had been to a great deal of trouble and expense, so it stood to reason the tunnels went *somewhere*, but they didn't seem to be in any sort of a hurry to get there. The nice thing about them was that they were deserted – deserted *so far;* that could, of course, change at any time, and when it did, there were no nooks or corners to hide in, though ample scope for running, if you were any good at that sort of thing, which Turquine probably was but she wasn't.

"I said," Turquine repeated, "what about that door?"

"What door?"

"That one."

Oh, *that* one. She'd walked right past it and not seen it, which only went to show how preoccupied she was. "I don't know," she said. "I don't like it."

"Really? Wrong shape? Not keen on the colour?"

She gave him a look which conveyed far more information about her attitude to sarcasm than mere words ever could. "I think it's a trap."

"Oh, I see. A trapdoor."

"Funny man." She looked at the door. It was rectangular, about right for her height-wise but Turquine would have to duck; just a door. "See if it's locked."

It wasn't. "Well?" he asked.

"Oh, why not? I'm bored with all these tunnels."

Turquine pushed the door open and stepped back to let her go through; chivalry, caution or both. She really wished she had her basket, with the hatchet in it. Ah well, she thought, and went through.

"Well?"

"Come on," she called back, "don't be such a baby. It's just a store."

She was fairly confident about that. The room she'd entered was square, about the size of the village green back home, and filled with wooden crates. Mountains of them formed canyons and ravines, overhanging narrow defiles you could walk along. All the crates she could see had the same letters stencilled on them, underneath a simple but eye-catching little line drawing of a swan;

Dynamite.

Handle With Care.

They looked at each other. "What's a dynamite?" Turquine asked.

"No idea. Let's open a crate and find out."

Dynamite turned out to be nothing but a fancy name for candles, about a foot long, with rather too much wick. For some reason, they were all individually wrapped in brown paper.

"He must've got a discount for bulk," Buttercup said.

Turquine frowned. "What does he want all these candles for? Everywhere we've been so far's been lit with the glowing yellow rocks."

"Maybe for special occasions," Buttercup hazarded a guess. "Dinner parties, that sort of thing. Or maybe he bought them in to sell, I don't know. Anyway, they're no use to us."

"Oh, I don't know." Turquine grabbed a dozen and struck them down the front of his shirt. "Always sensible to have a candle or two, in case we go somewhere dark."

"Have you got a tinderbox?"

"No, the guards took it off me."

She sighed. "Well," she said, "maybe we'll find another store full of tinderboxes. Come on."

He followed her back out into the tunnel. "Why should you need to handle candles with care?" he asked. "They're pretty robust things, as a rule."

She stopped. "Turquine."

"Yes?"

"It's sweet that you think I know everything, but if you don't stop asking me questions all the time, I'm going to hit you. Is that clear?"

Yet another door. Benny yawned, pushed it open and walked through. Then he stopped.

"Hello, Uncle Gordon," he said.

Gordon looked up from his desk. "Oh," he said, "it's you."

"What are you doing here, Uncle?"

He doesn't know, Gordon realised. Even though I'm sitting here in a sky-blue robe covered in arcane sigils, he hasn't figured it out. "Looking for you," he said, "what do you think? Bloody hell, Benny, what do you think you're playing at? I've been so worried."

"Were you looking for me in that box file?"

Ah, Gordon thought. "I'm trying to figure out what's going on around here, aren't I? To see if you'd been kidnapped or something. But you're here now, so let's get the hell out of this place and go home."

He felt in his sleeve and produced a doughnut. Benny looked at it. "What's the matter," Gordon said. "Haven't you ever seen a doughnut before?"

"You're the wizard," Benny said.

Sod it, Gordon thought. I could deny it, of course, but he's not that stupid, and I'll just make myself look devious and weak. "That's me," he said. "And you're Prince Florizel. You idiot."

"You're the wizard," Benny repeated. "And you've been doing all those horrible things to these poor people."

"Benny, don't be such a *girl*." He hadn't meant to shout. The book he'd bought the day after his sister died had specifically said, on page five, *do not shout*, and its authors had been leading experts on child management, who'd been on TV and everything. There are times, however, when only a full-throated roar will get the job done. "Look, I'm not going to sit here discussing value ethics with you when I've got a business to run and you've got exams to revise for. Get over here and we'll doughnut back home together."

Benny's eyes were fixed on the doughnut. "I can't do that," he said.

Here we go, Gordon thought. "Balls," he said. "You're coming home *right now*. Got that?"

Gordon had never owned a dog. If he had, 99 per cent probability it would've been the best-behaved dog in town. Gordon had the voice, when he cared to use it. Good boy, bad dog, *sit*! It had always worked on Benny, the way petrol always works on fires. But Benny didn't move. "Benny. Did you hear me?"

"Yes, Uncle."

"Look." As soon as he opened his mouth, Gordon knew he was making a mistake. Don't plead; it had always been a cardinal rule. It wasn't, he realised objectively, one of his best days for idiot-whispering. "Look," he repeated, "you've obviously got entirely the wrong end of the stick. We'll go home, I'll explain it all properly and then you'll understand. All right?"

"No, Uncle."

You don't plead, because when you then gear-shift from pleading to blustering, you're left with all the credibility of a government in mid-term. "That wasn't a suggestion," Gordon said, "it was an order. Get yourself over here and look through the doughnut. Now."

With an effort you couldn't begin to quantify in terms of joules and newtons, Benny tore his attention away from the doughnut and turned it on Gordon. "Uncle," he said. "How could you?"

"How could I what?"

"How could you do it? All those people. It's so *wrong*."

"Benny." Gordon pictured himself putting on the elements of his superiority, as though they were pieces of armour; the breastplate of wealth, the helmet of success, the shield of elder-and-betterness, the little lobster-tail arm and leg bits of emotional and intellectual maturity. "You haven't got the faintest idea what you're talking about. You don't know all the facts, you haven't thought any of it through, there are *Disney princesses* with a better grasp of the harsh realities of macroeconomics than you've got, and I'm not going to sit here listening to your half-baked self-righteous drivel. Now, are you going to look through the doughnut or do I have to call Security and have them make you do it?"

"I don't think you can make me do anything," Benny said.

Gordon laughed. "You reckon?"

Benny nodded, and with a movement surprisingly fluent for one so habitually clumsy, he drew the sword that hung from his belt. He didn't point it or anything; it was just there. Gordon found himself unable to look at anything else.

"Now steady on," he heard himself say.

Benny didn't seem to have heard him. "Just now," he said. "There were some armed Elves. They were going to attack me, but I drew this sword and they were *petrified*. At the time I thought, just as well they don't know I don't know how to use it. But what if I do? I've never tried. Maybe it's a sort of magic thing, and the sword knows what to do."

"Don't be stupid," Gordon said.

Suddenly, Benny grinned. "Rather more likely," he said, "is that I haven't got a clue how to swordfight, so if you call your Security people there'll be a brief struggle and they'll win. But any sort of a struggle with a big sharp thing like this involved is going to be very dangerous, and someone could easily get hurt. Almost certainly," he added, "me. Is that what you want?"

Gordon breathed out slowly through his nose. "No, of course not, don't be such a bloody fool. Put that thing away right now."

Benny shook his head. "You have no idea how much I wanted to go home," he said. "Once I realised I was stuck here, I mean. I'd have done anything. I tried so hard." A thought struck him and he frowned. "I guess you don't know anything about a unicorn."

"A what?"

"There was this unicorn," Benny said. "It told me I could find a doughnut in the Cradle of All Goblins, which is why I came here. But it said a funny thing. If I came here, I could never go home. I think I understand now."

Gordon sighed. "Benny," he said, "you do realise, you've got your final exams in *three days*. How long have you been here?"

Benny shrugged. "I don't know. Days, weeks. It doesn't matter, surely."

"Of course it matters, you idiot. You may have known all your exam stuff when you got here, but I'll bet you anything you like you've forgotten it all by now. You'd better get home and get some serious revision done, or you're going to fail. Is that what you want?"

"You haven't been listening, have you? I'm not going back."

"Benny? You're not making any sense. You can't stay *here*.

It's not *real*. This is not *real life*. This is just some place where you suspend disbelief and make money. You aren't even *you* here. You're some idiot with a palace full of falcons. That's not you. You know it isn't."

Benny breathed in slowly, then out again. The weight of the sword was hurting his wrist. "I think that may be where you've been going wrong," Benny said calmly. "This is real. It says so in the instructions for the YouSpace thing. It's not our real, but it's real. Real people and everything."

"Don't be bloody stupid."

"They're real people," Benny repeated, "and you're *hurting* them. That's the point."

"You know what?" Gordon said wearily, "you're really starting to annoy me. For the last time, these are not real people, and this isn't a real place. It's got dragons in it, for crying out loud, and goblins, and magic that works, it's *make-believe*. You can't hurt these people, and nothing that happens to them actually matters. This is just—" He clawed about in his mind for a word. "It's a *loophole*," he said, "it's a mistake made by reality which a clever man like me can exploit so as to make a fortune. None of it actually exists, any more than Amazon actually lives in Luxembourg. It's just something we pretend, to make money. For crying out loud, Benny, even a bleeding-heart big girl's blouse like you can't get all worked up about the rights of people who don't exist. What next? John Doe was framed?"

"You're wrong, Uncle. They're real. I've met them."

Gordon realised his fists were clenched; a warning sign which he'd learned to respect. "Fine," he said. "All right, let's suppose for the sake of argument that you're right. These people are really real, and so are the dragons and the Elves and the talking trees—"

Benny's eyes widened a little. "Talking trees."

"Yes, in the Old Forest beyond the Grey Mountains. I've

got forty thousand of them answering phones for MiniSoft. And you know what? They *enjoy* it. They *like doing* it. Before I came along, they just stood there, bored stiff. If a bird came and shat on their leaves, it was the highlight of their decade. Now, thanks to me, their lives are incredibly much better. They've finally got something to talk about, other than squirrels and the weather. They get a tremendous sense of fulfilment out of helping people whose screens have just frozen. They love what I've done. I'm their saviour."

"Do you pay them?"

"They don't *want* paying. Even if I did, what the hell can a tree spend money on? Same with all the rest of them. Before I came here it was all subsistence agriculture, scratching a precarious living from the dirt. Now they've all got shoes and woolly scarves and tea services. That's *progress*. That's what's so good about the whole outsorcery thing, everybody wins."

"You don't pay them."

"Actually, I pay most of them, the ones who want paying."

"You pay them pennies."

"Sure. And to them, it's unimaginable wealth."

"You're making them cut down all the trees. That's ecological suicide."

Gordon grinned. "We're talking primeval forest here, and men with axes. It'd take them ten thousand years to make a serious dent in it. And what they do clear is available to turn into farmland, to grow food, to feed people. You see? Everybody wins."

Benny shook his head. "But they're not growing food, they're working for you. You've got Santa's elves making guided missile components. That's *bad*. Even you can see that."

"They make them very well," Gordon said calmly. "Which means the missiles hit what they're aimed at, rather than the village school a mile further on. That's actually a good thing. And I make them very cheap, which means reduced defence spending, which means more money for schools and hospitals. Sorry, you're going to have to do better than that." Gordon found a smile from somewhere. It was a bit thin, creased and battered, but it would have to do. "Come on, Benny, you know me, I'm your uncle. Do you honestly think I'd do anything really bad? Well?"

Because everything here, this whole world, is about suspension of disbelief. "They seem happy enough," Benny said slowly. "Some of them, some of the time."

"Exactly. Like at home. Actually, if you look closely and think about it dispassionately, more of them, more of the time. I keep telling you. Everybody wins."

"Especially you."

"Yes." Gordon nodded vigorously. "Especially me, and what the hell's wrong with that? Who had the idea in the first place? Me. Who actually carried it through and made it happen? Me. Who's spent *three thousand years* arranging it all, so these people can have a better life? Me, that's who. So I make a lot of money. So I damn well should. And if you think there's something wrong with that, you may care to reflect what that money's all *for*."

"Enlighten me."

"For you, you clown. You want to know why I did all this? So you'll never have to do a day's hard work in your life." Gordon smiled. It was a terrible smile; pour it over sheets of lead, you've got a battery. "Because let's face it, you're a bright kid, you've got a very good mind, but in practical, ordinary, getting-safely-through-each-day terms, you're *useless*. You couldn't hold down a job for ten minutes. Which is why you need to be provided for. Which is what I'm doing, because you're my nephew, and I promised my sister I'd look after you, and because I love you, you halfwit. Right?"

Benny winced, as if he'd just been shot-blasted with chocolates. "So it's all my fault."

"Oh, for God's sake."

"Well, that's what you're saying, isn't it? You did it all for me. Therefore, it's my fault."

"For the last time," Gordon thundered, "there is no *fault*. No people, real or imaginary, were harmed during the making of this large amount of money. Listen to me. Thirty minutes' walk from here, there's a village with a shoemaker's shop. There you'll find a nice old man who makes shoes, all of which he sells to me. That makes him rich, in village terms; he can afford to eat well, he's got a clock on his wall and he's giving his nephew money to start up a carpentry business. He loves his work. The shoes he makes, him and fifty thousand like him, are either bright blue or pink, and they end up on the feet of a well-known brand of little girls' dollies. Now, before I got the contract, those dolly shoes were made in a sweatshop in south-east Asia, by kids half your age working sixteen hours a day for a handful of rice – that's if they still had hands to hold rice in, because the machines didn't have guards on them, to save a buck. You want cruel, you want barbaric, you go and look at the firms I put out of business. I tell you what, they made the goblins look like *sweethearts*."

Benny breathed in deeply, then let the breath go. "I never *wanted*—"

"Benny." Gordon's voice was softer now, firm but warm, a voice you could feel safe inside. "You don't know what you want, that's half the problem. Which is why someone who knows you better than you know yourself has got to want it for you. So I did. Believe me, you're going to have a great life. You reckon you want to be a professor, spend your life researching physics or pure mathematics? Fine, I'll build you a university. That's something you can *do*, something you'll be good at. Here—" He shrugged. "Sorry to have to break it to you, but you've been a rubbish Prince Florizel. Your people are that close to revolution, which in a place like this is—" Gordon made a vague, gentle gesture with his hands. "You get the idea. Stay out of politics, Benny, it's not your scene."

Benny gave him such a sad look. "But the way things are here, it's not *right*. It doesn't *work*. And people are starting to notice."

Gordon looked at him. "You mean that annoying girl in the village? Oh yes, I know about her. And she's not the only one. For a start, there's King Mordak, and several others. They're starting to think, ask questions, spoil everything. That's the point. So long as nobody thought or asked questions, it *did* work, and it will again once they stop doing it. And you know *why* they're thinking and asking questions? Go on. Three guesses."

"Uncle?"

"*You*, that's why." Gordon shook his head. "Hadn't you figured that out? It's ever since you came. There wasn't any of that stuff before you turned up. You're changing things, just by being here. That's why you can't stay. Not if you really care about these people. If you stay here you'll ruin everything."

Benny's eyes opened wide. "Me?"

Gordon nodded. "You," he said. "Some kind of instability in the transfer matrix, I don't know, you figure it out, you're the bloody scientist. All I know is, it's happening. And what's more, if you stay and it carries on, everything I've built here's going to collapse, in ruins, thud. And don't for one moment imagine—"

"Base theory," Benny said.

Gordon blinked twice. "You what?"

"Base theory," Benny repeated eagerly. "As formulated by

Sonderberg and Chen in the late nineties, but nobody listened to them. Essentially, it's like how there's different bases in maths – you know, like base ten is the default we all use, just because we happen to have ten fingers, but you can have base eight or base twenty or whatever. What Sonderberg and Chen did was postulate a theoretical model of the multiverse where the very fabric of reality is capable of being rebased, sort of like in maths only it affects *everything*, so that physical laws operate differently, or don't operate at all, depending on which base you happen to be in. So if you were to jump from, say, base six to base nine, suddenly magic would be possible, or you could have some clown in a red cape able to fly through the air and leap tall buildings in a single bound. The danger would be that an unadjusted base sixer intruding into base nine territory would create what they called a dynamic drag effect, a bit like poking a stick into a spider's web. It'd bend the fabric of space/time and eventually break it, and the first symptoms would probably be quite minor, such as elements of a base six mindset manifesting themselves in base nine consciousnesses, like a little voice in the backs of their heads, so to speak; like when I was back home, and suddenly none of the stuff I was revising for my exam made any sense any more, because I'd just been in a different base. I'm guessing there's some kind of self-calibrating Sonderberg compensator built into the root code of the YouSpace device, and if it's malfunctioning—"

"Benny."

"Yes?"

"Shut up," Gordon said. "Now, like I was saying, if you honestly believe that it'd all go back to how it was before I came, subsistence farming, some kind of primeval pastoral idyll, you're deluding yourself. Oh no. These people have got used to certain things; money, food, clocks, *things*. If something happens and all that gets taken away from them, they're not going to be happy. You really want to be responsible for plunging this world into civil war? I'm not kidding, Benny, I'm serious. That's what'll happen if you stay."

Benny stared at him. "Civil war?"

"Oh yes. Well, you're the one who reckons they're real people. What would real people do?"

"Start a war," Benny admitted.

"Start a war, that's exactly right. You'll have an army of woodcutters cutting wood nobody can afford to buy, you'll have dragons rampaging around the place and nobody to kill them, so growing crops or rearing livestock will be forget it. You'll have the goblins and the dwarves against the Elves, which will last roughly five minutes, and then they'll go back to slaughtering each other again, but without the mining to distract them, so they'll wipe each other out and be extinct, no great loss, you might say, but that's not exactly green thinking, is it?" He paused for breath, and studied his nephew's face. "That's a lot of tough challenges for a prince to face, if you ask me, especially one whose grip on power is decidedly tenuous. You think you'll be able to cope, and make everything all right for the people depending on you? Or would it be better for everyone if you went home, I sort out the mess and the people get a *real* prince, who knows what needs to be done? It's up to you, Benny. You're the one holding the sword, you choose. All I can do is offer a little bit of advice."

Benny had forgotten about the sword. He dropped it, and it clanged loudly on the floor. "Sorry," he mumbled.

"That's all right," Gordon said, in a forgiven-not-forgotten voice. "You were upset, you weren't thinking straight. We all of us do stupid things sometimes, the important thing is to stop once you realise you're being a total dick. You do realise that," Gordon added kindly. "Don't you?"

"Yes, Uncle."

"And now you're going to go straight home and get on with your revision. Aren't you?"

"Yes, Uncle."

"Good boy. You see?" Gordon picked the doughnut up off the desk. "If only everybody would do as I tell them, what a wonderful world this could be. Right, you know the—"

Just then the door flew open and a girl stumbled through, followed by a man. She saw Benny, and then Gordon, and then the doughnut.

"Hey," she said. "You're the wizard."

Gordon gave her a scowl that should've turned her into a silhouette on the wall, but she didn't seem to have noticed. "Get out," Gordon said. "This is a private meeting. Go away."

"You're the wizard," she said. "And Prince Florizel, too, surprise surprise. What are you doing with that *thing?* No, I don't want to know. We want a word with you."

Gordon looked over her head at the man. "Is she yours?"

"No," Buttercup snapped, "I'm mine. Turquine, get him."

Turquine surged past Benny, knocking him off balance, dived and scooped up Benny's sword. He seemed relieved to be armed again, and correspondingly unhappy when the sword turned into a carrot in his hand.

"Uncle?" Benny demanded. "Did you just do that?"

Gordon shrugged. "I'm a wizard," he said. "You two, piss off out of here before I call the guards."

Buttercup made a noise like a very angry pig, grabbed the carrot from Turquine's hand and threw it. To be fair, it was a big carrot. Also, in accordance with the sixth law of metempsychotic transfiguration, its appearance had changed, but not its mass. It hit Gordon on the side of the head, and he went straight to sleep.

"Oh for crying out loud," Turquine said.

"Be quiet," Buttercup snapped. "And anyway, he's not dead, he's just – oh no you don't." She darted in front of Benny, who was on his knees scrabbling for something. She assumed it was the carrot, which was why she didn't take particular care not to tread on the doughnut.

"No!" Benny yelled, but it was too late. Buttercup's robust, utilitarian footwear had reduced it to flattened dough and crumbs. The carrot, meanwhile (in accordance with the ninth law of metempsychotic transfiguration, concerning interruption of the power source to a catamimetic field), had turned back into a sword. Buttercup grabbed it and positioned the tip of the blade about three-quarters of an inch from the end of Benny's nose.

"So," she said. "You're his nephew, are you?"

"Yes," Benny said. "What's that got to do with—?"

Buttercup grinned. "Splendid," she said. "You're with us."

"You what?"

"I think she means you're now a hostage," Turquine explained. He was trying very hard not to look at the compressed wreck of the doughnut.

Benny shook his head. "That's my uncle lying there," he said. "I can't just leave him. He might be concussed or something."

"I wouldn't annoy her, if I were you," Turquine said. "She can be a bit—"

"Turquine!"

"Just do as she says," Turquine said. "It works for me, or at least, it has so far. Come on, let's get out of here before he wakes up."

Benny looked at his uncle, who was just starting to groan and twitch, then at the sword, then at the expression on Buttercup's face. She probably wouldn't hurt him on purpose, he decided, in cold blood; but see above, under sharp objects, strong emotions, accidents and collateral damage.

"If you've hurt my uncle," he said, "I'll smash your face in. Got that?"

Buttercup gave him a terrible scowl, then suddenly grinned. "You're not really a prince, are you? Admit it."

Benny shrugged. "Fine, I'm not a prince. Now, please stop waving that stupid thing about, and I'll come with you. All right?"

"They're so sweet when they suddenly grow backbones," Turquine said wearily. "Now come *on*. Both of you."

The chasm of Bhazad-glum, spanned until recently by a narrow stone bridge, is said to be bottomless, falling away into an abyss so profound that it transcends both space and time. Note the weasel words *is said*, which nine times out of ten translates as *can't be bothered to find out*. Just for once, though, what is said is entirely accurate. In the abyss of Bhazad-glum there are no dimensions; no x, y, z or t axes, nothing established, nothing at all to triangulate by. You can't climb down into it because there's no down to climb into. It inevitably follows, therefore, that only a complete idiot would try.

The tall, thin young man ate a hamburger and three Jaffa Cakes. Then he uncoiled his rope, secured one end to a crampon driven into the rock, and tugged on it with all his weight to make sure it was in good and solid. Holding on to the rope, he bent from the waist and peered down into the chasm. A surge of vertigo made him giddy; he tugged on the rope to straighten himself up. Then he looped the rope over his shoulder, ate a corned-beef sandwich, clamped another between his teeth, the way pirates do with cutlasses, and began to climb down into the abyss.

He went down so far that the pale light from the torches in

the wall sconces above failed; he climbed for so long that he left time behind, like someone crossing a frontier. At some point he reached the stage where there was no rock face to brace his feet against; so, pausing only to eat the second sandwich and half a packet of Rolos, he continued the descent the hard way, bracing his feet on the rope as he shifted handholds. He went further than any living thing had ever knowingly gone, passed the limits of memory and identity, leaving his past and even his name behind. The rope ran out, but he carried on climbing, his hands and feet gripping on nothing at all. Eventually, he left behind his reason for being there. Only one thing remained with him, kept him going, kept him strong. He was, he remembered, hungry; and if he carried on, maybe he'd find something to eat.

There came a moment, an isolated fragment of time utterly devoid of context, a sample of time on a sterile microscope slide, when he stopped and listened; and a voice said to him, "Art?"

It was dark. There was nothing. Who or what was Art, and could you eat it?

"Art? That you?"

A dim flare of memory lit a corner of his mind and he nodded. No light, of course, for anyone to see him do it by.

"Good lad, Art. I knew you'd come for me. Over here, son. Nearly there."

An arm grabbed him, looped round his neck, clung on, nearly strangling him. He felt weight on his windpipe, which shifted to his shoulders. "That's it, Art, I'm fine. You done well, boy. Off we go."

He started to climb. A hand brushed his neck, stuck a raspberry Danish in his mouth. He chewed it gratefully. "There you go, Art, got to keep your strength up, you're a growing lad. Nearly there, Art, nearly there."

There predicates *here*, and *here* was a baseless assumption, but he kept on going, feet together, hand over hand, until he felt rope against his palms and remembered, quite suddenly, who Art was. He made a gentle grunting noise and his uncle fed him a custard slice.

Light, when it came, was like a second birth. There was rock to brace his feet against, and he powered up the rope, fuelled by joy, hope and a small piece of cherry Bakewell. Before he knew it, he was hauling himself over the edge of the precipice. Job done.

"Cheers, Art," the old man said, straightening his cap and brushing nothingness off the knees of his trousers. "Right, we better get on. We'll just stop a minute and catch our breath." The young man was lighting a primus stove and pouring soup from a can into a saucepan "And then we'd better go and find King Mordak. We ain't out of the woods yet, Art, not by a long shot."

Mordak was pleased, though mildly stunned, to see them. "I thought you were—"

"Nice of you to be worried, sir, but here we are, safe and sound." The old man beamed at him. "Anyway, that's enough about Art and me. You want to be careful, King Mordak, sir. That wizard, he won't give up easily. He'll be coming for you, you can bet anything you like."

Mordak frowned. There was a sort of peace here in the woods (peace apart from the swishing of axes, the creak of rending wood, the occasional howl as a goblin mistook his shins for a sapling) that he'd never experienced down below in the mines; somehow, up here in the soft, dappled light, the wizard seemed far away, almost irrelevant. But he knew the old man was right. "What should we do?" he asked.

"Strike, sir, now, while you can." The old man was looking straight at him. "Attack him before he attacks you. It's the last thing he'll be expecting."

If so, then Mordak would be in a good position to

empathise, since he was just about to say the last thing he'd ever have expected to say, namely *now let's not be hasty*, when advised by a human to make war. "But he's got soldiers with magic weapons. We can't fight them. That's why I hired you."

The old man smiled. "Oh, I wouldn't be too worried about that, sir, not down in the tunnels, what with your people being so good in the dark and all. In fact, sir, I took the liberty of sending young Art with a message to King Drain, sir, asking if he wouldn't mind getting his army together and meeting us here in ten minutes. Hope you don't mind, sir, but I thought it'd save time."

Mordak opened his mouth, and his jaw moved up and down quite vigorously for several seconds, but no sound came out. Then he said, "You did *what?*"

"Well, sir, begging your pardon, but I fancy what's needed here is what you might call a united front, if you get my meaning. Goblins and dwarves together, it sort of says it all, really. When the wizard sees that, he'll know he's beaten."

Mordak shook his head, and his flapping jowls made a sort of slopping noise. "What in hell makes you think Drain'll— Oh. Oh my God."

A column of armed dwarves was threading its way through the trees towards them. All around the clearing, the goblins stopped what they were doing and stared. "God almighty," Mordak whispered. "What did you say in that letter?"

"Only what you'd have put if you'd been writing it, sir, I'm sure. There's King Drain at the front, look. Might be a good idea if you was to go and say hello."

And so it was that the king of the goblins and the king of the dwarves met in the greenwood, on the last day of spring, in peace. They looked at each other in silence for a long time. Then Drain said, "You lot look pretty bloody silly doing basket-weaving, like a lot of girls."

Mordak smiled at him. "Yes, but when we stop weaving baskets, we'll stop looking silly. I'm afraid it'll be that much harder for you. But there you go. You want to come and have a crack at the wizard?"

Drain shrugged. "Might as well, now we're here."

"That's the ticket," Mordak said. "You're not afraid of the magic weapons, then."

"What magic weapons? Nobody said anything about magic weapons."

"Ah. So you are afraid, then."

Drain scowled horribly. "Like hell we are. Dwarves aren't afraid of anything."

"Splendid," Mordak said. "Wish we were that brave. There's an old goblin saying; there is nothing to fear but fear itself and scary things. You lot can go first, in that case." He grinned, showing all his many and various teeth. "Well, go on, then. Age before beauty."

If looks could kill, the expression on King Drain's face would've wiped out all life on Earth. Clearly he was summoning all his powers for a thunderbolt of repartee so coruscating, it'd split the ground under Mordak's feet clear down to the magma core. Mordak braced himself and waited for it to come.

"You," Drain said, at last. "You think you're so damn *clever.*"

Mordak released the breath he'd been not so much holding as interning without due process. "Thank you," he said. "You're very kind. Well? Shall we?"

36

"**Y**ou know what," Turquine said suddenly. "I think I know where we are."

Buttercup put her back to the tunnel wall and slid down it until she was sitting on the floor. "You said that an hour ago," she said.

"Yes. But—"

"And fifteen minutes before that. And half an hour before *that*."

"Yes," Turquine said. "But I was wrong then and I'm right now. I know this place. I recognise the smell. It's the back end of the dragonmeat plant."

Buttercup had taken off her left shoe and was gazing sadly at her heel. "Don't be silly," she said. "That's miles away, on the other side of the—"

"Yes," Turquine said. "And we've been walking for hours. If you walk for hours, you end up miles away. Well-known fact."

Buttercup tried to put the shoe back on, but her foot seemed to have grown two sizes. "Well?" she said, turning her head to scowl at Benny. "Is that right? Is this the meat-packing place?"

"I don't know," Benny replied. "I've never been here before."

"Oh come on, you're the wizard's nephew. You must know these tunnels like the back of your hand."

Benny shook his head. "I keep telling you," he said. "I only found out the wizard was my uncle a few hours ago. Before that, I'd always believed he was something boring in shipping."

Turquine raised an eyebrow. "You thought your uncle was a teredo beetle?"

Buttercup sighed. "Please," she said to Benny, "don't try and be smart. When you do, it provokes him and he makes jokes, and I'm not sure I can stand it much longer. Do you know where we are or don't you?"

"Not a clue," Benny said. "Sorry."

"He may not know," Turquine said cheerfully, "but I do. We're out the back of the dragonmeat plant. I'd know that smell anywhere."

Buttercup clicked her tongue. "It'd help if it wasn't so dark and we could see."

"I've got a candle, remember," Turquine said.

"Yes, and nothing to light it with."

"I've got a tinderbox," Benny said, "if that's any help."

"Not that knowing where we are helps very much," Turquine added. "Because, if I'm right, the dragonmeat plant is on the other side of that wall, and there may be a door or there may not, and anyway, I'm not entirely sure I know what we're supposed to be doing."

"Running away," Buttercup snapped.

"Oh. I thought we were bearding the wizard in his lair or something."

"Running away," Buttercup amended, "with a hostage. Then, when we're a long way away and hiding safely somewhere, we open negotiations. Stop all the weirdness or your nephew gets it."

"Gets what?" Benny asked. Then he said, "Oh."

"She's bluffing," Turquine explained. "We aren't really going to hurt you." He paused and frowned. "Are we?"

Buttercup gave him an oh-for-crying-out-loud look, the full effect of which was dissipated by the darkness. "We negotiate," she repeated. "That way, nobody gets killed or turned into woodlice, and things can start to get back to normal around here." She sighed again, and propped her head in her hands, her elbows on her knees. "Assuming we can ever get out of here."

"Did you say you've got a tinderbox?" Turquine said.

"What? Oh, yes, right here." Benny fumbled in his pocket and handed it over. "I assume it works, I've never tried it. I'm not very good with them, to be honest."

"Nice bit of gear," Turquine said, turning it sideways to admire the mechanism. "Where'd you get it?"

"I think someone in a village somewhere makes them."

"We could shift as many of these as we can get our hands on," Turquine said. "If the price is right, of course."

"Turquine," Buttercup said. "Light the candle."

There was a soft gruntling noise as Turquine worked the little crank. "Just one thing," Benny said.

Buttercup scowled at him. "What?"

"Well," Benny said, "just now, when you said about things getting back to normal, if you can make the wizard stop what he's doing. I'm very sorry, but I don't think it works like that."

Buttercup laughed. "Says you."

"No, really." And Benny told her what his uncle had told him, about the irreversible nature of the move away from subsistence agriculture to a market economy. "So you see," he said, "it's not just a case of, get rid of the wizard and everything's going to be just fine. It's too late for that now. Sure, it can be made better. But it can't be put back how it was. It wasn't so bad when you didn't know something was wrong, you were being ripped off and exploited but you thought it was just a wizard, and wizards are *normal*. But when I came here, I did something to the way Uncle's magic works."

Buttercup gave him a look he could've shaved with. "You did something."

"Yes, me. Actually, I reckon it was something to do with base theory. You see, where I come from, there's two very wise men called Sonderberg and Chen, and they've got this hypoth—" He caught sight of the expression on her face, and the didactic urge melted away like ice on a hot stove. "I started something," he said, "something bad, just by coming here, and then the people here began *thinking*. Well, you two did, anyway. But pretty soon everybody'll start figuring it out, how it's all impossible, how it can't really work, and then eventually they'll understand, and after that everything's going to get really nasty. And that's not Uncle Gordon's fault," Benny concluded sadly. "It's mine."

Buttercup was silent for a long time. Then she said, "You're his nephew. Of course you'd say that."

Benny shook his head. "Before you two came in, I was yelling at him," he said. "I was really, really angry with him. I still am, I guess. I'm definitely not on his side."

"Odd," Turquine said. "I seem to remember something about faces getting smashed in. Oh, and this box of yours is no good. Moss is damp, probably."

"He's still my uncle," Benny said. "And all the family I've got. And he's looked after me since my mum died, and everything. But, no, I don't like what he's done, not one bit."

"Try turning the moss over," Buttercup said, "that sometimes works. Well, anyway, looks like we all agree about not liking what the wizard's been doing. So, you won't mind helping us stop him, then?"

Benny shrugged. "I think you're going about it the wrong way."

"I see. And the right way would be?"

"Sorry," Benny said, "no idea. When my Uncle Gordon wants to do something, he gets on and does it. I don't think anyone's been able to stop him, ever."

"You were right," Turquine said, with admiration in his voice. "It's going nicely, I must remember that one." He lowered his head to breathe on the glowing moss. "Right, let's get a candle lit and then we can see what we're—"

"Listen," Buttercup hissed. "Someone's coming."

Turquine snapped the tinderbox lid shut. "Keep still," he said quietly. "Maybe if we're lucky, we can jump them before they see us."

By now Benny could make out the crunch of heavy boots, reverberating down the tunnel like an oncoming train. It occurred to him that they must be his uncle's men, and probably they'd been sent to rescue him. Define *rescue*, he thought; one of those tricky, chameleon-like words that changes its meaning depending on which angle you're looking from. Do I want to be rescued? he asked himself. *We aren't really going to hurt you*, from the man with the sword, followed by *are we?* The alternative would be to go back to Uncle Gordon and get doughnutted back to Orpington and his revision notes. A few hours ago, he'd accepted that, and Buttercup and Turquine hadn't advanced any reasoned arguments to make him change his mind. On the other hand—

That bloody unicorn, he thought. That bloody unicorn, whose predictions have so far all come true. And some drivel about fires and rings of power. It's a terribly depressing thing, to realise that you don't have free will after all, and your destiny is being directed by badly written Robert Jordan.

The boots were getting close, and Turquine was winding

himself up to do something energetic. *One word from me*, he thought, and in thinking it realised it wasn't going to happen.

The boots stopped. It was too dark to see more than out-lines, but the sound Benny heard was unmistakable (though he'd never heard it in real life, only on TV) and distinctly out of place. Oh, he thought. Then he stood up and called out, "Over here, don't shoot."

"Bastard," Turquine observed, a foot to his left, just as a tiny dot of red light appeared in the exact centre of his forehead. Turquine couldn't see it, of course, and how do you explain laser sights to a knight in shining armour? Answer: you don't bother trying. Instead, Benny hissed, "Keep very still. Their weapons are magical. You don't stand a chance."

Turquine froze instantly. Buttercup thought about it, then saw the little red dot. It wilted her, like frost in June. "Magic?" she said.

"Afraid so, yes."

"Oh, nuts." She stood up slowly. "I'll get you for this," she said. "Trust me."

"I'm sorry," Benny said. "But they'd have killed you."

A soldier stepped forward into what little light there was, and Benny only just managed to keep himself from whim-pering out loud. It wasn't his modern, state-of-the-art assault rifle, though that was disconcerting enough, given where it was pointed. It was the soldier himself.

"Bloody hell," Buttercup murmured, staring. "What the hell are you supposed to be?"

The skeleton in combat fatigues didn't answer. Instead, he made a self-explanatory gesture with his rifle; *you're coming with us, no funny business.* "Dragons' teeth," Turquine said bitterly, slowly placing the sword on the ground and raising his hands. "Never occurred to me your disgusting uncle had figured out how to do *that*. And to think," he added. "I never charged him extra for a single tooth."

The soldier beckoned with his rifle and Turquine stepped forward. As he did so, a candle dropped from under his shirt, rolled across the floor and came to rest against the soldier's boot. Benny looked at it and thought: that's an odd-looking candle. Then a light came on in his mind and he knew what to do.

"Excuse me, officer," he said politely, taking a long stride forward. "I'm the wizard's nephew, Florizel. I assume you're here to rescue me?"

The soldier nodded, then (something of an afterthought) transferred his gun to his left hand and saluted.

"Jolly good," Benny said. "And about time too. Still, better late than never. Right, let's get moving, shall we? My uncle doesn't like being kept waiting. Oh, and would you mind lighting that candle? It's too dark to see where you're going, and I keep bashing my shins."

The soldier barked an order in what was presumably animated-skeleton language; another soldier stepped smartly forward, retrieved the candle and froze; nothing to light it with, does not compute.

"That's all right," Benny said. "Sir Turquine's got a tinderbox."

Turquine gave him a paint-stripper scowl and dropped the tinderbox in the soldier's fleshless hand. Trundle-trundle went the little crank. There was a faint flare as the moss caught, another as the soldier applied the glowing embers to the candle wick. Then Benny sprang. More by luck than judgement, he'd got it just about right. One outstretched arm knocked Turquine off his feet, the other one shoved Buttercup sideways, making her overbalance and fall. Benny hit the ground halfway between them, a split second before the tunnel filled with noise and orange light.

It was like having your face licked by a big friendly dog who just happens to be composed entirely of fire. When it was over, and Benny had come to the conclusion, improbable as it seemed, that he was still alive and mostly functional, he sat up and looked around.

What a big difference a few seconds and a firework display can make. For a start, there were no more walking skeletons; a few bones here and there, an empty helmet or two, a couple of thoroughly decommissioned rifles. Terribly sad, of course, but there you go. Buttercup and Turquine were lying face down; no, amend that, they were starting to move, excellent. Finally, where the wall had been there was now a hole, leading into a brightly lit space beyond.

"I'm guessing," Turquine said, "that those aren't your ordinary candles."

"Magic," Benny explained.

With all the spontaneity and vigour of a tooth leaving a gum, Turquine got up, then helped Buttercup to her feet. "Just to clarify," Turquine said. "You blew the dragons' teeth up."

"Well, yes."

"Ah." Turquine nodded slowly. "Thereby saving the both of us at great risk to yourself."

"At great risk to all three of us, but, yes, I suppose so."

"Mphm." Turquine gave him a long look. "Well," he said, peering sideways through the hole, "it's the thought that counts, I guess. Ah, told you so. The dragonmeat plant."

"What happened?" Buttercup said. "Did something just—?"

"He'll explain it all later," Turquine said.

"He'd bloody better."

"He will," Benny promised. "Right now, though, maybe we should make a move." He stepped towards the hole in the wall, then stopped. "Those candles," he said. "You wouldn't happen to have any more of them?"

"Yes," Turquine said. "Look, you seem to know about the horrible things, is it safe if I just dump them here? They won't go off or anything?"

Benny thought for a moment. "Bring them," he said. "Just in case."

"You bloody have them," Turquine said, thrusting five brown-paper-wrapped sticks into Benny's hands. He turned his head sideways and read *Dynamite. Danger. Consult manual before use.* Bit late for that now, of course. Still, he thought, I didn't do too badly, did I?

"Are you going to stand there all day?" Buttercup said.

"Sorry," Benny replied, deselecting hero mode. He leaned forward and put his head round the hole in the wall. "Is it safe in there?"

"I don't know. It looks all right at the moment, but who knows? Any moment, some lunatic might start letting off magic thunderbolts without warning the people he's with. I guess it's a risk we'll have to take. Well?" she went on, turning to Turquine. "Is it the meat place?"

"Oh yes."

No doubt about that at all. They were standing in a narrow aisle between rows of racks, taller than any cottage in the village where Buttercup had grown up. Huge pieces of what was recognisably dragon hung from the frames by massive S-shaped hooks. The smell was overpowering and the floor was sticky.

"Dear God," Benny said. "That's just—"

"Actually, it must be a fairly quiet week," Turquine said, trying to get the sword to go back in its scabbard. It must've got slightly bent in the explosion. He nicked his forefinger, swore and threw the sword away. "Won't be needing that, now we've got your thunderbolts. No, this is nothing like full capacity. I'm guessing a consignment's just been shipped."

"Shipped? Shipped where?"

"There." Turquine pointed. Benny followed the line of his forefinger and saw, set into the rock wall of the cavern—

"Ew," Buttercup said. "That's *gross*."

A doughnut. Fifty feet high, sparkling with sugar granules, in the middle a sort of swirly black nothing-at-all that was almost impossible to see. Something about it, maybe some sort of Higgs-chronaton field, generated alternating gusts of hot and cold air, as though the thing was breathing. Faint traces of oil glistened on the golden-brown fabric. It was the most outrageous thing Benny had ever seen in his life.

"I've watched them, from away over there," Turquine went on. "You're not supposed to, but sometimes they leave the front gate open, and you can just see. They wheel the racks over to that thing there, and a sort of crane arrangement swings the frames in through the hole, and they vanish. No idea where they go to."

"I know," Benny said quietly. "They go to where we come from. My uncle and me."

Deathly silence. Then Turquine said, "You know, I had a sort of feeling you weren't from around here. What is it? Big tunnel right through the mountain?"

"A bit like that," Benny said. He noticed the sticks of dynamite in his hands; somehow, he'd forgotten about them for at least twenty seconds. "But where you come out is a very, very long way from here. That's my home. Where I used to live."

"That's revolting," Buttercup said firmly. "I say we light one of your magic candles and stick it in the hole. Well, why not?" she added, as Turquine and Benny looked at her. "Stands to reason, if you ask me. The wizard uses this tunnel to take away all the stuff he gets over here, right? If we wreck the tunnel, he can't use it any more, there'll be no point him being here, he'll go away and we solve all our problems. And," she added as an afterthought, "nobody gets hurt. Ideal solution, yes?"

Throw the fire into the ring of power, Benny thought. Of course, the stupid unicorn couldn't have said *blow up the giant doughnut with dynamite*, too easy, not cryptic enough. Where would be the fun in giving advice people could actually understand? "What if he just builds another one?"

Buttercup shrugged. "Then we blow that up, too. There were *loads* of candles like those ones, back in that store place. I dread to think what he wants them for."

"Cheap way to scoop out all these tunnels, I guess," Turquine hazarded. "Why employ people when you can use magic?"

"Figures," Buttercup said. "Anyway, if we keep on destroying his stupid gateway, sooner or later he'll get the message and go and bother someone else. Let's do it," she said briskly. "Turquine, have you still got that tinderbox?"

"No, the dragons' teeth took it off me."

"Damn." Buttercup looked round. "It's all right, though, all we need is a bit of flint and something made of steel. I'm good at lighting fires." She stooped and picked up one of the S-shaped hooks. "Turquine, what sort of stone's that wall made out of?"

"Oddly enough, flint."

"Well, there you are, then. And I expect His Majesty Prince Florizel's got a dainty linen handkerchief or something like that we can use for tinder. Well, come on, you lot. There could be guards arriving any minute."

Turquine was sorting through the rubble on the floor. He picked up a chunk of flint. "This one do?"

Buttercup looked over his shoulder. "That's fine," she said. "No, that one, that one *there*. Right, give it here, where's that hanky?" She stopped and peered at something else.

"Turquine, did you know you've got a bright red spot on the back of your neck?"

Oh, Benny thought. "Everyone," he said, in as level a voice as he could manage, "keep perfectly still."

"Wasp?"

"Not as such, no."

Two dozen dragons' teeth emerged from the shadows at the edges of the cavern. Benny and Turquine slowly raised their hands. One of the dragons' teeth came forward, took the dynamite away from Benny and stowed it in a sort of knapsack thing. Reluctantly, Buttercup let go of the S-shaped hook and stepped backwards. "Well, don't look at me," she said, and raised her hands.

"Mind out, mind your backs, coming through." Someone was elbowing his way through the ranks of dragons' teeth. It proved to be a short, fat young man, thin on top and smiling, wearing a sort of pin-stripe monk's habit. "Let me through, please, I'm a lawyer. Right, then. You're Benny, right?"

Benny looked at him. "Yes. Who are you?"

"My card." The young man gave him a little rectangle of pasteboard. "John the Lawyer," he said. "I work for your uncle."

"Ah, right." Benny frowned. "You're here to read us our rights or something?"

John laughed. "I'm afraid that wouldn't take me very long," he said. "No, I'm just here to see to it that these gentlemen don't kill you by mistake. I'm also authorised to make this lady and gentleman a very substantial cash offer, provided they go a long way away and stop making trouble. You are, of course, completely at liberty to refuse, but if you do . . ." he paused and smiled. "Have either of you made a will, by any chance? If not, I can do that for you right now, very sensible thing to do at any time, but in your current circumstances, I should say it's essential."

Buttercup looked at him. "Get stuffed," she said.

"Mphm." John nodded affably. "I'll take that as a no. Is that in respect of the will, the offer of settlement, or both?"

He had something in his hand, Benny noticed; a sort of grey, flat something, roughly the size and shape of a mobile phone. *His* phone, the one he'd lost in the woods. He realised he was staring at it, and looked away.

"How about you?" John the Lawyer had moved away from Buttercup and was now obtrusively in Benny's space. "Of course the settlement offer doesn't apply to you and the need for a will isn't nearly as urgent as it is for your friends, but I always say to clients, it's never too early to think about testamentary dispositions and tax-efficient estate planning."

Benny felt something sliding into his hand. It was a revolting feeling, like a spider running across his face. He kept perfectly still.

"Well, no need to decide right this minute, think about it and get back to me any time. Now then, Sir Turquine, isn't it? How about you?"

Buttercup and Turquine were looking at John; hard to know what, if anything, the empty eye sockets of the Teeth were pointed at, but Benny decided to risk it. He glanced down at the phone in his hand, and on the screen he saw—

50/50 on suing Ur uncle Urside? Ur friends go free. Deal? Yes/No

He looked up. John looked back at him and grinned.

"I've changed my mind," Benny said. "Yes, I'm definitely interested."

"Splendid." John the Lawyer smiled at him, then came across and took the phone from him. "In that case—" He pressed a button, put the phone to his ear, waited, then said, "Any time you're ready." Then he handed the phone back to Benny. "You three might care to hide behind something," he added.

"You what?"

Same drill as before, only louder and much hotter; a fist of hot air sent Benny flying, and it was just as well that he hit a huge slab of dragon sirloin rather than the hard wall. It was snowing brick-sized chunks of rock, and the dragons' teeth were just an untidy scatter on the floor. Oh, and there was now another hole in another wall, through which a column of terrifying looking monsters were rushing, led by an old man in a flat cap and a tall young man with a phone in one hand and a half-eaten slice of *quattro stagione* pizza in the other.

"Just to confirm." John the Lawyer crawled out from under a large slab of dragon. "That is your phone, isn't it?"

"What?" Benny's eyes were glued to the advancing monsters. "Oh, yes, right. Yes, my phone."

John nodded. "Thought so," he said. "It was found in the young lady's basket, and your uncle was kind enough to teach me how it works. Not at all magic, I gather."

Benny turned and grabbed him two-handed by the throat. "Whose side are you on?"

"Mine, of course," John said, gently but firmly removing Benny's hands. "I'm a lawyer. Now then, do you know King Mordak?"

Mordak; the goblin. So these horrifying creatures were— "No. Look—"

"Then it's high time you met. He's your new best friend." John moved smoothly past him and advanced on the biggest and ugliest of the goblins, hand extended. "Your Majesty," he said. "Thank you so much for coming. My name is John the Lawyer, and this is Prince Florizel."

Mordak's face indicated that he felt about lawyers the way Benny did about goblins, which raised him considerably in Benny's estimation. "You said there was something we needed to see," he rasped, in a low voice that made Benny want to hide under the nearest bed. "Where is it?"

John smiled, apparently completely unfazed. Another advantage of his profession, presumably. "In just a moment, sir, if that's all right." He turned aside and smiled warmly at the old man in the cap. "Thanks ever so much," he said. "It's so nice when people are *punctual*."

"My pleasure, sir," the old man said, "and sorry about the mess. Art had to use C4, see, on account of gelignite isn't stable coming through the transdimensional vortex. The wizard not arrived yet, then?"

(And not just the hunchbacked, warthog-tusked goblins, either; there were equally terrifying short men with huge beards and axes. One of them was offering the tall young man a slice of cake from a battered tin box. Good cake, too, judging by how quickly the young man ate it.)

"He should be here any moment now," John replied. "I rang him just before we – ah, here he is. Over here, sir, if you'd be kind enough."

Benny swung round, and his heart nearly stopped as he saw his Uncle Gordon, with an escort of a dozen dragons' teeth, coming through the hole in the far wall. The Teeth tried to unshoulder their rifles, but there simply wasn't time; they were engulfed in a sea of goblins. Ten seconds later, the thigh bone was disconnecka from the knee bone, the knee bone was disconnecka from the leg bone, and only infinite patience and the latest edition of Gray's *Anatomy* would ever make sense of them again.

Mordak made a sound like two elephants disagreeing about politics, lifted his axe and advanced towards Uncle Gordon. A second later, Benny was horrified to realise he'd jumped up on the goblin's back with his arms round his throat. Wondering how he'd got there, he let go, slid to the ground and said, "Please don't hurt him, he's my uncle."

Mordak turned and glared at him. "So what?"

"He's my uncle. Don't hurt him. Besides, he can do magic."

He'd made a valid point. What with goblins, dwarves, dragon carcasses and Buttercup, the cavern was getting quite crowded. If Uncle Gordon started casting anti-personnel spells, he'd die quickly but by no means alone.

"Instead," John the Lawyer said, easing smoothly between them, "let's negotiate."

"Let's not," Mordak said. "That bastard tried to kill me."

"Quite," John said. "So, instead of just killing him, let's make him *suffer*. Why just disembowel when you can litigate?"

Uncle Gordon laughed. "Sure," he said. "See you in court. You haven't got anything on me."

John cleared his throat. It wasn't a particularly loud noise, even when amplified by the cavern's rather bizarre acoustics, but the dwarves and goblins fell silent and turned to look at him. "Actually," he said, "that's not entirely true. Gordon Gulbenkian, please accept this as formal notice that I shall be bringing an action against you for negligence, nuisance, breach of statutory duty, environmental pollution, attempted genocide and six thousand, nine hundred and forty-one separate violations of health and safety legislation. Without prejudice," he added pleasantly. "How do you plead?"

Gordon gave him a long, cool look. "I have no idea what you're talking about," he said.

"Really? Cast your mind back. When you first came here, there were no such things as dwarves and goblins, were there?" He paused for an answer; none came and he went on: "I checked the Elven records. No goblins, no dwarves, just the Elves and a few humans they kept as *pets*." He stopped, aware that his voice had changed. Then he went on as before. "Then you made a discovery. Under the mountain, you discovered a mineral; nothing of any interest to anyone here, but back where you come from, extremely valuable. Thanks to that extremely clever phone device you lent me, I was able to find out a bit about it; information from your side of the divide, not ours. I'm still not quite sure I understand what it is your people want it for, but *naturally occurring plutonium* is quite rare where you come from, isn't it? Rare, and valuable, and really rather dangerous. According to your clever machine, if you get too close to it, it does nasty things to you. If you're around it for any length of time, it kills you. Isn't that right?"

Gordon opened his mouth, then closed it again.

"Elves, of course, are tougher than humans," John went on, "as they never tire of reminding us. So when you hired Elves to dig up the shiny yellow rocks for you, they didn't die straight away, like men would've done. But it did do nasty things to them; so nasty that the other Elves didn't want anything more to do with them, so the miners took to living down here, in the caves. And, three thousand years later, here they still are, though properly speaking, they aren't really Elves any more. The mountain Elves got shorter and started growing beards, and the woodland Elves – well, I personally think Mordak and his people have a distinguished, commanding appearance, and you might care to argue that the extra eyes and the claws and so forth are actually useful developments and an improvement rather than a genetic mutilation. I'd venture to suggest, however, that a court might not agree. The grossly reduced lifespan issue is also somewhat moot, since because of the dwarf-goblin wars, very few goblins and dwarves ever live long enough to die of radiation poisoning. Since you deliberately started those wars, however, you may feel it wouldn't help your case too much to take that point in front of the judge. I don't know. Up to you." He smiled. "Well? Is that more or less how it happened?"

A loud sobbing noise made Benny look round, and he saw a short, bearded man with a gold crown on top of his helmet being led away in tears. Then he glanced at King Mordak and instinctively backed away three paces.

"Is that right?" Mordak asked, in a surprisingly quiet, calm voice. "Well? Yes, you, in the blue nightie, I'm talking to you."

Gordon shrugged. "I'm not admitting anything," he said. "But in any case it's all academic. All this stuff happened thousands of years ago. If your lawyer friend there was any good at his job, he'd know that there's such a thing as a statute of limitations, even in this godforsaken armpit of a reality. Sorry, boys, but you can't sue me, you're out of time."

For perhaps two seconds, Mordak was perfectly still and quiet. Then he roared and surged forward like a tidal wave, and nobody seemed interested in stopping him. Gordon sprang back, fumbling in the pocket of his robe. "Look out!" someone shouted – later, Benny was seriously upset to realise it'd been him – and a goblin soldier grabbed the thing that Gordon had pulled out; a small, round item of patisserie, with a hole in the middle. Gordon swerved sharply, kicked a goblin in the solar plexus and jumped over him, heading for the north wall of the cavern, where the fifty-foot giant dough-nut—

—Had been. But it wasn't there any more. Instead, there were just crumbs and a wall, against which the tall young man was leaning, chewing rhythmically and looking slightly guilty.

"Good *boy*, Art!" the old man yelled. "There, see," he told the world in a loud, happy voice. "Told you he'd make himself useful eventually."

Gordon stared in horror at the wall for a moment, then spun round to face the advancing phalanx of goblins. There was nowhere left to run, and Benny couldn't bear to watch. He was about to turn away when a movement caught his eye; Uncle was standing on one foot, rolling up his left sock, scrabbling for—

The goblins must've seen it too; they charged, and the first goblin to reach him was quick enough to knock the emergency backup Cheerio out of Gordon's fingers. It flew through the air, only inches from Gordon's nose. He had just enough time to stare at it, *through* it, and yell, "So long, idiots"; and then he vanished.

Some time later, when the cavern was almost empty, John the Lawyer said, "Damn."

Buttercup gave him a friendly smile. "It's all right," she said. "We all make mistakes."

John shook his head. "A *proper* lawyer wouldn't have forgotten about the statute of limitations," he said sadly. "A proper *Elf* lawyer. Ah well." He yawned, and stretched his arms. "You know, I don't think I'm really cut out for a career in the legal profession. I reckon I might go into local government instead. You can be just as nasty, but you don't have to keep getting things *right* all the time."

Benny cleared his throat. "Actually," he said, "if you want, I can give you a job."

Turquine, who'd been lying on the floor with his feet up on a dragons' tooth ribcage, looked up sharply. "Him? Oh come on."

"Why not?" Benny said. "He's smart, and his heart's sort of in the right place, and he did save us all from Uncle's soldiers."

John made a vague, bashful gesture. "Motivated by pure greed, I assure you."

"Yes," Benny said, "but to be honest, I don't think any of

us have exactly covered ourselves in glory over all this. I know I haven't, that's for sure. If it hadn't been for me barging in here without allowing for base theory distortion—"

The old man coughed gently. "As formulated by Sonderberg and Chen, sir? Bless 'em," he added indulgently. "Course, young Art helped them a lot with that, back in the day. Put 'em on the right lines, so to speak. Sorry, sir, you were saying."

Benny stared at him for a moment, then went on, "Anyway, the way I see it, this mess is just as much my fault as my uncle's, and someone's going to have to sort it out, and it's not the sort of thing you can fix with a few magic spells and a happy-ever-after, it's going to need solid hard work for a very long time. Really, I don't think there's any moral high ground, just a few low lying ethical foothills. If you want the job, you can have it."

"Thank you," John said. "Doing what?"

Benny shrugged. "Running things," he said. "Making sure everything works. One thing Uncle was right about, you people can't just go back to how things were. So instead, I guess you'll just have to carry on doing all the outsorcery stuff, or else a lot of people are going to starve. The difference will be, though, you'll get to keep the money, instead of Uncle grabbing it all for himself."

Turquine shook his head. "The portal thing," he said. "It's gone. *He* ate it." The young man blushed, and unwrapped a Snickers bar. "So we're cut off—"

"Not really, sir," the old man interrupted, "meaning no disrespect, but that shouldn't be a problem. Me and Art, sir, we can rig something up, if you'd like us to. I mean to say, patisserie's not really our line, strictly speaking, but it can't be all that different from metadimensional field inversion, and we're dab hands at that."

"Just so long as I don't have to watch," Buttercup said crisply.

"And just to make sure you don't make any careless mistakes in the accounts," Benny went on, "I'd like Buttercup and Turquine to keep an eye on them for me. If that's all right."

"Sure," Turquine said. "She's got a marvellous head for figures."

"Sweetheart."

"So she can do the sums," Turquine said, "and I can do the bashing-people's-heads-in if the sums don't add up. Though I'm sure they will," he added graciously. "Won't they?"

A wistful look flitted over John's face, and then he nodded. "Yes, why not?" he said. "After all, money isn't everything. It's helping people that matters most in the long run. What?" he added. "Why are you all looking at me like that?"

"Nothing," Benny said quickly. "Anyway, I'm glad that's settled. I'd like to think, after all the mess my uncle and I made, there'll be someone here to clear it up and make things run properly."

Buttercup frowned a little. "You're going back, then."

Benny nodded sadly. "I have to," he said. "I'd better talk to my uncle. Otherwise, he'll come storming back here casting spells and sowing dragons' teeth, and everything'll be ten times worse."

"You think you can stop him?" Buttercup asked.

"I think so, yes. He'd give it up, for me, if I make him see that's what I really want. He's not really a bad person, just—"

"An inhuman monster?"

"Thoughtless," Benny said. "Not much consideration for other people. I think it's because he uses up all his consideration on me, so there's none left for anyone else. I'll deal with him, leave it to me."

The old man coughed gently. "Excuse me, sir, but you can't."

"Oh, I don't know. If I can only make him see—"

"No, sir, if you'll let me finish. You can't go back to the other side, sir. You'll die."

Benny stared at him, but the old man nodded sadly. "Die? As in—"

"Yes, sir." The old man took his cap off and twisted it in his hands. "No disrespect, sir, but you weren't listening to what this gentleman here was saying. About the plutonium-302, sir. Particularly nasty isotope, the 302. Very bad for you, I'm sorry to say, and you were wandering about down there in the tunnels ever so long. Young Art's been down there with his Geiger counter, bless him, and he says the ambient level is ninety times the safe max."

With a sudden jolt of horror, Benny remembered the chunks of glowing yellow rock that lit the corridors. "Oh God," he whispered. "I'm going to die."

"Yes, sir," the old man said. "Eventually. Everyone dies *eventually*; well, nearly everyone." For some reason, the corner of his lip twitched; private joke, maybe. "But you should be good for another seventy-odd years, sir, provided you stay here. Not if you go back, though. That'd be a very bad idea."

"What?" Benny felt as though the inside of his head was full of water. "I don't—"

"It's the YouSpace field, sir," the old man explained. "Very clever, that Professor Van Goyen, he really knew his stuff. Got a built-in bioelectrical stasis compensator, see, keeps you safe from harmful radiation while you're within the effective area of the YouSpace effect. Once you leave it, though ..." He made a very sad face. "But so long as you stay here, you'll be fit as a fiddle, sir. So that's all right."

Benny's eyes opened wide. "Uncle—"

The old man nodded. "He'll be just fine," he said. "He used magic, see. Magicked up a personal bioshield, very impressive bit of conjuring, young Art says, more his line than mine, if you see what I mean. He can come and go as he likes and no harm done. Not you, though, sir. Sorry, but there it is."

There was a very long silence. Then John said, "Does that mean the job's off, then? If you're staying?"

"I'm stuck here," Benny said. "For ever and ever."

The sharp hissing noise proved to be Buttercup, sucking in air through her teeth. "Oh come on," she said. "Pull yourself together, for crying out loud. It's not so bad here, is it?"

"But it's . . ." Benny hesitated. A certain degree of tact, he decided. After all, this was their home. His too, now. "It's a bit of a shock," he said. "I've been trying so hard to go home, and now I've sort of *won*, but it turns out I can't go after all. It's just a bit unfair, that's all."

"Unfair." Turquine yawned. "Let's see. You're the absolute ruler of a relatively prosperous kingdom, with enormous personal wealth. Those two attributes alone are enough to pretty well ensure you'll find true love." He turned his head and smiled at Buttercup, who beamed back at him "And with John here and Buttercup and me running things, you won't have to do any work, so you'll have both the time and the money to do whatever the hell you like, always provided it doesn't involve food with holes in. Thanks to you, all the people in your kingdom will shortly be getting ludicrously rich, so you'll be incredibly popular and everyone'll love you, including the goblins and the dwarves, which I would find seriously weird, but maybe you're a bit more cosmopolitan in your outlook, I don't know. And there'll be universal peace, now the goblins and the dwarves have stopped fighting, and they'll be too busy sniggering at the Elves from now on to want to fight *them*. So, how's it looking? Yeah, it's a real bitch. If I were you, I'd write to someone about it."

Benny nodded slowly. "There's that, I suppose," he said. "I'll just miss my uncle, that's all. He's all I've got."

"All you had," Buttercup said briskly. "And that's what you want to go back to, leaving all this behind. Give me strength."

Suddenly, Benny laughed, and carried on laughing until everyone was looking at him. "Sorry," he said. "Yes, I think you're probably right. Stuff the unicorn. And stuff home." He grinned, so wide he nearly unzipped his head. "I think I'm going to like it here."

"Thank goodness for that," Buttercup said. "If I'd thought you were going to be stuck here rich, all-powerful and miserable, I wouldn't have been able to sleep at night." She looked round, then stood up. "What are we all doing sitting here surrounded by smelly dead dragons when we could be somewhere *nice*?" she said. "Come on. It's haggis night at the King's Head. You can buy us all dinner."

Something she'd said made the tall young man look up and grin. "Sure," Benny said, "provided you order the most expensive thing on the menu. I insist on that."

"There's only haggis on haggis night," Buttercup said. "And it's twopence. But there'll be other times."

"It's a deal," Benny said, and then he paused, and turned to John. "Looks like you're wrong," he said. "Money is everything, after all."

But John shook his head. "I don't think so," he said. "I used to, but I've changed my mind. I realised, there's something so much more beautiful and wonderful in this world than money, and it's going to be mine, and nobody will ever be able to take it away from me."

"Really?" Turquine said. "What?"

John picked a scrap of dragon fat off the sleeve of his robe. "The look on the Elves' faces when they find out they're intimately related to King Mordak and his goblins," he said. "In fact," he added, "I think I'll go and tell them right now. So long, everyone. And thank you. Ever so much."

And he walked away singing into the sunlight.

Gordon opened his eyes.

He saw a golden half-moon of sandy beach and a dark blue sea, bathed in the early afternoon light of a cloudless tropical sky. The warmth of the sun made his face tingle. He sank to his knees and roared like a bull.

How long he crouched there he had no idea; but, some time later, a simple bark canoe drew up and dropped anchor, and the fishermen got out and asked him if he was all right.

Gordon glared at them. "Where is this?" he asked.

They smiled at him. "Vanuatu," they said.

Well, he reflected, as he trudged along the beach towards where the fishermen told him there was a town, my fault. I was in such a rush, I didn't have a clear idea in my mind of where I wanted to go, and for some reason YouSpace saw fit to land me here. Not to worry. There's got to be a bakery somewhere, and then I can get back and make those bastards pay.

There was indeed a bakery, a very fine one, best in the islands, just off the town square in Luganville. Unfortunately, it was closed for a week during the John Frum festival, and when they said a week they really meant a fortnight. He could, of course, get a boat to Porta Vila, a mere two hundred miles away, and try there, but—

"Forget it," he said. "Where's the airstrip?"

Fortuitously there was a single-engine Cessna available for private charter. Yes, there was a bakery on New Caledonia, or New Zealand wasn't all that much further. Also, in New Zealand there were many excellent banks, which would be only too happy to arrange the transfer of the eye-wateringly huge cost of the flight from his main current account in Zurich. New Zealand it was, then. Hop in.

An hour and a half into the flight, the engine began to falter. That's all right, the pilot said, they do that. It faltered some more, and the pilot started to frown. No, he assured Gordon, there's absolutely nothing to worry about, I had the plane checked over before we set off, nothing could possibly go wrong.

Gordon glanced out of the window; nothing but blue, blue sea in every direction. The engine coughed, stalled and started again. The pilot had gone as white as milk. Absolutely nothing in the whole wide world to be concerned about, he said, frantically flicking toggles and hauling on levers, there's a pair of crackerjack new mechanics they've got now at Luganville, an old boy and his young nephew, they really know their stuff, if there'd been anything the matter they'd have spotted it straight away, no worries. Then the engine stopped dead, and inside the cockpit there was the most eerie silence Gordon had ever heard.

"Oh dear," the pilot said.

But it was fine, he went on, because look, over there, see, there's an island; not on the maps, but there's dozens of little islands out here that nobody's bothered to chart yet. Piece of cake to just glide in to land, then radio for someone to come and pick us up. All a bit of a laugh, really. How they'll tease me about this afterwards in the Planters' Club bar on Bora Bora.

For some reason, Gordon wasn't laughing, though it did

occur to him to ask if the old mechanic's nephew had a hearty appetite. The plane drifted on, light and graceful as thistledown, and gradually the island grew from a dot to a shape to a great green-brown slab that filled the windscreen as it rushed towards them ridiculously fast.

The island had a long, level beach, sheltered by a massive coral reef. The pilot put the plane down on the beach with scarcely a bump. He turned to Gordon and grinned, then picked up the radio. Stone dead.

It was perfectly all right, the pilot said. He had a tin box full of distress flares, and light aircraft like his own passed within sight of the island practically every week. All they'd have to do was listen out for an engine, and when they heard one, let off a flare or two. Meanwhile there was a good supply of emergency rations – freeze-dried chicken casserole and Snickers bars – in the overhead locker. It'll be more like a tropical beach holiday than being stranded, the pilot assured him, you'll be sorry to be rescued, trust me.

The flares box was gone. The overhead locker wasn't empty: it contained freeze-dried chicken casserole packaging and Snickers wrappers. But that's crazy, the pilot said, he'd checked them both just before he took the plane in for its pre-flight service.

"I don't understand it," the pilot said, "it just doesn't make any sense. There can be no rational explanation."

"Oh shut up," Gordon said, and set off to walk up the beach.

He'd gone a fair way, maybe as much as half a mile, when he suddenly got the unpleasant feeling that he was being followed. He turned and found himself facing a dozen men, tall and muscular-looking, armed with spears and blowpipes, and naked apart from white linen aprons and lace caps.

Gordon rolled his eyes. "Oh come *on*," he said. "Give me a break."

The men looked at each other. "He speaks the holy tongue," one of them said, in perfect English.

Gordon shook his head. "Sorry, guys, not interested," he said. "Whatever it is, I'm not buying."

"He came from the great silver bird," said another. "And he speaks the language of the Book."

Hm, Gordon thought. Even so, best not to jump to conclusions. He put on a big smile and advanced towards them. They flinched but held their ground. "Gentlemen," Gordon said. "I wonder, could you possibly tell me where this is?"

The men exchanged puzzled glances. "This is the world," said one of them.

"Sorry? This island is called *The World*?"

"What's an island?"

Oh boy, Gordon thought. "Quite," he said. "From that, I take it, you believe this is all there is and there isn't anything else. No other places, I mean."

They stared at him as though he wasn't making any sense. "There's this world," one man said, "and the other world. The one you come from."

"Where He came from," another said. "Where She is, and they speak the language of the Book."

Gordon turned the smile up a little. "Well," he said, "it's been a pleasure, but I really ought to be getting back now. Have a great day and, um . . ."

"No." The tallest of the men shook his head. "You must come with us."

Gordon looked at him, and then at the spears, which were now all pointing in his direction, and reflected on the fact that the men were between him and the Cessna, and that if there was anything fit for human consumption on this loathsome crumb of rock, these people either had it or knew where to find it. "Of course I will," he said, and allowed them to escort him off the beach and into the jungle.

The settlement, which they reached after half an hour of not unduly arduous walking along well-beaten paths, was made up of a dozen or so longhouses of classic Melanesian form, timber-framed with low overhanging eaves, which Gordon immediately identified from recollections of some TV documentary. When they politely ushered him inside, however; familiar, yes, very, but also about as wrong as it could possibly be.

"Welcome," said one of the men, "to the House of the Book."

History was one of Gordon's least favourite subjects, and furniture was another; but even he had no trouble at all identifying what he saw as archetypical mid-Victorian interior design. On a round three-legged occasional table, flanked by huge potted palms, he saw a book. He moved towards it, but a hand gently restrained him.

"One hundred and seventy-four winters ago," the man said, "a great ship was wrecked on the reef. All the people aboard were drowned except one man, a holy man, who brought with him two books. He lived just long enough to teach us the sacred language, and to read the holy words. Then he made us promise to live our lives according to the Book, and then he died." The man paused for a moment, then continued: "He neglected to say which of the two books was the holy one, but it wasn't too hard to figure it out. One of them was called the Bible, but it turned out to be nothing more than a history of war and politics in a faraway land of which we know little, so clearly it wasn't that one. The *other* one, however—"

He pointed at the spine of the book on the table. Gordon narrowed his eyes and peered, and read: *Mrs Beeton's Household Management*.

"In the Book," the man went on, "we found divine wisdom to guide us in every aspect of our everyday lives, from making a béchamel sauce to turning sheets side to middle. We knew at once that this was indeed a book to live by, with truly *practical* wisdom for every eventuality of our lives. Trusting in its holy precepts, we have prospered and flourished, so that we know that She is watching over us, Her apron protecting us, Her duster and wooden spoon comforting us. So long as we obey the true scriptures, our soufflés will rise, our sauces will not burn and our pots and pans will be spotless." He paused for a moment, visibly moved, then went on, "For a hundred and seventy-four winters we have lived thus, observing the Guidance, trying to be worthy. Now you have come, the first stranger to pass the reef. You speak the sacred tongue, your skin is the same unappetising shade of pinky-grey as His who first brought us the Book." He stopped and looked Gordon in the eye. "Well?"

"Well what?"

The man pursed his lips. "Presumably She sent you to see how we're getting on, or admonish us for our transgressions, or lead us forth into the Promised Scullery or something. So . . ." He shrugged. "What?"

"Actually . . ." Gordon hesitated. "Let's see," he said. "A hundred and seventy-four years since you last saw a stranger, right?"

"Indeed."

"Fine." He glanced at the Book, then went on, "I am indeed sent by Her to guide you in the Way. Now, the first thing I need you to do is bake me a plate of doughnuts."

"Of course." The man turned and barked a series of orders to his acolytes in some language Gordon didn't recognise. "The sacrament will take a while to prepare. In the meantime, can we offer you refreshment?"

Gordon shrugged. "What've you got?"

"It is the twelfth hour of the fourth day of the ninth Course," the man replied. "The *plat du jour* is therefore mutton broth with dumplings followed by terrine of pork with new potatoes, garden peas and celeriac." He frowned. "I thought you'd have known that."

Gordon smiled. "Just testing," he said. "Let the, um, sacrament be brought forth."

Actually it was really rather good, though the mutton was goat, the potatoes were some sort of grey tuber, and the celeriac was probably a variety of seaweed. Presumably something had got lost in translation somewhere. On the other hand, the gravy was just right. He was finishing up seconds of the terrine when three tall men in aprons came in carrying a tray.

"Behold," the man said. "Doughnuts."

Gordon looked at them. "Excuse me," he said. "Where's the holes?"

"Holes?"

"Doughnuts have holes in the middle."

He'd said the wrong thing. The man gave him a savage look, then crossed to the Book and turned the pages. "Behold," he said. "Her Word."

Oh snot, Gordon thought. "Ah well," he said, "that's really the reason I'm here, you see. The Book is, well, it's a bit out of date, to be honest with you, a touch behind the times in places. I've been sent to bring you up to speed on the changes. Such as doughnuts."

The man looked at him blankly. "Changes?"

"That's right," Gordon said, nodding vigorously. "Let's see, what you've got there is probably the third or fourth edition. Since then—"

"There can be no changes." The man's face had altered dramatically, and the acolytes were crowding forward. Some of them had flint knives, and others had heavy rolling pins. "Her word is immutable, and all change is deviance. The punishment for deviance—"

"Now hang on," Gordon said assertively. "I'm from over there, I came on the big silver bird, I speak the sacred tongue. If I say there's going to be changes, there's going to be— *ouch*."

He woke up in a small stone-walled barn. A thick rattan cable attached his ankle to the wall. Beside him was a gourd of water and a plate of cold roast pork with chutney, green beans and unidentified grey-tuber dauphinoise; prison rations, presumably, though in fact he'd had worse at the Dorchester. Opposite him sat the pilot, gnawing the last scraps off a chicken leg.

"Bastard," the pilot said. "You had to be clever, didn't you?"

Gordon sighed. "They're lunatics," he said.

"Yes, well." The pilot bit off a chunk of his crusty wholemeal roll. "They've got us down as tempters sent by the Great Abomination. You had to go and piss them off, didn't you? And now it looks like we're going to be stuck here in this barn for the rest of our lives, tethered to this wall, eating this really rather excellent . . ." He hesitated. "You want the rest of that pork?"

"Yes."

"Selfish git. Anyway, it's all your fault."

Gordon wiped his finger through the last of the dauphinoise sauce and licked it. "We could escape," he said doubtfully.

"Of course we'll *escape*," the pilot said. "First chance we get. I'll focus the rays of the sun through the lens of my specs, and we'll burn through these ropes, overpower the guards, leg it to the Cessna, jury-rig the carburettor and fly out of here." Already a thin plume of smoke was rising from the rope round his ankle. "I just want you to know I think you're an arsehole, that's all."

"Noted," Gordon said; and then a grim-faced warder

came in with two servings of peach and mango trifle, with whipped cream, passion fruit and dried coconut sprinkles. By the time Gordon had finished, the pilot had burned seven-eighths of the way through the rope. He hadn't touched his pudding. Gordon looked at it, and thought, Um.

"Well," the pilot said, as he broke the last strands of the tether. "It's now or never. You ready?"

Gordon looked at him, then at the trifle. He thought; well, young Benny can look after himself, apparently, and I never really *liked* doing it, if I'm perfectly honest with myself. And if I can't sweet-talk these buffoons into making me a god or something, I'm not half the man I thought I was. And the food . . .

"Tell you what," he said. "You go on. I'll catch you up."

extras

orbit

meet the author

Charlie Hopkinson

TOM HOLT was born in London in 1961. At Oxford he studied bar billiards, ancient Greek agriculture and the care and feeding of small, temperamental Japanese motorcycle engines; interests which led him, perhaps inevitably, to qualify as a solicitor and emigrate to Somerset, where he specialised in death and taxes for seven years before going straight in 1995. Now a full-time writer, he lives in Chard, Somerset, with his wife, one daughter and the unmistakable scent of blood, wafting in on the breeze from the local meat-packing plant.

For even more madness and TOMfoolery go to www.orbitbooks.net.

Find out more about Tom Holt and other Orbit authors by registering for the free monthly newsletter at: www.orbitbooks.net.

introducing

If you enjoyed
THE OUTSORCERER'S APPRENTICE,
look out for

DOUGHNUT

by Tom Holt

The doughnut is a thing of beauty.
A circle of fried, doughy perfection.
A source of comfort in trying times, perhaps.
For Theo Bernstein, however, it is far, far more.

Things have been going pretty badly for Theo Bernstein. An
unfortunate accident at work has lost him his job (and his work
involved a Very Very Large Hadron Collider, so he's unlikely
to get it back). His wife has left him. And he doesn't have
any money.

Before Theo has time to fully appreciate the pointlessness of
his own miserable existence, news arrives that his good friend
Professor Pieter van Goyen, renowned physicist and Nobel
laureate, has died.

By leaving the apparently worthless contents of his safety deposit to Theo, however, the professor has set him on a quest of epic proportions. A journey that will rewrite the laws of physics. A battle to save humanity itself.

This is the tale of a man who had nothing and gave it all up to find his destiny—and a doughnut.

"One mistake," Theo said sadly, "one silly little mistake, and now look at me."

The Human Resources manager stared at him with fascination. "Not that little," she said breathlessly. "You blew up—"

"A mountain, yes." He shrugged. "And the Very Very Large Hadron Collider, and very nearly Switzerland. Like I said, one mistake. I moved the decimal point one place left instead of one place right. Could've happened to anyone."

The Human Resources manager wasn't so sure about that, but she didn't want to spoil the flow. She brushed the hair out of her eyes and smiled encouragingly. "Go on," she said.

"Well," Theo replied, leaning back a little in his chair, "that was just the beginning. After that, things really started to get ugly."

"Um."

"First," Theo said, "my wife left me. You can't blame her, of course. People nudging each other and looking at her wherever she went, there goes the woman whose husband blew up the VVLHC, that sort of thing—"

"Excuse me," the Human Resources manager interrupted. "This would be your third wife?"

"Fourth. Oh, sorry, forgot. Pauline dumped me for her personal fitness trainer while I was still at CalTech. It was Amanda who left me after the explosion."

"Ah, right. Go on."

"Anyway," Theo said, "there I was, alone, no job, no chance of anyone ever wanting to hire me ever again, but at least I still had the twenty million dollars my father left me. I mean, money isn't everything—"

"Um."

"But at least I knew I wasn't going to starve, not so long as I had Dad's money. And it was invested really safely."

"Yes?"

"In Schliemann Brothers," Theo said mournfully, "the world's biggest private equity fund. No way it could ever go bust, they said." He smiled. "Ah well."

"You lost—"

"The lot, yes. Of course, the blow was cushioned slightly by the fact that Amanda would've had most of it, when the divorce went through. But instead, all she got was the house, the ranch, the ski resort and the Caribbean island. She was mad as hell about that," Theo added with a faint grin, "but what can you do?"

The Human Resources manager was twisting a strand of her hair round her finger. "And?"

"Anyhow," Theo went on, "it's been pretty much downhill all the way since then. After I lost the house, I stayed with friends for a while, only it turned out they weren't friends after all, not after all the money had gone. Actually, to be fair, it wasn't just that, it was the blowing-up-the-VVLHC thing. You see, most of my friends were physicists working on the project, so they were all suddenly out of work too, and they tried not to blame me, but it's quite hard not blaming someone when it actually is their fault." He grinned sadly, then shrugged. "So I moved into this sort of hostel place, where they're supposed to help you get back on your feet."

The pressure of the coiled hair around her finger was stopping her blood from flowing. She let go. "Yes? And?"

"I got asked to leave," Theo said sadly. "Apparently, technically I counted as an arsonist, and the rules said no arsonists, because of the insurance. They told me, if I'd killed a bunch of people in the explosion it'd have been OK, because their project mission statement specifically includes murderers. But, since nobody got hurt in the blast, I had to go. So I've been sort of camping out in the subway, places like that. Which is why," he added, sitting up straight and looking her in the eye, "I really need this job. I mean, it'll help me put my life back together, get me on my feet again. Well? How about it?"

The Human Resources manager looked away. "If it was up to me—"

"Oh, come on." Theo gave her his best dying spaniel look. "You can't say I haven't got qualifications. Two doctorates in quantum physics—"

"Not relevant qualifications," the Human Resources manager said. "Not relevant to the field of flipping burgers. I'm sorry." She did look genuinely sad, he had to give her that. "You're overqualified. With a résumé like that, you're bound to get a better offer almost immediately, so where's the point in us hiring you?"

"Oh, come on," Theo said again. "After what I've done? Nobody's going to want me. I'm unemployable."

"Yes." She smiled sympathetically. "You are. Also, you're a bit old—"

"I'm thirty-one."

"Most of our entry-level staff are considerably younger than that," she said. "I'm not sure we could find a uniform to fit you." He could see she was struggling with something, and it wasn't his inside-leg measurement. He betted he could guess what it would be. "And there's the hand."

Won his bet. He gave her a cold stare. "You do know it's against the law to discriminate on grounds of physical disability."

"Yes, but—" She gave him a helpless look. "Frankly, I think the company would be prepared to take a stand on this one. We've got our customers to think about, and—"

He nodded slowly. He could see her point. Last thing you want when you're buying your burger, fries and shake is to see them floating towards you through the air. It was an attitude he'd learned to live with, ever since the accident had left his right arm invisible up to the elbow. He wished now he'd lied about it, but the man at the outreach centre had told him to be absolutely honest. "Fine," he said. "Well, thanks for listening, anyhow."

"I really am sorry."

"Of course you are."

"And anyway," she added brightly, "a guy like you, with all those degrees and doctorates. You wouldn't be happy flipping burgers in a fast-food joint."

"Wouldn't I?" He gave her a gentle smile. "It'd have been nice to find out. Goodbye."

Outside, the sun was shining; a trifle brighter than it would otherwise have done, thanks to him, but he preferred not to dwell on that. He had enough guilt to lug around without con-templating the effect his mishap had had on the ozone layer. Cheer up, he ordered himself; one more interview to go to, and who knows? This time –

"Worked in a slaughterhouse before, have you?" the man asked.

"Um, no."

"Doesn't matter. What you got to do is," he said, pointing down the dark corridor, "wheel that trolley full of guts from that hatch there to that skip there, empty the guts into the skip, go back, fill another trolley, wheel it to the skip, empty it, go back and fill it again. And so on. Reckon you can do that?"

"I think so."

The man nodded. "Most of 'em stick it out three weeks," he said. "You, I'm guessing, maybe two. Still, if you want the job—"

"Oh yes," Theo said. "Please."

The man shrugged. "Suit yourself. Couldn't do it myself, and I've been in the slaughtering forty years, but—" He paused and frowned. "What's the matter with your arm?"

Theo sensed that the man probably didn't need to hear about the quantum slipstream effect of the implosion of the VVLHC. "Lost it. Bitten off by a shark."

"Too bad. Won't that make it awkward, loading the guts?"

"Oh, I'll have a stab at it, see how I get on."

"That's the spirit," the man said absently. "OK, you start tomorrow."

In the beginning was the Word.

Not, perhaps, the most auspicious start for a cosmos; because once you have a Word, sooner or later you find you've also got an annoying Paperclip, and little wriggly red lines like tapeworms under all the proper nouns, and then everything freezes solid and dies. This last stage is known to geologists as the Ice Age, and one can't help thinking that it could've been avoided if only the multiverse had been thoroughly debugged before it was released.

But things change; that's how it works. You can see Time as a coral reef of seconds and minutes, growing into a chalk island sitting on top of an infinite coal seam studded with diamonds the size of oil tankers; and each second is a cell dividing, two, three or a million roads-not-travelled-by every time your heart beats and the silicone pulses; and every division is a new start, the beginning of another version of the story – versions in which the Red Sea didn't part or Lee Harvey Oswald missed or Hamlet stayed in Wittenberg and got a job.

So; in the beginning was the Word, but ten nanoseconds later there was a twelve-volume dictionary, and ten nanoseconds after that a Library of Congress, with 90 per cent of the books in foreign languages. It's probably not possible after such a lapse of time to find out what the original Word was. Given the consequences, however, it could well have been oops.

The first week wasn't so bad. Well, it was; but at least he found the work so shatteringly exhausting that all he could do at the end of his shift was stagger home, stuff a pie or a sandwich in his face (for some reason, since he'd been working at the slaughterhouse he seemed to have lost his appetite), roll into bed and sleep like a corpse until it was time to get up and go to work. This suited him fine.

By the second week, however, he found he was coping with the exertion of gut-hauling rather better, which meant that he had enough stamina to allow him to sit staring aimlessly at the walls of his room for an hour before falling asleep. By the end of the fourth week, he could manage three hours of aimless staring with no bother at all. This wasn't good. Staring at the walls proved to be a primitive form of meditation, in the course of which he analysed his life so far, and ended up reaching the conclusion that it hadn't been going so well lately. Alone, all the money gone, living in a ghastly little shoebox and spending all day loading still-warm intestines into a galvanised box on wheels; it wasn't, he couldn't help thinking, the sort of life he'd quite reasonably anticipated five years before, when he was appointed as the youngest ever Kawaguchiya Integrated Circuits professor of multiphasic quantum dynamics at the University of Leiden.

introducing

If you enjoyed
THE OUTSORCERER'S APPRENTICE,
look out for

WHEN IT'S A JAR

by Tom Holt

Maurice has just killed a dragon with a bread knife. And had his destiny foretold... and had his true love spirited away. That's precisely the sort of stuff that'd bring out the latent heroism in anyone. Unfortunately, Maurice is pretty sure he hasn't got any latent heroism.

Meanwhile, a man wakes up in a jar in a different kind of pickle (figuratively speaking). He can't get out, of course, but neither can he remember his name, or what gravity is, or what those things on the ends of his legs are called... and every time he starts working it all out, someone makes him forget again. Forget everything.

Only one thing might help him. The answer to the most baffling question of all...

WHEN IS A DOOR NOT A DOOR?

PART ONE

When Is A Door—

Years ago, when he was a child, Maurice refused to go on the Underground because he was scared of all the dead people. His father had asked him a few questions and glanced at his bedside table, and explained that the Under*ground* wasn't the same thing as the Under*world* that he'd been reading about in his *Myths & Legends of the Ancient Greeks* book, which his aunt Jane had given him for his birthday. There were no dead people, three-headed dogs or sinister boatmen down there, his father promised him, just crowded platforms, unreliable trains, people in scruffy old coats who talked to themselves, a really quite small proportion of homicidal lunatics and a rather unsavoury smell. He'd been reassured (though he'd secretly quite fancied seeing a dog with three heads) and withdrawn his objection. Nevertheless, even now, there was something about it—

Especially at night, in the uneasy lull between the rush hour and the last junkies-drunks-and-theatre-goers specials, when the platforms are quiet and deserted and nobody can hear you scream; when the tiled corridors echo footsteps, and the trains, when they finally arrive, come bursting out of the darkness like dragons. Since he'd had to work late at the office recently – not because there was work to be done, but because the firm was rationalising, so everyone was sticking to their desks like limpets after nominal going-home time, to show how indispensable they were – he'd had more than his comfortable ration of nocturnal Tube travel recently, and it was starting to get on his nerves.

There were three people in the compartment when he got in, all women. There was an elderly bag lady in a thick wool coat, muttering to herself and knitting what looked like a sock. Opposite her was an elegant middle-aged businesswoman, with dark hair and glasses. She was knitting, too; that seemed a little out of character, but it was just starting to get fashionable again, or so his mother had told him. In the far corner there was a rather nice-looking girl, and *she* was knitting, which suggested his mother had been right about something, for once. In any event, they seemed harmless enough. He chose a seat in the middle of the carriage, sat down, opened his book and raised it in front of him, like a shield.

The windows were black, of course, so there was no visible world outside; all he could see in the one next to him was the reflection of the pretty girl, and it didn't do to dwell on pretty girls who might look up and figure out what you were doing. Instead, he looked up at the advertising boards. One caught his attention, as it had been designed to do—

WHERE IS THEO BERNSTEIN?

That was all: white letters on a black background. For a moment he allowed himself to wonder who Theo Bernstein was and what he was selling. Then he realised he'd been ensnared by evil capitalists and looked away. Out of the corner of his eye, he saw the elegant businesswoman bite through a strand of wool with her teeth. It was an incongruously savage act – though perfectly reasonable, when he thought about it; after all, you aren't allowed to have sharp things on you in a public place. Teeth, however, are the oldest and most basic weapons of all.

The train had slowed down to the point where, with no view through the window, it was impossible to tell if it was moving or standing still. He yawned. He'd had enough of this journey. He was in the kind of limbo, between the culmination of one sequence of events and the start of another, that you get in restaurants after you've finished eating, before they bring the bill. He looked around for something (other than the pretty girl) to graze his mind on. Not much of that kind of thing in a Tube compartment. Further down the carriage, he saw four more black advert boards with white lettering. The Theo Bernstein people were clearly determined to get their message across. He shuffled in his seat to get comfy, and tried to read his book. But that was no good. It was a self-help thing She'd given him to read, shortly before She'd stormed out of his life, slamming the door on the sunlight, and he really couldn't be bothered. *Coping with Rejection*, snickered the chapter heading. Yeah, right.

"All that time, he never realised."

The old woman had spoken. He winced. He hoped she wasn't going to make a nuisance of herself.

"He never realised," she repeated, "that she was carrying on with his worst enemy, behind his back."

Oh God, he thought, and glanced up to see how many stops there were still to go. But, since he hadn't been keeping track, he wasn't entirely sure where he was. Could be anywhere.

"Right under his nose," said the elegant woman.

She hadn't looked up from her knitting. Maurice peered at her round the cover of his book. Odd, he thought.

"He'll find out quite soon," said the old woman. "He'll be heartbroken."

extras

Actually, she didn't sound particularly batty. If anything, she sounded like a Radio 4 anchor. So, come to think of it, did the elegant woman, who now said, "That and losing his job."

Presumably, then, they knew each other. Then why were they sitting half a compartment apart?

"Of course," said the girl, "quite soon that'll be the least of his worries."

Um, he thought. So all three of them knew each other. The girl, who sounded like a trainee Radio 4 anchor, soon to make her debut seguing from the shipping forecast into *Farming Today* in the wee small hours, took a ball of green wool out of her pocket and, apparently without aiming, threw it across the compartment. The elegant woman caught it one-handed. She hadn't even looked up.

"Getting the new job will cheer him up," the old woman said.

The elegant woman threw her a ball of red wool.

"But not for long," the girl said. "He won't be able to enjoy it, because of the weird stuff."

The elegant woman frowned. "He'll find it suits him better."

"Up to a point," said the girl. "But then he'll make a big mistake."

"He always did have such a vivid imagination," sighed the old woman. "Even when he was a wee tot, bless him. Could I have the yellow, please, dear?" She raised her hand and a yellow ball sailed through the air, straight into her fingers. "Now I'm not quite sure what comes after that."

Something odd, really odd, about this conversation. "His friend," prompted the girl.

"What, the one who—?"

"His other friend," said the elegant woman. "Steve, in the army."

377

Maurice twitched. He had a friend called Steve, in the army. Of course, his Steve was a girl – Stephanie, at one time the boss barracuda in the Kandahar motor pool.

"That's right, silly of me. His friend Steve. She won't half give him a surprise."

A theory, born of desperation, floated into his mind: a variant on the old kissogram theme, he postulated, in which your friends hire paid performers to weird you out of your skull, while filming the whole thing on covert CCTV. Except he didn't have any friends with that sort of imagination or money, or who cared enough about him to go to so much trouble. In which case, it was just a coincidence. After all, lots of women called Stephanie get called Steve.

"He always did like her more than he cared to admit to himself," the old lady went on; and he thought, Coincidence? Seriously?

"Remind me," said the elegant woman. "What's the name of that boy they were both at school with? The one she eventually marries."

"You mean the one who became rich and famous? George something, wasn't it?"

George. Right, he thought, that's quite enough of that. He was just about to stand up, when he realised what the odd thing – the other odd thing – was. They were talking about the *future*—

"It doesn't last, though," the girl said.

"Now then." The elegant woman sounded reproachful. "We're getting ahead of ourselves. If we're not careful, we'll drop a stitch."

He wasn't a brave man, and the thought of accosting three strange women in a public place would normally shrivel him down to the size of a small walnut. This, though, was different.

He had no idea what was happening, he definitely didn't *want* to know, but he knew, with a kind of fatal clarity, that he was going to have to ask. He cleared his throat and said, "Excuse me."

They didn't seem to have heard him. "After he's killed the snake," the elegant woman said.

"*Excuse me.*"

The old lady frowned. "Oh, it's a snake, is it? Must've got in a bit of a tangle."

"Definitely a snake," the elegant woman said. "Well, sort of a snake. Anyhow, after he's done that—"

"*I'm talking to you.*" Maybe, but they weren't hearing him.

"Is that before or after he gets fired from – what's the name of the firm?" the girl was asking.

"Overthwart and Headlong, dear. You remember. Before, definitely," the old lady said authoritatively. "Then the snake." She paused. "I think."

Overthwart & Headlong, whose offices he'd just come from. Fired? Oh *shit*...

"Damn. I'll have to unpick."

The old lady smiled sympathetically. "Some of these plait-stitch patterns can be a bit confusing," she said. "It was so much simpler in the old days, when everybody was either plain or purl."

There was a gentle but perceptible jolt. The train was moving. "Ooh," the girl said, "we're nearly there; we'd better get a move on. Where had we got to?"

"The snake," said the elegant woman, as she polished her glasses on her sleeve.

"What about the choice?" the old woman said.

"Oh *hell*." The young woman pulled a savage face. "Now I'm going to have to unpick three whole rows."

"Excuse me," Maurice said weakly.

"Are you sure the choice comes before the snake?" the elegant woman said. "I thought the choice came in between the bottle and healing the wounded king."

The *what?* He opened his mouth, trying to say *Excuse me*, but no sound emerged.

"She's right," the old woman said. "Stupid of me. I've got the pattern upside down."

The girl shot her a furious glare. "So it's the snake, *then* the bottle, *then* the choice and *then* the king and presumably the goblins after that. Or is it the choice and then the bottle?"

"EXCUSE ME." He hadn't intended to roar, but it was the only way he could get his mouth to work. He roared so loud they could probably hear him in the street above. The women took no notice.

"Check," the elegant woman said. She glanced at the window, which was still completely black. "Well," she went on, "we cut that pretty fine, but we got there in the end."

The girl was stuffing her needles and wool into her bag. "Talking of which," she said.

"Sorry, dear. Oh yes, of course." The old woman nodded eagerly. "The end. How will it end?"

"Badly," said the elegant woman.

The girl clicked her tongue. "Well, of course *badly*," she said impatiently. "But how exactly? We can't just say *badly* and leave it at that; they'll want details. Like, for instance, what's the cause of death?"

The old woman frowned. "Entropy?"

"*His* death." The girl sighed. "Precisely when and how does he—?"

With a strangled cry, Maurice jumped to his feet, grabbed at the elegant woman (who happened to be nearest) and felt his fingers close on the lapel of her jacket. On and *through*.

The sound they made was like those fireworks that scream as they shoot up into the air; appropriately enough, because that, as far as Maurice could tell in the circumstances, was what the three women did. It was as though they'd all been simultaneously sucked into the thin nozzle of an invisible, exceptionally powerful vacuum cleaner; they sort of *compressed* from three dimensions to two, into straight vertical lines, just before vanishing with a sudden bright blue flare and a distant roll of thunder. At which point, the train stopped, the doors slid open and three Japanese tourists and a bald, fat man in a raincoat got in. Through the window, Maurice could see a sign saying *Piccadilly Circus*. The automated voice said, "Mind the gap", the doors closed and the train gently moved forward.

Maurice's eyes were very wide. Piccadilly Circus was where he'd got on. He fumbled with the sleeve on his left arm and dragged his shirt cuff off his watch. He'd left the office at 7.45. It was now three minutes to eight—

Oh hell, he thought. Here we go again.

At exactly the same time as Maurice got off the train, in exactly the same place, but at ninety-one degrees to that time and place in the D axis, a man in his mid-thirties rolled onto his back, grunted and opened his eyes.

He lay quite still for a moment, looking up. Then he frowned. "Hello?" he said.

There was no reply apart from a slight and unusual echo. The precise qualities of that echo meant more to him than it would to you or me, because the man had once been a physicist – a great one, a Nobel laureate. True, he couldn't remember anything he'd learned during his twelve years at the University of

Leiden, not even his room number or where they keep the washing machines, but his brain was still as sharp as ever. Imagine a Porsche, mechanically perfect but its gas tank completely empty.

He was working, therefore, from first principles, rather like Archimedes or one of those guys. Also, he wasn't consciously trying to account for the slightly odd properties of the echo. Even so, his subconscious got onto the problem straight away, and, in the time it took the man to sit up and rub his eyes, it had come up with a viable hypothesis that happened to be perfectly correct. The echo sounded funny because he was inside a cylinder – a cylinder, moreover, that tapered dramatically somewhere out of sight overhead. Sort of a bottle shape.

Because of the way the mind works, he wasn't conscious of all the calculus and equations he'd just performed. Instead, he attributed the flash of insight to intuition, which he'd been brought up to mistrust. That's all the thanks his subconscious got for all that hard work. It's an unfair world.

I'm in a *bottle*, he thought.

Then he realised that that thought was the only one he'd got, like the very first stamp in a brand-new stamp album. His frown deepened. Once again, his subconscious raced. It realised that it occupied a brain equipped with vast memory-storage capacity, a very big stamp album indeed; therefore, wasn't it a bit odd that all that space had just one thought in it?

Well, now there were two, but that wasn't the point. Surely there ought to be, well, *dozens*. And, while he was at it, he couldn't help noticing the substantial quantity of intellectual plant and machinery cluttering the place up – logic and cognitive processes and arithmetic, and God only knows what that one over there was supposed to be for. Unless the inside of his head was just warehouse space, presumably they'd been put there for a reason. I must be somebody, he realised. With a thing, *name*, and a personality and a, what's that other thing, a *history*. And what, now I come to think of it, am I doing in a bottle?

If he really was in a bottle. He looked around. There was nothing to see, absolutely nothing at all. There was light, quite a fair amount of it. What was lacking was anything for the light to play with.

Now then. All from first principles, of course, but it didn't take him long to come up with a theory. I'm in a glass bottle, or just possibly a jar; and the bottle or jar's in—

Nothing?

That's where a frame of reference is so devilishly useful. A frame of reference lets you know instantly if being inside a glass bottle inside nothing at all is normal, the same old same old, just another day at the office; or whether it's odd, a bit strange, possibly even a cause for moderate concern. But, as far as he could tell, he had no frame of reference, not even a scrap of a corner of one. Awkward. And, since he was stuck in a bottle surrounded by nothing at all, it wasn't immediately obvious how he was supposed to go about changing that. In which case, presumably, all he could do was wait patiently in the hope that the frame of reference he must once have had would at some point return and start making sense of things. Well, of course it will. It'll come back when it's hungry. They always do.

At which point (from first principles) he realised he'd discovered the concept of time. For about two and a half seconds he felt rather excited about that, though he wasn't sure why. A small part of him was trying to tell him that finding out stuff about how the world works is a good thing and something to feel pleased with yourself about. Quite why, he couldn't say, but the instinct was surprisingly strong. Maybe that's what I'm for, he told himself; after all, I must be for something, or else why the hell bother having me in the first place? Assuming I exist, of course, but I'm pretty sure I do. Well, of course I exist. I'm thinking, aren't I? And if you think, you exist, surely. Stands to reason, that does.

He stood up and peered down at himself. He was, he noticed, a sort of drab pink colour, in striking contrast to everything else, which was no colour at all. When he patted the top of his head, he felt something soft and sort of woolly; it felt a bit like the thin black hair on his arms, legs and body, but longer. He tried to think of a reason for it – how being partially thatched could possibly make him a more efficient pink entity in a bottle – but maybe he was missing pertinent data, because nothing sprang immediately to mind. Also, there were hard, vaguely scutiform plates on the ends of his fingers and toes. Crazy.

Am I alone?

Now where, he wondered, had that thought come from? For one thing, it meant he'd invented mathematics, simply by postulating that there might be such a thing as more-than-one. But of course there was, because he had ten fingers and ten toes; therefore, plurality exists. Any damn fool could tell you that. In which case, given the possibility of multiple entities, there might be more like him, maybe as many as five, or ten even, out there somewhere. Out where? He peered, but all he could see was nothing, with more nothing just beyond it, set against an infinite backdrop of zilch.

Now here's a thought. I'm in a bottle, but I can't see it. I know it's there, because of the echo. Therefore, things can exist without me being able to see them. Therefore, even though I can't see other entities like myself, there may be some, somewhere. Whee!

Enough of the abstract theorising; time for some practical experimentation. He walked forward in a straight line (which, for the sake of convenience, he decided was probably the short-est distance between two given points). After three paces, he simultaneously banged his nose and stubbed his toe—

Ouch. Pain. That made him frown, because he wasn't sure he liked it. But of course, it must be an inbuilt warning mech-anism, to keep you from damaging yourself by, for example, walking into one of those things that exist but can't be seen. Ingenious and effective, he decided; my compliments to the chef. Still, probably a good idea to reduce one's exposure to it as far as conveniently possible.

"Hello."

The echo again? No, not possible. It sounded all wrong for that. He turned round, and saw – his reflection? Good guess, but apparently not, because the entity he was looking at, though similar to him in many ways, was subtly different in others. Par-tially covered in white fabric, for one thing; also longer hair and two curious sort of bumps, or swellings, on the front.

The entity spoke. "It apologises," it said, "for any inconve-nience."

That made no sense, but he was prepared to make allow-ances. "Do they hurt?" he asked.

"Excuse it?"

"The swellings on your front. Are you ill?"

The entity's face moved, producing an expression he intu-itively suspected was meant to convey displeasure. "It's sup-posed to be like that."

"Really? Why?"

"Presumably you perceive it as female. Would you mind ter-ribly much not staring? If it's female, it doesn't like it."

"Sorry." He turned away, then turned slowly back and delib-erately focused a hand's span above the top of the entity's head. "Is that better?"

"Marginally," the entity replied, "though it's not easy having a conversation with someone not looking at it. But that's fine for now," the entity added quickly, as he started to turn away again. "It'll just have to get used to it."

Hang on, he thought. A million questions were bubbling away inside his head, but there was one he just had to ask. "Excuse me."

"Yes?"

"Why do you talk about yourself in the third person?"

The entity's face showed an expression designed to convey perplexity. "Say what?"

"Well," he said, "there's three persons in speech, right? Apparently," he added, as it occurred to him to wonder how the hell he knew that. "There's the first, like I, and the second, you, and then for some reason there's *three* thirds. But you don't seem to be using the right one."

The entity looked at him for a moment, shook its head and said, "It wouldn't worry about that right now if it was you. There are..." the entity hesitated. "More pressing issues."

"Are there?"

"You bet."

"Wow. Such as?"

"Your identity," the entity replied. "Your current status. Talking of which, it would like to assure you that you're perfectly safe."

"Ah." It hadn't occurred to him that he might not be. "Well, that's good."

"And, more to the point," the entity went on, "while you're in there, so is everyone else."

"Excuse me?"

The entity looked mildly embarrassed. "It's been instructed to tell you that you're being held in temporary isolation, pending a review. In another time, place and context, your status here would be aptly conveyed by an annoying hourglass, or an even more annoying running horse. There is no cause for concern."

"Great," he said, trying to sound pleased. "So I'm just—"

"Here."

He nodded. "And that's all right, is it? I mean, that's how it's supposed to be."

A MIS VIEJOS AMIGOS DEL PUEBLO DOMINICANO,

CON LA ESPERANZA

DE QUE UN DÍA ENCUENTREN LA JUSTICIA Y PROSPERIDAD

QUE USTEDES SE MERECEN

Y A TALIA FEIGA, QUE TIENE UN CORAZÓN

TAN GRANDE COMO UNA MONTAÑA

(¡Tanto arrojo en la lucha irremediable

Y aún no hay quien lo sepa!

¡Tanto acero y fulgor de resistir

Y aún no hay quien lo vea!)

—Pedro Mir, "Si alguien quiere saber cuál es mi patria"

CONTENIDO

SEGUNDA PARTE • DÓLARES

LAS ESTRELLAS ORIENTALES

Gracias, Presidente

Este es un libro sobre lo que en Estados Unidos se conoce como "triunfar". Y al igual que muchas de esas historias, esta también es una historia sobre no triunfar. En el pueblo dominicano de San Pedro de Macorís, la diferencia entre lo uno y lo otro se reduce al béisbol.

Para quienes no triunfan está la caña de azúcar, aunque sólo durante la mitad del año.

En algún momento entre la Navidad y el 27 de febrero —fiesta nacional de la República Dominicana—, y dependiendo de lo lluvioso que haya sido el verano, los *pendones* (semejantes a brotes blancos) sobresalen entre los cañaverales verdes y ondulantes de San Pedro de Macorís. En las islas del Caribe de habla inglesa, de las cuales provienen muchas de las familias de los trabajadores azucareros de San Pedro, se dice que el campo está "enflechado" cuando los pendones apuntan hacia arriba.

Esto significa que la caña de azúcar está lista para el corte, y que puede comenzar la *zafra*, es decir, la cosecha de la caña.

Es un momento emocionante porque la mayoría de las personas que trabajan en las plantaciones azucareras sólo tienen empleo durante los cuatro a seis meses que dura la zafra. En un año electoral como 2008, al comienzo de la cosecha se ve un aviso en el Ingenio Porvenir, que está controlado por el partido gobernante. Dice: "*Gracias Presidente por una nueva zafra*", como si Leonel Fernández, el político educado en Nueva York que se lanzaba de nuevo como candidato, tal como lo había hecho en 2004 y en 1996 (la última vez que los dominicanos creyeron que les estaba ofreciendo algo nuevo), y que exhibía la misma sonrisa de un vendedor de enciclopedias en los carteles que inundaban las plazas, hubiera hecho brotar la caña de azúcar personalmente.

Algunos ingenios de azúcar de San Pedro —Santa Fe, Angelina, Puerto Rico y Las Pajas— ya no están funcionando. Actualmente hay cuatro ingenios de azúcar que permanecen activos, aunque no en toda su capacidad: Quisqueya, Consuelo, Cristóbal Colón y Porvenir. Cuando llega la época de la zafra, los resplandores rojos se divisan por todo el norte de San Pedro, donde los ingenios arden toda la noche cocinando el jugo de caña.

Al igual que los otros ingenios, Porvenir estaba situado originalmente en las afueras, pero la ciudad fue creciendo a su alrededor y actualmente los camiones repletos de tallos de caña rojos como la uva deben atravesar el congestionado centro de San Pedro para entregar el producto en la fábrica.

Niños indígentes, que sobreviven en las calles lustrando zapatos o lavando los parabrisas de los coches que paran en los semáforos, corren detrás de los camiones y sacan cañas para chupárselas. A veces agarran los tallos como si fueran bates. De todos modos, los niños de las calles de San Pedro se mantienen en postura de bateadores. Y al tener un palo en la mano, algunos no pueden resistirse a practicar el bateo con piedras pequeñas, un hábito peligroso en las partes más concurridas de la ciudad. Pero si cometieran un error y golpearan la flamante camioneta SUV de un hombre adinerado, lo más seguro es que el conductor, oculto detrás del cristal ahumado, sea un beisbolista que no muchos años atrás había bateado piedras en ese mismo lugar con una caña de azúcar.

La carretera que sale de la ciudad y conduce a otros ingenios comienza en el Estadio Tetelo Vargas, de color verde, blanco y ocre —el hogar de las Estrellas Orientales. El equipo de béisbol de San Pedro, a pesar de haber atravesado por grandes dificultades, siempre ha sido un equipo consagrado. Fundado en 1910, es más antiguo que muchos de los equipos de las Grandes Ligas de Estados Unidos. El muro del jardín central de su campo de juego mide 385 metros, lo mismo que uno de las Grandes Ligas, pero con el mismo número de asientos de un estadio de la Triple A.

Detrás del muro del jardín se acumulan las hojas marchitas de las enormes palmeras, y puede apreciarse en la distancia, elevándose por detrás del jardín derecho, la chimenea de Porvenir. La carretera que pasa a un lado del estadio va directamente hacia el Norte, en lo que alguna vez fue una vía pavimentada de dos carriles y que actualmente está llena de baches. Atraviesa la zona rural de San Pedro, en medio de las aldeas que han crecido alrededor de las fábricas de las que toman sus nombres: Angelina, Consuelo, Santa Fe. Todavía en San Pedro, el camino

semeja una calzada que se abre sobre un mar vegetal de olas pla-
teadas y verdes de caña de azúcar. Algunos campos desbrozados
recuerdan a un mal corte de cabello. Las garzas, esas aves zan-
cudas de patas largas y blancas, se alimentan allí hasta la caída
del sol, cuando anidan en los árboles que bordean los cultivos.
Al mediodía, la garzas aún se posan en los campos y los cortadores de caña de Consuelo descansan bajo los árboles, resguar-
dándose del sol canicular. En la República Dominicana, cortar
caña es el peor trabajo imaginable, el más duro y el peor remu-
nerado. Siempre se ha dicho que ningún dominicano jamás rea-
lizaría esta labor, y menos aún sería visto mientras la hace. Las
personas necesitadas de otras islas azucareras con producciones
en franco descenso fueron traídas aquí para cortar la caña. Por
esto, poblaciones como Consuelo tienen una cultura políglota,
donde el inglés de las Antillas y el criollo haitiano se unen con
el español —el idioma predominante—, entremezclándose a
menudo en una misma frase.

Pero eso ocurrió en los siglos xix y xx, cuando la República
Dominicana era un país poco poblado y con una pujante industria azucarera. Hoy es todo lo contrario; el mercado laboral se
encuentra en una situación desesperada. En este lugar, todos
los cortadores de caña que descansan a la sombra nacieron en
República Dominicana.

A nadie le importa la brevedad del almuerzo. No pueden
darse el lujo de descansar mucho tiempo porque se les paga
por tonelada cortada y no por horas. Sin embargo, necesitaban
descansar un poco, especialmente cuando el sol estaba en el
cenit.

Se cultivan varios tipos de caña, y este campo había sido sembrado con una variedad conocida como *Angola pata de maco*, un

tallo duro y rojo que tiene que recibir fuertes golpes de machete antes de ser cortado; con frecuencia, centenares de machetazos en el transcurso de un día. Pero a los cortadores de caña no les importa la dureza de esta variedad, sino su densidad y contenido líquido. Algunas variedades de caña son considerablemente más pesadas que otras, y un cortador se esfuerza para trabajar en un cañaveral como este, con buena caña, porque se le paga por peso.

Reciben 115 pesos por cortar una tonelada de caña de azúcar y apilarla en los vagones abiertos del tren, con barras a los lados para evitar que la caña se salga. Ciento quince pesos equivalían a unos \$3,60 en 2009. En un día, dos cortadores pueden llenar un vagón de cuatro toneladas. Una locomotora pasa regularmente para llevar el vagón hasta el ingenio. En la industria azucarera dominicana, el cortador de caña debe hacerlo todo manualmente, por lo cual es considerada una de las industrias menos productivas del mundo. No se trata de falta de capacidad de trabajo, sino de intensidad. La optimización del trabajo, un concepto normal en el desarrollo de cualquier industria, no existía en la producción azucarera dominicana. Ecuaciones tales como el número de horas de trabajo requeridas para producir una tonelada de azúcar eran de poco interés para los aventureros informales que vinieron a la República Dominicana para producir azúcar. El costo de la mano de obra era tan bajo, la cantidad de azúcar que podía producirse era tan grande y las ganancias de tal magnitud, que nadie pensaba en mejorar los medios de producción. Después de las primeras décadas, cuando los empresarios del azúcar llegaron y desarrollaron ingenios de última tecnología, no se hizo ningún esfuerzo para actualizar los equipos.

Así, mientras en otras zonas los cultivos son incendiados para quemar las hojas antes de la cosecha, en la República Dominicana un solo trabajador debe cortar los tallos verdes y duros al ras del piso en tres partes iguales y subirlos a un vagón. En Jamaica, donde la caña se quema primero y el cortador de caña no tiene que ocuparse de la carga, el promedio de corte es de siete toneladas diarias. Mientras tanto, un buen cortador de San Pedro puede cortar dos toneladas al día.

Los cortadores trabajan desde las siete de la mañana hasta las cinco de la tarde, pero al mediodía, cuando el sol arrecia, necesitan ampararse en la sombra, comer y atender otras necesidades. Sería fácil imaginar que los hombres que hacen este trabajo deben ser grandes, fuertes y musculosos, pero esto requeriría de una dieta rica en proteínas, algo que ellos no están en condiciones de procurarse. Elío Martínez, uno de los cortadores, no es un hombre grande. Delgado, de estatura mediana y voz suave, tiene cincuenta y siete años de edad y ha cortado caña desde los dieciséis. Su padre, que también fue cortero, y su madre eran haitianos.

Su almuerzo consiste básicamente en el jugo de la caña, que, a pesar de su poco valor nutritivo, es dulce y refrescante. Además, el azúcar genera una carga momentánea de energía y produce una sensación de llenura. El secreto está en encontrar la parte más madura, que él busca entre los cientos de tallos rojizos que sobresalen de la pila de dos toneladas que hay en el vagón, listo para ser enganchado a la locomotora. Cuando encuentra uno jugoso —reconocible al tacto y por su intenso color marrón—, Elío hala la caña de 5 pies de extensión que sobresale del vagón. La sostiene horizontalmente con la mano izquierda y la golpea varias veces en el centro con un palo. Le da

vuelta y la sigue golpeando hasta que las fibras del medio pare-
cen ligeramente trituradas. Luego inclina su cabeza hacia atrás
y, sosteniendo la caña entre sus manos, la retuerce hasta que el
jugo verde llena su boca como si saliera de una llave. El repite
el mismo proceso con varias cañas cuidadosamente escogidas.

A unos 5 kilómetros de distancia, en el centro de San Pedro,
hay un edificio de apartamentos de dos pisos, semejante a un
motel. Tiene una puerta de malla metálica para proteger los
apartamentos y las numerosas camionetas SUV último modelo
estacionadas frente al edificio, así como la privacidad de sus
inquilinos, todos ellos ampliamente conocidos.

Un hombre de aspecto atlético con una camiseta con escenas
de pesca juega en el jardín delantero con una jaula de metal sin
base. "Mira esto, es gracioso", le dice a otro hombre musculoso.
Un extremo de la jaula está amarrado con una cuerda de nylon
azul a una botella de agua para sujetarla al suelo. El hombre con
la camiseta estaba sentado a 15 pies de distancia, sosteniendo
la cuerda. Había echado maíz en la jaula a manera de cebo.
Algunas palomas se estaban acercando.

Su nombre es Manny Alexander, y creció no muy lejos del
centro de San Pedro. Su familia era tan pobre, su casa tan pequeña y hacinada, que compartía la misma cama con varios
hermanos y hermanas. Entonces, en febrero de 1988, cuando
tenía dieciséis años, firmó un contrato con los Orioles de Bal-
timore como campo corto. Le pagaron un bono de $2.500 por
su firma, una pequeña bonificación en la actualidad, pero una
suma muy respetable en 1988.

"Lo primero que hice fue comprar una cama", recuerda

Alexander. "Yo quería una cama sólo para mí. Luego compré un radio, algo de ropa y comida". A esto le siguieron otros enseres. Si bien su carrera en las Grandes Ligas no fue ilustre y él no era un jugador que recibiera el salario más alto, en sus once años en las Grandes Ligas ganó más de $2 millones, que aquí en San Pedro podrían durarle mucho. Si Manny trabajara, ésta sería su hora del almuerzo. Pero Manny no tiene horario alguno que cumplir. Quería mostrarle su trampa de palomas a su amigo José Mercedes, nacido en El Seibo, al noreste de San Pedro, que se había mudado a San Pedro a finales de los años ochenta. Era un pitcher que también había jugado con los Orioles. Su carrera en las Grandes Ligas comenzó en 1994, a la edad de veintitrés años, y sólo duró nueve. Pero le alcanzó para ganar varios millones de dólares. Él estaba descansando después de haber iniciado el juego de la noche anterior para Licey, el equipo de Santo Domingo que había derrotado al equipo de casa, las Estrellas Orientales, disminuyendo aún más la ventaja que tenía la escuadra de San Pedro en los últimos juegos de la temporada. Licey tenía una gran cantidad de pitchers de las Grandes Ligas.

Manny se puso en cuclillas, sosteniendo la cuerda, listo para darle un tirón a la botella y atrapar a las palomas mientras renuían el valor para aventurarse en entrar a la jaula a comer maíz. Las aves avanzaron lentamente hacia la trampa con pasos bruscos, cuando de pronto una camioneta Ford de color cobrizo, nueva y brillante, se detuvo y un merengue —la música nacional por excelencia— comenzó a sonar a todo volumen. Las palomas, que no tenían sensibilidad dominicana, huyeron despavoridas.

Atrás del vehículo había dos números grandes: 47, el número

del uniforme de Joaquín Andújar, un pítcher excepcional que ayudó a los Cardinals de St. Louis a ganar la Serie Mundial de 1982, donde abrió dos juegos con éxito. Curiosamente, muchos de los ex peloteros le habían instalado ventanas oscuras a sus autos para que nadie los reconociera, como intentando preservar su anonimato, pero al mismo tiempo pintaban los números de sus uniformes en sus autos para asegurarse de que todo el mundo supiera quiénes eran. Muchos de los antiguos jugadores de las Grandes Ligas oriundos de San Pedro tienen autos lujosos. Sin embargo, su verdadero estatus no se mide por el valor comercial de sus autos, sino por el costo de la gasolina que consumen. La mayoría de los habitantes de San Pedro no podrían llenar los tanques de estos autos aunque se los regalaran.

Las palomas no fueron las únicas en sorprenderse por la súbita llegada de Andújar a mediodía.

Era bien sabido en San Pedro que Andújar, quien todos los días salía hasta altas horas de la madrugada, rara vez se despertaba y salía de su apartamento antes del mediodía. Sus días comenzaban generalmente por la tarde.

Andújar, un hombre que con sus 6 pies de estatura no era particularmente grande para ser pítcher, iba cuidadosamente vestido aquel día con un suéter amarillo —algo inusual para un mediodía en la República Dominicana a menos que uno pase todo el tiempo bajo aire acondicionado—, se acercó y habló con Mercedes sobre la trampa de Manny. Éste insistió en que la cuerda debería estar atada a la jaula y no a la botella. Hicieron eso y las palomas regresaron, pero estaban demasiado cautelosas como para aventurarse al interior de la jaula.

Los tres hombres bromearon acerca de comerse las palomas que atraparan. Pero ellos no se las comían, simplemente las mantenían en una jaula grande como mascotas. Era sólo por diversión. Manny Alexander se rió.

"Es por eso que nos gusta tanto la República Dominicana: aquí somos libres", señaló.

En el cañaveral de Consuelo, Dionicio Morales, conocido entre los corteros como Bienvenido, se dirige somnoliento a almorzar a un lado de su vagón. No es tan delgado como Elio y los demás que descansaban bajo los árboles. Una pequeña panza es sinónimo de una posición un poco más cómoda en la vida. Hijo de padre haitiano y de madre dominicana, tiene la misma edad que Elio, pero seis años más de experiencia. Comenzó en los cañaverales cuando tenía diez años. "He hecho todos los trabajos", dice, aunque parece más una queja que un alarde. "He cortado, sembrado y despejado los cultivos".

Ahora Dionicio era un supervisor de campo, y este día estaba a cargo del puñado de cortadores cansados que reposaban allí. Ganaba 8.000 pesos mensuales, alrededor de $250, casi $1 más al día de lo que gana un trabajador que corta un promedio de dos toneladas. Pero se daba el lujo de tener un sueldo estable, al menos durante los cuatro meses de la zafra. A mediados del siglo XX, su padre atravesó la isla desde Haití para cortar caña por tres centavos de dólar la tonelada. Dionicio recuerda aquellos días más difíciles aún cuando un simple camino de tierra conducía desde Consuelo a la ciudad y los trabajadores del azúcar nunca salían de los cultivos. Las empresas azucareras ofrecían viviendas en las plantaciones, dispuestas en pequeñas aldeas llamadas batey, una palabra indígena que antes de la llegada de los españoles designaba un juego de pelota. Los trabajadores y sus familias vivían allí y compraban insumos y alimentos en la tienda de la compañía, que les otorgaba un crédito. Estas compras terminaban consumiendo la mayor parte o la totalidad de su exiguo salario. Si los trabajadores de la caña querían que sus hijos estudiaran, estos tenían que caminar varias millas para ir a la escuela más cercana, pero esto supuso una mejora considerable con respecto a épocas anteriores cuando sencillamente no había escuelas. La carretera asfaltada marcó una gran diferencia, pues el estadio de béisbol, localizado en el centro de San Pedro, quedó a tan sólo quince minutos de distancia. Los cortadores aún no poseían medios de transporte, sin embargo, con el dinero que ganaban tras cortar unos pocos cientos de libras de caña —unos cuantos pesos— podían viajar al centro de la ciudad en el asiento posterior de una motocicleta. Éste, conocido como motoconcho, era el principal medio de transporte de San Pedro.

Al igual que varios centenares de familias de trabajadores, Dionicio y Elio vivían cerca de este campo, en el Batey Experimental. Allí los trabajadores no vivían en barracas, tal como sucedía en algunos de los peores bateyes, sino en casas de concreto separadas, con techos de hojalata, con una a tres habitaciones pequeñas. El agua corriente y la electricidad funcionaban de vez en cuando. Las familias siembran algunos de sus alimentos en los bateyes, especialmente plátanos, yuca y chícharos, todos ellos productos básicos que crecen con facilidad en el Caribe. Algunas ganan un dinero adicional comprando y vendiendo naranjas por las calles sin pavimentar del batey.

"No es tan malo si ganas buen dinero", dice Dionicio refiriéndose al batey, al que considera su hogar. "Si no ganas mucho dinero, es difícil". Un gran número de personas del Batey

Experimental —especialmente entre las zafras, período conocido como el "tiempo muerto"— no ganaban nada.

No existen muchas opciones de trabajo en San Pedro de
Macorís. Al preguntarle si le gustaba su trabajo, Elío Martínez
negó con la cabeza enfáticamente, como si hubiera ingerido
una sustancia amarga. Luego se apresuró a agregar: "Pero tengo
que ganar dinero".

No todos en San Pedro cortan caña. Algunos trabajan en los
ingenios de azúcar. Otros son pescadores, venden naranjas o
conducen motoconchos. Algunos juegan béisbol, una actividad
por la que es cada vez más conocido San Pedro ahora que la
industria azucarera está desapareciendo.

El azúcar y el béisbol han intercambiado lugares. Una ciudad
donde se jugaba un poco de béisbol, y que era conocida en
el mundo sólo por su industria azucarera, se había convertido
en una ciudad con un poco de azúcar, reconocida mundial-
mente gracias a los grandes equipos de béisbol y a sus segui-
dores. La ciudad azucarera de San Pedro se había convertido
en San Pedro, la ciudad del béisbol. También es, por supuesto,
un lugar donde la gente escribe poesía, se enamora, engendra
niños, tiene matrimonios felices o desdichados, pescan en el
mar, siembran otros cultivos, abren tiendas y negocios y practican incluso otros deportes como el baloncesto y el boxeo. Pero
quiso el destino que San Pedro fuera conocido en el mundo por
una sola cosa. Que una ciudad de ese tamaño alcanzara la fama
en un país pequeño y pobre que rara vez llamaba la atención
del resto del mundo, salvo para ser invadido, es algo notable.
Un siglo atrás, si San Pedro se mencionaba en el extranjero y se
recibía respuesta, probablemente era: "Ah, sí, el lugar del azú-

car". Hoy en día básicamente es: "Ah, sí, esa ciudad de donde provienen todos los campo cortos".

En la época en que San Pedro era una ciudad azucarera, el béisbol echó raíces en las plantaciones de caña. La historia del azúcar en San Pedro —una historia de pobreza y de hambre— y la historia del béisbol —una historia de millonarios— siempre han estado estrechamente entrelazadas. Las compañías azucareras fueron las que llevaron el juego, y los trabajadores de las Antillas Menores que jugaban cricket, proporcionaron los jugadores. En algunos casos, el azúcar suministró incluso el insumo básico del béisbol, una pelota dura elaborada con las melazas. Más tarde, cuando el juego llegó a otras partes del país, se utilizaron pelotas diferentes. Bajando por la costa, en Haina, al otro lado de Santo Domingo, donde crecieron los Alou —una de las grandes familias de beisbolistas—, no había azúcar pero si cultivos de limón, y los limones se convirtieron en pelotas mucho más efímeras que el azúcar.

Esta es una historia acerca de alcanzar el éxito; sobre los giros y vicisitudes que determinan el éxito o el fracaso, y cómo cada uno de esos aspectos puede cambiar la vida de una persona; una historia sobre un mundo donde un simple gesto del entrenador del equipo de una granja, así llamado por sus ubicaciones en lugares apartados de Norteamérica, pueden marcar la diferencia entre ganar varios millones de dólares al año o regresar a casa y ganar unos pocos cientos de dólares. Y esa es una diferencia que determina, a su vez, la vida de más de una docena de familiares. La vida es un entramado muy frágil que se decide con frecuencia por la fuerza de un brazo, la fluidez de un bateo, o la firmeza de una mano enguantada. Incluso en San Pedro, no todo el mundo tiene el talento para ser un beisbolista. Casi siempre la vida se reduce a lo bien que jugamos las cartas que nos reparten. Al igual que el póquer, la vida es un juego de habilidades derivado de la suerte. La mayoría de nosotros no piensa que la vida es esencialmente injusta. Es por eso que admiramos tanto a los que saben jugarla.

En todo el Caribe, los pobres viven de sueños. Pasa una generación tras otra y la vida sigue siendo difícil. Pero siempre existe la esperanza. En Jamaica, los niños de los tugurios de Kingston practican el canto con la esperanza de ser el próximo Bob Marley o Jimmy Cliff. En San Pedro de Macorís, practican su bateo y el sueño de ser como Sammy Sosa.

En 2008, setenta y nueve habitantes de San Pedro ya habían llegado a las Grandes Ligas, donde el salario promedio era de $3 millones. Pero Elio Martínez no jugó béisbol. Golpeó otra caña y la exprimió en su boca para beber un último sorbo. Muy pronto, su almuerzo habría terminado. *Gracias, Presidente.*

EL AZÚCAR

La caña triturada, como una lluvia de oro,
en chorros continuados, baja, desciende y va
allí donde la espera la cuba,
para hacerla miel, dulce miel, panal.

El sol que la atraviesa con rayo matutino,
de través, como un puro y terso cristal,
sugestiona, persuade, que se ha fundido
la misma luz solar.

—Gastón Fernando Deligne, "Del trapiche".